COLD BLOOD

A THOMAS SHEPHERD MYSTERY

DAN PADAVONA

GET A FREE BOOK!

I'm a pretty nice guy once you look past the grisly images in my head. Most of all, I love connecting with awesome readers like you.

Join my VIP Reader Group and get a FREE serial killer thriller for your Kindle.

Get My Free Book

www.danpadavona.com/thriller-readers-vip-group/

1

The slot opened on the cell room door, and Officer Kevin Newman slid the dinner tray inside. On the cot, a monstrous man with an unshaven face glared at him, as if wishing death on the officer and his family. Newman looked away. It was critical not to show fear around the inmates, but this was Victor Bacchus, lord of a Rochester crime syndicate.

Rumors claimed Bacchus had murdered more than a hundred people. Newman didn't believe the rumors, yet he never questioned the danger of approaching the convict's cell. He worried the mob boss, who maintained ties with the outside world, would put a hit on him. Or a loved one. He couldn't wait to be rid of the killer.

"Last meal, Bacchus. Eat up."

Newman snapped the slot shut and backed away. Bacchus growled and rose to his feet. Standing, the man towered above the officer.

"You make it sound like I'm going to the electric chair," Bacchus said.

"New York doesn't do that anymore."

"Can't wait until I leave, can you, Newman?"

"Smile, Victor. You want a change of scenery, right?"

"Buffalo," Bacchus spat. "Who the hell wants to spend eternity in the great north?"

"Look at it this way: When the guards let you wander the yard during recess, you'll see nature in the distance. Better than here. We have nothing but concrete and skyscrapers."

"I like New York City."

"But Buffalo is closer to your people."

Bacchus stood before the shatterproof glass and gave Newman an evil grin.

"Think my people, as you so aptly described them, don't come this way?"

Officer Newman didn't want to think about the state's most dangerous crime syndicate moving through New York's boroughs.

Bacchus snatched the tray and carried it back to his cot, where he chiseled through a hunk of bloody meat. When he chewed, the juice dripped down his chin like a cannibal's rictus. There was something unsettling about the mobster. Not just because he'd murdered his enemies. He walked the razor's edge between stability and insanity. Prison had pushed the man closer to the brink. One more nudge, and there was no telling what Bacchus would become.

"Don't miss me too much," he said between mouthfuls.

Newman shook his head in disgust. He was thankful he only had to spend one night playing nursemaid to Bacchus before they escorted the convict to Buffalo.

"No chance of that happening," Newman mumbled.

He moved to the next cell and placed the dinner tray in the slot. By the time he reached the end of the cell block, he saw Officer Fleming going from door to door, ensuring everyone was locked in for the night. Fleming stopped at Bacchus' cage and shot him a grin. For whatever reason, Officer Fleming got along with the mob boss. Fleming was part of the team charged with transporting Bacchus to Buffalo.

As the second officer moved down the hall, it occurred to Newman that everyone was afraid of Bacchus except Fleming. He should have been relieved he wouldn't have to deal with the killer after tomorrow. Instead, his stomach twisted into knots at the thought of someone getting friendly with a man he viewed as a monster. He forced himself to return to his rounds, trying not to dwell on the fact that Officer Fleming might be in over his head. Never cozy up to a shark.

As he reached for the door, a shout rang out from the upper corridor. The alarm blared, and the exits at either end of the cell block locked. Newman's radio squawked.

"Dead body on the fourth level. It's Dimuzio."

Officer Newman shuddered. Anthony Dimuzio was a member of a rival crime syndicate. Bacchus had every reason to murder the man, but Dimuzio was locked behind a cage door. How had Bacchus gotten to him?

He removed his gun and watched the corridors. In his mind, he pictured Victor Bacchus' door sliding open, then the killer stepping into the hallway with that bloody, toothy grin.

But the door remained closed. From down the corridor, someone whistled a haunting tune—"The End" by The Doors.

The whistling came from the killer's cell.

2

The headlights of the patrol car sliced through the predawn darkness as it descended the hill. There was no moon, and the stars were merely pinpricks of light in the inky black sky. The winding country road twisted and turned, shadows pooling in the dips and hollows of the land.

The driver of the car, Sheriff Thomas Shepherd, sighed and slowed to a stop in the parking lot behind the station. A cough was going around the office and two of his junior deputies were out sick, requiring him to work overnight. With the graveyard shift almost over, he slogged inside, where he found Deputy Aguilar arriving for work.

"Morning, Thomas," Aguilar said, setting her keys and hat on the desk.

"Good morning, Aguilar."

She shook the flurries off her jacket and laid it over the chair.

"Rough shift?"

"That's the first midnight I've worked since October. I need to get used to them again."

"Be thankful. You can drive home and sleep like a baby, then wake up and start your vacation."

Thomas scratched his head. "I've been thinking about the vacation plans, and with two deputies sick—"

"Oh, no. Stop right there. Thomas, when is the last time you took a vacation? And I mean a real vacation, not a long weekend."

He stammered. "It couldn't have been too long ago."

"It's been over a year. You're going on vacation, and so is Chelsey. No more excuses from either of you about falling behind on work."

Thomas laughed. "You're just excited to run the office without me looking over your shoulder."

"I'll rule the department with an iron fist."

"Please don't."

She waved his concern away. "Not on my life. The sheriff's department is in safe hands, and I have Lambert to back me up."

"Are you sure it's all right? I don't want to leave you shorthanded."

"Thomas, if you and Chelsey don't go on vacation, I'll knock your heads together. Laurel Mountain is spectacular this time of year, and you can't get your deposit back."

"It's only money," he said. "The department is my priority."

"No, your future wife is your priority, and you are hers. Spend time together. Think about it: no pets to worry over, no LeVar knocking on your door and asking if it's okay to do laundry, no midnight shifts. Just a cozy cabin in the forest and a woodstove to snuggle beside."

"You strike a hard bargain."

"Be honest. It was the part about LeVar that convinced you."

Thomas shook his head and gathered his belongings. "I'll stop by before we leave."

"You don't have to."

"Aguilar, are you kicking me out of my department?"

"Why, yes, I am."

The sheriff arrived home before the first light of day broke on the horizon. A brisk wind made him bundle his jacket as he rushed from his pickup to the door. Jack, their dog, lifted his head and thumped his tail against the mattress when Thomas opened the bedroom door. Chelsey lay sound asleep.

He fell asleep as soon as his head hit the pillow. Upon wakening, he whiffed eggs and toast cooking downstairs. With a stretch, he read the alarm clock. Nine thirty. He'd only slept three hours, but that was fine. With vacation looming, now wasn't the time to mess up his sleep pattern. Tonight he'd catch up.

Chelsey had breakfast ready when he came downstairs. She kissed his cheek and removed a bottle of beet juice from the refrigerator. Jack was looking for handouts, and their cat Tigger drank from his bowl and padded under Chelsey's legs.

"Did you get enough sleep?" she asked.

"Long enough. I don't want to fall asleep after midnight tonight. We have a long drive ahead of us tomorrow."

"When is check-in time?"

"Three o'clock. We can pick up the key from the ranger's office after then. It's a two-hour drive, so I'd like to be on the road by one."

"Perfect. That will give me a chance to stop at the office."

Chelsey owned Wolf Lake Consulting, a private investigation firm. Her partner Raven would kick Chelsey out of the office, as Aguilar had Thomas. Chelsey and Thomas were overdue for a vacation.

Thomas carried their plates to the dining-room table. The lights were off in the guest house behind the A-frame. LeVar, who rented the house, must be at the community college taking class. Final exams were fast approaching, and the teenage deputy wanted to ace his tests and improve his chances for another scholarship after he transferred to Kane Grove University.

"Thomas," Chelsey asked between bites, "did you check the weather report?"

"Sure did. Chilly with breaks of sun. Maybe a few snow showers tomorrow afternoon. Why?"

"I worry about that storm moving up the coast. The forecast says it's supposed to miss us, but you can never be sure."

"You're searching for an excuse not to go, and I should know. I pulled the same act with Aguilar this morning, and she all but tossed me out the door."

"Let's monitor the news, okay?"

"Of course, but there's no reason to worry. My F-150 cuts through winter weather, and I put on the snow tires."

Preoccupied with thoughts of their upcoming trip, Thomas failed to notice it was colder than the forecast had predicted. They had planned this trip since summer. He pictured the little cabin in the woods, the striking views from the mountain, the powdery snow that would be perfect to hike and snowshoe through. Who cared if the storm shifted westward and dropped half a foot of snow? His truck would handle it, and the winter weather would add to the ambiance. In Upstate New York, you learned to enjoy the snow and cold, or you vacationed in Florida until April.

Jack sat beside Thomas and eyed him expectantly.

"No eggs for you," he said. "You ate your breakfast. Let me eat mine."

The dog woofed and lolled his tongue out.

The phone rang. Noticing it was Darren Holt, Thomas answered. Darren and Raven had agreed to watch Jack and Tigger in the ranger's cabin at Wolf Lake State Park.

"Darren, how is your morning?"

"Quiet. We don't have a single cabin rented this week."

"All right, Ranger Holt. You're trying to convince me to cancel the trip to Laurel Mountain and rent from you."

"You know all my tricks. Are we still on for tomorrow? What time are you dropping Jack and Tigger off?"

"We're leaving around one. How about noon?"

"Perfect. That's my lunch break; not that I'll have a darn thing to do tomorrow besides chop wood for the stove. Did you read your thermometer?"

"Can't," Thomas said. "Last week's windstorm blew my weather station over."

"Before you walk outside in shorts and a T-shirt, I should warn you. It's five above. I was outside for two minutes and my nose hairs froze."

"Ah, good old nose-hair weather."

"That's pretty cold for two weeks before Christmas. It's supposed to drop to ten below overnight."

"I'd better put an extra comforter on the bed."

"You're telling me." The television played in the background. "Thomas, did you know the coastal storm shifted westward?"

"I haven't checked since last night."

"It's still supposed to miss Wolf Lake, but it's coming closer. The forecast says three feet for the Catskills. Philly and New York City are supposed to receive flooding rains and tropical-storm-force winds."

"Glad I'm not a county sheriff down there. Can you imagine the power outages?"

"I don't want to think about it," Darren said. "Anyway, I wanted to warn you that the storm is coming closer. Best keep up to date in case the track changes."

"I will, Darren. And thanks again for watching Jack and Tigger. See you tomorrow at noon."

Chelsey glanced at Thomas after he ended the call.

"What did Darren want?"

Thomas didn't want to mention the storm shifting. She'd use any excuse to cancel their vacation and work with Raven.

"He asked what time we wanted to drop off the pets. I told him noon."

"What was that about your broken weather station?"

"Apparently, it's in the single digits outside. If you step out, wear an extra layer."

Chelsey shivered. She wasn't a fan of winter, but he hoped the tranquility of Laurel Mountain would change her mind.

"We should finish packing," she said. "I don't want to rush tomorrow morning."

"Great idea. That will give us an excuse to stay inside."

As Chelsey finished eating, Thomas looked across the lake. The water hadn't frozen, but at this rate a solid layer of ice would cover Wolf Lake before the new year. Hills blocked his view to the east, but he could see a layer of dark gray massing above their peaks.

Maybe he should check the forecast again.

3

The next morning, Thomas drove the F-150 from the lake to the sheriff's department. Chelsey sat in the passenger's seat and shivered despite the roaring heater. Beyond the windshield lay a wonderland of ice and snow. The defroster worked double-time to keep the windshield clear.

"Tell me again why we're visiting the station?" Chelsey asked.

"I just need to grab a few things before we pick up the pets and bring them to Darren and Raven's."

"You mean you want to check up on Aguilar? You're hoping she'll have a change of heart and talk you into staying."

"What, me?" He wore a look of mock offense. "Like you didn't do the same at Wolf Lake Consulting."

"That's between me and Raven."

While Chelsey shared an eye roll with Aguilar, who worked at her desk, Thomas removed his jacket and hung it from the coat rack.

"What are you doing here, Thomas?" Aguilar asked without looking up from her computer.

"Just checking on a few things. There's a case on my desk I need to file."

"I filed it."

"And a list of winter weather supplies I should check."

"Checked it."

Thomas cleared his throat. "You really want me to leave, don't you?"

The lead deputy turned off the monitor and swiveled her chair to face him.

"What I want is for you and Chelsey to have an amazing trip and forget about work." She glanced around the sheriff and held Chelsey's eyes. "That goes for you too. Forget about work."

"I'm cooperating," Chelsey said.

"No looking at your phones, no calling back to the office. Raven can cover the work at Wolf Lake Consulting, and Lambert and I will run the sheriff's department. Neither of you has anything to worry about."

Thomas turned to Chelsey. "She doesn't want us around."

"Now you understand. Oh, and that rule about not staring at your phones and calling Wolf Lake? The coverage on Laurel Mountain is terrible. Plan on communicating like humans used to do before mobile connectivity ruined the world."

Thomas chuckled. "Fair enough. Are we free to go?"

They hugged Aguilar goodbye and drove away in the F-150. Yesterday's cold had made the road treacherous; Thomas navigated the icy path back to the A-frame. LeVar was waiting inside and helping himself to hot chocolate.

"You're sure you don't want me to watch Jack and Tigger?" the teenager asked, scooping his dreadlocks off his shoulder.

"Positive," Thomas said. "Concentrate on passing your finals."

"I'll do a lot better than pass, Shep Dawg."

"You always make me proud."

LeVar bent to pet Jack. "You won't miss me, little bro. I'll visit you at the ranger's cabin." He stood as Chelsey coaxed Tigger into a crate. "Once you get to Laurel Mountain, gather supplies and hole up. Never know if this coastal storm will move inland."

"Trust me. Between Chelsey and Darren, everyone has me checking forecast updates on the hour. It looks like the Catskills are gonna get crushed."

"Three feet of snow, four to six on the peaks."

"Incredible. Glad we don't have to deal with that."

Chelsey placed a hand against her forehead. "Well, that was fun. Not."

"Tigger wasn't into the whole crate idea?"

"Nopers."

LeVar bumped fists with Thomas and hugged Chelsey before kneeling to pet Jack again. If Thomas was correct, the teenager would spend half the week at the ranger's cabin, playing with Jack and eating Darren out of house and home.

"See you in a week," Thomas said. "Feel free to hang out in the A-frame. The guest room upstairs won't be as chilly as your place."

"I may take you up on that offer. Now hit the road before you change your mind."

Jack piled into the cab and sat between Thomas and Chelsey. She held Tigger's crate on her lap as the cat eyed her with derision.

After a quick trip up the hill, which the F-150 handled without slipping, Thomas pulled into the parking lot of the visitor's center. Darren welcomed them inside the toasty cabin, where Jack ran back and forth, sniffing every inch as if he hadn't visited a hundred times. As soon as Chelsey opened the crate, Tigger scurried away and perched on top of the couch. To Thomas's dismay, the television played the latest weather forecast. Some weather reporter with a death wish gripped a flagpole on Long Island as wind and rain whipped him to and fro.

"Welcome back," Darren said, patting Jack on the head.

The dog lolled his tongue out and panted, happy as a clam.

"I don't think he'll miss us," Thomas said.

"Nah. I'll keep Jack busy. We'll take plenty of hikes through the woods. If it isn't too cold, we might make it to Lucifer Falls."

"Have the falls frozen?" Chelsey asked.

"Not for a few weeks yet. But if we get another arctic outbreak like yesterday, they might freeze by Christmas."

She looked around the cabin in puzzlement.

"Where's Raven? I saw her at the office this morning. She planned to bring a laptop home and work from the cabin."

"Raven will be here within the hour. A client stopped by and talked her ear off."

"Ugh. I hope it wasn't Mr. Feinstein. She'll be there all afternoon if that's the case."

"Can I offer you something warm to eat? I cooked meatballs and have rolls for subs."

"We should get on the road."

"Are you sure? Once you leave Nightshade County, it's nothing but hills and country until you reach Laurel Mountain. Don't expect any diners on the way."

Chelsey shared a glance with Thomas. "He has a point."

"If you insist," Thomas said, "I could go for a meatball sub."

Darren rubbed his hands together. "That's the spirit. I'll fill you up before you get on the road."

"You'll make a wonderful parent someday," said Chelsey, and Darren's cheeks reddened.

For months, Raven's mother Serena had dropped hints that it was time for Darren to marry her daughter.

The woodstove kept the cabin at 75 degrees, and the subs

tasted like the best Thomas had eaten in years. The coziness made him want to stay. There was something so comforting about being surrounded by those you loved, who could make you feel like everything would turn out fine no matter what happened beyond these walls. But the day grew late. If they wanted to purchase supplies in Laurel Mountain and make it to the cabin before dark, they needed to hustle.

Before they left, Darren bundled supplies for the journey. Blankets, canned goods, first-aid kits, lighters, flashlights—all items that one needed in nature. He even threw in a few books of matchsticks in case they encountered wet tinder on the trail.

"We have all of this," Thomas said.

"Trust me, you can never take enough. This is a state park ranger you're talking to. Don't question my authority."

"Yes, sir."

"Here are extra containers of fuel for your lanterns. Don't use too much at once or you won't have enough if you get stuck in the cabin. There aren't many stores around that carry supplies, and the shop in Laurel Mountain charges an arm and a leg. Better safe than sorry."

Chelsey glanced out the front window and saw the obscured sun had tracked to the western sky. She frowned and gave Thomas a meaningful look.

Taking her cue, Thomas shook Darren's hand and thanked him for the supplies and hospitality. Chelsey put on her coat and boots, ready for the journey ahead of them.

With one last wave from Darren, who stood in the doorway, they packed their gear in the cab and Thomas backed out of the parking lot. Sadness tugged at Thomas's heart as he watched the cabin grow smaller in the mirror. It was only a week, but he already missed Jack, Tigger, and their friends.

As they exited the village of Wolf Lake, unexpected flurries dropped from the sky. The gray had thickened since morning, with a sheet of black hanging over the land to the east.

Chelsey reached for the radio and searched for a weather update.

4

Five minutes after three o'clock, Aguilar drove her cruiser out of Treman Mills, where she'd responded to a land dispute between two farmers. The police radio was quiet, except for the occasional traffic violation. A text from Thomas confirmed the sheriff and Chelsey were halfway to their destination. Soon he would lose coverage.

On the way back to Wolf Lake, she eyed the eastern sky with trepidation. It wasn't gray anymore but black. The AM news channel kept her up to date on the forecast, which reiterated the storm would miss Nightshade County. But there were seven counties under new winter storm warnings, and the alerts were coming closer.

Wind buffeted the cruiser, and she realized her speed was only 50 mph into the headwind. When she'd left Treman Mills, the wind had been from the west, and now it roared out of the east. She knew what that meant. The forecast was wrong.

Picking up speed, she weaved around slow-moving vehicles and hurried back to base. When she entered the department, Deputy Lambert had just arrived for shift and was holding court with a junior deputy. They were attempting to outdo each other with raunchy jokes.

"Settle the battle between the Hatfields and McCoys?" Lambert asked.

"Talk about a waste of time. One farmer parked his tractor a foot over the property line, and all hell broke loose." She tossed the keys on her desk. "You work until eleven, right?"

Lambert nodded as the other deputy filed paperwork. "I'm on swing shifts until Tuesday. What's up?"

"Did you bring extra food?"

"Enough for dinner. Why?"

"Maybe you should run out and grab everyone sandwiches at The Broken Yolk cafe. I'll pitch in."

"That's no problem, but I'm curious. What is making you so nervous?"

"I'm worried the storm will hit us."

"The nasty coastal storm that's tearing up Long Island?"

"That's the one. Did you know the county east of us is supposed to receive a foot of snow? If this storm shifts ten or twenty miles, we're screwed."

Lambert peeked between the blinds covering the window.

"It's almost like night," he said.

"I noticed as well."

"What about the wind?"

"Easterly around 20 or 30 mph."

Lambert removed his hat and scratched his head. "I may not be a meteorologist with NOAA, but that tells me a coastal storm is coming. How do you want to handle this?"

Aguilar pursed her lips and propped herself on the corner of the desk.

"The plows can keep up with a foot of snow. That's not the issue. If those tropical-storm-force winds reach Nightshade

County when the snow and ice arrive, we'll lose power. Wolf Lake has a large elderly community, and we'll need to think about those who need electricity to survive."

"That's an impossible task. With so many people to care for, we can't protect everyone."

"But we can ensure they prepare. If my hunch is correct, we have three to six hours before the storm hits us. That gives us enough time to pound on doors and tell people to gas up their generators."

"And if they don't have a generator?"

"Find someone in the neighborhood who does. Know where to go if we lose power. The largest issue will be the homes with electric heat. Most everyone is on propane or natural gas. Anyone on electric heat risks freezing to death if the power goes out."

"The gas and electric company can tell us who is on electric heat," Lambert said. "I'll get on the horn."

Aguilar turned to the junior deputy. "Call the radio and television stations. Everyone in Nightshade County should have enough nonperishable food to make it through the next forty-eight hours."

As the junior deputy made the calls, Aguilar pinched the bridge of her nose. She felt a five-alarm headache coming on. So much for telling Thomas that she had everything under control. By tonight, Wolf Lake might be under a state of emergency, and two deputies were out sick.

"Damn," she said.

Lambert lifted his head. "Now what?"

"Once the public hears about my order to stock up on food, everyone will flock to the grocery stores. I've seen riots break out because two people wanted the same loaf of bread."

"You really believe something like that will happen in our county?"

"Keep in mind I just responded to a land dispute because a tractor was a foot too far to the north. Yes, it can happen here. What did the power company say?"

"The best they could do was send me the residents who don't use natural gas. That's not to say they're on electric; many order propane from an independent supplier. Some own woodstoves and fireplaces. Those folks will be fine."

"Good enough," Aguilar said. "We'll hit as many residences as we can."

"What would you like me to do in the meantime?"

"Check the supply room. Thomas left a list. Gather as many flashlights and batteries as you can find. Call around and order nonperishables. The counties to our west appear safe from the storm. Hopefully they can help us out with generators."

Aguilar gave the weather out the window one last look. The flurries had increased to light snow showers, and already the wind was driving drifts across the street.

They were in trouble.

⁓

"What's with Jack?" Raven asked, sitting on the couch with her legs propped up and the laptop balanced on her thighs.

Darren folded his arms and studied Jack, worried that something was wrong with the dog. He'd acted skittish since Thomas and Chelsey left, whining one moment, rushing from the door to the window and back again, then cowering behind the bed. The dog might be homesick, but he worried something more was going on. Before the pets arrived, Darren had ensured there was nothing poisonous left out. He'd even taped the cable and electrical cords to the floor, discouraging the dog from chewing.

Rounding the bed, he stared at the dog, who lay on his belly with his snout buried between his paws. Jack gave him a frightened look. Every time the wind blew, the dog whimpered and tried to dig himself under the carpet.

"I think it's the weather," Darren said.

"He didn't get into anything, right?"

"I put the cleaning supplies on the top shelf. There's nothing to get into."

Raven closed the computer and joined Darren beside the dog. Tigger appeared no worse for wear. The cat had found its place on top of the couch and was content to stay there.

"Well," said Raven, "if Jack is worried about the weather, it must be one helluva storm coming."

Darren watched the warnings scroll across the bottom of the television screen. Still no alerts for Nightshade County, but the forecast now predicted three inches of snow overnight. The previous forecast had claimed a dusting would fall.

"We should prepare for the worst," Darren said.

"How can I help?"

"Follow me."

Without another word, he hustled to the closet and grabbed a box of plastic sheets, along with a roll of duct tape and three rolls of twine. He ripped open the supplies and walked around the cabin, checking for loose boards and shutters, securing everything to the wall.

Using Raven's help, he opened each window in the cabin and draped a sheet of plastic over it, then used a staple gun to hold them in place

"We'll leave tiny air vents near the windowsills so fresh air enters the cabin without the snow getting inside," he said.

"Roger that."

Once finished, Darren stood back with Raven at his side and surveyed their work with satisfaction.

"That should do it for now," he said, wrapping an arm around her shoulders.

They returned inside to find Jack had come out from under the bed and was pacing restlessly near the door.

"Has he ever reacted this way to inclement weather?"

"I'd call Thomas and Chelsey," he said, "but I don't want to bother them on their trip."

"Smart. Knowing Chelsey, she'll talk him into turning around and canceling their vacation."

The prospect of being stuck indoors for the duration of the storm had Darren and Raven thinking of activities to keep them busy. It was likely to be a long night, since there was no way they could leave the cabin if a blizzard raged outside.

"We can catch up on Netflix shows," Raven said. "I still haven't watched the last season of *Stranger Things*."

"And I'll make popcorn. Might as well make the most of the opportunity."

As he walked toward the kitchen, she grabbed his arm.

"I know of a few fun activities we could do locked in the cabin."

The craving in her eyes made his knees weak. "Easy, Xena. We're assuming a lot. This storm is supposed to miss us."

"Who needs a storm for play time?"

He glanced from Jack to Tigger. "In front of the kids?"

"I'm sure they'll be fine."

"Hey, before we get caught up in other activities, help me bring in enough firewood to get us through tomorrow."

"I'll put on my jacket."

They breathed condensation clouds as they worked. Despite his gloves, Darren's hands grew numb before they finished. Back inside, Darren opened the closet and pulled out three board games. Placing them on the kitchen table, he suggested that each pick whichever game sounded most fun. A cheerful debate led them to select Uno.

"I haven't played this game since I was a kid," said Raven.

"After dinner and fun times. First, we should get Jack out of the cabin."

Raven grabbed Jack's leash, and they took him for a walk around the campgrounds. After the dog did his business and worked off his nervous energy, they returned to the ranger's cabin. Darren started dinner—pasta with tomato sauce and the meatballs he'd made this morning—while Raven turned on Netflix.

While they digested their food, Jack and Tigger cuddled between Darren and Raven. In addition to *Stranger Things*, they also cued up *The Princess Bride* and *Indiana Jones* before snuggling under blankets.

Outside, the wind quickened and rattled the windows. The woodstove kept the cabin warm, and Darren was thankful they'd brought in wood before the storm hit. He was about to write off the potential for snow when a tone alert turned on his radio.

The synthesized voice said, "The National Weather Service in Binghamton, New York, has issued a Winter Storm Warning in Nightshade County. Snow, heavy at times, will reach Nightshade County after 7:00 p.m. Snowfall rates of two inches per hour are expected, with ten to twenty inches of snow accumulation by tomorrow evening. Easterly winds will increase to 20 to 30 mph, with gusts over 50 mph possible. Expect whiteout conditions and power outages. Do not travel unless it is an emergency."

When the message ended, Raven turned to Darren. "I guess the storm is coming after all."

"I'm glad we prepared before the warning came out."

Just then, a gust of wind issued a werewolf's howl. Something crashed against the cabin—probably a tree branch. Raven wore a worried expression.

"Darren, what if the storm is worse than they're saying?"

"We'll be okay."

But as the howl grew to a roar, he wondered if the cabin would hold up.

5

The pickup truck snaked along the winding road that ascended Laurel Mountain. Armed with the key, Thomas looked forward to peace and quiet: just him and Chelsey, with nowhere they needed to be for the next seven days. A sudden gale shoved the truck around, but he kept a grip on the steering wheel and did his best not to appear anxious about the weather.

A quilt of black lay in the eastern sky. The clouds had followed them since they drove out of Wolf Lake. He was sure it was snowing to beat the band under those clouds, yet the storm was supposed to remain well east of here.

Chelsey glanced over her shoulder. "What do you think? It looks pretty dark back there."

"It might be an optical illusion," he said, hiding the lie behind his smile. "There's only an hour until sunset. We're losing light to the east."

"I don't know, Thomas. Those look like storm clouds."

"Even if they are, we can't turn around. No sense driving into the snow."

She redirected her gaze out the windshield. The wind blew

harder, bending trees beside the road. Thomas bit his lip and pressed the gas a little harder. This was the only road to the cabin. If a tree fell and blocked their path, they were stuck.

The conifers opened to a snowy mountainside with a spectacular view of the valley below. Chelsey inhaled in wonder, and he was relieved to see she no longer focused on the weather. Theirs was the only cabin on this stretch of land, and it sat in a clearing in front of a standing army of fir and oak trees.

"This is even better than the pictures on the website showed," she said.

A snow-covered dirt road led to the cabin, and he was thankful for four-wheel drive and snow tires. He pulled the truck beside the cabin and hopped out. She helped him carry the bags to the front door.

Thomas worked the key into the lock as the wind thickened, blowing their hair around. Chelsey bounced on her toes to stay warm and her teeth chattered. The door opened to a rustic cabin, the walls dark with the smell of old wood and organic material. The air almost seemed colder indoors, saturated with an old smell, sour and musty. An icy draft made Chelsey pull her coat around her torso. The living room was small and had a rough stone fireplace along a solid wall near the back. They would need to get a fire going, and soon. An ancient-looking couch, an even older-looking recliner, shelves that held more books than decorations, and two bright throw rugs were the only furnishings.

"It's certainly minimalistic," Chelsey said, glancing out the window.

The ranger had left several logs and a pile of kindling in a bucket beside the fireplace.

"That's enough to get us through the night," Thomas said. "We'll need more by tomorrow."

"Maybe we should hit the store while it's still light out."

"Not a bad idea, but I'll start a fire before we leave. That way, the cabin will be warm by the time we return."

"Is it safe to run the fireplace unattended?"

He tapped the stone. "Absolutely. How do you think people stay warm when they're asleep?"

"Point taken. Can I help you start the fire?"

"Sure. Dig out the matches Darren gave us. I'll set up the kindling."

He stacked sticks and thinly chopped wood in a teepee shape. The ranger had left newspaper in the bottom of the bucket, but they didn't need it. Once Chelsey lit the base, the teepee caught fire. She helped Thomas layer the split logs over the blaze. Soon the fire grew large enough for the warmth to pour into the cabin.

Thomas brushed off his hands. "A job well done."

"So much better. You know, this place is kinda cozy."

"That's the idea."

"Can we go to the store now?"

"We'll gather firewood before we go. There's a stack out back we need to carry in, then I'll grab fallen limbs from the woods and stock up on kindling."

Beyond the window, light faded from the sky, and the army of darkness to the east marched closer.

~

A HALF-HOUR OF DAYLIGHT REMAINED, Jack was preoccupied with a squeaky toy on the couch, and Darren led Raven away from the pets, a forefinger pressed against his lips. She gave him a conspiratorial giggle.

As she sat on the edge of the bed, he shook his head. She held her palms up in question, and he yanked the comforter off the bed and tossed it in front of the woodstove, along with two pillows. She silently clapped. He searched one last time for the pets and found them as they'd been—Jack gnawing on the toy, Tigger sound asleep and purring from his perch.

Raven was pulling Darren's shirt over his head when headlights swept across the windows. She groaned.

"Who can that be?" she asked.

"A camper looking to rent a cabin?"

Fixing her beaded hair, as if they'd done anything to mess it up, Raven peeked out the window and palmed her forehead.

"It's my brother."

"LeVar?" Darren asked. "What's he doing here?"

"He probably smelled the meatballs."

Before the door opened, Darren tossed the comforter and pillows on the bed and did his best to appear casual. As soon as LeVar entered, Jack leaped off the couch and hurried to meet him.

"Jackie boy," LeVar said, ruffling the dog's fur behind the ears. "Long time, no see. What's it been? Half a day?"

"LeVar," Raven said, clearing her throat. "What made you stop by?"

"Just wanted to ensure you heard about the storm."

"Yeah. Shouldn't you be home? If the storm hits, you'll get stuck here."

The teenager set his hands on his hips and glanced at the woodstove.

"Would that be so bad?" When he noticed Raven's mouth falling open, the boy held up a hand. "I'm kidding, I'm kidding."

"Now that you're here," Darren said, "you could help me prepare the other cabins for the storm." Raven's shoulders sank. "Which won't take more than an hour. Right, LeVar?"

"If the ranger says so."

"So don't take off your jacket and boots. Let's get to work."

"*Aight*." LeVar eyed Raven. "Sis, you don't look so good. You sick or something?"

"Uh, might be coming down with a cold," she fibbed. "It's best if you keep your distance."

Darren struggled to keep the smirk off his face.

She hugged him and whispered in his ear, "Yeah, lovesick."

"Come on, LeVar. Before it gets too dark to work."

It didn't take long before Darren regretted the idea. Though he wanted to cover the cabins' windows as he had his own, the temperature had plummeted since the last time he went outside, and the air held a heaviness, as though the atmosphere might drop from the heavens and bury them where they stood.

LeVar, who'd learned home repair under Thomas's tutelage, was a tremendous help. Working together, they stapled plastic sheeting over every cabin window in less than an hour. By then, a grayish gloaming had settled overhead, lowering with the clouds. Light snowflakes drifted from the sky and left a dusty blanket over the land.

"I'm thinking this storm will be a lot worse than the forecast said." LeVar shivered. "You guys in good shape up here? Thomas's A-frame is open. I'm sure he wouldn't mind if you moved in."

"Thanks for the offer, but I'm tied to the state park. The ranger can't abandon his post for days on end."

"Days on end? Are you worried it might last that long?"

He lifted a shoulder. "Everything is happening too quickly. They're in a bad way from Philly up through Long Island, and the people east of us are prepared for three feet of snow. If that makes it in here, we might be stuck for a long time."

"I hear you. As soon as I get home, I'll secure the guest house like we did here."

"Smart." Darren turned his face away from the blowing snow. "In fact, I intend to drive into the village and load up on supplies. You should too."

"I will. Call me if you run into trouble."

"Thanks, LeVar. Please do the same."

6

Darren didn't trust the weather. With the wind intensifying, he imagined the storm trapping them in the cabin for days on end. They needed food. There was no telling how dangerous the storm would become. Though he wanted to stay inside with Raven, enjoy their time together, and make love after the pets fell asleep, duty called. With his girlfriend in the passenger's seat, he navigated the Silverado down the hill and into the village.

A light snowfall covered the ground, not enough to slow them down, though a glaze of ice glistening beneath the fresh powder worried him. Testing the village speed limit, he reached the store before the storm became severe. A garbage can rolled back and forth across a crowded parking lot, colliding with vehicles.

When they stepped out of the truck, a sight far more chaotic than they could have expected materialized. People crowded around the shelves, desperate to get their hands on whatever supplies they could find before the storm hit full force.

The checkout lanes were strewn with discarded baskets and forgotten items as people raced out with whatever groceries they could grab. The shelves were nearly empty by this point—the few remaining items seemed to be swarmed by dozens of villagers competing for those last cans of beans or cartons of milk. It was like a scene straight out of a disaster movie, where everyone stopped caring about manners and focused on getting what they needed. So much for neighbors helping neighbors.

Realizing the clock was ticking against them, Darren and Raven went into survival mode. Grabbing a cart each, they snatched canned goods, bottled water, cereal boxes, pasta kits, and any food that looked easy enough to prepare in case their cabin became inaccessible during the storm or they lost power.

"The shelves are picked clean," Raven called over her shoulder.

"Tell me about it," he said with a grunt. "This is as good as we're going to do. Follow me to the checkout lane. If anyone gets in my way, I'll knock them aside."

"No, you won't. I only date nice guys."

He smirked at her. "I thought you liked bad boys."

"Only inside the cabin."

Darren purred. He would never push someone aside, no matter how belligerent they acted. Everyone needed to band together, not fight.

There weren't many cashiers left—likely because the frantic crowd that waved bills at them before darting away with supplies had already swept some up—but one came free. Raven spotted the opening and shouted at Darren. He was one step ahead of her. Unloading the food items onto the conveyor belt, he searched his pockets. His wallet. Where was his wallet?

Sweat broke out on his forehead a second before his hand closed over the wallet. It was under his keys. The boy at the checkout counter had a scrawny build and thick, dark hair that flopped into his eyes. He wore a bright blue shirt with a store logo stitched on the lapel, and his hands flew as he scanned the groceries and bags of supplies. He spoke quickly and efficiently in a low monotone. The boy apologized for the wait and asked how everyone was doing, even though he couldn't keep up with the flood of customers. He checked each item before totaling the order.

Darren spotted the panic in the boy's eyes.

"You're doing great," he said. "Don't rush. We'll all get through this together."

"I wish the others were as patient as you."

A look over his shoulder told him what the boy meant. The people next in line tapped their feet, cursed, and stared bullets at Darren, Raven, and the checkout clerk.

"Easy, people," he said. "There's no reason to get angry."

A man opened his mouth to argue, took one look at Raven, who dared him to say something, and shut it with a click of his teeth. The woman beside the man lowered her gaze, suddenly interested in her shoelaces.

But the wait and underlying tension became too much. Arguments broke out between the customers, while others shouted at Raven and Darren to move faster. Some even threatened to jump ahead of them if they didn't hurry. Even so, Darren kept his cool, never losing sight of his goal: complete the purchase and drive home before the storm worsened.

After what felt like an eternity, their items were scanned, bagged, and paid for. Not a moment too soon either; a crash of thunder roared as they stepped out of the store with their supplies. People ran around in chaos, rushing back to their cars or scurrying past, carrying armfuls of groceries. Wind kicked the snow into the air, obscuring everything except fleeting shapes—shadows in constant motion.

"Was this supposed to happen?" Raven asked, staring up through the windshield. "I can't recall the last time it thundered while it snowed. Maybe when I was a teenager?"

"We'd better get out of here while we can."

Snowflakes whistled past the windows. A runaway shopping cart raced toward the Silverado. Darren shifted into drive and escaped before the cart could strike his truck. He steered onto a side street, away from the traffic. A second later, Raven yelped. He stomped the brakes.

A power line dislodged from its pole in front of them, blocking the road. The sound of splitting wood and buzzing electricity filled the air as sparks flew from its severed ends.

"Back up!" she yelled.

He reversed the truck as the live wire snaked toward them, hissing fire. Momentum threw them against the seats. The Silverado skidded to a stop just feet away from disaster, both passengers shaken but unharmed. Darren stared wide-eyed through the windshield, his heart drumming against his ribcage. He blinked back tears and swallowed hard before finally turning to Raven. He wore a smile despite it all—the storm, the chaos, and whatever else tonight would bring.

"Well, that was easy."

"Get us out of here, or I'll knock your block off."

"Yes, ma'am."

7

The glow of the dashboard panel turned Officer Newman's face red. The sky grew darker by the second, and the rain they'd encountered in New York City had changed to a snow and sleet mix as the police transport van motored westward along I-90.

Now and then he checked the mirror. Victor Bacchus' stare was expressionless. His wrists were cuffed behind his back, and chains clamped his ankles to the bottom of the seat. Whenever the headlights of a vehicle coming in the opposite direction lit the mobster's face, Newman caught the man glaring at him. The officer concealed the tremors rippling beneath his skin.

Don't show fear.

Officer Fleming manned the seat behind Newman. Two officers, not counting the driver, to watch one man. It seemed a waste of time and fuel to drive Bacchus to his new home in Buffalo, but Newman was thankful to rid himself of the killer. After fifteen years working in the federal detention center, he'd never encountered a prisoner who gave him nightmares until Bacchus came along.

Boots shifted. Newman turned his head and watched

Fleming make his rounds. The other officer checked the cuffs and chains while Bacchus ignored him. Fleming nodded at Newman and returned to his post.

"Glad he's about to be someone else's problem?" Fleming asked. Newman didn't answer. "Wonder why the feds want him in Buffalo."

"Doesn't matter." Newman peered through the windshield as snow hurtled like shooting stars at the glass. "As long as we make it there in one piece."

"Worried about the storm?"

"It's snowing hard up ahead. We won't break through until we're west of I-81."

Fleming bobbed his head.

Brake lights flared on the thruway, and Newman spotted two cars in a ditch. The drivers conferred on the shoulder, and he prayed the transport van wouldn't hit an icy patch and skid into them.

"Officer Newman," the guard in the driver's seat said, "I received word they're closing the thruway ten miles up the road."

"We have to transport the prisoner to Buffalo. Do we have an alternative route?"

"I'm checking now."

Newman crawled into the front of the van as the guard surveyed the GPS.

"Looks like this road will take us past I-81," Newman said, poking his finger at the screen. "Then we can hop back on the thruway."

"That should work, but the way this snow is coming down, I'm nervous. The plows hit the back roads last."

"I don't see another choice."

When he returned to his seat, Fleming was telling Bacchus

to wipe the smirk off his face. As far as Newman could tell, Bacchus wasn't showing any emotion.

"What's the deal?" Fleming asked.

"We'll take the next exit and hope the alternative route will get us out of this storm. They're closing the thruway for a twenty-mile stretch. We don't have a choice."

"Can the van handle the snow?"

"We're about to find out."

Fleming had a white-knuckle grip on his seat with the belt over his shoulder. The van slowed and traveled down the exit ramp. Another driver had the same idea. That car skidded and slalomed through snow drifts, battling to stay on the road. The snow was an impenetrable wall now, blocking the way forward and making it impossible to see more than a few feet in front of them.

The driver inched the van forward, tires wobbling over patches of ice. Branches trembled in the wind, and debris shot across the road. Lights from cars in the opposite lane blazed past. The transport van shook as Newman grabbed the door handle.

The van safely avoided a car in the ditch, but as they neared an intersection they hit a patch of ice, making the vehicle skid into a spin. Officer Newman cursed at how close they had come to hitting the stranded vehicle head-on before, then braced himself for whatever would happen next.

Tires squealed, snow swept beneath them like waves flooding a beach, and dizzying lights spun around them until finally their transport came to a stop. The rear of the van pitched downward, stuck in a culvert. Thankful they hadn't collided with a vehicle in the oncoming lane, Officer Newman exhaled and released his grip on the handle. He unlocked his safety belt and twisted toward Victor Bacchus to make sure he was secure in their truck's backseat before speaking again. The madman stared at him with beady black eyes.

The engine shut off. The van was still and frozen in a lake of snow.

"Why did you kill the engine?" Newman asked, pulling himself up a slight incline to reach the driver. "It's freezing out there."

"I didn't. The damn thing just died."

"Try it again."

Newman shifted forward as the driver turned the key, testing the engine. All he heard was a clicking noise.

"It ain't working," Fleming said behind them.

Newman glanced back at the other officer. "I can see that. Just watch the prisoner."

Fleming held up his hands.

"This is just great," the guard behind the wheel said. "Stuck in a ditch, no heat, and the snow is falling harder than ever."

The guard kicked at the dashboard with indignation before settling into his seat again.

"Calm down. We'll find a way out of this."

Icy tendrils seeped through every crack, chilling their bodies to the core. Newman looked around for another driver to help but saw none. They were stuck in a frozen wasteland, with no hope of rescue.

He checked his phone, hoping to find something other than static on his maps app, but all that met him were dead airwaves and flickering bars of 1%.

The three officers exchanged helpless glances before Fleming spoke again: "We have to send out an SOS signal or call someone who can help us get back on track."

"Can't," Newman said. "No coverage."

"We could light a flare."

"Good idea. Last thing we need is a semi losing control and running into us."

Bacchus coughed from the rear compartment and began laughing crazily until Newman slammed his fist against the door, silencing the psycho. Fearing further issues if they stayed put much longer, Officer Newman got out of the van. Through numb fingers, he cranked at the wheels with little success. They were stuck in knee-deep snow, and the storm was intensifying.

"Toss me that flare," Newman yelled, but no one responded. "Fleming! Are you listening?"

Freezing, the officer climbed into the van and found the driver checking underneath the ignition panel while Fleming crawled on his hands and knees to reach the flares in the back. Bacchus continued to giggle.

"Keep laughing," said Newman. "You'll freeze to death like the rest of us."

Bacchus lunged forward. He had a knife in his hand. The cuffs and chains lay in a pile under his seat.

Newman reached for his gun. Too late. The blade ripped his throat open, and he fell into the wall, gushing blood over the seats. The driver spun and removed a gun from his holster, but Bacchus was already on him, plunging the knife into the man's chest and making the blood geyser.

As Newman clutched his gushing throat, his sight failing, Fleming struggled up from the rear of the van with a gun in his hand. Instead of shooting Bacchus, he handed the weapon to the man.

"Thanks for the assistance," the killer said.

"The pleasure is all mine. Your people funded my early retirement. But how are you going to get out of here?"

"I'll find a way."

"Take me with you," the officer said. "I don't intend to freeze to death with a couple of corpses."

"I'm afraid there's only room for one person on this journey. It was nice knowing you, Officer Fleming."

Fleming's eyes widened in shock a moment before the knife slit his throat. The officer gagged and tumbled backward. He twitched and spasmed as the lifeblood drained from his body.

Bacchus cranked the engine in vain while Newman crawled out from under the seat. The interior of the transport van was blurry and indistinct. He could only make out shapes and shadows.

When his strength gave out, he collapsed on his belly. His arms lay outstretched. Bacchus buried his shoe into Newman's hand.

"Don't you have the decency to die?"

Bacchus aimed the gun and pulled the trigger.

∼

VICTOR BACCHUS MOVED from one dead officer to the next and stole their guns. He snatched their phones as well, but none displayed a service bar.

Ignoring the cold, he stepped out of his prison uniform and stood naked except for his socks and underwear. The driver was the tallest of the three corpses, so he stripped the man and concealed himself in the guard's uniform. The boots proved to be a tight fit, but they would keep his feet warm and dry. He might have a long walk before he found cell service.

His second-in-command would send someone to pick him up. Blake Skelton had run the crime syndicate since the killer's arrest. The henchman had also orchestrated the escape, paying off Fleming and convincing the officer to unlock the cuffs and chains while no one was looking. The accident had provided the perfect opportunity, and now he was free.

Which wouldn't help him if he froze in the storm. The tall

guard's jacket would keep him warm for an hour or two. Eventually, he would need to find shelter.

The icy wind blew snow into his face as he stepped outside. With the van pitched upward, he leaped from the door into a foot of snow.

Ahead of him lay freedom and the black coat of night.

8

With the haunting echo of thunder still ringing in his ears, Darren drove through the village, winding around snow-covered streets, watching for danger and other stranded drivers. It didn't take long before they found one: a car stuck in the snow with its frazzled driver standing outside, pleading for help.

The man wore a suit with a tie visible beneath his winter coat, which he had thrown over his head to protect himself from the snow. His cheeks flushed, and his eyes begged them to pull over and save him from the abyss. His briefcase lay at his feet, likely forgotten in his attempt to push the vehicle out of its deep rut.

Darren parked the Silverado, jumped out, and ran to the man. The stranded vehicle's wheels churned snow as Raven followed close behind him with an armful of rope from the back of the cab.

"What happened?" Darren yelled over the wind.

"The squall blinded me," the man said, "and I didn't see the ditch. The rear tires dropped in. I don't think I can push her out."

"Let me see what we can do. Three of us might get the job done."

Together they pushed, Raven and Darren straining with veins popping out on their heads. The suited man did his best, but his dress shoes kept slipping on the ice. The vehicle wouldn't budge. A tractor trailer drove past, kicking up ice and salt. Their proximity to the road drummed home how dangerous this job was, but they had to help the man.

"Here," Raven said, handing Darren the rope. "Tie his vehicle to the back of the truck. We'll drag him out."

Darren wasn't sure it would work. Was the rope strong enough, or would it snap?

"It's worth a try," he said. "Sir, get behind the wheel and keep her in neutral."

Darren attached the rope. The motorist didn't appear confident, but he climbed into the car, relieved to escape the cold. Darren felt the same once he entered the Silverado. The heat ran, keeping the interior comfortable. Raven shivered beside him and brushed snow out of her beaded hair.

A few tugs forward and he yanked the motorist free from his icy prison. The car sat on the shoulder, where it wouldn't get stuck again, but other vehicles skidded past. What if one lost control and rammed into them?

"Thanks so much," the man said, leaning his head through the open window.

"Anytime," Raven said as the pickup sat beside the car. "Get moving. We're vulnerable if we stay on the road."

After untying the rope, Darren drove into white nothingness. The drive up the hill to Wolf Lake State Park had him questioning if his truck could make it. No salt trucks had visited the road, and he suspected the plow and salt trucks wouldn't come out this way for hours. His tires slipped and skidded as the Silverado fishtailed along the incline. He wrapped his fingers around the steering wheel and willed himself to relax. Losing his cool would guarantee an accident. Scattered houses stood along this stretch of road, but he couldn't see them through the storm, only the lights at the windows. Raven held the door handle in worry.

Both issued sighs of relief when the truck motored into the parking lot outside the guest center. Darren cursed himself for not attaching the plow to his truck. It would have come in handy on the hill. The snow was lightening up, but he knew the initial squall was just the beginning. They needed to hurry before the storm smashed into the village.

"Go inside and warm up," he said. "I'll bring in the groceries."

"No way, Mr. Chivalry. We're in this together."

He unclasped the cover from the back of the truck. Side by side, they slid and stumbled from the parking lot to the cabin. Each unloaded a bag on the kitchen table before rushing out to the storm to retrieve the rest.

Darren and Raven tightened the hoods of their coats and rushed back to the truck. His boots sank into drifts, nearly slipping off his feet. The wind brought a chill he hadn't experienced in years, adding to his discomfort. Sheets of blowing snow blasted their faces, stinging like little needles that reminded him of the danger outside. Even so, they moved quickly, tugging grocery bags from the truck bed.

Thunder rolled in with a gust of icy wind that stopped Darren in his tracks. He had seen enough storms to know this wasn't right; the squall was moving with an intensity he hadn't expected.

Raven grabbed hold of him and shouted over the growling thunder, "Get inside! Don't worry about reattaching the cover."

He nodded.

The last of the bags tested Darren's endurance. It was

jammed with canned foods, though he suspected Raven had thrown a boulder into the bag to weigh it down.

Once inside, he closed the door and leaned against it in relief. They were safe from the elements for now. He had seen similar storms before and knew this one was only getting started. A blanket of snow would soon cover all of Wolf Lake.

Jack ran to greet them. Tigger stirred, then went back to sleep. The cabin walls creaked in protest as the wind roared around them. It howled like a wounded animal and poured through the trees surrounding the cabin, shaking their branches and sending a cascade of snow down on all sides. The temperature dropped, and Raven threw more logs on the fire while he bundled up by wrapping himself in an old blanket.

The wind increased its ferocity with each gust, picking up speed as if trying to tear Wolf Lake out of the earth and claim it as its own. Darren had to steady the window frame more than once to prevent it flying loose from the wall.

He glanced at Raven, who stared out at the blizzard.

"Perhaps we can stay put for the next few days and wait for the road crews to clear the village," he said, hoping she wouldn't sense his underlying fear. "We're safe here, and I'm sure Thomas and Chelsey are fine."

She turned and met his gaze, her eyes glinting with understanding.

"I think that is an excellent idea."

Darren exhaled, happy she had agreed. He put an arm around her shoulder and squeezed, then looked out the window at the raging storm and thanked the heavens they had made it to the cabin.

9

Teenager Scout Mourning parted the curtains over her bedroom window and gasped. Ten minutes ago, the warning had popped up on the emergency management website she monitored on her laptop. The snow was intensifying, and already two inches covered the road. She knew it was worse east of here, where the authorities had shut down a large stretch of the thruway.

What frightened her more was the radar loop. The snow was spreading westward at an alarming rate, and the National Weather Service had extended the warnings to Aldridge County, which included Thomas and Chelsey's cabin on Laurel Mountain. They were under the assumption that the storm would miss them, and she didn't want them to be caught unprepared.

Attempts to reach Thomas and Chelsey by phone failed. Not surprising. They would be lucky to find coverage atop Laurel Mountain, especially after the storm struck. There had to be a way to warn them.

The desktop radio connected her to LeVar, Darren, and Raven, the members of her amateur investigation team. She pressed the call button to alert Darren and Raven at the ranger's cabin but got no reply. If the phones failed, the radios would keep her in communication with everyone, but nobody was answering at the cabin. After two other attempts, Darren answered.

"I read you loud and clear, Scout."

"Darren, they just issued a winter storm warning for Laurel Mountain. Thomas and Chelsey are supposed to get a foot of snow, and by the looks of the radar, that prediction might be on the low side."

"We can't reach them. I doubt their phones will operate that far into the countryside."

"I don't want them to be caught unawares. The storm should hit the mountain in an hour."

Darren blew out a breath. "Best I can do is call Deputy Aguilar. If she tracks down someone from the Aldridge County Sheriff's Department, they can get word to Thomas. Everything all right in the valley?"

"The snow is coming down harder," she said, "but Mom hit the store yesterday. We have enough food to get us through the week."

"Let's hope the power doesn't go out. You're on gas heat, right?"

"Yes, and so is LeVar, but the guesthouse is frigid unless he runs the space heater. I'm worried he'll lose electricity."

"Raven and I loaded up on groceries. It's insane out there: people pushing each other to grab milk and cereal, checkout lines running halfway into the store. I hope people keep their heads."

"Me too."

"Okay, Scout. I'll contact Deputy Aguilar and see if she has any ideas about reaching Thomas. Let us know if you and your mother need help."

"Thanks, Darren."

Scout set aside the radio and padded in socked feet through the kitchen, where her mother was sliding a pumpkin pie inside the oven. She peered through the sliding glass door, cupping her hands over her brow to block out the light. LeVar had come home before the weather worsened.

"Who were you on the radio with?" Mom asked.

"That was Darren. The storm is spreading toward Laurel Mountain, and we're figuring out how to contact Thomas and Chelsey."

"They can handle themselves, hon."

"But what if they get two or three feet of snow and can't make it down the mountain?"

"I doubt they'll receive that much."

Scout nodded, though Mom didn't appreciate how strong this coastal storm was. Albany had received two feet of snow since morning, and it was still storming there. Meanwhile, half of Long Island was without power, and the news showed waves scouring the shore and homes falling into the ocean. As she considered how bad the storm would get in Wolf Lake, LeVar passed by a window. He wore a winter coat.

"Hey, Mom, do you mind if I see what LeVar is up to before the snow gets too deep?"

"No, but you'll want to hurry back before the pie finishes baking. This might be my best yet. And invite LeVar over. He's always good for two or three slices."

Scout laughed. "At minimum. See you in a few."

～

Bare-chested, Darren walked back from the radio and crawled into bed with Raven. They had the rest of the night to themselves. With the groceries stuffed into the refrigerator and enough wood to fuel the stove for the next few days, he could finally relax.

"Was that Scout?" she asked.

"We never should have given her a radio."

They shared a laugh. She ran a playful finger down his chest. "Where were we?"

"I believe you'd gotten to the part where you tell me I'm the Greek god of park rangers."

She slapped his shoulder. "Wise guy."

On the couch, Jack snored beside his chewy toy, and Tigger's tail curled mid-dream.

"First LeVar. Then Scout. Now Thomas and Chelsey."

"Thomas and Chelsey?" she asked. "How are they interrupting our play time?"

He pushed the hair off his forehead. "It seems the storm is heading towards Laurel Mountain, and nobody knows how to warn them."

"They'll be all right. That's what the cabin and fireplace are for."

"Yeah, but I hope they have enough firewood and food before the snow starts."

"I suppose you're right."

He pushed himself up, and she gave him a disappointed look.

"Don't look so glum. I'll be back." He spoke the latter in a poor rendition of Arnold Schwarzenegger in *The Terminator*. "I'll try Aguilar and see if she can help."

Raven sighed and rolled on her back. She scrolled through her phone, passing time as he pressed the deputy's speed dial and waited for her to answer. Aguilar picked up. In the background, he heard vehicles passing by.

"Hey, Darren. You two all right up on the hill?"

"We're in tip-top shape. I'm more worried about your boss."

"Thomas? What's going on with the sheriff?"

"Seems the warnings cover Laurel Mountain now."

"I didn't realize that, though it doesn't surprise me. Things are getting nasty in Wolf Lake."

"Would it be too much to ask if you contacted the Aldridge County Sheriff's Department and had someone check on Thomas and Chelsey?"

"I can do that," Aguilar said, "but it might take a while. Between alerting people with electric heat and policing the grocery stores and gas stations, we're up against it."

"The gas stations too?"

"Oh, yeah. Everyone wants fuel. Gas for generators, gas for plow trucks. It's as if everybody in the county lost their minds at once." Lambert said something to Aguilar. "Darren, I don't want to impose, but if this storm gets even worse, we might need your help."

"Raven and I will be there for you," he said. "Whatever you need."

"I appreciate it. Hopefully things won't come to that. I only pray I'm wrong about this storm."

"You think it will get worse?"

"A lot worse. It won't surprise me if we see two feet of snow in the village, and with this wind, we're looking at power outages countywide."

Darren wiped a hand across his mouth. "Let's hope it doesn't come to that point. If you need us, you know where to reach me."

"Thanks, Darren."

Aguilar ended the call. He stared at the phone, wondering if she was right. The wind whipped over the roof and the kitchen light flickered.

"What did Aguilar say?" Raven asked, rising onto her elbows.

"They're shorthanded and might need help. I volunteered our services."

She looked out the window and scrunched her face.

"Can your Silverado make it down the hill?"

"My truck can make it through anything."

"Two feet of snow?"

"If we take it slow," he said, his voice lacking confidence. "I hate to extend our intermission, but I should attach the plow to the Silverado."

"Is that code for play time?"

He burst out laughing. "No, but that's a good one. Even LeVar would be proud."

"Please. I don't want to think about my brother when I'm in the mood for love."

"Sorry to be a buzz killer, but we might need it to get out of here. The plow takes precedent."

She pulled a shirt over her head. "I'll help."

"Stay inside where it's warm."

"No, this is important."

Before he could argue, she stepped into her clothes and hurried to the closet for her winter gear. Being locked inside a cabin with a beautiful woman during a snowstorm had its advantages, yet it seemed there was always an interruption.

He put on his coat and walked into the storm. The wind shoved him around like a plaything. He lowered his head, gripped his coat together around his neck, and treaded through the snow and ice.

Could he find the plow in a blinding squall?

10

The first thing Deputy Aguilar did upon arriving at the station was remove her snow-covered jacket and place it over the heat vent. She shook the ice out of her hair. Only two inches of snow had fallen, but the storm's intensity increased by the minute. Outside the window, the snow shot past on a horizontal plane as the wind strengthened and shook the trees.

Lambert was still in the field with two other deputies and going from door to door. Her anxiousness grew. Most of the village residents had acted surprised by the storm. Either they weren't paying attention to the reports on television and radio, or they hadn't bothered to look outside. She didn't know what she would do for all the people on electric heat who lost power.

One idea popped into her head, and she picked up the phone to contact the school superintendent, Jackson Brower.

"Mr. Brower, this is Deputy Veronica Aguilar with the Nightshade County Sheriff's Department."

"Good evening, deputy. If you're calling to warn me about the storm, I already know. School is canceled tomorrow."

"Actually, it's about the village residents. We have a few thousand people on electric heat, with no backup source. If we lose power, and we certainly will, many lives will be at stake."

"I understand your concern, but I'm unsure how I can help."

"What if we converted the school gymnasium into a shelter? You're on the emergency manager's list of potential shelter sites."

"Under any other circumstance, I'd say yes in a heartbeat. But a pipe burst in the gymnasium two days ago, and the structure isn't safe."

"Shoot. I wish I'd known."

"We could use the auditorium, but that seats two hundred people, and there's no room for cots."

"Understood. I'll put the auditorium down as a last resort and check into other possibilities."

"I'm sorry, Deputy Aguilar."

She hung up and cursed. Where would she put all these people? And could she even get them from their homes to a shelter if the roads became impassable? If only Thomas were here to figure this out. She wasn't sheriff material. How many times had he told her she had the tools to run the county? Nonsense. She was a grunt—a hired hand that worked hard and always gave her best. Deputy work was her specialty. If someone wasn't telling her what to do, she became lost and directionless.

Thinking of Thomas made her remember the conversation with Darren Holt. Outside, a plow rumbled past, while a salt truck followed. She dialed the Aldridge County Sheriff's Department, and a deputy put her through to Sheriff Donner.

"Deputy Aguilar," Donner said. "I haven't spoken to you since last year."

Aguilar pictured Donner, who looked like a sheriff from the Wild West. His white handlebar mustache and matching bushy eyebrows made him appear ten years older than he was, and he was lanky, like the good guy facing the villain at high noon. His ten-gallon hat completed the getup.

"How are you, Sheriff Donner?"

"Never been better, though I hear this storm is supposed to hit us in an hour or two. How are things your way?"

"The storm is here, and I'm afraid we'll wake up to snow drifts past our windows."

"Brrr," Donner muttered. "Winter is just starting and I'm already over it. Where's Thomas?"

"That's why I'm calling, Sheriff. Thomas is up your way, staying in a cabin outside Laurel Mountain Township with Chelsey."

"Beautiful place to be when it storms."

"When they left Wolf Lake, he was under the assumption the storm would miss them, and I'm worried they won't make gathering firewood and stocking up on supplies a priority. Plus, if you get as much snow as our county expects, driving down the mountain will become impossible."

"I see your point. Here's what I'll do: Right now, all my deputies are busy, but I'll contact the ranger and try to get a deputy up to Thomas's cabin before the storm hits."

"Appreciate it, Sheriff."

"Not at all. Wish we had more sheriffs in New York like Thomas Shepherd. He's a loyal friend."

The conversation made Aguilar worry less about Thomas. He and Chelsey had people looking out for them.

In the distance, the truck turned into a neighborhood, spraying salt over the road. The snow grew heavier.

∽

FRIGID. Shivering.

Victor Bacchus held the guard's jacket together and struggled through the snow. The stolen boots kept his feet dry, but the cold bled through the boots and gloves as if he weren't wearing them. All around him lay the deepening blanket of winter.

The idiot driver who'd lost control of the transport van deserved his fate. That van could have gotten Bacchus out of this mess. Removing his gloves, he blew on his numb hands then into the gloves, puffing them up with warm breath like balloons. After he slipped on the gloves, the added heat thawed his hands, but now that the feeling was returning pain replaced the numbness. He was going to die in the storm. So much for paying off Fleming and escaping. The plan was to drive the van to a meeting point, where his second-in-charge would pick him up. Without cell service, he couldn't contact his men.

The wind tossed a spray of snow into his face. He turned his head too late, and the grains found their way inside the coat and down his shirt. It felt as if someone had doused him with a bucket of ice water.

Service. He had to find cell service.

Or a house. No way he would survive the storm unless he located shelter.

Bacchus glanced over his shoulder as he marched up a gentle incline. The storm had covered his tracks—not that he could find his way back to the van. Huddling inside the vehicle would only prolong his death. If freezing was the only option, he might as well get it over with in a hurry.

This was a wasteland. Nobody lived out here. He hadn't wanted to leave the road, but there was no choice. He wouldn't risk the police spotting him, and by now the authorities must be searching for the van. When they discovered the dead bodies, they would know he was on the loose. Could dogs follow fugitives through the snow? He wasn't sure, and he didn't wish to find out.

Ahead, the trees thinned, and he swore a shadow loomed in a clearing. He quickened his pace, thinking about someone spotting an oasis while lost in a desert. Was his mind conjuring illusions?

His feet plunged into a trench, his ankle twisting as he pitched forward. The powder covered his face and crept into his gloves and boots. He was in trouble.

"Help!" he cried out.

Fighting his way to his feet, he pushed on. Invisible blocks of cement encased his legs. When he made it past the trees, he would discover nothing but a clearing. That would be the end of him. He'd heard that dying from hypothermia was peaceful.

But as he pushed through the branches, he spotted the farmhouse. Abandoned? The windows were dark, and no vehicles sat in the driveway. If tire tracks existed, they lay buried under half a foot of snow.

He limped toward the house, unable to place his weight on his left foot. The porch steps squealed. He removed the gun, though his hands were too numb to fire the weapon.

The killer tested the doorknob. Locked. No problem. It was a flimsy door and wouldn't hold up against his strength. With a shove of his shoulder, he burst into the house and fell to his hands and knees in the entryway. At first, he thought he'd written his death warrant by finding an abandoned house. Then he realized the chill came from the wind blowing in.

Kicking the door shut, he rolled onto his back and panted at the ceiling. Something hummed beside him. A heat vent.

He threw himself on the register, tucking his hands under his stomach. Grunting, he removed the coat, hat, and gloves, then pried off the boots with his toes. As the heat enveloped his body, he glanced around.

The farmhouse was a cozy space, with worn furniture, faded floral wallpaper, and sun-bleached curtains drawn across the windows. The floors were creaky and unevenly stained, and thick layers of dust lay in the corners. This place needed a woman's touch. A bookcase filled with tattered novels stood against the far wall. The interior stank of must, like old newspapers and forgotten memories. An underlying scent of damp earth and wood smoke lingered in the air.

He got to his feet and listened, ensuring he was alone. His hands no longer trembled. If anyone was hiding upstairs, he'd take care of the problem.

The killer crept from room to room until he was sure he was alone. A check of the landline made him cuss. No dial tone. Were the lines down, or had the homeowner switched to a mobile service?

The bedroom held a chair beside the window. He sat down, wanting a warning if anyone approached. Another vent blew blessed heat across his flesh.

Bacchus checked the gun. In his mind, he pictured the map. From reading the exit signs, he felt confident that he was somewhere east of Laurel Mountain. The township stood at the base of the hill. There would be businesses and working phones. It couldn't be more than an hour's walk, even in the storm.

But could he find the township in the dark?

11

When Scout pounded on LeVar's door, nobody answered. She could see him through a part in the curtains, wearing headphones as he affixed plastic sheeting to the windows.

Testing the knob, she found it unlocked and peeked her head inside.

"Knock, knock," she said.

He sensed someone in the house and spun around with alarm on his face.

"Scout, I didn't hear you come in."

"That's because you're wearing headphones."

"Very observant. Nothing gets past you."

"What are you up to?"

He gestured at the windows. "Trying to keep the cold air outside where it belongs. These old windows can't handle the wind."

"Can I help?"

"Are you trained in the art of using a staple gun?"

"I've been known to use a stapler from time to time."

"No," he said. "A staple gun. It's a gun that shoots staples."

"Just kidding, LeVar. Mom taught me to use a staple gun. I helped her lay carpet in the basement."

"*Aight*, we're cooking with fire. I finished the interior, but I've been putting off the exterior, hoping the storm would let up."

"Fat chance of that happening. This is turning into a blizzard."

"Do you mind working outside? It's gonna be cold."

"No problem. I've got layers on. One more won't hurt. Let's get cracking."

"If your skin numbs, get your butt inside, understand? I don't want you getting frostbite."

They stepped into the wind. Despite the cold, they moved with precision around the guesthouse, stapling the plastic sheeting to lock out the snow and wind.

"Won't it tear off in the storm?" she asked.

"Probably, but every hour I can keep the house warm counts. That gas furnace doesn't help much."

"What if we lose power? You won't be able to use the space heater."

"I'll think of something."

After several minutes, they finished covering the windows, and their fingers were numb from the frosty temperatures. Exhausted but satisfied with their work, Scout and LeVar rushed inside and kicked off their boots.

"I have just the thing that will warm you up," he said. His cheeks heated when he recognized the double entendre. "Hot chocolate."

"So we'll dance around to hits from the seventies?"

"Funny. No, I'm talking about organic cacao. It will warm you to your toes."

"Then pour me a mug. I feel like a snowman."

LeVar made a beeline for the kitchen and prepared hot chocolate in two large mugs. Scout helped. He noticed how effortlessly she navigated his kitchen, as if it were second nature to her. He smiled to himself as he watched her prepare their beverages. She was like his sister.

Once they settled down with their cups of hot cocoa cradled between their hands and the heat filled their bellies, peace deepened inside LeVar. He'd grown up wondering what the meaning of family was. All he'd had was Raven to keep him company before Mom threw her out of the house. Now he had two sisters, and he grew closer to Scout every day.

They sat across from each other at the card table. Outside, snow whipped against the windows, but the extra layer of plastic was already paying dividends. He turned down the space heater before the room became too hot—a nice problem to have.

"What are you looking at?" she asked over the rim of her mug.

"Just thinking how close we've become since I moved in."

"You're not gonna get all sentimental on me, are you?"

He chuckled. "Nah. It's just that all those years I survived without a family, and now I have one that's larger than I ever imagined."

Her eyes misted over. "That's nice of you to say, LeVar. You're like family to me as well."

"You know what I went through. What was your childhood like? Was Ithaca nice?"

Her smile held a hint of sadness. She must be thinking about her parents' divorce.

Scout seemed content with the quiet, the low buzz of the heater providing white noise as she reminisced about her past. While LeVar had grown up in a household lacking warmth, hers was loving and cozy. Holiday dinners included ten to twenty guests, conversations lasted well into the evening, and aromas of freshly cooked meals lingered for days. She'd enjoyed summers at the creek swimming, playing catch, or acting like a kid. He'd spent his vacations hoping a gang would recruit him.

"I remember building a treehouse with Mom and Dad and hanging out days on end. There was always a new adventure." She lowered her gaze. "Until the accident."

"Which you survived."

She thought for a second and lifted her chin. "You're right. I did."

"What was your mom like?"

"She was all about respect, loyalty, honesty; all of which helped foster a bond between us. That's why she got so upset after I lied to her about Halloween night. Until then, I'd never broken her trust."

LeVar wondered how his life would have been, had he grown up in Scout's household. In Scout's family, disagreements arose when everyone wanted something different, but they compromised because that's what family did. They supported one another no matter what happened.

"But you have that now, LeVar," she said, reaching across the table to take his hand. "You don't have to harp on the past."

"True, and I'm totally proud of the way Mom and Raven turned out."

"You should be, but don't forget how proud they are of you."

12

Darkness fell over the mountain. Thomas and Chelsey picked their way through the dead leaves, gathering enough kindling and logs to get them through the night. The clouds were rolling ever closer, and Thomas wished he had a television to alert him about the weather.

The wind picked up, making it hard for the two of them to stay on their feet as they scurried from tree to tree in search of fallen branches. Thomas took the lead, carrying an armload of logs towards the cabin while Chelsey followed with an ax, cutting away any limbs she found that might serve their purpose.

When they returned to the cabin, they were out of breath. Though it had only been a few minutes, the sky had lowered and blackened, and Thomas swore he saw a flicker of lightning to the east. The region rarely received thunder snow, but when it happened, the accumulation piled up in a hurry. They fed the fire and left the logs to dry inside. The wind howled around the cabin.

"The storm is coming our way," Chelsey said.

"Not according to the weather reports. It might be a squall."

"Does that look like a squall to you? If you intend to make it to the store and back before the weather hits, we better get moving."

He couldn't argue with her logic. Bundling up, he led her to the truck. They hunched over so the wind didn't drive them backward. It only took a few seconds for his nose and ears to freeze. They'd brought enough food to get them through a day or two.

As the truck bounced down the mountain road, he kept looking to the east, worrying Chelsey was right. What if the forecast had completely changed while they were out of radio coverage? The bigger the storm, the harder it was to predict, and this cyclone was a monster. Lightning flickered again, making it difficult to concentrate on the road.

"Thomas, look out!"

He had enough time to slam the brakes as a tree tipped over and crashed across the road. It lay in their way like an insidious creature, guarding the mountain and preventing them from making it down the hill. They sat with the truck for a moment. His heart pounded through his chest. Had Chelsey not alerted him, the tree would have crushed the truck.

"Maybe we should turn back," she said.

"Not if you want enough food and emergency supplies to get us through the next several days."

She swallowed. "Can we move the tree out of the way?"

"It's a young tree. If we work together, I think we can push it to the side."

They climbed down from the cab. Thomas left the engine running. He needed the headlights to see what they were doing. The tree proved heavier than it appeared, but with Chelsey's help, he broke the largest branches and tossed them into the field. Grunting, he shifted the fallen tree. With every tug, his muscles bulged under his coat and sweat poured down his forehead. After what seemed like an eternity, they cleared a large enough path to drive through.

The first flurries wet his nose and danced before his eyes. The full brunt of the storm couldn't be far behind.

"Hurry, Thomas," she said after they climbed into the truck.

She didn't have to ask twice. He shifted into drive and stomped the gas pedal, hoping they would make it to the store in time.

∼

SHERIFF DONNER PUFFED out his mustache. He'd lived through too many winter storms like this one. Snow didn't scare him, but he knew when to be afraid. This was one of those times.

Deputy Barton sat at the next table, using a ham radio to raise awareness about the storm. Aldridge County had over a hundred people trained by the National Weather Service. The amateur ham radio network would allow the spotters to send snow totals and damage reports to the sheriff's department, even if the phone lines went down.

Trees swayed and danced outside his window. He looked over at Barton, the proud father of three newborns. Triplets! Robert Barton and Becky lived five miles from Laurel Mountain Township.

"Deputy, I need you to stop what you're doing and take a drive up the mountain."

"Anything you need, Sheriff. What's on the mountain?"

"Sheriff Thomas Shepherd from Nightshade County is staying in a cabin with his girlfriend. You won't meet a finer lawman than Shepherd, but I'm afraid this storm will catch him off guard. If anything happened to the sheriff of a nearby county under my watch, I'd take it personally."

"Understood."

"You'd best be going, deputy. The weather is only going to worsen."

Barton placed the hat on his head and buttoned his coat. After the deputy left the station, Donner stared at all the darkness beyond the window, as if impending doom were rolling forth. He had a bad feeling about Thomas and Chelsey out in this weather, and he hoped their vehicle wouldn't slide off the road or become stuck in a snowbank. It never took long for hypothermia to set in when temperatures hovered in the single digits.

He looked out the window at the swirling flakes racing past the glass. The snow had already piled up around most of the buildings and slicked the roads in the township. For Thomas and Chelsey to get to their cabin, they needed time—time they didn't have with the weather worsening at each breath. If they got caught in the storm, they would need God to see them through.

∼

DEPUTY BARTON DIDN'T ENJOY DRIVING in winter weather. He'd grown up in Georgia, where a dusting of snow was enough to close the highway for days. Up here, winters were severe and unforgiving, dumping mountains of snow and ice that didn't melt until spring. And some people actually skied through this stuff. To each their own.

A mile outside of Laurel Mountain Township, Becky called. He put her voice through the speakers.

"What's all this I hear about a winter storm warning?" she asked. His wife still had her Georgian drawl.

"It might be the worst in years, babe. Whatever you do, don't go out."

"Didn't plan to."

Three babies cried in the background. He felt guilty for abandoning her, but at least her parents were there to help. Neither had ever seen more than an inch of snow, and he pictured them huddled around the window and looking excitedly at the building storm.

"Mom and Dad helping you with the kids?"

"Yeah, and thank goodness. Three are a handful."

"I wish I could be there, Becky, but the office needs all the help it can get."

"You stay safe and worry about doing your job, Robert. That's all I care about."

The call ended, and he peered up at the night sky. Clouds raced westward, shredded into tags by the jet stream.

The terrain of the mountain was more dangerous than it appeared. Trees hid treacherous ledges and crags, while massive boulders obscured the view of the valley below. The occasional sapling blocked his path, and Barton used a handsaw to clear a passage wide enough for the vehicle to pass. He felt his muscles stiffening as he worked, but he pushed forward, determined to make it to the sheriff's cabin.

When he was halfway up the mountain, a tall pine tree chose this moment to slam across the road. Barton strapped on gloves and grabbed an ax from inside the SUV before stepping into the cold. His breath quickened as he approached the stillness of the woods. He knew that time was against him now; if he couldn't move this tree quickly, the worst of the snow might catch him before he reached the cabin.

Barton dug deep into the snow-covered roots and yanked. With a groan, he lifted the trunk and tossed it into the oncoming lane. Now there was room for one vehicle to pass, and he climbed into the SUV and continued upward.

The wipers struggled to clear the increasing snow. A slam of thunder made him draw a breath. He'd seen snow and thunder before, but never at the same time.

Wind whistled from the heavens. Or perhaps it had come from below.

A crack brought his head around. An oak tree that must be a hundred years old fell along the road.

He prayed the weather hadn't blocked his only return route off the mountain.

13

Mother Nature couldn't decide if she was angry or docile. As Thomas drove the F-150 into Laurel Mountain Township, bursts of snow rained from the sky, then the clouds thinned before the snow started again. Lightning flashed in the distance, unusual for December and unheard of when the temperature hovered near zero. Chelsey kept her eyes on the sky. She seemed to expect the worst, and he trusted her intuition.

They pulled in front of the only store in the township, an old wooden building, weathered by years of exposure to the elements. The paint around the windows had faded and cracked, and the door was slightly ajar. The porch creaked as he stepped on it, and a thin sheen of dirt covered the windows.

Inside the store, shelves of canned goods lined the walls, and an old cash register sat on the counter. The air was heavy with the musty scent of dust and old wood.

A grizzled man behind the counter pointed at Thomas and said, "I know you. You used to camp on the mountain years ago."

"Excellent memory," Thomas said, offering his hand.

"Sheriff Thomas Shepherd. And this is Private Investigator Chelsey Byrd."

The man's eyes widened. "You're a sheriff now? Sheriff Donner stops in every week, but never anyone from outside the county. And a private investigator? You're not chasing criminals, are you?"

"Not this week. I'm renting a cabin on Laurel Mountain. A little rest and relaxation."

"Be careful, Sheriff Shepherd. The roads are getting slick, and the wind is the devil incarnate."

"I'll grab us some food," Chelsey said, touching his arm.

"Listen to the private investigator, young man. I won't slow you down. You'll want to return to your cabin before the worst of the storm hits."

Thomas gathered food staples like oatmeal, water, sandwich fixings, coffee, canned goods, and extra blankets. Chelsey filled a basket with bread, condiments, and water. Beyond the window, a loose paper bag rocketed down the street. Night blanketed the sky, and it was becoming difficult to make out the approaching storm, were it not for the lightning.

"Yeah," the man said as they laid the groceries on the counter, "when the weather hits hard, it's always worse on the mountain. You have enough firewood to keep you warm for a few days?"

"We do," Thomas said.

"You know, it's not too late to drive into Astralon and reserve a hotel. Might be a wise idea. If we get a foot of snow, it might be a week or more before anyone arrives to plow you out."

Chelsey gave Thomas a hopeful glance.

"I've got an F-150."

"Hope it makes it through the storm. If you ask me, it will take a snowcat to get down that mountain."

As they set the bags inside the cab, Chelsey stared at him.

"Maybe he's right, Thomas. A hotel sounds kinda nice."

"We'll be fine. You're not used to living in the wilderness."

"But if it snows like he said it might?"

"You'll love it. Wait until you see the views. Until you see a snow-covered township from that mountain, you haven't lived."

"If you say so."

∼

DARREN YAWNED and stretched his arms above his head. Making love to Raven never failed to leave him exhausted.

Jack and Tigger curled beside him as they lay on a comforter tossed in front of the woodstove. The heat of the fire relaxed his body and melted the tension from his muscles. There was something exciting about the storm. He enjoyed being inside with the woman he loved. Yet an underlying nervousness provoked by the snow and wind prevented him from drifting off to sleep.

All around the cabin, the wind howled, prompting Jack and Tigger to move closer to Darren in search of comfort. Raven stirred beside him, and he felt the heat from her body along his legs. He liked that feeling—the heat and the weight of her body against him. He snuggled closer to block out the sound of the wind trying to break down the door.

Somewhere to the west, Thomas and Chelsey were inside their cabin on Laurel Mountain or battling the elements. He prayed it was the former. If only he could reach his friend by phone and warn them. He trusted Deputy Aguilar was doing her best to get word of the storm to Thomas. If they didn't know by now, it was too late.

He watched with half-closed eyes as Raven slowly opened her own. Her brow furrowed, and she squirmed under the blanket. The wind grew stronger by the second, rattling windows and howling at the threshold of their home.

"My God," she whispered, though a thunderous gust drowned her voice, shaking the house like an angry fist pounding on the door.

Protecting them from the storm would take all of Darren's energy, yet he wouldn't have it any other way. He was determined to make sure Raven and the pets were safe.

At a clap of thunder, the kitchen light flickered and went out. Darren cursed the lightning and grabbed flashlights and candles, filling their home with a soft glow.

Thankfully, they had plenty of blankets and the woodstove to keep them warm while they waited for the power to return.

He could wait no longer. Darren grabbed his coat. He had to see the wrath Mother Nature had brought upon the state park.

Darren opened the door and stepped into a snowdrift, bracing himself against the howling winds and blinding snow. The view made him hiss. Two trees lay prone around them, wrestled to the ground by the storm's intensity. Drifts piled high, blocking the parking lot from the road. A blizzard had smashed through their sleepy community with a vengeance.

But even in all that destruction, there was beauty: snow covered bare branches and icicles hung from trunks like jewels dangling from a necklace. The wind sang a haunting dirge.

Darren stood, lost in wonder at nature's force, before returning to Raven. He shook the snow from his boots and took her waiting hand. Her eyes were wide with awe as Darren told her about the fallen trees.

Wrapped in coats, gloves, and hats, they ventured into the winter wonderland. As Darren pulled open the door, a gust of searing cold blasted their faces and nearly knocked him off balance, but he held on to her hand and stood firm against the wind.

Together they marveled at the power of nature and its ability to destroy yet also create something so beautiful. The snow had blanketed their world in crystal whites and icy blues, leaving them breathless as they surveyed the damage.

"There must be six inches of snow on the ground," she said. "That's ridiculous. The storm began two hours ago."

"And it's still coming down."

Jack joined them in the doorway. When it became obvious Tigger wanted no part of winter, Darren closed the door to conserve heat. The three stood and stared. Flakes the size of silver dollars wet their hair and faces. The dog barked and shook the snow off his coat, then ran and bounded through the snow.

"He won't run away, will he?"

Darren shook his head. "Jack is just having fun. He's never seen it snow this hard."

Jack stopped and stared back at them with a huge grin. The dog wanted them to join him.

"I don't think so, buddy," Raven said. "It's too cold for me."

Darren formed a snowball, tossed it to Jack, who leaped skyward and snatched it out of the air with a puff of powder. She couldn't stop laughing. He kept tossing snowballs at Jack until the dog tired of the game and trotted back to them, covered in white.

"I bet you want to hang out beside the stove," Darren said, petting the dog.

Raven grabbed his arm. "Darren, those trees only missed the cabin by a hundred feet. Do you think the other trees will hold up to the wind, or are we in danger?"

Last month's fires had weakened the forest. Fortunately, he'd taken down the deadwood, anticipating that a storm might put the cabin at risk.

"We're okay for now."

"For now?"

"Don't worry about it."

But as Darren entered the cabin with Raven and Jack, he wondered if he could justify his confidence.

14

An inch of snow covered the ground as Deputy Robert Barton stopped his cruiser outside the cabin Sheriff Thomas Shepherd had rented with his girlfriend. There was no sign of a vehicle out front, but smoke curled out of the chimney. It didn't appear anyone was here.

Approaching the cabin, he called out.

"Sheriff Shepherd? Ms. Byrd? Anyone out back?"

Nobody answered. The snow was falling more heavily now, and the wind leached the heat from his body, shoving the deputy around and bullying him.

"Hello?"

He pounded on the door until the hinges shook. Still no answer. Barton hurried around the side of the cabin toward the wood chopping area, scanning for any sign of the missing people. He kicked through a patch of snow that had gathered between two rocks, small ice chips exploding in all directions.

The snow was coming down even harder, and Barton had to squint to see more than a few feet in front of him. His police radio squawked, and he heard Donner's voice.

"Can you hear me, Barton? Everything all right?"

He hollered back into his radio, "Yeah, I can't find Shepherd and Byrd."

Barton ducked under some low-hanging branches and stepped over logs, which someone had dragged—presumably for wood splitting—near an old shed. Snow had piled up against the base of the structure; he pushed clumps from the door as he bent down to peer inside. Nothing but tools and planks of wood. He thought he heard something, like a faint whisper or moan coming from deeper in the woods, but it quickly faded away with the wind.

If the sheriff of Nightshade County and his girlfriend had lost their way in the storm, how would he find them? He needed help. Barton grabbed his radio and contacted the police in Astralon, the closest town with its own force.

"I need assistance in locating two missing citizens. Requesting other units to join the search for Sheriff Shepherd and Ms. Byrd, both of which have recently been reported missing from their cabin on Laurel Mountain."

With no response from his fellow officers, he adjusted the frequency and tried again. "This is Deputy Robert Barton calling on behalf of the Aldridge County Sheriff's Department. We need help locating Sheriff Thomas Shepherd and Ms. Chelsey Byrd, who are believed to be lost somewhere near Laurel Mountain."

He waited, listening for any sign that someone was responding to his call. A faint reply crackled through the radio. It was Chief David Meyer's voice coming from the nearby town of Astralon—they were sending two officers to search the roads, but their department was having a hard time keeping up with the wind damage.

Just as Barton was about to thank Meyer, he heard Sheriff Donner.

"Barton, abandon your search and regroup with the Astralon force," he said. "An escaped convict is in the area. State police located a prison transport van two miles from Laurel Mountain. There were three dead officers in the van. The man they were transporting is Victor Bacchus, a murderer with a Rochester crime syndicate. Will forward you his picture."

Barton gasped. He'd never heard of Bacchus. How could one man take out three armed officers? Somewhere, a dog howled. The photograph arrived. The psychopath in the picture made Barton forget about the wind and cold.

Reversing course, he drove down the mountain, hoping no more trees were blocking his path. The tires spun on the ice, and he felt the back end fishtailing. Righting the wheel before he ended up in a ditch, Barton continued down the hill.

He thanked the sky when the SUV arrived in the township. Astralon PD had congregated near the abandoned van. As he exited Laurel Mountain and reentered the wilderness, something dark flashed in front of him. It could have been a deer. It might have been anything.

The deputy jammed the brakes and radioed his position to Donner. Removing his gun, he moved through the woods. Snow-covered trees stood guard, as if warning him away from unseen danger. He heard twigs snapping underfoot and glimpsed fresh animal tracks, but no signs of the escaped convict.

Barton thought about the state troopers who'd happened upon the slaughter; he couldn't imagine what they were going through. Law enforcement was a tightknit community. They may have known the prison officers.

Deeper into the woods, Barton noticed a break in the snow near a fir tree. Kneeling, he found tracks that led into the distance. The prints were too large to be those of a bear or wolf, and when he followed them with his flashlight, they led him to a pile of sticks and leaves, as if a person had considered making a fire and run off. Someone had been here. Victor Bacchus.

The tracks were easy to follow, as it appeared Bacchus had been dragging one leg behind him. Then, suddenly, the tracks zigzagged, as if changing direction multiple times before returning to their original heading. Had the escaped convict become confused in the storm and lost his sense of direction?

Tracking forward with his gun drawn, Barton followed the trail until it ended at a broken down shed in an open field beside Laurel Mountain. He stopped when he got close enough to make out movement inside. Was that whistling? As he drew nearer, he could tell someone inside was humming an old waltz while working on something, blowing on it as if trying to start a fire. He recognized the song—it was one his grandmother had taught him when he was just a boy: "On Top of Old Smokey."

As Barton approached, a figure lumbered out of the shed, and Barton lowered the gun in relief.

"Don't shoot," the hunched-over man said.

"Sorry to alarm you. There's a dangerous escaped convict on the loose, and I followed footprints from the woods to the shed. Was that you?"

"No." The man scratched his beard. "I came straight from the house."

Barton followed the man's gaze toward a farmhouse on the edge of the clearing.

"You see anybody in the storm?"

"Can't say as I did, but I noticed something. I had an ax for splitting wood outside the shed. It's gone."

Barton mulled over the possibility that the escaped convict had taken it. The ax would serve as a weapon and help him chop wood. Nobody could survive for long in this cold without building a fire.

The deputy warned the man to lock his doors and report suspicious activity to the sheriff's department. He searched for footprints leading away from the shed, but if Bacchus had come this way, the storm had covered his tracks.

Then Barton spotted another set of prints crossing the field. If they belonged to the convict, it appeared he was heading toward the township. Following them further into the woods, he saw the tracks heading in all directions, yet each eventually returned to a single path. It was as if Victor Bacchus had been going around in circles. Barton moved faster, pressing through the snow until a light shone in the distance. He continued to follow the trail and soon realized he was closing in on something. Another house.

Farmhouses were scattered throughout the countryside, and any would serve as the perfect hiding spot for the killer. He thought about the dead officers and worried what Bacchus would do if he came upon a homeowner.

Deputy Barton radioed Donner. The sheriff sounded as if he was telling Barton to convene with the Astralon police, but the feed kept breaking up. It was foolhardy to enter a home without backup, but duty pulled him forward.

Barton hurried toward the light.

15

Sheltered from the storm, Scout scrolled through social media posts on the computer she'd donated to LeVar and the amateur investigation club. He was outside, clearing a path from the guesthouse to the concrete walkways. The scrape of metal against ground continued every few seconds. She wished LeVar would stop worrying about the storm and come inside. There was no keeping up with it. As soon as he opened a path to the door, the snow covered it. Wind shrieked, and a sheet of white fell outside the window, falling from a tree.

LeVar ran inside, cussing as he pulled off his jacket.

"What happened to you?" she asked, spinning around in her chair.

"The wind. It knocked a pile of snow out of a tree, and half of it fell down the back of my shirt."

She tried not to laugh, but it was impossible. He yanked the shirt over his head, ran into the bathroom and shut the door. A second later, the shower ran. When he returned to the front room, he was wearing his Batman pajama bottoms and a fresh shirt.

"What's the latest on the storm?" he asked, toweling his hair dry.

"The internet is losing its mind. People are reporting crazy snowfall totals. Check this out. Kane Grove University has half a foot of snow on the ground, and the storm just started three hours ago. Someone in Treman Mills reported nine inches, though that might be an exaggeration."

"Not based on what I saw outside. I've never seen it come down so hard." He gave her a concerned look. "Scout, maybe you should head home while you can. I can't keep the walkways clear."

"Trying to get rid of me?"

"Not at all. I'm just saying the longer you stay, the more difficult it will be to get back."

That was a valid point. Still, she'd walked through a foot of snow before. There was time.

"How is the storm east of here?" he asked.

She switched tabs and displayed a weather radar. The bright oranges and reds highlighted a squall.

"That wasn't there before. Those storms must have popped up in the last ten minutes."

"Where are they heading?"

She zoomed in on the town names.

"Laurel Mountain. I don't like this, LeVar. We don't have any way to reach Thomas and Chelsey, and the storm is about to smash into them."

"Have you tried their phones in the last hour?"

"No, but the coverage around Laurel Mountain is horrendous. I'll give it a shot."

She tried Thomas's cell, then Chelsey's. No answers. Her throat went dry, as if a caterpillar had crawled inside.

"Look, I talked to Aguilar earlier. She got through to the Aldridge County sheriff, who knows Thomas. He'll get word to them and ensure they're okay. Besides, it's not like Thomas hasn't driven through snow before."

"He's never driven through a storm like this one."

The squall marched toward Laurel Mountain like a monstrous army. She returned to the reports and searched for information. Her heart stopped.

"What's wrong?"

"LeVar, when the squall went through Ithaca, it produced 70-mph winds at the airport and ripped a roof off a house."

"Geez."

"According to a storm spotter in Cortland, the squall dropped four inches of snow in less than an hour. That's dangerous."

"As I said, Thomas and Chelsey can take care of themselves."

She noticed the lack of conviction in his voice.

Scout continued to search the internet for information about the snow. She came across a news report concerning a prisoner, Victor Bacchus, who had escaped from custody during the storm. The authorities believed he was outside Laurel Mountain Township.

"Are you seeing this?" she asked.

He stared over her shoulder, reading along.

"What else could go wrong?"

"LeVar, this guy is a murderous psychopath, and he can't be more than a few miles from Thomas and Chelsey's cabin."

He raised a hand.

"All right, calm down. What are the odds they'll run into this guy? Why would he head up the mountain?"

"Gee, I don't know. Maybe to search for cell coverage or find a nice, cozy cabin to hide in while the police searched for him?"

"You're jumping to conclusions."

Though LeVar was trying to keep her calm, she saw worry creeping into his eyes.

"Call Deputy Aguilar."

"Scout, if it's on the internet, every law enforcement officer in the northeast already knows about this Victor Bacchus guy. There's no point in calling Aguilar and bothering her. Heck, I volunteered to work tonight, and she bit my head off and told me to stay inside."

LeVar was right. The chances of Thomas and Chelsey encountering Victor Bacchus were low. Still, she couldn't help but worry because he was close by. The news report claimed Bacchus had murdered five people over the past two years.

Scout tried Thomas's cell phone again with no answer. She tried to calm her nerves as best she could while thinking through worst-case scenarios. If Bacchus happened upon Thomas and Chelsey in their cabin, would he murder them to steal their shelter?

"You're overthinking this," he said. "If you intend on staying, let's shut down the monitor and avoid the reports. At least for the next hour."

"What do you have in mind?"

He held up a finger and ran to the hallway closet. She smirked when he returned with a board game tucked under his arm.

"Scrabble. I'm about to take you to school, girl."

"You think so, do you?"

He set the board on the card table. Scout stared at the pieces, her mind in another place. How could she enjoy a game when her friends were in danger? LeVar laid out the tiles as she stared through the window into the black night.

LeVar folded his hands and sighed. "Scout, I understand your worry, but we have no control over what's happening in Laurel Mountain. Either we put the game away and worry ourselves sick, or you watch me kick your butt all over Wolf Lake with my superior intellect."

"You're pushing your luck."

"Am I? You're looking at a dean's list student."

"Yeah? And you're challenging an honor roll student."

He was right. She needed to distract herself with a game while they awaited a response from Thomas or news of Bacchus' capture.

Scout picked up the letter tiles and mixed them around in her hand, as if they held significance beyond providing options in the game they were about to play. She knew it was irrational, but she had used this trick often when faced with an impasse before; getting herself out of her own head by focusing on something completely unrelated. And the challenge provided brain stimulation, perfect for taking her mind off her worries.

A clap of thunder made her jump. Lightning gave her a brief view of the outside world. This was less of a winter storm and more of an apocalyptic event. She'd never seen flakes so large. The snow obscured the houses along the lake, and the gale slammed waves against the shoreline.

"It's up to you," LeVar said. "Let's do this. We'll call Thomas again after we finish playing."

Scout exhaled, then smiled as she set up her tiles. She'd never seen LeVar passionate about board games, and that made her laugh.

"You're on," she said. "Prepare to lose."

16

The snow fell so hard Thomas couldn't see the road ten yards in front of his truck. He moved at a snail's pace, the tires grinding and crunching through the fresh powder. At least they weren't spinning. He had that going for him.

He maintained a stoic expression, hiding his worry as best he could, but it grew more difficult by the minute. Chelsey held the handle with both hands and darted her eyes from one obscured stretch of pavement to the next.

They were near the highway. That was Thomas's best estimate. Whether they were two miles or two hundred feet from the on ramp, he didn't know.

A flashing red light appeared in the haze, and he touched the brakes, making the back end of the truck slide into the oncoming lane.

"Careful, Thomas," she said. "It's the police."

"The police?"

"Maybe they're turning people around because the roads are too dangerous."

After Thomas lowered the window, a gruff-looking officer

with a thick mustache shone a flashlight inside. The man glanced at Chelsey.

"Where you folks headed?"

"Up Laurel Mountain," Thomas said. "We had to double back to reach the road."

The officer, who wore a navy-blue Astralon PD uniform, spoke into his radio before turning his attention to the cab's interior, as if searching for something.

"See anyone along the road while you were driving?"

"No, officer." He thought about producing his badge and ID, but the man appeared intense and stressed. Now wasn't the time for Thomas to throw his weight around. "Should we be worried?"

"Under no circumstances should you pick up anyone on the road. As far as the weather goes, you're best off jumping on the interstate and heading to the city. Even with four-wheel drive, your truck won't make it up the mountain."

Before Thomas could thank the officer, the man waved him through. The truck passed between two cruisers. Another officer watched the F-150 with suspicion.

"What was that about?" Thomas asked after raising the window.

"If you ask me, they're searching for a fugitive."

"That was my impression. Maybe I should radio the Aldridge County Sheriff's Department. I know Sheriff Donner. If something is going on, he'll tell me."

The truck slid, and Thomas turned into the skid.

"How about you just concentrate on getting us out of this mess? You can radio Sheriff Donner afterward."

She was right. It took all his concentration to keep the F-150 on the road. Still, he disagreed with the officer. If they made it back to the mountain, the pickup could handle the conditions.

The snow was only a few inches deep. He had to hurry before the weather worsened.

"Thomas," she said, "we should take the officer's advice and drive to the city. Forget the cabin. If the weather clears, we can try again in a few days."

"We can't."

"Why not?"

"Our belongings. We left everything in the cabin."

"But we have our IDs, credit cards, and enough bags of groceries to feed ourselves for two days. Let's find a hotel before they all fill up."

"Chelsey, there's a reason I drive this truck. It cuts through the snow, and I've made it through countless winter storms since I returned to New York."

She pressed her lips together and turned away in disagreement. Was he making a mistake?

"Honey, we'll be fine. A half hour from now, we'll be sitting in front of the fire and eating dinner. Trust me. We'll make it."

"I don't know."

"Once you experience winter on Laurel Mountain, you'll see this was worth it."

She chewed a nail and looked through the window. Thomas knew he'd upset her; talking would only dig a deeper hole for himself.

With both hands gripping the steering wheel, he stared into the white maelstrom.

∼

THE NO-NONSENSE GLARE Deputy Aguilar gave the customers in the checkout lines made people look away or study their shoes. She'd never seen the citizens of Wolf Lake act like this.

Boxes of cereal, bread, and canned goods lay scattered in the aisles. It appeared a tornado had struck the inside of the grocery store. The manager, an overweight man with a red face, was on the fast track toward a heart attack. He thanked Aguilar for showing up.

"I need you to keep the peace," she told a junior deputy with a boyish face. The kid swallowed and nodded. She wished LeVar was here. He wouldn't blanch under the pressure. "You can handle this. If you need anything, contact me."

The junior deputy straightened his back and lifted his chin. He would do fine with a little encouragement.

Before Aguilar walked away, she eyed the customers. "What's wrong with you? All the years I've lived in Wolf Lake, I've never been so embarrassed. You're in this together, people. The same person you're fighting with over a loaf of bread might be the one who pulls you out of a ditch or offers you a warm place to sleep after your power goes out. I suggest you act with decorum, or so help me, I'll come back here and ensure you do."

Aguilar may have stood a foot shorter than some men in line, but to them, she was an angry giant.

"They'll behave for you," she whispered to the deputy. "Don't show fear."

"Yes, Deputy Aguilar."

She left the store and lowered her head against the blowing snow. Fifteen minutes ago, she'd brushed off her windshield, yet an inch of new snow covered the cruiser. Groaning, she cleared the glass with a gloved hand and slid into the seat.

The radio activity had increased tenfold since she'd last listened. Something about an escaped convict, though it was difficult to hear over the passing plow. She turned up the volume and recognized Sheriff Donner's voice. Escaped convict Victor Bacchus was somewhere near Laurel Mountain. He'd murdered three officers and left their bodies in the transport van.

The killer was near Thomas and Chelsey.

"Sheriff, this is Deputy Aguilar in Nightshade County."

"Having a hard time hearing you, deputy," Donner said. "The radio keeps breaking up. Must be this storm."

"Any chance you contacted Sheriff Shepherd?"

"Afraid not. With the snow and a fugitive on the loose, we're up against it."

"Understood. Do you believe the convict is coming our way?"

"If he steals a vehicle," Donner said, "anything is possible, but if I were him, I'd head away from the storm, not into its teeth."

The sheriff's voice crackled, and she only caught bits and pieces of what he said. Her first thought was to call Thomas and warn him. There were two problems. One, Thomas would throw aside his vacation and rush to aid the searchers. Two, she couldn't get a hold of him. All attempts to call Thomas and Chelsey had failed.

With the radio on the fritz, she called Lambert's cell.

"Did you get Sheriff Donner's report?" she asked.

"I heard it. Laurel Mountain. I've been trying to contact Thomas."

"No can do?"

"Nope. He's beyond the coverage radius."

"I wish someone could get up that mountain and let him know what's going on."

"I hear you, but Thomas is sheriff for a reason, and Chelsey is a tough cookie herself. They'll be all right."

"Thanks, Lambert. I'm coming in. Meet you at the office in ten minutes."

17

"What did you say?" Chelsey yelled.

"I said we made it back to Laurel Mountain Township," Thomas said.

They raised their voices to hear each other. The whistling wind drowned out all sounds except the crunch of the tires digging through the snow.

He didn't tell her everything, choosing to leave out the part about not knowing where they were in the township. The houses looked the same, and he swore this was the third time he'd turned down this street. It was impossible to read the roadsigns.

"Are you sure this is Laurel Mountain Township?" she asked.

"Positive. What else could it be?"

In truth, all these little townships looked the same. Maybe he was way off course. Her suggestion to throw in the towel and get a hotel for the night kept ringing in his head. Either way, they would spend time together. Why risk their lives to find their mountain cabin? The storm wouldn't last that long, would it? They could try again tomorrow. Or the next day.

No. All their clothes were in the cabin, and he'd left a warm fire blazing. *You have your father's stubbornness,* a voice whispered in the back of his mind. True, but that stubbornness had led his father to build Shepherd Systems into a regional powerhouse after everyone told him he couldn't compete with a technology company backed by Wall Street. He could do this. What was a little snow?

"All right, we're just about there," he said, passing a pale-yellow house for the third time.

"I swear we've been here before."

"It's probably just the storm fooling us. If I'm not mistaken, the village store is on the next block. We're safe now."

"Are we?"

The tires spun as the truck pushed through the falling snow. The flakes were growing larger. They struck the window with wet splats and drizzled down the glass like blood pouring from open wounds. Something appeared out of the darkness and bounded across the road. He slammed the brakes and reached across the cab, though the seatbelt held her in place.

"What was it?" she asked, peering toward where the creature had disappeared.

"Deer. A buck, given the antlers."

"In the middle of town?"

"It's probably lost and confused because of the storm."

"That makes three of us."

All the houses were dark, the villagers snug and secure in their beds. Back home, his family and friends were inside their houses, laughing and out of the elements. A pang of jealousy hit him in the chest.

He focused on the task at hand. He searched for the store, allowing his headlights to lead the way. Still, it was difficult to tell where the road ended and the parking spaces began. Visibility was poor and getting worse.

"I see it," she said, pointing out the window.

Yes, they'd reached the Laurel Mountain store. Except the light drawing his eyes turned out to be a streetlamp. Were they even on the main road? If this wasn't the store, where was it?

The look on her face told him she was too frightened to argue.

"Are you ready to put this adventure of ours to bed?" she asked, her voice strained.

He intended to finish what he'd started, but his stubbornness collided with his sanity. He wanted to press forward, but he held back. The storm was getting worse, and they were driving in circles. Much as he hated to admit it, she was right about finding a hotel, but reaching the highway might prove even more difficult than locating the mountain road.

He pulled the truck beside a curb and shifted into reverse. "We'll find a place to stay," he said. "We'll give it another go tomorrow."

Chelsey exhaled, relief flooding her face. "You're a good man, Thomas."

He chuckled, letting the truck move backward. "Just a stubborn one."

As he turned the vehicle around, he glanced out his window, certain they were in Laurel Mountain Township and a turn away from driving to the cabin. He searched for a recognizable landmark and found nothing.

∼

Victor Bacchus spat and shivered. He never should have abandoned the farmhouse and tried to reach town. Inside, he'd had heat and a pantry full of food to keep him from starving. But he'd also trapped himself. If the police showed up, they could have surrounded the house. And he needed to find cell service. Too bad this backwards township had none.

Now he was starving and freezing to death, with no place to go. His booted legs struggled through the deepening snow, and his twisted ankle shrieked with agony. Every house he passed tempted him to break inside, murder the owners, and thaw his body. At least no one would recognize him. He could barely see the street from the sidewalk, which meant the police couldn't see him either. Good thing since he looked out of place carrying an ax over his shoulder.

The rectangular structure emerged from the storm like an island trapped in a fog bank. An abandoned store stood in the shadows, dark and dilapidated. He shuffled forward, almost colliding with two smaller rectangles that protruded from the ground. Pumps. He'd located a gas station.

Bacchus yanked the door and found it locked. He jammed the ax handle through the glass, reached in, and twisted the locking mechanism. It was cold inside, but nothing compared to the chill of slogging through the storm. He stumbled in, cackling with wild joy.

"Nothing can kill you," he said to himself.

He locked the door behind him and studied the interior. The gas station was dingy, with a tiled floor coated in a layer of grime. Posters covered the walls, and an empty, decrepit vending machine that had once served salty and sweet snacks stood upright. Dust littered the counter, and cobwebs hung from the ceiling. Shelves once stocked with candy, cigarettes, and chips stood bare and uninviting. The stench of mildew and gasoline leached out of the walls. There was also an underlying scent of stale cigarette smoke that refused to dissipate.

Bacchus grinned. This was exactly what he had been looking for—an abandoned business that he could use as a temporary refuge. All he needed to do was warm himself, but how? Starting a fire in the back was a terrible idea—old motor oil covered the floor in inky blotches, and smoke would draw the police.

He crossed to the counter and searched for a telephone. No luck. He tried his cell phone again, found a bar, and issued an expletive when it vanished.

Bacchus shook his head. He needed rest as much as he required a plan to contact his home base.

He found a half-open door at the rear of the building, stepped through, and couldn't believe his luck. A moth-eaten couch stood against the far wall, and someone had left a blanket on the cushion. Perhaps the former owner had taken catnaps between jobs.

The killer collapsed on the couch and drew the blanket over his shoulder. He was exhausted; sleep crept up on him. Snow pattered against the window, and he closed his eyes. Beyond the refuge, the wind howled. He would rest and formulate a plan upon awakening.

18

The blinding snow, the plows speeding past, Chelsey's constant warnings to get off the road—they all wound Thomas into a knot and made him wish he could block out the world. All he cared about was keeping the truck on the road. Wherever the road was. He seemed to be in the correct lane. It was impossible to tell. She wanted him to give up and take her to a hotel. He gladly would, if he could find the highway in this mess. It was hard enough searching for the mountain road.

"I'm doing my best," he said through clenched teeth.

"I know you are, Thomas, but neither of us knows where we are. Admit it. The roadsigns are invisible. There's no telling how to reach the cabin."

"Repeating that won't change anything."

She turned away, and he instantly regretted snapping at her. If he'd listened to her in the first place, they wouldn't be in this mess. He should have driven to the store before the snow hit, and when she suggested they find a hotel, he could have listened. Instead, he'd been dead set on making it to the cabin, and now he was paying for his foolishness.

A salt truck passed, heading in the opposite direction. For a long second, the wake left him completely blinded. Visibility didn't improve after the truck disappeared. Having surrendered to the inevitable, he just wanted to find somewhere to stop. A store, a hotel, anywhere. Sheriff Donner would let them hang out in the department until the weather cleared, but he would need to find the interstate, and that was proving impossible.

The tires struck something in the road, and the truck hopped. Chelsey yelped and looked behind her. She was worried they'd hit an animal . . . or a person, but the mirrors revealed a chunk of ice that had fallen off a vehicle.

He leaned over the wheel and squinted, scanning the darkness. Nothing. Then something emerged from the shadows—a rectangular structure in the middle of an empty road. He gasped and slammed on the brakes. No, not an empty road. He'd lost control and was hurtling across an icy parking lot toward two gas pumps.

"Thomas, the pumps!"

"I see them, I see them."

He turned into the skid, and the opposite side fishtailed. The pickup's momentum carried them toward the pumps. He cranked the wheel again as sweat broke on his brow. The wheels caught, and the truck jerked and came to a stop.

"Oh my God." Chelsey clutched the door handle with one hand and the center compartment with the other. "How did we end up in a parking lot?"

"Your guess is as good as mine."

That was close. Had he not recognized the structure as a gas station, he would have driven through the pumps and smashed into the building.

"Where are we?"

"Still in Laurel Mountain Township. The good news is I know where we are now."

"You recognize this place?"

"I've stopped here before. Cheapest gas in the county."

"I don't think it's open."

Thomas blinked and released his seatbelt. He hadn't expected to find anything in this storm. But here it was—a beacon in the night, beckoning for them to pull over. He drove the truck closer, parking it halfway between the road and the building. He pushed the door open and stepped outside. The wind roared in his ears and frosted his skin.

"An abandoned building," Chelsey said through the open window. "There isn't anyone here who can help us."

"We're two miles away from the mountain road. I can get us back now."

"You think the F-150 can make it to the cabin in this mess?"

"It's worth a try. The entire township shut down after the storm hit. Wait here and keep the engine going. I'll check it out."

He approached the storefront. The windows were black. The door was locked, and flakes of snow gathered on the pane. Someone had broken the glass. Vandals?

Cupping his hands around his eyes, he peered inside and searched for signs of life. Water congealed on the floor. That could have come from a leak in the roof. Either that or someone had broken in and tracked snow through the front room.

Before he reached for the handle, he caught Chelsey staring at him through the windshield. She motioned for him to return. Giving the abandoned gas station one last glance, he climbed into the truck.

∼

Victor Bacchus sprawled on the couch with the blanket covering his face. He teetered on the edge of a dream about freezing to death. A noise brought him awake, and he sat up, rubbing his eyes and reaching for his gun. The police? Impossible. Nobody knew he was here.

He remembered smashing the glass on the front door. Someone had reported a break-in.

The killer crawled off the couch and stood beside the door. Outside the gas station, a truck motor rumbled. He slipped down the hallway and crouched behind the counter. From here, he could make out a pickup truck beyond a wall of falling snow. The wipers ran back and forth.

There were two people in the pickup. He couldn't tell if they were law enforcement or ordinary citizens. Either way, if they approached the gas station he'd kill them both.

He checked the gun for ammunition, stepped away from the counter, and waited for them to enter. Minutes passed, but the truck didn't move. They were deciding what to do, or they knew he was inside. For the first time since his escape, his confidence waned. He had to take control if he ever wanted to find cell service and rendezvous with his henchman.

He crept to the entrance and peered through the broken window. The truck was still there, but the driver had changed seats and the passenger was now behind the wheel. Was this his chance?

Now that he was closer, he could see a man in the passenger's seat and a woman with long curly hair behind the wheel. Nothing but a couple lost on the road and trying to escape the snow. As long as they left him alone, he'd allow them to live.

A thought occurred to him. What if they knew he was hiding behind the counter and were about to call the police? Every law enforcement officer in the state was searching for him. He couldn't take chances.

Then he heard something—the sound of doors opening, of voices in the parking lot. The two were talking, but he couldn't hear what they were saying.

Bacchus felt his heart speed up. They were coming. He had to act fast. He hefted the ax and assessed its weight. The blade craved fresh blood as he prepared himself to strike. That was safer than firing the gun and drawing attention. This way, they'd die in silence, and none would be the wiser.

"I'm telling you, the door is locked and the lights are off," the man said outside. "Even if there's a phone in the building, it can't be connected."

"Someone broke the glass, Thomas."

"I see that."

"If worse comes to worst, this is shelter."

"No, thanks, Chelsey. That place is crawling with rats. I'll take my chances on the road."

Bacchus aimed the gun around the counter and sighted it on the man. One squeeze of the trigger would take his life. The other hand gripped the ax handle.

Kill them both.

The woman reached for the door, and the man coaxed her back to the truck. A second later, they left the parking lot. The headlights blinded him.

As they drove away, he slumped against the wall. He was the only rat in this building, and he was trapped.

19

Deputy Robert Barton watched the farmhouse from behind a tree. With an inch of new snow accumulating every twenty minutes, he couldn't tell if anyone had approached the residence in the last hour. He estimated Victor Bacchus had been on the run for about ninety minutes, and it would have taken him a long time to reach this house. No vehicles stood in the driveway, yet a lone light shone from upstairs like a warning.

He stooped and adjusted his gloves, ensuring he protected his wrists and fingers from the biting cold. Snow encased his shoes as he approached the back door. There were no footprints, but that didn't mean someone hadn't come through the yard.

He detected a peculiar smell in the air, like smoke, but saw no evidence of a fire. He scanned the property and found nothing.

Barton rounded the south side of the house when snow thundered off the roof and piled a few steps away from him. Another two feet, and the avalanche would have crushed him.

He raised his gun and moved around the house. The front door was closed, but something seemed strange about its appearance. Climbing the steps, he noticed the warped frame and the splintered jamb, as if someone had muscled his way inside. All of Barton's instinct told him to call for backup, but he moved forward anyway, knowing there might be someone in the home. Even if he contacted the Astralon PD officers, it would take them thirty minutes or more to reach the house.

He rapped his knuckles on the door and announced his presence.

"Aldridge County Sheriff's Department. Is anyone inside?" After a pause, he reached for the knob. Unlocked. "I'm coming in."

The musty scent was the first thing he noticed upon entering. Beyond the entryway, a grate cut into the floor blew dry heat upward. He wanted to stand over the grates and let the warmth wash away the snow and ice, but he sensed he wasn't alone. A living room with a bookcase stood to his left. No one inside. He checked the kitchen and dining room and found them empty. A staircase climbed to the second floor.

"Aldridge County Sheriff's Department," he repeated.

The moaning wind answered. Gun in hand, he ascended the steps and paused on the upper landing. An open door displayed a bedroom with a chair beside the window. He started forward and came to a halt when the gray light through the windows glistened off something wet on the floor. Kneeling, he touched the water stain. It was still cold. Someone had marched through the upstairs with snow on his clothes.

Heart beating in his ears, Barton peeked around the corner, expecting the escaped convict to leap out. He was making himself crazy. Anyone could have dripped snow and ice in the hallway, including the homeowner. Jumping to conclusions wouldn't help him catch Victor Bacchus.

A call came over the radio. Donner's voice.

"Yeah, Sheriff?"

"Dammit, Barton. I've been trying to reach you for ten minutes. A second later, and I would have sent the National Guard to find you."

"The radio is on the fritz. Must be this weather."

"Where are you?"

Great question. He had to be almost a mile from the cruiser.

"I came across a farmhouse with signs of forced entry. No one inside."

"Give me the address." Barton did. "You were supposed to meet Astralon PD at the abandoned transport van."

"I understand, Sheriff, but I saw someone run across the road and thought it might be the escaped convict."

"Listen to me, Barton. Under no circumstances are you to approach Victor Bacchus without backup. What part of three dead guards don't you understand?"

"I know, but—"

"No more unnecessary risks. I'll send two deputies to check the area around your location, but I want you back in your cruiser by the next time we talk."

"Yes, sir."

He set the radio on his hip. The shadows were all wrong through the upstairs. They lurched off the walls like something black and faceless, and they seemed to move in the periphery of his vision. This place was giving him the creeps.

"If I were Victor Bacchus, what would I do after escaping from the van?" He felt stupid querying himself, but it helped to hear his own voice. The sound quieted the malevolent spirits trailing him through the upstairs. "I'd come this way and find somewhere to escape the cold. Then I'd head to town and use the stolen cell phone to call for help."

The thought of Rochester's crime syndicate slinking through the night around Laurel Mountain made Barton tremble. They had enough problems with the storm and a mass murderer running loose. He pictured a map of the surroundings. If Bacchus was heading for the township, he'd pass several more houses on the way. The residents who lived there were in danger.

After clearing the attic and basement, Barton confirmed no one was inside. He hoped Donner would send those two deputies. If they hurried, they might close in on Bacchus and prevent him from escaping.

Barton stepped outside and faced the cold. The snow refused to stop, and the wind seemed to hold a personal vendetta against him. He high-stepped through the banks and hurried toward the next house between here and Laurel Mountain Township. A road lay a quarter mile ahead, but he couldn't see it because of the storm. Already the chill leached the heat from his body. Slush crusted on his nose and lips; water doused his eyebrows.

He wouldn't have found the road were it not for the headlights beaming through the darkness. Donner's deputies, a rookie and an experienced detective named Gilbert, stepped out of their vehicles, wearing heavy winter jackets. The rookie gripped an assault rifle while the detective was busy studying the surrounding area.

"Deputy Barton," the rookie called.

"Over here."

Barton ran faster. The officers exchanged words regarding Bacchus' whereabouts.

"We'll split up," Gilbert said. "We'll take the east side of the woods. Barton, take the west side. If you see anything, radio me."

"Got it."

They split up. The snow crunched under Barton's boots as he crossed the road. How long before the plows reached these back roads? It might take hours or days. The Fullers lived just over the ridge. If he followed the road, he'd find their house along the right. But if a vehicle came this way and couldn't stop, he was as good as dead.

Flashlight aimed at the ground, he pushed onward. The possibility that Victor Bacchus had broken into the Fullers' house and gutted them the way he had those guards made ice form on his spine.

The wind howled as snow billowed around him. His legs protested from fighting through the banks. Through the gloom, he caught sight of something shining in the night. A window lit up with a soft yellow glimmer. He'd found the Fullers.

Barton radioed his position to Detective Gilbert and hurried up the road, praying he wasn't too late.

20

The headlights vanished into the storm as the F-150 drove away. Victor Bacchus set aside the ax and stared into the night. He'd trapped himself and made it easy for the police to surround him. A shame. He was getting used to the gas station. Not that it was warm inside, but huddled in his jacket with the blanket over him, he'd finally stopped his teeth from chattering. Now he needed to go back out there.

He removed the cell phone from his pocket and tapped the screen. Still no service. He was trapped in prehistoric times, unable to escape this nightmare of a township. All he needed was a brief connection to contact his men, and he could finally get out of here.

Maybe he'd been wrong to head to the town. What he needed was height. The terrain rose in monstrous shadows down the road. That was Laurel Mountain. If he climbed to the peak, he was bound to find service. Or freeze to death. He had to be strategic about this. All the houses and cabins between the town and the peak meant he could take breaks and warm up. He'd already done so once. If he found an occupied house, he would murder the owners, steal their food, and enjoy their heated home. The police were looking for him, but they'd have a helluva time tracking him through the wilderness. They probably thought he'd head for the interstate, but that wasn't a viable option. Stealing a vehicle would cause him to get stuck in the storm. He pictured himself behind the wheel of a car and stuck in a ditch, with the police swarming around the vehicle. No, that wasn't what he wanted.

Bracing himself for the cold, he zipped the jacket, pocketed the gun, and grabbed the ax. He trudged up the street, and with each step he imagined his men arriving to help him escape. The blizzard could be his greatest ally. He could find abandoned cabins and hide until he'd regained strength. Soon enough, he would pick up the phone, contact his men, and host a surprise party for the Astralon PD and sheriff's deputies swarming the countryside. It would be a bloodbath. The thought made him grin as he vanished into the night.

Bacchus crouched behind a mailbox and waited for the snowplow to pass. Why did they bother? As quickly as they cleared the streets, more snow replaced it. Good. He needed the storm to cloak his presence, though the wind ripped the heat from his body, froze his nose and ears, and pushed him toward the brink of insanity. Well, he was already there. Death surrounded him, and wherever he looked, he saw the faces of his old victims. He could barely keep his eyes open. But that was because of the cold. He had to stay alert, as once he made it to the peak no one would locate him, and he might find cell service. Even if the connection only lasted a few minutes, that was all he needed.

~

DEPUTY BARTON MARCHED along the street, following the path carved by a snowblower. The light from his flashlight revealed patches of white, and now and then his boots stirred a flurry of powder. The wind seemed to laugh, mocking him—just one man patrolling a blizzard the size of the Appalachian Mountains.

His partners had knocked on several doors. Barton didn't know how long the fugitive had been outside in the storm with a coat that wouldn't provide much protection, and he doubted Bacchus knew much about hiking and outdoor survival. If the killer had gone too long without shelter or food, he could enter a state of delirium. But he could be anywhere.

Barton followed the road to the end, gazing into windows. He was checking the houses near the base of the mountain when he heard it. The faint sound of laughter, originating from the woods behind him.

He froze.

Someone was out there.

He took cover behind an oak tree, drew his gun, and scanned the darkness beyond the edge of the woods. The laughter echoed again, muffled by the snow.

Barton stepped toward the sound, pulse racing. He was about to call for backup when he spotted a figure. The person was standing in a clearing, bathed in moonlight, unaware that someone was watching him. Still, Barton was taking no chances; he edged closer until he glimpsed the glint of metal. A gun stuck out of the figure's back pocket, and there was something in his hand. An ax, like the one stolen from the shed he'd come across.

The deputy took out his gun and silently cocked it. Allowing himself one more second to assess the situation, he stepped forward. The wind whipped snow into his eyes. He blinked, and the silhouette was gone. *What in the hell?*

"Deputy Barton," someone called.

He spun around to Detective Gilbert, with the junior deputy alongside him.

"There was someone in those trees," Barton said.

Gilbert shielded his eyes from the wind and followed Barton's gaze.

"I don't see anybody."

"He was right there, dammit. I think it was Victor Bacchus."

Gilbert shared a glance with the deputy and shrugged. They thought he was delirious from the cold.

"All right then. Show me."

Barton kept his weapon ready as he hurried to the woods. He stopped where the laughter had come from and turned his head left and right.

"There's nobody here, deputy," the detective said.

"But I saw him."

"Where are the footprints?"

Barton scanned the ground and saw nothing but a blanket of snow. Had the storm covered the prints in a matter of minutes, or was he losing his mind?

"I swear I—"

"Keep going from door to door, Deputy Barton. If you spot anything out of the ordinary, radio me." Gilbert started away and turned back. "And Barton?"

"Yeah?"

"Keep a level head. You're hunting a fugitive through the worst winter storm in decades. There's no shame in imagining killers in the dark."

Gilbert's words burned in Barton's ears as the detective disappeared up the street. Had he mistaken the howling wind for laughter?

∼

WATCHING FROM THE FOREST, Bacchus waited until the officers separated. He slipped through the woods and broke into a wide smile as he thought of how he'd evaded the deputies. His joy turned to desperation when his ankle began to hurt and the chill worked into his bones. Though he'd left the gas station fifteen minutes ago, he was already pushing toward hypothermia and needed to get inside. Warmth. He would pay any price for it.

A road cut through the woods and gave way to a clearing. One two-story house stood in the dark night. A light glowed downstairs. He could already smell wood smoke from a fireplace. This was what he needed.

He made his way to the house. The path grew clearer as he approached, and the faint glow from a table lamp lit the window. Peering through the glass, Bacchus saw an elderly woman rocking in a chair by the fire. The woman was small and frail; white hair hung around her face. Her skin displayed the wrinkles of age, and silver glasses framed her bright blue eyes. She wore a simple dress and slippers, her hands clasped together in her lap as she rocked back and forth. The woman had her back turned and appeared lost in thought. Bacchus gripped the ax hilt.

He quickened his pace, no longer feeling the cold, only the blood-fueled adrenaline pumping through his body. Approaching the door, he heard a noise inside—the sound of metal cocking into place. His heart beat faster as he envisioned himself with nowhere to run or hide should the woman come onto the porch with a weapon.

So she'd heard him. He wasn't concerned. If he acted fast, he could kill her before she called the police. Ah, yes. A phone. He needed a phone almost as much as he wanted to warm up.

Bacchus kicked open the door and stepped inside with the ax in hand.

The elderly lady gave a startled cry as she leaped out of her chair. He had to hand it to the old bat. She'd heard him and grabbed a gun, a little peashooter revolver that wouldn't frighten a mouse.

"You're . . . you're the man the police are searching for. I called them. They're coming now."

He didn't believe her. The phone sat on the other side of the room, and she didn't possess the agility to race across the floor and place a call.

An unholy roar came out of his chest. She screamed and aimed the gun, but her trembling arms failed her. The bitch couldn't keep the gun straight.

He swung the ax and drove the blade through her chest. There was the sickening sound of bones cracking and a splash of blood. She fell in a heap and bled out on the living room floor. Bacchus stood over her twitching corpse as tiny red streams trickled between the floorboards.

He wiped the blade on his pants and made his way to the phone. Picking up the landline, he listened to utter silence on the other end. Punching the hangup button with his forefinger, he waited. The damn phone lines must be down.

Bacchus heaved the phone across the room. It struck the plaster and shattered into multiple pieces.

At least he had the fireplace to keep him warm.

21

Through the window, LeVar watched the waves of Wolf Lake pound the shoreline. The snow was a foot deep and still falling, and the path he'd shoveled from the guesthouse to the concrete walkway had vanished under a blanket of white.

Behind him, Scout sat at the card table, one leg crossed over the other and a book open on her lap. He did his best not to look, but it was difficult. She'd grown into a beautiful teenager over the last few months, as if the spinal surgery had released a butterfly from its chrysalis. But it was wrong to have those thoughts. She was only sixteen, and he was days away from turning twenty. Heck, he was teaching her to drive. She was the younger sister he'd never had, and he refused to see her in any other light.

Still, it was impossible not to notice. The glasses that had once made her appear studious and nerdy accentuated her beauty. And now he was alone with her in the house as a winter storm raged outside. He cleared his throat.

"Scout, shouldn't you call your mother?"

Without looking up from her book, she said, "If I do, she'll only tell me to come home before the snow gets too deep."

"Isn't that a wise idea?"

She closed the book and studied him with a mischievous grin. "You really are trying to throw me out of the house."

"I'm not. It's just that ... well ..."

"Ah, this is about people getting the wrong impression because we're alone," she said.

"That's my worry."

"LeVar, my mom trusts you, and we both know we're friends and nothing is going on. What do we have to worry about?"

"I suppose you're right. Still, if you stick around, you'll have a harder time getting back. The storm is getting worse."

She walked to the window and looked out at the lake.

"It's kinda exciting, isn't it?"

"The snow?"

"And the two of us working together to ensure we don't freeze to death in your house."

"Hey, it gets cold, but it's not *that* bad," he said.

Scout glanced at him from the corner of her eye. "You know what we should do?"

He didn't want to give her an answer. The question was too open-ended, considering their situation. Here he was, locked inside his house with no one to see, and a girl who grew more beautiful every day was his guest.

Stop it. She's practically family. Not to mention her age. What kind of monster am I?

"We should prepare the front room for a sleeping area in case I can't leave," she said, answering her own question.

"Let's hope it doesn't come to that. I'm sure we can come up with something more fun to pass the time."

She turned to him with her hands clasped behind her back as she bounced on her toes.

"Like what?"

"How about we cook together?"

"But we both ate dinner," she said.

"Didn't anyone ever tell you about second dinner?"

She threw her head back and laughed.

"That tummy of yours is a bottomless pit. How is it you don't look like Eddie Murphy in *The Nutty Professor*?"

"Now you're dropping 90s comedy references."

"I know my music and movies, yo. That works. If you want to pass the time by cooking, that's what we'll do. What should we make?"

"I have all the fixings for pizza," he said.

"You sure eat a lot of pizzas, L."

"Okay. How about tacos?"

"It's not Taco Tuesday, but you have me interested."

"What if I told you I have an unopened jar of mango salsa?"

"Now you're talking," she said.

As the storm raged outside, they passed the time by dancing around the kitchen, laughing, and making dinner. LeVar placed a speaker on the table and blasted his favorite old-school hip-hop playlist, and they found themselves competing over who could rap along with Erik B and Rakim.

But even as he grew more comfortable spending time alone with Scout, he grew more wary of the wind shrieking over the lake. The trees behind the Mournings' house bent almost to the point of snapping. Branches littered the ground, slowly vanishing under a sea of white, like bones beneath the gravedigger's soil.

As he plated the first round of chicken and mango salsa tacos, she paused and looked his way.

"You've lost your mojo again," Scout said. "Please say you aren't worried about cooking dinner with me."

"That's not it. This storm is bothering me."

"Yeah, I can't stop thinking about Thomas and Chelsey, especially with that escaped psycho near Laurel Mountain."

"Hundred percent. And now I'm worried about my sister and mom. Raven has Darren to take care of her, but they're way up on the ridge with only one road back to the valley. Mom lived in an apartment most of her adult life and never had to deal with snow removal."

"What about Buck? He owns a truck."

LeVar narrowed an eyebrow. "Buck is an exceptional dude, and he loves Mom, but he's not exactly handy. This is a guy who needed my help to start his lawnmower this summer. I had to drive over and teach him how to change the oil. He doesn't own a plow, and if he has a snowblower, chances are he won't know how to start it."

Scout retrieved a bottle of fruit juice from the refrigerator. "Have you called your mother?"

"I should check on them."

"Why don't you take care of that while I set the table?"

"Bet," he said.

He carried the phone to the bedroom and closed the door. Despite what he'd told Scout, it comforted him to put distance between the two of them. He loved her more than mere words could express, yet he couldn't prevent himself from viewing her as a young woman, someone he might ask on a date if he were a few years younger. Or if she had turned eighteen instead of sixteen in October. Though she was mature enough to acknowledge her mistakes—she never should have lied to her mother and broken into an abandoned house with Liz during an ill-fated ghost hunt—she was also old enough to test her limits.

LeVar shook his head. He saw no sense in driving himself crazy. Under no circumstance would he ever betray Scout's or Naomi's trust. They were two of his favorite people, as close as his actual family.

Speaking of which, he dialed his mother and waited for her to answer.

"LeVar, this snow is really something. We've gotten over a foot here. How is it on your side of the lake?"

"Just as deep. Ma, does Buck have a snowblower?"

"He's got one out back. Why?"

"Does he know how to use it?"

"I'm sure he does."

"Just to be sure, why don't you ask him to fire it up and test it out before the snow gets any deeper?"

"I guess that isn't such a bad idea," she said. "Are you worried about your ma?"

"I always look out for you."

"We're all right, LeVar. The house has natural gas heat, so if the power goes out, we'll be fine."

"Ma, if the snowblower doesn't start, call me. I'll drive over and help him out."

"Baby, I don't want you risking your life. Nobody should drive tonight."

"I can make it."

"No, you can't, and if you don't listen to your ma, I'll tan your hide."

He snickered. "Duly noted. But if there's an issue—"

"Which there won't be."

"Have Buck hit me up on FaceTime. I'll walk him through the steps."

"That's kind of you. You stay safe, LeVar."

"You too, Ma."

A moment after he ended the call, an earsplitting crash came from outside.

22

He didn't want to leave the comfort of the old lady's home.

Victor Bacchus kept the blinds closed, peeking between them every few minutes to ensure the police weren't converging on the house. Here, the fire kept him warm, and he'd found leftover lasagna in the refrigerator. It occurred to him that this was the first home-cooked meal he'd eaten since his incarceration. As he forked the last of the food into his mouth, he grinned at the corpse splayed in the middle of the living room. Her bleeding had stopped, but it wouldn't be long before she stank.

Again, he checked the stolen phone for a signal and found nothing. There was no choice but to climb the mountain, and he didn't relish venturing into the cold. Even with the guard's jacket, gloves, and boots, he couldn't survive the storm. He would need to repeat the process—break into homes and murder the owners until he reached a higher elevation and found service. Then he could finally escape this arctic hell.

He picked up the bloody ax and wiped the crust on the woman's clothes.

"It was nice knowing you. Too bad I never learned your name." He dropped the dinner dish on her face, her eyes open and frozen in horror. "Thanks for the fire and the lasagna."

Snow swirled into the entryway when he opened the door. He braced himself against the chill and stepped outside, scanning the horizon for signs of the deputies.

"Show your faces, little piggies," he said with a maniacal grin.

Bacchus held the ax blade beside his face and drank in the scent of the woman's blood. It had been too long since he'd killed a citizen. His taste for murder returned. He wanted more. As the gale screamed through the forest, he cackled.

The night was the devil's belly, and he its teeth.

∽

Finding the Fuller family alive didn't quiet Barton's worry. There was a madman stalking through the darkness, and the deputy imagined a trail of bodies between the escaped killer and his destination. For the second time tonight, he considered where he would go if he was in the convict's position. Heading into the township made sense, but so did finding a path up the mountainside. The mobster had contacts who would rescue him, but Bacchus needed a working phone. He might find fleeting coverage on the mountain.

Barton was certain someone had watched him from the edge of the forest. Let Detective Gilbert think what he wished. He wasn't crazy, and he hadn't imagined the laughter.

After he departed the Fullers' house, he pictured the houses and cabins between the valley and the mountaintop. All those people were in danger.

Ignoring the frigid conditions, he set off toward the next house.

"Gilbert," he said into the radio.

No response came.

"Deputy Barton to Detective Gilbert. Come in."

"Gilbert here," the detective said, sounding irritated.

"I'm heading up the hillside and will check the residences on the way."

"If you ask me, Victor Bacchus stole a vehicle and drove to the highway."

"In this weather? Doubtful."

"If you're intent on freezing to death, I won't stop you. Let me know if you find anything."

Gilbert ended the radio call. Idiot. Why Donner had promoted Gilbert to detective, he'd never understood.

Barton held his jacket together at the neckline and pushed through the snow. He cut through the forest and followed the killer's likely path. The winding road would get him there quicker, but Bacchus couldn't afford to let anyone see him. Under normal conditions, tracking the killer would be as simple as following his footprints, but the storm covered them within minutes. It was Barton's instincts against the killer's.

The Dennel family owned a home a quarter mile up the ridge. Reaching the house wouldn't be easy with the storm blowing into his face. Barton ducked his head and struggled forward. Like the Fullers, the Dennels would invite him inside while he warned them about strangers in the dark. Thinking of their fireplace got him moving.

The darkness was an impenetrable blanket of pure black, and the trees were obscured by the night. The wind became a cacophony of high-pitched screams that filled the air with dread, accompanied by the creaking of trees bending to its will. It carried a chill deep into the deputy's bones.

After what seemed like hours, the lights of the Dennels' house appeared after the trees. He hurried, so cold he might be minutes from hypothermia. His teeth chattered, and his body trembled beyond his control.

As he circled the property, laughter came out of the trees as before. The sound drew him upright, and he removed his gun. Overhead, a branch groaned seconds before it crashed into the snow. Barton waited for the laughter to come again, but it didn't. Detective Gilbert had claimed it was all in his head. Was it?

The deputy studied the looming forest. He swore it was staring back at him.

∼

BACCHUS WORE A DEMENTED grin as he hefted the bloody ax and pushed through the snow. He could see lights in the distance. Somewhere ahead stood a home, another stop on his trek up the mountain. It had been ten minutes since he'd searched for cell service, and he wasn't about to try now. Removing his gloves would lead to frostbite. Instead, he muscled onward, delirious and freezing. This was how he'd felt before finding the farmhouse. He had to escape the elements. Each second in the storm brought him closer to death.

Yet the light told him he wouldn't find an empty house this time. He'd have to murder the occupants as he had the elderly woman. No matter. He would do whatever he needed to survive.

Hurrying to the house, he approached from the side, where open curtains lent him a clear view into the dining room. He heard chatter and excited voices. How many were in the home?

Creeping up on the window, he peered around the corner. A middle-aged couple sat at a table. Playing cards lay face down in front of them. But it wasn't the couple who drew the killer's attention; it was the deputy he'd watched from the woods. The man had removed his hat, and he sipped from a mug as he spoke with the occupants. Was the deputy warning them about the escaped killer? Bacchus smiled. The deputy had reason to alert the couple. After all, the murderer stood right outside their window.

He touched the ax blade. Could he risk killing three people at once? If he took out the deputy, dealing with the couple would be easy.

Something had changed within Victor Bacchus. Though he still felt the cold, he was a part of it now. One with the night; one with the forest. More a force than a human presence. The back of his mind whispered and urged him not to kill unless he had no other choice. Each murder increased the risk that the police would catch him.

But he had a taste for it now. A taste for blood and killing. And so did the ax.

"Come out and play, little deputy."

The wind screamed in terror.

23

It was becoming impossible to traverse the village roads. Deputy Aguilar hissed when the cruiser skidded over a mound of snow and spun. Ice lay hidden beneath the powder, and the snow was past her tires. She would be lucky to make it back to the station, let alone warn the community.

She'd taped Deputy Lambert's list to the dashboard. These were people on electric heat, with asterisks marking the elderly. Above the cruiser, the power lines swayed like rope for skipping, and ice hung off houses, congealing around the roof and gutters. Nobody had reported an outage yet, but that time was coming.

Outside a brick ranch, she stopped the cruiser and struggled up the sidewalk to reach the door. Even on the porch, the snow rose past her boots. At most of the homes, she'd encountered people who didn't believe the storm would be as dangerous as she predicted, as if the pictures outside their windows couldn't convince the skeptics. She pressed the doorbell and waited.

A man in his eighties opened the door a crack and flinched every time the wind blew.

"Mr. Zado?"

"How can I help you?"

"I understand you're on electric heat."

A woman in the background asked who was at the door.

"It's the sheriff's department, Kristin. Go back to sleep." The man turned to Aguilar and shook his head. "Always nosy, that one. Yes, we have an electric heating and cooling system."

"Do you have a backup heating source? Maybe a fireplace or woodstove?"

"I have a heater I plug in when I'm working in the garage."

"What about something that will work if the power goes out?"

"No," he said, eyeing the power lines. "You think the electricity will fail?"

"With this wind, it's possible. Do you have anywhere you can go if you lose heat?"

"The Adinolfi family will take us in."

"And where do they live?"

"Three houses down the street."

"Mr. Zado," Aguilar said, "there's a foot of snow on the ground, and it's getting deeper. Are you sure you and your wife can make it to the neighbor's house?"

He scratched his head. "I can, but I'm not sure about Kristin."

"Do you have a snowblower?"

"We pay a guy to plow."

"I don't want to alarm you, sir, but your plowman might not make it to the house. We're issuing a state of emergency and banning unnecessary travel, and many of the roads are impassable."

"The snow will stop soon, won't it?"

"Don't get your hopes up. The storm is slamming Cooperstown right now, and all that snow is heading our way. If you think your wife can make it to your neighbor's house, leave now before the storm worsens."

Had a shovel stood on the porch, she would have cleared a path for them. Instead, as soon as the door closed, she rushed back to the cruiser to escape the elements. The wind chill had fallen well below zero, and the blowing snow made it difficult to see the road.

The cruiser fishtailed up the street as she searched for the next address on the list. What would she do with all these people after the power failed? She liked the idea of sending everyone to an emergency shelter, but the school couldn't take them, and it was too dangerous to transport the elderly across the village.

While she had supplies, she handed out blankets to anyone who lacked a place to go if they lost power. She even handed out energy bars to people who hadn't purchased enough groceries to make it through the next three days. This was a nightmare. If the department had received warning before the storm struck, she could have prepared the county. Now it was too late, and she was fighting an unwinnable battle.

A benevolent force must have been watching over her because she reached the sheriff's department without sliding off the road or colliding with a salt truck. There was one bit of good news: The emergency workers were the only people on the roads—salters, plows, the occasional sheriff's cruiser. She hoped the storm had convinced everyone to hole up inside and allow the village laborers to do their jobs.

Coincidentally, Lambert arrived in the parking lot at the same time as Aguilar. He yelled to her, but she couldn't hear over the wind. With their heads lowered, they rushed inside.

She had plenty of gripes about the outdated heating system. During the winter, the temperature inside the department hovered several degrees below the thermostat setting. Despite the cool interior, it seemed like a sauna compared to the outdoors. Peeling off her jacket, hat, and gloves, Aguilar set the winter gear near a register to dry.

"I covered the north and east end," Lambert said, brushing ice out of his buzzed hair. "Nobody is prepared. This storm took them by surprise."

"I found the same."

"As if things couldn't get any worse, all the grocery stores closed. No telling when they'll reopen."

Aguilar perched on the edge of the desk. "I suppose it doesn't matter. You'd need to have a death wish to drive to the store in this weather. I spoke to the principal at the school. We can't use the gymnasium as an emergency shelter because a pipe burst, but the auditorium is an option."

"The auditorium can't take that many people."

"That's what the principal said. If worse comes to worst, and it probably will, we could set up cots in the classrooms and cafeteria."

Lambert gestured at the window. "But how will we get everyone to the shelter? I barely made it here in one piece."

"I haven't come up with a solution yet. Dammit, if I need to drive them to a shelter one by one, I'll do it. I don't want anyone freezing to death on my watch."

"Nor mine."

Aguilar slapped her forehead. "We can recruit volunteers to transport people to the shelter. The village already has a volunteer fire department, so we have folks who can handle the task."

Lambert considered Aguilar's suggestion and nodded in agreement.

"That's a workable idea. Let me make some calls."

He dug his radio from his pocket and contacted volunteers while Aguilar diversified their resources by calling the sheriff's departments and state police barracks outside of the storm. If their officers could make it to Nightshade County, they could help.

As she worked the phones, her confidence sank. The state police and neighboring sheriff's departments were aiding other counties because of the storm, and officers remained on watch for escaped convict Victor Bacchus. Lambert raised a thumb, signaling he was having more luck than her.

Working inside Thomas's office, she turned her head so the deputies wouldn't see her uncertainty. Until now, she'd believed herself capable of filling in for the sheriff. She was failing her county and letting Thomas down.

Why hadn't she seen the potential for the winter storm to strike Wolf Lake?

24

Encased in ice, Victor Bacchus stood within the shadows of two pine trees. Snow crusted his hair, melted, and dripped down his face, freezing over his lips, as though he'd grown a set of vampire's fangs. He felt the cold less and less, and the quiet voice of his instinct warned him to get inside or flee.

Another voice spoke to him. It came from the black sky, the shadows, the storm. The voice told him to kill them all.

And he would.

The branches groaned above his head, or maybe it was his body swaying in the wind. In the brief time he'd stood here, the snow had risen another inch up his frame. The cold comforted him. He was a part of it now.

Across the clearing, the deputy was speaking with the couple in the house.

It must be warm inside.

It doesn't matter. Let them taste the ax.

When his mouth opened in a haunting grin, the ice shredded his lips and left him bleeding. The killer's tongue flicked out and drank the blood. It tasted like eternal life.

Strange that the storm sapped his energy, yet he believed he could run a marathon. Climbing the mountain wouldn't challenge him. Why had he wanted to reach higher ground?

Oh yes, the phone. With a cackle, he dug the cell phone out of his pocket and checked for service. Still nothing. He needed his second-in-command to rescue him from Laurel Mountain.

Or did he? What if he stayed here forever?

Get inside. You're losing your mind.

Except he wasn't. He'd never been so sure of his intentions. Here, he was more than the leader of some crime syndicate. He was a god, an immortal, a beast who grew more powerful every time he killed. The guards had been first. Then the old woman. Now the deputy and the homeowners. Three at once. All that wonderful blood.

Run, his mind whispered.

Feed me, said the night.

Bacchus collided with a tree. The ice glazed over his body, acting as an insulator. He crouched in a shallow cave formed by snow-covered boughs. The air seeped through the walls and coated his skin.

No one could see him here. He was unstoppable. Unbeatable.

When his moments of clarity faded, Bacchus embraced the darkness and smiled. He would stay until the voices commanded him to kill.

Ice clung to him, and he accepted it. He was a deadly wind, a storm that fed on pain. He would find his prey and savor their terror. The weak would be taken, the strong slaughtered. He was the god of winter's wrath, and no one dared question his power.

It's time.

With a snicker, Bacchus raised the ax and stepped out from behind the trees.

∼

"Are you sure you can't stay?" Mrs. Dennel asked. "I want to hear more about the triplets."

"I wish I could, ma'am," Deputy Barton said, setting the hat on his head. "Your neighbors need to know who's out there and what he's capable of."

"Bah," the husband said, waving his hand. "Nobody could survive in this cold. The wind chill has to be thirty or forty below. You'll find what's left of him come spring. That is, if the animals don't consume him and bury the bones."

"Ansel," the wife said, "that's a horrible thing to say."

"He deserves it for killing those innocent guards. Who knows what else he's guilty of?"

The woman apologetically shook her head at Barton. "At least tell me you'll get inside as soon as possible."

"I wouldn't have it any other way," said Barton. "This is the coldest I've ever seen it up in New York."

"And it will get worse through the night. You take care of yourself, deputy."

Barton didn't want to leave, but someone needed to alert the Dennels' neighbors about Victor Bacchus. When the door closed behind him, he realized how dark it was beyond the home's lights, how freezing it had become. The woman had given him hot chocolate and sent him away with a sugar cookie. The treat was warm in his pocket.

The deputy blinked and focused on his surroundings. He was alone in the woods with a madman on the loose. The eerie darkness of the night made him twitch. The forest was watching him.

At the far edge of the clearing where the trees climbed skyward and danced in the wind, he glanced back at the house. He could see Mrs. Dennel through the window as she carried a tray of drinks into the kitchen. Ansel sat down and dealt the cards.

A twig snapped, and he spun around with his gun raised. As he stared, a branch tumbled off a pine and stabbed a snowbank. Just the wind snapping a bough off the tree.

Yet there was something else hiding among the shadows. The hair standing on his arms told him he wasn't alone. Which made no sense. The escaped convict was on the run, not hunting sheriff's deputies. He raised the radio to his lips and called Gilbert. The detective didn't reply. After a wait, he tested the radio and contacted the junior deputy. Again, no one answered his call.

Barton couldn't tell if it was the cold or his nerves making his arms tremble. No way to hold the gun straight. A darkness blacker than a bottomless pit pooled between two pine trees. The void swam with movement his eyes couldn't see yet his brain perceived.

He took one step forward. Then another.

The deputy was close enough to yank the boughs aside and reveal what lay hidden. His mind conjured images of a demonic figure, blood dripping from its fangs, deadly talons that shredded flesh.

The snow crunched in the dark. Now.

Barton pulled the bough aside and yelled, "Freeze!"

The figure sprang at him. Something pierced his coat and tore his skin. Like razors, the weapons sliced through his face.

He fell backward and landed in the bank. The buck bounded past, his blood dotting its antlers.

Barton half screamed, half laughed. The wind tore his voice away and hurled it up the mountainside. Climbing to his feet, he thought of what he'd tell his wife and her mother. This would make an amazing story once his children grew old enough to understand.

He brushed the snow off his jacket and pants, removed his gloves, and blew into his hands. Barton slid on the gloves, checked the gun and ensured it was still functional after his near brush with death.

It was a long walk to the next house. His bones had already stiffened, and he couldn't feel his ears. He passed the pine trees and slogged up the ridge. The residence was nothing but a hulking shape in the night.

The guttural roar came out of the dark. Blood dripped from the maniac's mouth as he swung the ax. The blade buried itself in Barton's chest.

A fountain of red drenched the sky as the deputy dropped to his back. With a grunt, the madman yanked the ax free and raised it over his head. There was no time for Deputy Barton to scream before the blade split his throat.

25

Two road closures left Thomas turning in circles. The only path to the mountain was a country route that ran parallel to a gorge. The drop was a hundred yards, but he didn't mention that to Chelsey, who fidgeted in her seat. He wished he'd taken her advice and driven to Astralon before the storm worsened. Now he didn't know whether he'd make it to the cabin. If the sheriff's department closed this road too, they were stuck.

In the whirling darkness, the flakes grew larger and splattered against the windshield. Despite four-wheel drive and snow tires, his pickup slid as if he drove on an ice rink, which wasn't far from the truth.

"You're doing great," she said. "Drive slowly and keep us on the road."

"I'll get us back. Don't worry."

"At this point, I don't care where we stop. All I need is civilization."

The wipers couldn't keep up with the storm. Snow piled along the base of the windshield and blew across his vision.

Each swipe left a streak of ice that made him squint and lower his head, battling to see around the obstruction.

Two red lights appeared in the night. They blinked twice. What lay ahead of them?

Thomas pulsed the brakes. The guardrail would keep the F-150 from sliding into the gorge, but he wasn't taking chances on the slick road. The lights flashed again, and the long rectangular hulk of a slow-moving tractor trailer materialized.

The pickup slowed to a crawl; his speedometer read 5 mph, and that was plenty fast considering the conditions. Nevertheless, there was no getting around the 18-wheeler.

A thick fog of blowing snow enveloped the truck, obscuring their vision and making it challenging to stay in one lane. The tires slipped and slid as he followed the trailer, his headlights a dull sweep through the icy mist. Thomas kept enough distance to get out of the way in time if the semi veered.

The gray soup grew thicker as they inched along the mountain pass; visibility dropped below twenty yards. Despite Thomas's best efforts, they were running low on gas, and he didn't know where to refuel.

To make sense of where they were, he lowered his window and cocked his head through the opening. The semi's exhaust made him gag.

"I take it the driver knows where he's going," Chelsey said. "He's sitting higher than we are."

"Based on his speed, I doubt he can see the road much better than we can. If we make it another mile, we'll—"

The trailer bucked upward. Thomas gripped the wheel as the semi spun out of control, the back end sweeping across both lanes and hurtling at the guardrail. Metal shrieked and crunched. In the chaos, he heard her yelling for him to stop.

He pumped the brakes. The pickup kept sliding. Ahead of

them, the jackknifed tractor trailer formed an impassible barricade.

"Thomas!"

"I'm trying to stop."

He touched the brakes again, willing the pickup to stop before the underside of the trailer took out their windshield. If he didn't regain control, they would die.

The rear of the pickup led the way until it struck a massive tire and came to rest. His heart pounded in his throat. He was thankful they were alive.

"Are you all right?"

Unable to speak, Thomas nodded. He closed his eyes and leaned his head back, composing himself. That was close. He never should have attempted to make it to the cabin. After he gathered his senses, he blinked at her.

"We should check on the other driver," he said.

"Is it safe? I can't see the guardrail."

He lowered the window again and peered outside. The driver's side stood against the rail; he would have to climb across the cabin and exit through her door.

"Get out on your side. I have to scoot across."

He struggled over the center console and winced when his trailing ankle got stuck beneath the steering wheel. She grabbed his hand and helped him through the doorway.

On the barren road, they stood in the frigid cold as snow dotted their hair and shoulders. His boots slipped out from under him when he tried to move. Hooking arms, they steadied themselves and worked their way toward the semi. The door was closed. They could see the silhouette of a man inside. He wasn't moving.

Two steps led Thomas up to the cab. Holding on to the safety bar, he pounded on the glass. The man inside sat motionless, his head resting against the window. He wore an old denim jacket and a pair of jeans ripped on one knee. His gaunt and drawn face made his prominent jawline stand out; deep circles lay under his eyes, his hair unkempt.

"Hello? Can you hear me?" Thomas knocked again and received no response. He shouted down at Chelsey. "He's unconscious. I think he hit his head on the window."

"Is he alive?"

Thomas cupped his hand over his eyes and peered inside. He caught the slow rise and fall of the driver's chest.

"He's alive, but the engine stopped. If I don't get him out of there, he'll freeze."

"How do you want to do this?"

"Climb up beside me. I'll support his weight while you open the door."

"Maybe I should go back to the pickup and grab a rope, just in case."

"I'll go with you."

"No, Thomas. I can handle it."

"It's too icy. Let me help."

She gritted her teeth before accepting his aid. It occurred to him another vehicle might come along and strike them. On their way back to the pickup, he searched for another driver, wary of a collision yet hopeful someone would appear and help. He wasn't sure if the pickup was drivable; they'd struck the 18-wheeler hard enough to click his teeth together.

Just steps away, he couldn't see the semi anymore. The wind forced him to lower his head and shiver. Snow blew in miniature twisters, and ice crusted his eyebrows. He couldn't even see the pickup, though he was certain they were moving in the right direction. They had to be.

"I'll get flares out of the back," he said.

"What?"

The wind shrieked more loudly, swallowing their shouts.

"I said I'll set up flares so nobody runs into us."

"Smart."

"What did you say?"

"Never mind. Just find the flares. I'll search for the rope." She stared in confusion. "Thomas, shouldn't we have found the truck by now?"

He looked around. Had they walked past their vehicle without noticing?

"It must be—"

The ground gave way. In the confusion, neither had realized how close they were to the rail. One second, they were talking. The next, Chelsey screamed. Snow fell out from under her.

Avalanche.

He reached for her arm. Too late. The last thing he heard was Chelsey calling his name before she toppled over the rail. She disappeared into the gorge.

"Chelsey!"

With no concern for his safety, he rushed to the guardrail. Nothing but black lay below. She was gone.

26

The ax wanted to eat.

A twisted grin curled Victor Bacchus' bloody lips toward the sky. He stood over the dead deputy's husk. Like the elderly woman, the man's eyes lay open in a silent shriek.

Bacchus stood in the storm as the snow piled around him. He couldn't recall where he was or why he was in the woods. As if part of a long ago dream, he remembered needing to climb the mountain. For what? So he could find more people to kill? A quiet portion of his mind warned him to get inside before he died, but that made no sense. He didn't feel the cold. Not anymore.

He was about to march up the hill when his gaze stopped on the house. There were people inside. He'd known that, hadn't he? Bacchus looked from the home to the deputy and back again. He couldn't just knock on the door and expect them to let him in, right?

An idea occurred to him. Grabbing the dead man's foot, he dragged the corpse into the pines. As the wind swirled around their bodies, the killer stripped off his coat and shirt and replaced them with the deputy's. Now he was a member of the local sheriff's department, a trustworthy servant. He eyed the badge; it read *Barton*. At night, the black lifeblood across his chest looked like spilled water.

Numb to the elements, Bacchus limped toward the house, dragging his injured foot behind him. In his hands, the ax pulsed heat. He cackled with delight.

Much as it pained him, he set down the ax and leaned it against the house so the homeowner wouldn't see. He raised a hand and pounded on the door, which rattled against his might and fury. A man with a hunch to his shoulders answered and peaked out.

"Yes, deputy?"

"Sorry to bother you, sir," Bacchus said, "but I'm searching for my partner. Did Deputy Barton come this way?"

"Why yes, he was here moments ago. I'm surprised you didn't pass him on the way in."

The old man's eyes landed on the badge, and a look of confusion came over his face, soon replaced by one of terror. He'd read Barton's name and spotted the splotch of blood across the chest.

"Who's at the door, Ansel?" a woman asked from inside.

"It's him!" Ansel said, swinging the door closed.

Not fast enough. The killer blocked the door with his foot. He grabbed the ax and muscled his way into the home. Screams . . . glorious screams . . . filled the house. He raised the ax above his head, so high it drew blood from the heavens.

Ansel stumbled and raised an arm to shield himself. The handle shattered his bones. With a crunch, the blade chopped his head in half. Red spatter doused the killer's face. Bacchus' tongue slipped from his mouth and tasted the blood.

Crying in horror, the wife staggered out of the living room and shuffled down a dark hallway. In no rush, he dislodged the bit from Ansel's head and limped after the woman. The house was his now. Demonic chanting followed him through the hall, haunting and operatic, as if a madman's orchestra trailed his every step. His eyes flicked to each room as he continued after her. One door stood closed at the end of the hall. Was she limber enough to climb through a window?

The ax blew the door into splinters. It hung off the jamb like a deformed limb. He kicked it aside and found the shrieking woman trying to pry open the window. In her haste, she'd forgotten to unclasp the locks.

The ax cut through the back of her skull and stopped the screaming. She crumpled to the floor.

Until a sound came from beyond the windowpane. A police radio. One second later, a flashlight beam swept across the glass.

Hide the woman, a voice warned him.

He grabbed the lady's feet and tugged her into the hallway. Then he placed his back against the wall and stood in the darkness. In the living room, Ansel lay on his back, his head fanned out like a smashed pumpkin. Bacchus tried not to laugh. It was hard not to.

Someone knocked. More deputies? Perhaps he should answer and kill them too.

No, hide. Now isn't the time.

He didn't argue with the voice. It had served him well tonight. As the deputies pounded on the door, the feeling returned to the murderer's extremities. The blissful heat warmed his body. Not that he required heat. He'd adapted to the storm and become part of it.

More knocks.

"Come inside," he whispered. "I have a surprise for you."

He reached into his back pocket and removed the guard's gun. Tossing it aside, he licked the blood off the ax. This was the only weapon he needed; it was an extension of his black soul. The weapon hissed and steamed like an extinguished match, and then flared once more, a fresh yellow flame that roared with life, spraying blood everywhere he carried it. None could stand against him.

Footsteps and raised voices faded as the deputies gave up. He stalked out of hiding and stood beside the window. In the distance, their silhouettes vanished into the night.

Something dug into his hip, and he reached into his pocket and removed the cell phone. Why did he need it? Confused, he touched redial and pressed the phone against his ear. Nothing. Just a faraway hum, as if the sound came from a parallel universe. He removed the phone from his face as a ringing tone came through the speaker. That was unexpected.

A trickle of excitement moved through his bones. The ringing was important, though he couldn't recall why. He stared at the alien device. A man answered.

"Bacchus. Bacchus, is that you?"

My name is Bacchus, is it not?

"Hello? Victor, tell me where you are, and I'll come get you."

The killer didn't reply. Doing so would put him at risk. This might be another deputy trying to fool him.

"Dammit, Victor. Why won't you say anything? Are you injured?"

He ended the call and searched for somewhere to hide the phone. His eyes landed on the couch, where he stuck the device under a cushion.

As the killer backed away, he couldn't help but feel he'd committed a grievous error. But what? All that mattered was keeping himself alive so he could kill again.

He found a refrigerator in the kitchen and opened the door. An uneaten sandwich lay inside, so he took it. Satiated, he curled beside the fireplace.

There would be more killing tonight. But first he wanted rest.

27

Venturing outside didn't appeal to Darren, not when he was warm in the cabin. Nor did he want to separate himself from Raven. But he understood what needed to be done. If he didn't act, they would never get out of the parking lot, let alone make it back to the village.

"Where on earth are you going?" Raven asked.

He fixed a ski mask over his head and face and pulled on his jacket.

"To start the truck and plow the parking lot."

"We're safe inside."

"Yeah, but how will we get out of here? I don't know if you've noticed, but the snow isn't slowing down."

Indeed, it wasn't. The drifts outside were almost up to the windows. He wondered how difficult it would be to open the door.

"Then I'm coming with you."

"Raven, it only takes one person to plow the parking lot."

"What if something happens to you?"

"Like what?" he asked.

"Like the abominable snowman comes out of the woods and takes you."

"I'll smack him with a shovel."

She wouldn't take no for an answer. Before he could leave, she shrugged into her jacket and donned a hat and mittens. At that moment, Jack woofed and leaped off the couch, tail wagging as he joined them at the door.

"It looks like someone else wants to help," she said.

Darren threw up his hands. "I take it everyone is joining me. Tigger?" The cat turned its head and lay beside the woodstove. "No, I don't suppose you want to come. You're the only sane one among us."

The ranger muscled the door open. After they stepped into the night, he closed it so the snow wouldn't fall into the entryway. The chill struck him like a slap across the face. He'd experienced northern winters throughout his life but remembered nothing like this. The arctic air took his breath away, and the wind made it seem ten times worse. The logical portion of his brain told him to go back inside and huddle near the fire. He couldn't. Not with the snow higher than the Silverado's tires. It would take effort to dislodge the truck from the powder.

Raven opened the door, and Jack jumped inside and sat between them. The engine groaned when Darren turned the key. Before long, the Silverado obeyed his command, though it too wanted to hibernate until the storm ended. Shifting into drive, he went nowhere.

"Should I jump out and shovel the snow away from the tires?" she asked.

"Stay in the truck. I don't want you catching pneumonia."

"Darren, you're worse than my mother. Bacteria and viruses cause pneumonia, not chilly weather."

"You mean all those times my parents were wrong when they told me I'd catch a cold if I didn't wear a hat and scarf?"

"Pretty much."

"Gosh, science really is advancing quickly," he said.

Jack glanced back and forth, enjoying the banter.

"I'll ask again. Should I get a shovel?"

"Nope. I've got this."

He put the truck in reverse, moved a few inches, then shifted into drive. After rocking back and forth, he cleared enough room for the pickup to gain a foothold. The Silverado's tires caught the pavement, and the truck pushed forward.

Once the pickup gained momentum, Darren lowered the plow and carved a path.

"The question is, where should I put all this snow?" he asked. "I can't block the entrance to the welcome center, and campers need a path to the cabins."

"Better plow it against the far side of the parking lot."

He agreed. The plow struggled to move all that snow, but after several sweeps of the lot, he formed a new mountain range in front of a thicket. That pile wouldn't melt until May.

"I'm tempted to drive across the grass and plow a way to our cabin."

"So do it. You're the ranger. That means you can do anything."

"Absolute power corrupts absolutely."

He held his breath, hoping the pickup wouldn't bog down on the snow-covered grass, but there was no reason to worry. The truck muscled forward and pushed the snow aside, giving them a clear path to the cabin. He'd need to repeat the process every several hours until the storm let up, but at least the snow wouldn't confine them to the state park grounds.

"Now can we go inside? Even with the heat cranked, it's freezing in here."

"Not yet. I doubt the county cleared the road down to the valley."

"You intend to plow the entire hill?"

"Why not? God forbid there's an emergency, but I can't depend on a plow truck coming by."

Night surrounded the vehicle as Darren peered through the windshield. He took it slowly and ensured he kept the pickup on the road.

The wind lifted, kicking frozen powder into the air before sending it over the hood. Every few minutes, a gust swept off the hill and further worsened their plight. Darren hunched behind the steering wheel and squinted ahead while Jack lolled his tongue out. The storm escalated, and visibility dropped to almost nothing as snowflakes flew across their path.

The cab rocked with each gust, making it difficult for Darren to maintain control. He maneuvered around curves, knowing a shift in direction could send them careening off a steep embankment or into another driver. As if anyone was crazy enough to be on the roads tonight. Black ice made the tires spin. He felt the truck drifting and sliding, but with the plow scraping the macadam, he cleared one lane on the hill.

Raven let out a sigh of relief when they reached the bottom and turned around on the lake road. He could see Thomas and Chelsey's A-frame. Lights shone in the guest house where LeVar lived. After executing a three-point turn, he reversed direction and plowed the other lane on their way up the hill.

Though the Silverado battled harder to move the snow without sliding backward, the trip was less hair-raising. If Darren lost control, he had the clear lane to fall back on. The second job took twice as long as the first, but after fifteen minutes, the welcome center came into view.

"I feel better now," he said, removing another inch of snow from the parking lot. "At least we know we can get out of here if we need to."

"I can't believe it's still snowing. When will this storm end?"

He wanted to tell her it would all be over in a few hours, but the easterly wind showed no sign of abating, and he knew it was dragging ocean moisture off the Atlantic and into Wolf Lake. There was no telling when or if the snow would stop.

28

The public reported the first power outage a little after nine o'clock. Seconds later, all the lines flashed. Aguilar rubbed the tension headache out of her temples.

"Nightshade County Sheriff's Department," she said.

"Yes, I'd like to report a power outage on Smithville Road in Wolf Lake."

"I'm sorry, sir. You need to call the gas and electric company and let them know."

"But my wife and I are on electric heat. What do we do if the power doesn't come on tonight?"

"Do you have a neighbor with a gas or oil furnace?"

"I suppose, except I don't want to walk down the block in this cold. Nobody shoveled their sidewalk, and we're still waiting for the snowplow to come by."

"I understand, but I suggest you go somewhere safe before the snow deepens."

"It's already deep."

"My apologies. I wish I could help, but there's nothing the sheriff's department can do about an electrical outage."

The man hung up in anger. Seated at two other desks, Lambert and a junior deputy answered similar calls. She'd reached out to as many people as she could, but her efforts seemed fruitless. Another failure on her part. The next time Thomas went on vacation, she'd tell him to leave Lambert in charge. With his military background, he knew better how to lead others and respond to pressure. She was nothing more than a leaf blowing in the wind.

"It sounds like about twenty-five percent of the east side of Wolf Lake lost power," he said, setting a muscular forearm on his desk. "If this continues, the entire village will lose electricity before midnight."

She prayed he wasn't right.

"The roads are impassible," she said, "and the snowplows are having a helluva time clearing them."

The junior deputy chimed in. "I heard over the scanner that a plow truck is stuck in a snowbank near the Wolf Lake village plaza. Even the plows can't stay on the road."

"That's all we need. If we can't clear the roads, we can't transport people to safety."

Another call came over the scanner. There was a chimney fire near the lake, and the village fire department was en route. A second later, the phone rang, and the fire chief requested Aguilar send a deputy to help control the scene. She promised to try, but with deputies sick and Thomas on Laurel Mountain, there was no one to call in.

"We have to get another deputy in here," Lambert said.

"Who? Besides calling the midnight shift in early, we're out of bodies." A thought occurred to her, and she snapped her fingers. "Darren Holt and Raven Hopkins. They offered to help. Maybe I should call them. Even though they're only private investigators, they can perform tasks."

Lambert walked to the window and glanced out at the storm.

"Do it. We'll need as many bodies as we can find to help residents without power."

While Lambert and the other deputy followed up on the fire and the abandoned plow driver, Aguilar retreated to Thomas's office and closed the door. Sitting down, she thanked the gods that the sheriff didn't keep a mirror in the room. The last face she wanted to see was her own. She didn't deserve to sit in his chair or walk in his shoes. What a mess. How many people would die tonight because of her incompetence?

As much as she hated calling Darren and Raven, she didn't see a choice. They were busy keeping up with the storm and didn't have time to save her hide. She dialed and hoped for the best.

"Aguilar, how are things in the village?" the ranger asked.

"You don't want to know."

"That bad?"

"We're losing power on the east side, and it won't be long before the outages spread. The wind is taking down lines everywhere."

"Our power is on at the cabin, but I expect it won't be by morning."

She heard an engine in the background.

"Are you on the road?"

"Just made it back to the parking lot. I cleared the lot and moved the snow off the road into the village. Didn't want to get stuck up here."

"Darren, thank you so much. You don't know how much that helps."

"What's going on?"

"The snowplows. They can't keep up with the accumulation, and one slid off the road near the village center. I don't have anyone who can help get it going."

"Say no more, Aguilar," he replied. "Raven and I are in my pickup, and Jack is willing to help."

"Jack is with you?"

"Oh, yes. He's sitting between us and staring at me like he wants to drive."

Aguilar couldn't help but snicker. Thank goodness for Darren. Like Thomas, the state park ranger knew how to make her laugh. A tiny portion of pressure tumbled off her shoulders.

"I hate to ask, but if you can free the snowplow and help us get people to safety, I'll be eternally grateful."

"Hey, it's our village too. We'll do anything you need us to."

"Thank you, my friend, and please thank Raven as well."

"Will do. See you soon."

After the call ended, she leaned back in the chair and stared at the ceiling.

"That went better than expected," she said to nobody in particular.

What would the sheriff's department do without Wolf Lake Consulting and Darren Holt? Between their investigative skills, experience, and willingness to help, they provided an invaluable service. Darren gave them an extra truck to clear the roads. She needed to use her head and stop feeling sorry for herself. For better or worse, she was in charge.

Returning to the operations area, she slid into her own chair, happy not to play the role of pretend sheriff anymore.

"Darren and Raven agreed to help," she told Lambert.

"Perfect. We need them."

"And Darren has a plow on his Silverado. He already cleared a path from the state park to the lake road. After he gets our stuck driver moving, I'll send him to help everyone with a plow on their vehicle."

"That's smart."

She took a breath. Yes, she could still make sound decisions.

Lambert deserved to be in charge, but she would make the best of the situation.

"Go online and find every plowing service in Wolf Lake. If they're willing to help, we can clear the village roads, then branch out and take care of the countryside."

Lambert set his hands on his hips.

"For every volunteer we free, that's another person who can clear the roads and help others."

"Exactly. We'll concentrate on freeing as many volunteers as possible."

"Damn, Aguilar. By morning, we'll have an army at our disposal."

A warm feeling billowed through her chest. She fought to contain her smile.

"If everyone helps, we might get through this mess." She shook her head and straightened her back. "No, we *will* get through this mess."

Lambert grinned.

"That's the badass I know. I wondered where she was hiding."

He raised an open hand and invited her to give him a high-five. She slapped his palm, unable to contain her happiness.

As she grabbed her coat off the rack, she felt something new coursing through her veins.

Confidence.

29

Tears streamed down Thomas's face. Every time he called to Chelsey, the wind answered. She was gone. Because he'd wanted to help an injured driver, he'd lost the only woman he ever loved. With his hands on the guardrail, he leaned over the edge and stared into the gorge. A boiling pit of black lay below, vast and consuming, a caustic pit of stone and darkness that endlessly swirled and churned. Thick and jagged rocks jutted out from the walls of the pit, the bottom shrouded in shadow. Wisps of forgotten night snaked up from the depths as if the gorge were alive, breathing and waiting for fresh bodies to plunge to their deaths. It was a miracle the truck hadn't spun off the cliff and into the abyss.

His mind refused to accept the inevitable—that she was dead. If he wanted to find her, he would have to descend into the pit himself. Terror coursed through him; there was no other way. He turned from the edge and began trekking through the deep snow towards an old pine tree that hung over the gorge. In tatters, its thick branches provided just enough protection against nature's chill.

Bit by bit, Thomas inched down the side of the gorge,

clinging to every branch and rock ledge with grim determination. The wind roared as it battered his body with angry fists, trying to knock him loose from his perch. Despite its efforts, Thomas remained true to his mission.

"Chelsey!"

No reply.

She couldn't be dead.

Thomas realized what he had to do next; putting one foot in front of the other, he threw caution and fear out of his head and lowered himself another foot towards what he could only describe as hell on earth—an unforgiving landscape that seemed eager for another sacrifice.

"Chelsey!"

The wind shrieked in his ears. But there was something else in the wind. A call. He wanted to believe it was Chelsey, but it could have been an animal, the storm, or his mind playing a cruel trick. As he climbed lower, his boot slipped, and his legs flew out over the nothingness. This was it. He would die too.

He held on to a sapling. The young tree was the only thing saving him from instant death. His hands grew tired of supporting his weight.

Swinging his legs, he searched for the rocks and found them, but his boots slid off the icy wall and left him hanging over the gorge again.

The darkness was more intense in the pit, except for the occasional shred of gray light finding its way through a fissure or crevice in the rocks. The gorge concealed lurking shadows that Thomas could only guess at; an added layer of dread kept him vigilant while traversing this abyssal landscape without a single source of light or protection from the jagged bottom.

Then he heard it again—the faint call of a woman's voice.

Hope surged through Thomas' veins and he found the strength to climb along the wall, clinging to anything that provided purchase. He searched until his gaze fixed on two trees jutting out from the cliff wall, their gnarled branches entwined around a lone figure suspended between them.

It was Chelsey. Alive.

Thomas shouted her name, and she peered over at him with eyes filled with tears and wonder. Agony swam under those tears. He climbed towards her, his heart pounding as he realized how close he had come to losing her forever.

His booted foot sought purchase. None existed. He wasn't sure how to reach her.

"Hang on!" he shouted. "I can't reach you from here. I'll have to climb higher and find a ledge."

"Go back, Thomas. It's too dangerous."

"Like hell. I'm not leaving you alone."

"The trees will hold me," she said. "Climb to the top and call the sheriff's department."

"They'll never make it down the road. Not in this weather. Hold on, I'm coming."

The muscles in his hands and arms protested, yet he conjured his energy reserves. Hope pulled him upward. Hope and desperation. No matter what she said about the trees, the wind might blow her into the gorge or cause her to lose her grip. He couldn't get the pained look in her eyes out of his head. Was she injured? She'd fallen fifty feet and must have struck the rock wall. How could she survive the drop unscathed?

After pulling himself halfway back to the guardrail, he found a razor-thin ledge, just deep enough for his boots to stand on. There were more trees growing out of the cliff to his left. If he reached them, he could climb down to her.

"Almost there," he said. "Hold on a little longer."

She gritted her teeth without replying.

"Are you injured?"

"It's just my ankle. I'll survive."

Thomas started along the ledge. His boots slipped on the ice. One wrong move, and he'd be the next one to fall into the gorge.

When he was within arm's reach, Chelsey reached out a hand, trembling like a leaf in the wind as he grasped her forearm between his freezing fingers. They held on to each other, swaying together like children at the mercy of the unforgiving storm.

"I can't pull you up the wall," he said.

"You don't have to. If you get me started, I can climb."

He shook his head.

"We'll have to climb down."

"But your truck. How will we get back to it?"

"There has to be a way. We'll find a road or another way to the top. The important thing is we save ourselves. We'll figure out the rest after."

She bit her lip.

"How far down?" she asked.

"It must be another hundred feet. Maybe more. A river runs along the bottom, but I'm sure it's frozen."

"Rocks?"

"Jagged ones. We can't risk jumping. Hold on to me."

She wrapped her arms around his chest and hung on. Little by little, he worked his way down the side, moving from tree to tree and ledge to ledge. It was almost impossible to see the features unless he was right up against them.

"That's far enough," she said. "I can make it now."

"Chelsey, I'm doing fine."

"Let me climb on my own. The ankle isn't so bad."

He knew she was hiding her pain, but she'd already taken her arms from around his shoulders and grabbed hold of a ledge.

"I'll go first; you follow me down."

Thomas took it slow. He was paying just as much attention to her as he was his footing, and that was dangerous. They were still high enough that a drop would kill them.

Ten minutes later, his arms were screaming from exertion. He was thankful she could descend the wall on her own. He didn't think he could support her weight. At least he hadn't dropped his firearm. The gun jabbed into his hip every time he moved.

Then he heard the river. The gurgle beneath the ice was faint, yet it was unmistakable. They were almost at the bottom.

Finally, his boot touched solid ground. He exhaled and caught her as she dropped.

"We're alive," she said, hugging him. "Thank you for not giving up on me."

Her teeth chattered as she spoke. The wind made him tremble.

"We have to keep moving."

"How far to the township?"

He wasn't sure. In the darkness, everything looked the same. Staring up, he couldn't see the road or his lost truck.

"The river winds toward the mountain. If we follow it, the terrain might take us to the cabin."

"I don't care if we wind up in the township or at the cabin. All I want is heat."

"We'll make it. Keep the faith."

The wind picked up and blew her hair around as she wrapped her arms around her body. She glanced ahead.

"Thomas, we need to build a shelter. I don't think either of us is ready to walk a few miles or climb a mountain. Can't we build a fire?"

"The matches are in the cabin."

"So we'll do it the old-fashioned way. Find me dry sticks."

"By the time we make a fire, we might be better off locating a way out of here."

"Then lead the way. If we don't move, we'll freeze."

He wondered if they wouldn't freeze anyway. Even dressed in layers, there was no stopping the cold.

They hooked elbows as they walked, supporting each other. Chelsey had a noticeable limp. He admired her for never slowing down. She didn't know the meaning of surrender.

Following the river, he spotted the forest in the distance. They were heading in the right direction. At least he hoped they were.

But there was something else in the snow. Tracks.

Someone had come this way.

30

A crash brought Victor Bacchus awake. His eyes fluttered open, and he rolled over to stare at the smoldering fire. Already the temperature had plummeted inside the house. Rising, he dragged his injured leg to the window and looked out. The snow appeared several inches deeper than before.

It didn't take long to find the source of the clamor. An avalanche of snow had tumbled down the mountain and crushed a shed in the backyard. He peered between the curtains, searching for more deputies.

The killer tossed another log on the coals and stoked them until a flame curled around the bark and grew into a blaze. He rubbed his hands in front of the fire. Behind him, Ansel lay on the floor with his head split open. He wasn't bleeding anymore, but the body was beginning to stink. Or maybe the stench came from the dead wife down the hallway.

Above the home, a churning mass of gray and black clouds spat snow upon the mountain. It was as if the storm acted on his behalf, concealing his presence as he sought new victims. His eyes landed on the ax. Blood and hair crusted the blade.

He glanced down at the uniform, forgetting where it had come from.

Barton.

The name stirred something dark inside the killer. Was that a man he'd killed? Yes. Then came Ansel and his screeching wife. He had to be careful. The deputies hunting him carried guns.

But he had the ax. The blade drew blood and took lives.

He stumbled to the door, knowing that this hunt would be treacherous. Part of him feared death, but more of him wanted it. The life he had known was gone, and his only solace came from hunting.

Grabbing the ax, he stepped into the night, letting the biting winds slash his face. The snow had already erased his footsteps from earlier. He would make new ones. His own trail of terror.

The killer had one goal in mind—find the deputies and kill them. He didn't know how far away they'd gotten, nor did he know how he would find them in such a vast and wild landscape, but he was determined. Nothing else mattered but killing.

He took a deep breath and set off, following his instincts and the howling wind. It seemed to give him direction. The storm was part of him. It craved fresh bodies as much as he did.

For the first time since his incarceration, he felt alive.

~

Sheriff Donner stopped his cruiser beside Barton's abandoned vehicle. For the last two hours, he'd failed to contact his deputy. Detective Gilbert said he'd last seen Barton near the Flemings' home, and that the deputy was dead set on visiting every residence to warn them about Victor Bacchus. Gilbert could learn a few things from Barton. For one, commitment. Barton always went the extra mile.

But as Donner stared into the swirling snow, he worried his deputy had gone one mile too far this time. This storm could kill, and Barton wasn't a native New Yorker. Hell, even the sheriff shivered from the frigid air. He couldn't remember such a combination of cold and snow. And the storm was still raging.

"Gilbert, come in."

A second later, the detective responded over the radio.

"Yes, Sheriff."

"I'm having no luck reaching Barton. Where are you now?"

"With Astralon PD at the crime scene."

"Dammit, Gilbert. There's a psychopath loose on Laurel Mountain. What more can you learn from investigating an escort van for prisoners? Bacchus isn't coming back."

"What would you like me to do?"

"Find Barton and the escaped convict. I don't pay you to stand around, playing cops and robbers."

"Right away."

Gilbert ended the call, but not before Donner caught the frustration in the man's voice. He never should have promoted Gilbert to detective. If only Barton had joined the department sooner. The deputy was a model lawman, and Donner wasn't about to lose him to this storm.

Donner climbed into his cruiser, grateful to be inside. The heat ran on high, and it was barely enough to thaw his numb fingertips.

He gave the vehicle gas and shifted it into gear. He had to locate Bacchus before the killer found his deputy.

∼

IN THE DEAD OF NIGHT, stalking inside the black heart of the storm, the killer limped from tree to tree. He could see lights up the mountain—another home and more victims. It occurred to him he'd murdered several adults, including the elderly. Didn't children live in any of these houses? Yes, killing the young would bring a smile to his face.

He stepped through the deepening snow, his face crusted in ice and flakes. The cold didn't seem to touch him. As much as he'd relished resting beside the fire, he felt comfortable in the storm, as if the clouds acted as blankets. The snow masked his tracks, covering them minutes after he trekked through. He was invisible.

A cabin came into view, the one he'd spied through the forest. From inside the home, the killer heard laughter. He allowed the sound to fill his ears, but his fingers tightened around the ax. Though hunger stirred inside him, most of all he wanted to dance in blood.

He stepped up to the door. The snow never crunched beneath his boots. Inside, a woman and a man sat around the table. They were discussing something, but he paid them no mind. He wanted their blood and their screams.

Bacchus raised the ax and smashed it through the door. The force sent it crashing against the wall. He burst in, swinging the blade. The woman shrieked and flung herself forward, pushing her husband out of harm's way.

The killer rushed toward her, ignoring the pain in his leg. His cold eyes never left the woman. She cowered against the wall, clutching her terrified and useless mate.

"Don't worry," Bacchus muttered. "This will be over soon."

31

With each step Chelsey and Thomas took, their boots sank into the snow. She was slowing him down. He would never admit it, but it was true. Her ankle.

"How much further?" she asked.

They must have walked for an hour without a glint of light on the horizon. Did he know where he was going? She couldn't blame him for losing his way. The snow and darkness made everything appear the same.

"Another mile. Difficult to tell."

She nodded, though she doubted his conviction. He was doing his best—they both were—but if they didn't find shelter or build a fire soon, they wouldn't survive. No longer able to feel her nose, fingertips, or toes, she did her best to keep her limbs moving. If her bones locked up, she was as good as dead.

Thomas was following tracks in the snow. They were barely discernible, yet he could see them. But who were they following? Another lost soul leading them to their doom?

Chelsey fought to stay positive. Giving up would mean the end. There was a way out of this predicament.

"I can't see the tracks anymore," he finally said, turning back to her.

That wasn't good. He'd abandoned the river to follow the tracks. They might be anywhere.

"What now?"

"We'll keep going."

Her breaths came in gasps. "Thomas, I don't think I can."

"You can, and you will."

"We need to stop and build a fire. We're dying."

He looked away, ashamed he'd led her in the wrong direction. Logic stated the township and mountain had to be just ahead, but nothing made sense tonight. It was as if the valley kept spinning beneath their feet, sending them in different directions.

"I doubt I could keep a fire going, even if we build one. The wind. It's too strong."

He was right, but they had to generate heat. As they walked, she fell forward and landed in the snow. The ankle kept giving out on her, and he had to help her up. She didn't want to be the helpless victim. It was her fault she'd fallen into the gorge and injured herself, and she didn't want to slow him down.

A bulk emerged from the night. It seemed to be the mountain in the distance, but as they moved forward, Chelsey realized her perspective was wrong. The shape appeared close. It was a barn.

"We found someone," she said, hurrying forward.

He grabbed her arm to stop her from running.

"It's better to stay cautious. We don't know who lives here."

The frigid air poured inside her clothes. There was no stopping the cold. Her eyelids drooped, and as she opened her mouth to respond, her words came out slurred. He eyed her with concern.

"I'll be all right," she said, lying.

Chelsey was in trouble. She felt her movement slowing; each step required more effort. The house near the barn came into view, and her heart sank. The roof of the farmhouse had collapsed through the downstairs, and the windows were blown in and shattered. Nobody lived there. Judging by the dilapidated frame, the owner had abandoned the home years ago. Maybe decades ago.

Yet, by some miracle, the barn remained standing. It leaned slightly, and she was sure there were holes in the structure. She didn't care. All she wanted was to shield herself from the wind for a while.

"Can you make it?" he asked.

"Of course."

But the struggle to keep up with Thomas grew more difficult, and the storm refused to show mercy.

∼

THOMAS KNEW he was losing Chelsey. He recognized the signs of hypothermia, and if he didn't warm her up, she might lose consciousness. Or worse.

Her speech was difficult to understand, and she'd slowed since climbing into the gorge. The barn would help with the wind, but it wouldn't blanket them from the cold. For that, they needed to find an occupied house and someone who would take them in.

The farmhouse stood as still as a skeleton. From the front door, he couldn't see a single light, didn't notice signs of life. The barn, however, was casting a sharp silhouette against the black sky. It was the only one of its kind in the valley, mystifying and magnetic.

Thomas forced himself to take a step, the thin layer of snow crunching beneath his boots. His coat flapped in the gale, and he felt the cold seeping into his bones. He was relieved when they finally made it to the barn.

The door wouldn't open; over the years, the hinges had rusted against the clasp. A swift kick would break the door down, but he didn't want to do that. There were already holes in the walls letting the chill inside. He didn't wish to invite the elements into the barn.

Chelsey shivered beside him. Her lips appeared blueish, but it was difficult to tell in the dark. She stepped in place to keep her body moving, but it was a losing battle. He had to get her inside.

From his pocket, he removed a multi-tool and worked the knife between the clasp and hinge. After applying elbow grease, the door creaked open. She stumbled, and he caught her. The grimace on her face told him she was angry with herself. She didn't want to be a burden or depend on him to save the day.

A pile of snow lay in the center of the barn. Thomas glanced up and discovered the source—a hole in the roof. Any hay in the barn had long since composted and become part of the dirt floor. Old tools hung from the far wall, including a saw with brownish-red teeth and a flimsy handle.

"The hole in the roof," he said. "We need to start a fire, and the hole will act as a chimney."

Chelsey nodded, her teeth chattering. "C-can you start a fire? With w-what?"

"We'll find something. There's a copse behind the farmhouse."

He helped her lie down on the packed dirt, then he began digging through the broken tools and rusty buckets. He found an old cloth and put it to one side. Then he collected some pieces of wood and fashioned them into a teepee that would act as kindling. Now he just needed fuel to keep the fire going.

Thomas didn't relish exiting the barn and leaving her alone, but she needed heat. He had to hurry. Running through the snow, he crossed behind the bulk of the farmhouse. Like a dying beast, it groaned with each gust of wind.

In the copse, he spotted what he was looking for. The evergreens created a patch of snow-free ground. Here, he gathered branches. He knew from experience that the pine would light quickly. Seeking a slower-burning fuel, he gathered oak limbs. Once he had an armful, he carried it back to the barn.

Chelsey's entire body trembled, and she didn't even look up at him as he set the branches beside the kindling.

On his second trip to the copse, he spotted a silver birch glowing under the gray light of the storm, as if a benevolent being shone a spotlight on it. Perfect. This was just what he needed. Scraping the bark, he came away with a handful that shredded like paper. In his palm, it looked and felt like cotton or feathers. All he needed was a spark, and the tinder would produce a flame.

"Chelsey, you won't believe what I found," he said upon returning.

She didn't answer. Her eyes were closed.

He dropped the tinder beside the kindling and rushed to her. Touching her neck, he confirmed she had a pulse. He was losing her.

"Stay with me. I'll warm you up in no time."

He considering removing her jacket and shirt and lying on her to combine their body heat, but he was better off starting the fire.

Please, let this work.

He rubbed two sticks together for what seemed like hours. His hands blistered, but he couldn't slow down. When he was close to giving up, a spark fell off the sticks and landed on the birch. Shielding the tinder, he puffed a few breaths into the pile.

A flame started; it was small, but it was enough to ignite the kindling.

Thomas thanked the gods for their mercy. He arranged the wood and cloth around the fire and moved away—too close to the flames, and he would go up in smoke.

With each passing minute, the heat filled the barn and Chelsey's body relaxed. Thomas stoked the flame and wished he had more wood, but even with the little he had, the fire was doing its job.

He stretched next to her and rested his head against the barn wall, relieved he'd been able to create a heat source. She would wake up despondent that she'd needed him to save the day. But that's why partners existed: to pull each other up in times of strife.

Outside, the wind howled in anger. They'd escaped the storm for now, and it wanted to consume them.

The hole in the roof acted as the perfect chimney, drawing the smoke upward so they could breathe. Once he was sure she was safe, he'd run back to the thicket for more fuel.

For now, he was thankful she was alive.

32

Though he hadn't looked at the clock, LeVar knew the hour grew late. Midnight must be approaching, and Scout still hadn't left. Every hour, she phoned her mother to let her know she was safe, promising to come home soon, yet there was always an excuse to stick around. They'd finished a game of Monopoly, and now she couldn't stop asking about what college was like, as if LeVar could tell her. Yes, the community college provided an invaluable education, but he'd never lived on campus and wouldn't when he transferred to Kane Grove next fall.

Not that he was sorry for her company—having her around lightened his heart and warmed his soul—but temptation lingered in the back of his mind. She no longer looked like the awkward girl he'd met last year and was a little too comfortable around him, not the least bit self-conscious about changing clothes. He couldn't ruin their friendship. It was important he kept his distance.

The sweet scent of marshmallows wafted through the guesthouse. Without chocolate, they couldn't make s'mores. Instead, they made do by melting marshmallows between graham crackers. Personally, he could go for an ice cream sundae with all the toppings, but fat chance anyone would be open during the storm. Yeah, ice cream. Or a double cheeseburger. There was a tub of ice cream in the freezer, but he didn't want to think about frozen food with the cold seeping through the windows, even after he'd storm-proofed the glass.

"Should we melt more marshmallows?" he asked as she cruised the internet.

She read the snow totals and storm reports as if she were giving him the night's sports scores.

"I'm down for another round."

"After that, I'll walk you back to your—"

He didn't get the words out of his mouth before a crunching sound came from outside. A sonic explosion that made him leap out of his chair followed the noise. They shared a wordless glance and rushed to the window.

"Oh, man," she said, pushing the hair off her forehead. "That's not good."

An oak tree that must have stood for a hundred years had fallen from the Mournings' yard and landed a short walk from the guesthouse. A little further, and it would have crashed through the roof. Skeletal branches lay outside the window, like the shriveled hand of the undead. A light sparked beneath the tree. LeVar stood on tiptoe to see what was causing the sparks.

No sooner did he identify the fallen electrical wire than Scout's cell phone rang.

"Yeah, Mom, we're looking at it right now," the girl said. "Thank goodness it missed the houses . . . It hit the wires? Is that what's causing the spark?" Scout placed the phone against her chest. "Mom says the tree took down the wires. She lost electricity."

LeVar could see the windows were dark in the Mournings' house.

"We still have electricity," he muttered, peeking up to see one wire clinging to his house like a lifeline. "But for how long?"

She spoke to her mother for another minute and asked him, "Mom doesn't want me leaving your house because of the live wire. She wants to know if it's okay if I spend the night?"

LeVar, who was sipping from a bottle of kombucha, spat. He bent over and coughed as she eyed him in confusion.

"I think he said it's okay," Scout told her mother.

As she finished the conversation, he held up his index finger and retreated to the bathroom, locking the door behind him. His reflection stared back at him. This was wrong. What would everyone think?

Then again, her mother trusted him and had given her consent.

But did he trust himself?

He ran a hand through his dreadlocks before splashing water on his face. They were going to sleep together. No, that sounded bad. They were going to *sleep under the same roof*, and if he had anything to say about it, she would take his bed while he crashed on the couch. Or on the floor. Heck, he had a blowup mattress in the closet that might come in handy.

Good lord. Was this happening?

"LeVar?" she called from the other side of the door. "Everything okay in there?"

"All fine," he squeaked. Clearing his voice, he said, "Just brushing my teeth."

"Before you eat marshmallows and graham crackers? Weird."

The floor creaked as she padded away. They'd planned none of this, so it wasn't like she'd brought pajamas with her. He pictured her removing her clothes before bedtime and wanted to vomit. Was this a test? Or was someone above the clouds pulling a joke on him?

He shook his head, not wanting to entertain the thought. The storm was bad enough without someone watching them, testing their faith.

LeVar stepped out of the bathroom, ready to jump back inside if she was changing, only to find her sitting on the bed, wearing his wool sweater and a pair of his sweatpants that she had rolled up.

"I hope you don't mind," she said, gesturing to the clothes. "I thought it would be better than sleeping in my jeans and t-shirt."

"No, no," he stammered. "It's fine."

She smiled, then busied herself with fixing her hair in the mirror. He tried to keep his focus, remembering how important it was to protect their friendship, as well as her virtue. And his. He went to the closet and retrieved the blow-up mattress, then dragged it into the front room and set it on the floor.

"What are you doing, LeVar?" she asked.

"I thought—I was going to sleep on the floor. You know, just so you have privacy in my bedroom."

"You're the host. I can't kick you out of your own bedroom and force you to sleep on the air mattress. Besides, it's cold near the window."

"No way. You're my guest. I won't have it any other way."

She shook her head and pointed at the mattress. "You can sleep on the bed. I'll be fine in the front room."

He thought of objecting, but she wasn't taking no for an answer. Guilt rolled through his heart. How could he allow her to sleep in the front room, knowing how chilly it would get? He didn't want to keep the space heater on while they were asleep. That was dangerous. First a fallen tree, then a house fire. No, thanks.

"Look," he said. "This is the compromise. I'll stay up and

ensure the space heater is working. You sleep on the air mattress."

She hesitated. "That's not fair. Why should you have to stay up all night?"

"Because I'm a sheriff's deputy, and I'm the law. What I say goes."

She snorted. Outside, the wind railed against the glass.

"How about we eat the last of the snacks? We'll formulate a plan over our food. You think better while you're eating."

His stomach growled and her lips curled up.

"All right, but this is my place. House rules, *aight*?"

"*Aight*."

He shook his head. She never said it as well as he did.

33

The bloodthirsty monster that had once been Victor Bacchus, leader of a Rochester crime syndicate, glared through the window at the storm. He'd stacked the couple's bodies in the hallway closet like cordwood. Red seeped under the door and spread into the corridor. The heating system strained to keep up with the draft. He'd shoved the front door back into its frame, but the chill bled through the cracks.

In the back of his mind, his old self whispered warnings of what he should do. Something about finding a phone and contacting a man named Skelton, who would take him from this place. He didn't want that. This night belonged to him.

The killer crossed the room and peered out another window. Beyond the glass, the mountain steepened and rose until the top vanished behind a shroud of precipitation and fog. It was there he would go. When he reached the top, he would become an invincible god. He would be free.

The grin soon faded. The deputies were out there too. Since escaping from the van, he had been stalking them. He tried to ignore it, to focus on his goal, but it was getting harder by the second. He wanted to eliminate his enemies, to rid himself of them.

But he had to be careful. He could sense their presence, and they could sense his. He glanced out the window one last time before turning away, his heart beating faster and faster.

A smile broke out on his face.

Soon, he thought with a wink. Soon.

Tugging on his coat, he stepped into the storm and resumed his trek up the mountain. Something drew him toward the top. Destiny. Nothing could stop him now.

∽

DEPUTY BRIAN RHOADS shook his head and turned away so Detective Gilbert wouldn't see his face. Since ending the radio call, all Gilbert had done was complain about Sheriff Donner's orders to find Barton. It was a shame Gilbert wasn't the one missing in the storm. Here was a man who'd been promoted beyond his level of competency. If anyone deserved the role of detective, it was Barton.

Rhoads held his coat together and shivered. He wanted to be inside where it wasn't so freezing, but an escaped convict ran free in the night, and a well-liked deputy was missing. Duty called, and he would do anything to find his fellow deputy, even if Gilbert groaned about the task.

Astralon PD had fanned out to search the other side of the valley, believing Victor Bacchus was heading for the highway. Rhoads wasn't so sure. The highway was impossible to reach in the snow, and unless the convict had stolen a vehicle, he couldn't get far.

"If you ask me, Barton is probably inside someone's house, running his yap," Gilbert growled. "That's all he's good for."

"Sheriff Donner wants us to find him."

"Donner can kiss my ass. Let him stomp through the snow in sub-zero temperatures."

Gilbert wouldn't talk so tough around the sheriff. Though Donner was twenty years Gilbert's senior, he could whip the detective with an arm tied behind his back. Donner had come up through the department, working as a deputy and detective before winning the sheriff's role. Gilbert had transferred from Albany PD and thought himself above Aldridge County.

They started through the forest, Gilbert leading the way and grumbling nonstop about Barton and the sheriff's incompetence. Unlike the detective, Rhoads didn't believe the missing deputy was visiting the locals and warming himself by a fire, shirking his duty. Between the storm and Victor Bacchus, too many dangers existed in the night. He hoped Barton was safe, but his instincts told him otherwise. Why wasn't the deputy responding to radio calls?

Around them, the trees swayed and groaned. The storm tossed snow into their faces, and Rhoads tucked his head as low as it would go in his jacket. Gilbert cursed.

"When I find Barton, he'll wish he never met me," the detective boasted.

They all wished they'd never met Gilbert, but it wasn't out of fear. The detective was an all-knowing pompous idiot.

Rhoads shivered and prayed for daylight. He was tired and he wanted to go home, but he wouldn't rest until they located his friend. As long as Bacchus was out there, no one was safe.

A sound drifted on the wind. Was that laughter?

Surely the wind was fooling him. Yet he recalled Barton's claim that a man had watched him from the woods. Gilbert couldn't stop lampooning the missing deputy for seeing ghosts. Hadn't Barton said the stranger was laughing at him?

A twig snapped. Rhoads swung toward the sound with his gun drawn, but Gilbert marched on without slowing.

"It's the wind," the detective said. "There's no one in the woods."

Rhoads trembled and prayed for daylight. The laughter came again, this time louder and closer. Rhoads froze in his steps, his breath coming quick and fast. Gilbert appeared not to hear. He glanced back at Rhoads and scowled.

"Are you coming or not?"

A figure emerged from the forest, walking calmly towards them.

Rhoads turned his gun on the silhouette, only to see that it was a man wearing a deputy's uniform. The stranger grinned, his eyes glinting in the reflection of the swirling snow. He lifted his arms, palms facing outward to show he was unarmed.

Rhoads glanced at Gilbert, who went still. Gilbert's cheeks had gone ghostly pale. The detective blinked, recognition dawning on his face.

"Victor Bacchus," Gilbert breathed.

Bacchus smiled, revealing a set of sharp yellow teeth. "You're looking for your friend?" he asked. "I know where he is."

It was then Rhoads spotted Barton's name on the badge. Now he knew what had befallen his friend. Without waiting for Gilbert to act, Rhoads moved his finger toward the trigger. A gust of wind kicked the snow into the air. Ice sprayed against his face and stung his eyes. The maniacal laughter started again.

"You understand?" Bacchus yelled. "I am the storm, and the storm is me."

As the deputy cleared his eyes, he saw a blurry form walking forward. Gilbert screamed. Blood splashed against the deputy's face. He blinked and righted the gun, but no one was in front of him. As he spun, the madman swung the ax.

The blade dug into his shoulder, making the gun fall from his hand. Bacchus reared back and brought the ax down on the deputy's head.

The night faded behind a scarlet curtain.

34

The fire sparked and popped on the damp logs Thomas added to the pile. Fortunately, the wind struggled to find a path inside the barn. He worried about a gust tossing embers against the walls, which would go up faster than the kindling. Building the blaze in the barn was risky, but he didn't have a choice. All that mattered was keeping Chelsey alive.

She was awake and sitting up now, her hands cupping her elbows. The dancing light threw elongated shadows against the barn and drew out her features. Her lips were blue, her face pale and sickly.

"How are you doing?"

"Better," she said, staring at the fire.

He didn't believe her. Chelsey wouldn't want him to worry, but he couldn't help himself. She was his soulmate, his everything. He'd gotten her into this mess, and somehow he'd see her through.

"Don't sit too close to the flames."

"I can't feel the heat, Thomas."

He tossed yet another limb on the fire. The flames consumed

it and threw off more warmth. It scared the hell out of him that she didn't notice.

"Here," he said, peeling off his coat.

"You need your jacket. The fire isn't hot enough to keep you from freezing."

"I'm warm."

She glared at him, but he wouldn't take no for an answer. Hiding the fact that he was cold, he draped the coat over her shoulders and eased her down to the ground so she lay in the direct path of the heat.

Chelsey shivered and pulled her knees toward her chest. The color hadn't returned to her face, and worry that he was losing her grew. Why hadn't the fire turned her around? She seemed to worsen by the minute. He needed to get her to a hospital, but there was no chance of that happening. Heck, he didn't even know where they were.

Eyeing the pile of wood, he saw their stock was running low. The last thing on his mind was to leave her, but his priority was feeding the fire and warming her.

"Do what you need to do," she said through chattering teeth.

"I'll only be gone a minute."

"Don't worry about me, Thomas. It's not like I'm going anywhere."

She snickered, and he put on his best smile. Keeping her calm and positive was important. Leaning over, he kissed her cheek.

"See you in a second."

Without his coat, he strode into the storm. The snow was a few inches deeper than before, and the wind had strengthened, bending the trees and pulling shingles off the dilapidated farmhouse. Debris spun in the air like a murder of crows. He folded his arms, doing everything he could to ward off the arctic blast. Head lowered, he ran toward the thicket. One good thing about the wind: he would find an endless supply of fallen branches unless the snow had already covered them.

The trees shielded him from the gale, but the cold followed him everywhere he ran. He kept telling himself it would only take a minute for him to carry an armful of fuel back to the barn and join Chelsey beside the fire. His limbs shook so hard he kept dropping the branches. There was nothing he could do to prevent his teeth from chattering.

"You're okay, you're okay."

The wind shrieked. There was another sound in the night. He swore he heard laughter, but that couldn't be. Nobody was out in the storm except him.

Twice he fumbled with the branches as the gusts whipped him back and forth. He didn't want to drop them in the snow and risk dousing the fire.

A part of him worried he would find the barn empty, but as he entered, Chelsey lay in the same position. She didn't respond when he called her name.

Setting the fuel on top of the fire, he kneeled beside her.

"Can you hear my voice?"

She nodded once.

"I'm so cold, Thomas."

She looked worse than before. Her lips remained discolored, and her face appeared drawn in the firelight. Seeing no other choice, he lay on the chilly ground and wrapped his arms around her body. She snuggled against him, her limbs shaking like those of a newborn calf. He rubbed her arms and legs, working heat into her body through friction. A sob came out of her throat.

"You don't have to cry, Chelsey. I'll get you out of this."

"I'm sorry."

He turned her face toward his.

"What do you have to be sorry for?"

"For slowing you down, for falling into the gorge because I wasn't looking where I was going, for hurting my ankle, for this."

She gestured at the barn.

"Shh. You have no reason to apologize. I'm the one who caused this. If I'd taken your advice, we would be in a hotel by now."

Her body trembled. Even looking in her eyes, he couldn't tell if she was laughing or crying.

"Remember my first suggestion?" she asked.

"For vacation? You wanted to go to Costa Rica. That was a much better choice than a cabin on Laurel Mountain during the worst storm of the century."

"Costa Rica. Sun and sand would feel awfully nice."

"I promise if you stay with me, I'll get you back to civilization, and our next trip will be to somewhere tropical."

"I'm holding you to that promise, Thomas."

"Next time, we'll complain about sunburns and jellyfish."

She turned toward the fire. It seemed wise to keep her talking. Much as she needed rest, he was wary of her drifting off while on the edge of hypothermia. When would the fire's heat warm her bones? This close to the blaze, his forehead beaded with sweat.

"How long do you figure it will take to find the cabin?" she asked.

"Less than a day. If you feel up to it, we'll leave after the sun rises."

"Do you think the storm will be over by then?"

"Of course. It can't go on like this forever."

Was that true? The snow hadn't slowed since they'd departed the store.

A gust of wind shook the walls, but Chelsey clung to him and held on. He whispered more promises in her ear and stroked her hair until she relaxed. He held her tighter, praying for her survival, willing the heat to transfer from his body to hers.

Thomas would do whatever it took to save her. Even if it meant admitting he didn't know where they were or if the township lay ahead. Should the storm abate for a few minutes, he could study the horizon and search for Laurel Mountain. For now, they were stumbling blindly. Better to stay put until the weather cleared.

He hoped it would soon.

35

The cruiser skidded and spun as Deputy Aguilar struggled to keep it on the road. Lambert sat beside her wearing a stoic expression. Nothing ever rattled her partner. Yet tonight he gripped the door handle and swallowed every few seconds.

A starburst of snow hurtled at the windshield and obscured the way forward. The flakes were the largest she'd ever seen.

Even after Darren and Raven had rescued the snowplow and gotten the driver on the road, it remained a fruitless battle to clear the village. As soon as one driver plowed a neighborhood, the storm dumped another few inches of snow, and the wind caused banks to drift across streets, preventing emergency vehicles from reaching their destinations. An entire village of volunteers worked to plow the roads, but there was only so much they could do.

Lambert set his phone aside. "That was Darren. He and Raven are working on the north end of the village. After they finish, he'll head into the village center and clear a path toward the hospital."

She eyed the dashboard clock.

"It's two in the morning. I can't ask them to work all night."

"Let them work in the village center, then I'll tell them to head home. Hopefully they can make it back to the state park."

A black shape darted in front of the cruiser. Aguilar stomped the brakes, but the cruiser kept sliding. Lambert set his hands against the dash and clenched his teeth. The tires barely missed the cat, who scurried across the road and leaped onto a porch. Her heart pounded in her throat.

"Remind me never to say anything positive about cats again."

"You kept the cruiser under control," he said. "That's all that matters."

"What's the number on that house again?"

"Mrs. Katsuro lives at 26 Elmwood."

Back at the office, Aguilar and her barebones staff had spent the last hour phoning everyone on electric heat who'd lost power. Katsuro was the only one who hadn't answered.

As far as Aguilar knew, the woman might be asleep beneath a stack of blankets—it was certainly late enough—or at a neighbor's house, warm and safe. But Aguilar needed to be sure. Katsuro was eighty-one and had a history of heart ailments.

She sped as much as the road allowed, but the tires kept slipping and spinning. Halfway down Elmwood, the single-story house appeared on the right.

Mrs. Katsuro's house had been swallowed by the storm. The snow was piled up to the windows, and the porch on one side of the house had collapsed from the weight. A drift of snow blocked the front door. Aguilar killed the engine and stepped into the snowdrift. Despite her thick coat and boots, she felt cold seep through her veins as she pushed forward.

The snow was so deep that her legs felt weighed down with each step, and the flakes clung to her face like tiny stars. "We have to make sure she's okay," Lambert said when they reached the door. "Let's clear a path."

Taking shovels from the back of their cruiser, Aguilar and Lambert dug a tunnel to the entrance. The sky was thick with snow clouds, muffling any sound from outside the bubble of light cast by their headlamps. She pounded on the door and prayed someone would answer, though she remembered Mrs. Katsuro didn't speak English.

Lambert adjusted his flashlight and peered into the window. He gasped.

"It's Katsuro. She's unconscious on the floor."

A thin blanket lay over her body, tucked between her neck and shoulder. Lambert broke the window, his thick winter gloves absorbing most of the impact. Knocking the shards out of the way, the lanky deputy climbed into the living room. A moment later, the lock disengaged, and Aguilar followed him to the unconscious woman. Katsuro's face was pallid and lifeless, and a purplish tinge made her lips stand out in the flashlight beam.

"She needs an ambulance," Aguilar said.

"There's no time. Even if an ambulance makes it into the neighborhood, there's no way they're carrying a gurney through all that snow."

"Now what? Take her to the hospital ourselves and hope we make it in time?"

"I see no other choice."

She radioed the hospital and alerted the staff that they would soon be en route with an elderly, unconscious woman who'd succumbed to the cold. That is, if they could make it to the facility. Half the roads in Wolf Lake were closed and impassable.

Already, the pile of snow they'd shoveled aside had

collapsed and blocked the door again. Lambert lifted the woman's frail body into his arms, the blanket dangling off her body and flapping in the breeze through the open doorway. Aguilar didn't need to check Katsuro's pulse to know her heart was beating too slowly.

Grabbing the shovel, she pushed the pile aside and cleared a narrow pathway. She supported Lambert as he descended the steps. Ice covered the stairs, and the walkway to the cruiser would be just as treacherous.

They set the woman in the back of the vehicle. Aguilar sat with Katsuro, stabilizing her on the seat and speaking in soft tones. The victim might not understand a word she was saying, but if she could hear the deputy in her unconscious state, the conversation might keep her alive.

Lambert pulled off the curb, and the tires immediately spun. Parking for fifteen minutes had buried the cruiser. He eyed her in the mirror.

"No worries," he said. "I'll get us there."

Lightning exploded overhead, and a roar of thunder was the defiant answer from the storm. After rocking between drive and reverse, the tires gained traction and the cruiser lurched forward.

The trip across the village pushed Aguilar's heart into her lungs. Her partner kept reversing direction after encountering blocked roads. It would take divine intervention to reach the hospital. When they were a block away, Lambert cursed.

"What's wrong?"

"Debris blocking the way. It appears part of a roof blew into the road. I'll contact the county and ensure they know. Vehicles need an unobstructed path to the hospital."

Katsuro's head lolled on her neck. Aguilar searched for a pulse and found nothing.

"No time. We'll have to carry her."

Lambert gave her a worried look in the mirror before stopping the vehicle as close to the curb as the storm allowed. With a grunt, he lifted Katsuro out of the back.

As the storm screamed in anger, they struggled down an uncleared sidewalk, praying they weren't too late.

36

LeVar didn't know what time it was when he sprang awake. Outside, the relentless blizzard battered the guesthouse and lowered visibility to nothing. Even the shoreline had vanished behind the maelstrom.

He was on the floor in the front room and covered in a blanket. His back ached from sleeping on the hard surface, and the pounding in his head told him he'd end up struggling with a migraine before light returned to the sky. Not that there would be much light from that canopy of black. He couldn't believe the storm hadn't slowed down. If anything, it was increasing in intensity.

Why was he sleeping on the floor? Oh, right. Scout had refused to take his bed, and he hadn't wanted to leave her alone while she slept on the blowup mattress. Sleeping in the same room as his friend reignited his worries. This wasn't right. Her mother had given her consent, but was there any choice? Sending Scout home was a terrible risk, especially with a live wire hanging across the backyard. The power was out in the Mournings' house, but the space heater was still running.

No one could ever learn about this. Not his sister and mother, and definitely not Scout's teenage friends. They would assume the worst. So many people prejudged LeVar based on his past. Would anyone give him the benefit of the doubt if they found out he'd shared his house with a pretty girl during a storm? He didn't want to imagine the terrible things kids would say about her. Sleeping with a nineteen-year-old black man who'd struck fear in the hearts of Harmon residents for several years? The truth would forever ruin her reputation. She didn't understand. As intelligent as she was, she didn't appreciate how cruel society could be. The racial component would rear its ugly head. In situations like this, it always did.

Now he noticed her. She sat and stared out the window. Coming through the glass, the silvery-gray glow haloed her hair.

"Why aren't you asleep?"

She turned to him, and he recognized the tears wetting her cheeks. He came to her side and sat on the edge of the mattress.

"Scout, what's the matter?"

"I'm scared, LeVar."

He wasn't sure if he was supposed to set an arm around her shoulder, give her a hug, or keep his distance. The latter was the path of least regret, so he took that trail without looking back from where he'd come.

"What are you afraid of? Talk to me. Let me help."

She shrugged. "The snow, the wind, my mother alone in the house."

"Your mom can care for herself."

"I tried to call and text. She isn't answering."

Scout sniffled and wiped her cheeks with the back of her wrist.

"Look, there are two possibilities. Either she's sound asleep and didn't know you'd messaged her, or the cell towers aren't functioning. I wouldn't be surprised if the entire county has lost service."

"What if the power line catches fire and a spark lands on the house? She's all alone."

"Do you want me to check on her? Just ask, and I will."

She shook her head, causing her tear-dampened hair to swing from side to side.

"I won't let you risk your life. We can't leave the guesthouse until the power company fixes the wire or we confirm the electricity is dead."

"I'm not afraid, Scout. Say the word, and I'll check on your mother."

"It's not worth it. I'm acting like a baby."

The girl sniffled again, and this time he rubbed her shoulder without thinking. He'd comforted her hundreds of times, but never under these circumstances.

As though he'd touched a hot pan, LeVar pulled his hand away. She gave him a curious glance before brushing a tissue across her nose.

"You aren't being a baby. Think I'm not worried about my ma and sister? Ma is sleeping with a guy who can't run a toaster without reading the directions, and God knows what Darren and my sister are up to. Bet you anything they're driving around in his Silverado and helping people survive the weather. If they're at the cabin, it's only to check on Thomas's pets and catch an hour of sleep."

"Are you frustrated because you want to help, but you're stuck babysitting a teenager?"

"Stop that. Now you're just feeling sorry for yourself. Scout, your mother is safe, and we can see the house through the window. It's not as if she lives on the other side of Wolf Lake, *aight*?"

"I wish I wouldn't stress myself over all this stuff," she said. "Sometimes it seems like my life is nothing but a hot mess."

"Seriously? This is the girl who willed herself to walk again after paralysis?"

"That was the surgeon's doing."

"Oh, really? Who was the one keeping a positive mindset throughout the ordeal and battling through days and weeks of physical therapy? Who was the girl who said to hell with learning to walk first and took long jogs to the state park and back? You're an inspiration."

"I'm also the girl who lied to her mother and sneaked out on Halloween, and as intelligent as you think I am, you haven't watched me flounder in physics class."

"You made one mistake," he said. "Stop beating yourself up."

"College is a few years away. By spring, I should send out applications. I can't afford to screw up again."

"You won't. I'll keep you on the straight and narrow. No more ghost hunts in abandoned buildings with Liz. Listen, the storm will stop, then it will be safe to go home. Things will look different in the light of day."

She averted her eyes and pushed the bangs off her forehead. The wind took an inopportune time to shriek over the guesthouse. LeVar had just calmed her down. A groan came from outside, and he imagined another tree toppling over, this time crashing through his roof.

Scout shivered and lay on her side, head resting on the pillow. A tremor ran across her shoulders. Without thinking, he lay beside her and set a comforting hand on her side. Before he could pull it back, she grasped his wrist and dragged him closer.

Now she snuggled beside him, seeming so vulnerable, so young. He knew this was wrong, but there was no turning around the ship of fate.

As the wind built to a frightening crescendo, he lay beside

the girl. Her protector, her friend and brother. He would never do wrong by her.

Lulled by the gentle rise and fall of her breathing, he promised himself he would only close his eyes and stay with her until she drifted asleep.

Yet exhaustion pulled him under.

37

The pop of damp fuel burning brought Thomas awake. He'd forced himself to stay up all night and feed the fire so Chelsey would get warm, and he'd failed her. The fire was on its last legs, crackling and smoldering as it collapsed into coals and pushed a narrow plume of smoke skyward and through the hole in the roof. Snow fell through the opening, searching for the fire, intent on snuffing out their only source of heat.

He checked her before rising. She curled on her side like a sleeping child. He didn't trust the color of her cheeks. She no longer appeared her vibrant self.

Thomas couldn't tell if she was breathing. A frightened jolt rushed through his body, and he kneeled so his face was beside her wan lips. A weak puff of air touched his cheek, and he sighed. Alive. For now.

He hurried to toss branches on what remained of the fire, then left his jacket hanging over her shoulders and entered the frigid doom that waited beyond the barn. To his shock, the visibility had further degraded. Forget finding Laurel Mountain; he couldn't even see the farmhouse. The snow, which had reached his knees, stood waist-high. Walking forward proved impossible. How would he reach the thicket and carry the fuel to the barn? Better question: If Chelsey recovered—no, *when* Chelsey recovered—how would they reach civilization?

The wind bit his exposed skin. It was too much. Shivering, he retreated into the barn and closed the door. Feeling useless, he leaned against the frame. They were trapped. Even if the storm let up, they couldn't walk through all that snow. And it was still coming down.

His eyes darted around the barn, searching for anything that might get them out of this mess. All those rusty tools hung from the wall. A scythe wouldn't do him any good, though it might serve a purpose if a hungry animal decided they would make a filling meal. The spade might clear a path out of the barn, but then what? He couldn't shovel until they found a town.

Then his gaze landed on a pole saw. The teeth looked brittle and bronzed with age, yet he cared little about the saw. It was the polyester rope dangling from the tool that drew his attention. Eyeing the fire, which would burn out if he didn't act quickly, he hurried to the tools and yanked the saw off its hook. A weathered piece of wood, which may have once been part of the roof, would keep the fire going a little longer. He piled the plank on the coals, and a flame rose phoenix-like from the ashes.

There were more boards on the ground. Testing them, he smiled when they supported his weight. Yes, this would work. It had to.

Removing the multi-tool from his pocket, he sliced the rope into manageable lengths. The boards were several inches longer than his shoes. As he stood on them, he knotted the boards in place. If this worked, the snowshoes might be their tickets back to civilization.

First he had to find fuel for the fire. Ensuring the snowshoes were strapped to his feet, he pushed open the barn door and stepped outside. Now he could climb on the snow rather than sink into it. He shuffled his way forward, worried that the shoes wouldn't work and that he would collapse into the bank. They kept him afloat.

Despite the storm throwing snow at him, he crossed the field and reached the thicket without incident. Snow covered the fallen limbs, but standing high on the banks, he broke branches off the trees, tucked them under his arm, and carried them back to the fire.

He made three trips until he had the blaze roaring again and the smoke billowing through the hole in the roof. Chelsey issued a contented sigh and snuggled closer to the blaze. Thomas lay beside her before going back for more firewood.

Yes, this would work. They finally had a plan for reaching civilization. He checked her pulse and found that it was normal. Her color appeared better, although that might be wishful thinking, and her forehead was beading with sweat.

Thomas feared the extra jacket thrown over her shoulder was too much. That was a good sign. The fire was doing its job and breaking through her hypothermia. He pulled the jacket off and slipped his arms into the sleeves. Perfect. Now they were both warm.

He would have to wait until sunrise and see if she could regain her strength and walk. Either way, he could reach the thicket and keep her warm.

~

At the hospital, Deputy Lambert rubbed his arms, which were sore from carrying Mrs. Katsuro from the cruiser to the emergency room. Without his help, Deputy Aguilar never would have saved the woman. Now Katsuro was safe and in the hands of a doctor.

As suspected, the elderly woman was suffering from hypothermia, and it would be touch and go for the next several hours. The doctor remained optimistic and told Aguilar she could go back to the station, but the concerned deputies stayed.

After ten minutes of sitting in the waiting room, they stood when a doctor in a white lab coat opened the doors and made a beeline toward them.

The doctor wore glasses and had thinning hair, which barely fell to his forehead. He looked too young to be balding, but he had kind eyes and a lean physique that told them he spent time at the gymnasium. He removed his glasses, folded them, and hung them from the top of his lab coat.

"Mrs. Katsuro is recovering," the doctor said. "We believe she can go home within twenty-four hours. Of course, if the power doesn't return, it won't be safe for her."

Aguilar agreed.

"Have you treated many patients suffering from hypothermia tonight?" she asked.

The doctor shook his head.

"I suspect there are quite a few people suffering from the cold, but with the storm spinning out of control, I doubt anyone can make it to the hospital. I'm afraid of what's going on behind those closed doors. There are so many elderly in the Wolf Lake community who might be sick and trapped inside their houses, and too many rely on electric heat."

"That's a problem when the power goes out. Most of the time, it's a convenience."

"It's important to have a backup heat source," Lambert added. "A fireplace, a woodstove, or a kind neighbor who will take you in when you lose power. Unfortunately, with the snow so deep, it's impossible for someone Katsaro's age to make it to a neighbor's house."

The doctor nodded. He took their cell phone numbers and

would contact them as soon as he had more information on the woman's condition.

Holding their coats closed, Aguilar and Lambert skidded through the snowbanks and struggled down the sidewalk to reach the cruiser they had abandoned along the curb. Snow already blanketed the windshield, and the storm showed no sign of slowing down. The last time Aguilar had checked, the radar had promised more squalls would reach Wolf Lake and the surrounding countryside. They couldn't take any more snow. The plows couldn't keep up. Even with volunteers like Darren and Raven helping, there was only so much they could do.

Aguilar took the keys this time. Lambert seemed relieved to sit in the passenger seat after the hair-raising drive from Katsaro's house to the hospital. When Aguilar pulled off the curb, the tires spun, and it took some doing to regain traction and get them on their way. Reports continued to come in through the radio of stuck plows and salt truck drivers quitting for the night. There was no reason to salt the roads when the plows couldn't clear enough snow to expose the macadam.

"I can't imagine what's going on at Laurel Mountain," Aguilar said.

Lambert didn't respond, but she could see the concern on his face. Thomas and Chelsey were stuck somewhere on top of the mountain. God willing, they had learned about the storm before it struck. The reports claimed the snow was even deeper over the high elevations. And that meant Laurel Mountain must be in worse shape than Wolf Lake. That seemed impossible to conceive.

But without a way to reach Thomas and Chelsey, they could only hope that the sheriff and his fiancée were indoors and safe.

38

Darren didn't remember falling asleep. One second he was returning to bed after taking Jack outside, and now he was blinking at the hazy gray of morning. Raven snored beside him with the covers pulled up to her shoulder. Jack curled at the bottom of the bed while Tigger watched from the couch, his tail flicking back and forth.

He checked the time and realized that they had slept past six a.m. Only his watch served as a clock, because the power had gone out in the middle of the night. The light over the stove no longer shone, and the digital alarm clock on the nightstand didn't blink.

Darren rubbed Raven's shoulder.

"Wake up. It's already morning."

She blinked and looked around in surprise, then sat up with the covers falling down to expose her sports bra. How was it a woman who'd spent the last three hours tucked under the covers could look so beautiful before showering and cleaning up? She amazed him every day, and he realized he loved her and wanted to spend every moment of his life at her side.

"Is the power out? Wasn't the light on over the stove?"

"It was. From what I can tell, the electricity failed in the last three hours."

Jack raised his head. It was time to take the dog outside to do his business, then feed the pets and get back on the road. To Darren's shock, snow was still falling outside the window.

That didn't seem possible. By his estimation, three feet of snow covered the ground. How could it still be snowing this hard? The wind refused to let up, and he noticed two fallen trees in the forest. Since the cabin sat so close to the woods, he worried about a large oak toppling through the roof.

"What should we do about breakfast?" he asked. "I can't cook on an electric stove until the power returns. Cold cereal?"

"I have a better idea. Do you have a pan that can take high heat?

"I own a few that fit the bill."

"Grab your best pan and bring it to me."

He gave her a curious look before swinging his legs off the bed and padding across the cold floor. He rummaged through the cabinets until he found the pan he sought. From the pantry he grabbed the non-stick cooking spray, and from the refrigerator a carton of eggs, which were thankfully still cold. He didn't waste time shutting the refrigerator door. If worse came to worst, he could put the food outside. With the temperature hovering below zero, there were no worries about anything spoiling. Freezing the food into ice blocks was another problem. They would cross that bridge when they came to it.

He handed Raven the pan, and she slicked the surface with the olive oil spray.

"Now watch and learn."

She cracked two eggs and dropped them in the pan, setting it on the woodstove.

"I see what you're doing," he said. "Great idea."

"How do you want your eggs? Sunny side up, sunny side down, or scrambled?"

She cracked three more eggs into the pan.

"Sunny side up is the only way to go."

Because of the woodstove's intense heat, it didn't take long for the eggs to cook. After she plated the food, he set two slices of bread in the pan and let them sizzle. Jack looked on with his tongue hanging out, hoping for a treat.

While Raven monitored the pan, Darren took Jack outside. The dog leaped through the snow, yelped, and quickly did his business. Though the wolf-like dog loved being outdoors, the cold was too much. After squatting, Jack raced inside and shook off his coat in the entryway.

Huddled in front of the woodstove, they ate breakfast and occasionally tossed pieces of toast to Jack. Maybe it was the excitement of being locked inside with this beautiful woman, but Darren couldn't recall enjoying a meal so much. The excitement soon faded when he remembered the work ahead of them. He would have to plow the parking lot and road just to make it to Wolf Lake. He shuddered at the thought of what he might find in the village.

When Lambert had told Darren and Raven to go home and get some rest last night, the plows were struggling to keep up. The snow fell too quickly for the emergency workers to clear paths. Making things worse, a roof had blown off a house across the street from the hospital and blocked the entryway for three hours.

As she ate, Raven checked her messages. She raised an eyebrow and glanced at Darren.

"Did you hear about an escaped convict near Laurel Mountain?"

"Aguilar mentioned nothing to me."

"I received a message from Scout in the middle of the night.

Between her snowfall reports and her weather reporting, she sent a story about a mob boss from Rochester named Victor Bacchus escaping from an escort van. Apparently he was on his way to Buffalo."

"That's news to me."

Darren worried. Thomas and Chelsey had enough on their plates between the storm, the cold, and the isolation. Was a dangerous criminal in their midst?

"At least our phones are still working," she said. "I'll try to contact Chelsey and Thomas again." After dialing their numbers, she frowned and set the phone aside. "Same as before; the phone just rings and nobody answers. I don't think they have coverage on the mountain."

"A cell tower might be out as well."

"I don't want to bother Lambert and Aguilar with this, but they should know if Thomas is in danger."

"I'm sure the sheriff took a firearm with him, and knowing Chelsey, she armed herself as well. Even though you don't expect an escaped convict to threaten you in the middle of paradise, there are always bears and coyotes to worry about. What are the chances that this Victor Bacchus character will attack Thomas?"

"Low, but if Bacchus needs food and shelter, he'll look for occupied cabins."

That was a troubling thought, one he couldn't brush off.

"There's not much we can do about it now. Here, give me your plate. I'll wash the dishes. Get changed. I'm sure they need help in the village."

While Darren fed the pets and Raven changed, he thought about Victor Bacchus. Scout was prone to overreacting, as teenagers often did, but this sounded serious.

After he washed the dishes, he got on the computer and logged on to a private forum which catered to current and retired law enforcement. He kept quite a few contacts in the forum, and it didn't take long for him to find a thread on Victor Bacchus. He'd never heard of the man, but perhaps he should have. Bacchus was the most feared mob leader in Western New York and ran a crime syndicate out of Rochester. A former officer discovered that the convict had stolen a firearm from an armed guard and shot everyone inside the van. Nobody believed Bacchus would make it far, not with the temperature plummeting below zero and snow falling at two to three inches every hour.

There was another troubling report. The Aldridge County Sheriff's Department was searching for a missing deputy. An unconfirmed report suggested someone had murdered an elderly woman inside her house at the base of Laurel Mountain. The same poster claimed someone had stolen food from the refrigerator and warmed himself by a fire.

Concerned, Darren made a note for himself to contact Aguilar and ensure the Aldridge County Sheriff's Department knew Thomas and Chelsey were staying in a cabin on the mountain. More than anything, he wanted to drive to Laurel Mountain and find his friends. But the storm had other ideas.

39

LeVar awoke with a start. He was sleeping beside Scout and had one arm dangerously close to hers. She gave a contented sigh and rolled over on her back, and the covers fell down to expose her bare shoulder. For a moment, he lay frozen, unsure how to react.

Working up the courage to move, he pulled himself off the blow-up mattress, stood, and looked down at her sleeping body. He knew he had done wrong, yet he'd felt a need to comfort her and keep her company. Raising her spirits would prevent her from worrying about her friends and family.

Moving with care so he wouldn't awaken her, LeVar entered the kitchen, turned on the stove, and was relieved to see the lights still functioned. Somehow, the guesthouse continued to receive power. Looking out the window, he thought it seemed half the neighborhood had electricity while the other half did not.

The wire hanging beside the guesthouse was too close for comfort. They still couldn't leave until the power company removed the line or verified it wasn't live. Checking the time, LeVar saw it was fifteen minutes past eight o'clock. He'd slept later than usual. Then again, they'd stayed up late last night, talking through their problems and gaining a better understanding of each other. They'd grown closer, if that was possible. Their fears had pulled them together. He worried just as much as she did about what was happening to their families and friends. Were Thomas and Chelsey safe on top of Laurel Mountain? And what about Victor Bacchus? Was the psychopath still alive and loose near the township?

A quick glance out the window confirmed it was snowing. There had to be four or five feet of snow on the ground, yet it was still coming down. The wind might have let up slightly, but it was gusting hard enough to make the lines overhanging the street rise and fall and spin in loops.

Quietly, he removed a pan from the cupboard, slicked it with butter, and cracked four eggs. The sizzle made her stir, and after a second Scout sat up, bleary-eyed. Confused as to where she was, she rubbed her eyes and pushed the hair off her forehead. After that moment of confusion, she gave him a smile. But there was something sheepish behind her grin, which told him she was just as embarrassed as he was. Did she realize they had slept side by side all night? If so, would she blame him?

"That smells good," she said. "You're up early and cooking breakfast for us."

LeVar smirked. "Nah, I ain't cooking breakfast for us. *We're* cooking breakfast for us."

"Understood."

She reached below the covers and grabbed something. To his shock, it was her sweatpants. She had been sleeping beside him without them. She pulled the pants over her legs. He turned away and pretended not to notice. Then she joined him beside the stove and they fixed breakfast without saying much.

"Got some fresh fruit in the refrigerator," he said, tilting his chin.

She nodded and pulled out the strawberries, cantaloupe, honeydew, and a pint of blueberries.

"Why don't you whip up a fruit salad while I work on the eggs?" he asked.

"That seems fair."

She ran the berries and fruit under the water while he flipped eggs, added more to the pan, and stuck bread in the toaster. He still wasn't sure how to begin the conversation. How long would they dance around the issue that they'd slept together, and she hadn't even been wearing her sweatpants?

Every few seconds, he cleared his throat, and she could tell he was uneasy.

"Have you checked with your mother and Buck?" she asked

"Not yet. I should call them. If they were smart, they stayed in all night. I'm just worried that Buck didn't figure out how to start the snowblower, and now there's five feet of snow sitting in their driveway. They'll never get out. What about your mother?"

She pressed her lips together, and it was clear she was nervous about what was happening next door. The power was out inside the Mournings' home. LeVar searched Naomi's windows for a sign of the woman, but she was nowhere to be seen. At some point, he needed to get to her house and confirm she was all right. For Scout's sake, and for his own. He cared about his neighbor. She had been like a mother to him.

After Scout mixed the fruit in a bowl, she moved beside LeVar and stared across the yards toward her own house. Even without the live wire, they could not cross the yard. There was simply too much snow; shoveling was no longer an option. The snow and ice came up to their shoulders.

"You better get used to it," he said. "The eggs and fruit, I mean. I'm running low on groceries, and there's not much chance I can get to the store."

"I'm happy with what we have. Besides, I like fruit, and I like eggs. I get my healthy carbohydrates and complete protein. What more can a girl ask for?"

"I just wish I could do more."

"LeVar, don't act like you need to save the world. You're doing enough by giving me a place to stay. And by the way, it's my fault that I'm stuck here. I should have left when you warned me yesterday."

"I *did* tell you."

"On the other hand, had I gone home and followed your advice, I'd be stuck with no electricity. At least everything functions in your house."

"Yeah, for now."

"And for what it's worth, it's been nice to spend time with you."

LeVar swallowed, unsure how to respond. He felt the same way. It seemed he knew more about her now than ever before. Yet they'd crossed a line, and there was no path back to the way things used to be.

"Scout, I uh . . ."

"Don't say another word. Thanks to that wonderful space heater of yours, I got hot during the night and kicked off my sweatpants without realizing what I was doing. I should have known you were sleeping in the same room."

"I was sleeping right next to you."

"Because I was frightened. It's not your fault. Nobody has to find out. And just so you know, I'm not the least bit uncomfortable about what happened . . . or what didn't happen."

"You won't tell anybody? Not your mother?"

"Are you kidding? She would so freak."

"What about Liz?"

"LeVar, you fool. I won't gossip about myself. That would be ridiculous."

"So what do we do now?" he asked.

"There is nothing to do. We'll go on being friends, like we've always been. You know nothing happened; I know nothing happened. Our relationship is purely platonic. You're not after more, and neither am I. We're just two friends who took care of each other last night. Just because we shared the same mattress doesn't mean it was anything inappropriate."

"I feel ashamed."

"Well, don't. I knew you were there all night. Had I wanted you to leave, I would have elbowed you off the bed."

"Why didn't you?" he asked.

"For the same reason I wouldn't push any friend away in a time of need. We were both scared. Admit it; it wasn't just me. You're concerned about your mother and Buck, Raven, and Darren, and I'm worried about my mother."

LeVar caught movement out of the corner of his eye.

"Speaking of which, I see your mother right now."

Scout followed his gaze. Her eyes widened and her shoulders relaxed upon seeing her mother beside the sliding glass door that led from the kitchen to the back deck. She wore a bathrobe, and from the way she held it together, LeVar could tell she was cold. The Mournings' house had gas heat, so that shouldn't be a problem, but people who had heat were uncomfortable with the wind pushing the arctic air into their houses. He was lucky the space heater was working. If it failed, the guest house would become unbearably cold.

"She's waving to you, Scout. I think she wants you to come outside."

Scout bit her lip. Was she nervous about what her mother would say? Did Naomi somehow know what had happened between them last night? There was no explaining a mother's intuition.

"I'll go with you," he said. "We should do this together."

They pulled on their jackets. After LeVar plated the eggs and turned off the stove, he opened the door and pushed aside a mound of snow that stood as tall as his face. He formed enough room for them to squeeze outside.

Wearing slippers, Naomi opened the sliding glass door and called to them. "Are you two okay?"

He waved an arm over his head and raised a thumb. "Power is still on over here. It's warm, we're safe, and we're staying away from the wire."

She cocked her head toward the roof of her own house.

"There's a wire hanging over the eaves on the front of the house. Whatever you do, don't come over. It's not safe."

"What about the power company?" Scout asked. "Will they move the wires so you can exit the house?"

"I'm sure they have their work cut out for them. When they get to me, they get to me. Until then, I want the two of you to stay inside where it's safe. Don't cross the yard. There's no power here, so there's no point, and it's an unnecessary risk with all this snow. I don't know how you would get here anyway."

"I can shovel a path," he said.

"LeVar, I love you like a son. I won't watch you shovel five feet of snow and give yourself a heart attack. I trust you to take care of Scout and keep her safe, and that's what I expect you to do."

Guilt curled around his throat.

"I will, Ms. Mourning. Have you heard anything from Chelsey or Thomas?"

She shook her head. "I don't suppose that they have cell service where they are. From everything people in town are saying, Laurel Mountain got it even worse than we did. It's still snowing hard there. Now get inside before you catch hypothermia. It can't be warmer than zero degrees, and the wind is ferocious."

"You stay safe. If you need anything, and I mean anything . . ."

"I know. I'll get a hold of you if it comes to it. But I think we're best off staying where we are."

LeVar opened the door for Scout and returned to the kitchen.

Whatever fear he'd had that Scout's mother somehow knew they'd slept side by side was replaced by lingering regret. She trusted him, and expected LeVar would do right by her daughter.

That wouldn't be easy. They might be stuck here for days.

40

Though the black clouds hanging over Wolf Lake blocked out most of the light, there was still enough to make Aguilar pinch her eyes and blink upon waking up in the back of the sheriff's department. She lay on an uncomfortable cot with no mattress in the storage room, which had an east-facing window. The scant morning light barely made it past the dusty glass, and she could see flakes floating down from the sky.

When would this storm finally end? Knowing she had to get moving, she sat up, ruffled her mussed hair, and pulled on her boots. She'd slept in her uniform with an old blanket tossed over her shoulders.

"This isn't like Wolf Lake Consulting," she muttered to herself.

Wouldn't it be nice to have bedrooms like Wolf Lake Consulting when they worked overnight and couldn't make it home? In a situation like this, where duty required officers to remain at the station for days on end, they needed a place to sleep. She didn't expect hotel accommodations, but something a little more homey than a storage room would be nice. She glanced around at the boxes of old cases and wondered how this event would be remembered.

A message awaited on her phone. She cleared her eyes and read it, pleased the doctor from the hospital had confirmed that Mrs. Katsuro was making a full recovery. They would keep her through the afternoon for observation. With the storm continuing, they couldn't send the woman home.

Aguilar shuffled out of the storage room and down a dimly lit hallway. She could hear someone snoring from Thomas's office and wondered if that was where the junior deputy had holed up for the night. In the operations area, she found Lambert leaning back in his chair with his feet propped on top of his desk and his eyes closed. He snored to beat the band.

Sensing her presence, the former military man opened his eyes and looked at her in alarm before realizing where he was. One deputy worked the phones. Few people had called in the last hour, probably because the phone lines were down and many of the cell towers had ceased functioning.

"Sorry," Lambert said. "I was only asleep for an hour."

She waved a hand in front of her face. "As long as you brush your teeth, I don't have a problem with how long you slept."

He gave her a wry smile and lifted a thumb.

"I hate to throw more work upon your shoulders, Aguilar, but we need help. I kept in contact with the plow drivers all night. They can't keep the roads clear. Plus, we have two pages' worth of people to check on."

"Elderly without electricity?"

"Yep. We reached some of them by phone, but most aren't answering. I'm unsure what to do. None of the other deputies can make it in, and we still have that bug going around the office to worry about. With no Thomas and nobody at Wolf Lake Consulting to fall back on, I wonder if we shouldn't call LeVar."

Aguilar nodded. "Thomas didn't want us to call him, but these are extreme circumstances."

"How will LeVar get to work?"

"That's a question we'll answer once we reach him. Hopefully he still has phone service. Otherwise, we're really up the creek."

"Darren and Raven are ready to return to the job. I just received a text from them."

"Did they clear the hill from the park into the village?"

"Not yet, but they will. That Silverado of Darren's can handle any task. Once he makes it here, he'll help any of the plow drivers who are having difficulty and bail out a few more volunteers so we can work together."

"I'm worried what we'll find at these houses, Lambert. There are too many people trapped inside, and with our aging community, that's a recipe for disaster."

"I wonder how many tried to shovel and ended up with chest pains," he said. "Nobody can make it to the hospital."

"This is the worst storm I've ever experienced. If we make it through this, we can make it through anything."

"Truer words have never been spoken. I'll get on the horn with LeVar and see if he can come in."

"No, work on Darren and Raven, and I'll call LeVar."

"What should we do about the other deputy who is asleep?"

"How long was he up?" she asked.

"Till about five or six in the morning."

"Let him sleep, Lambert. He's no good to us if he's dead tired. Besides, nobody should have to work without sleep."

In LeVar, Aguilar was down to her last hope. She needed the deputy to come in. The question was, could he make it to the station? The field reports that had come in suggested the snow was heavier near the shoreline where the lake added moisture to the clouds. She dialed his number and waited; the phone rang several times, then LeVar answered.

"What's up, Boss Lady?"

"LeVar, I hate to ask this of you, but we're really up against it at the Sheriff's Department. I need someone to come in and you're the only available deputy."

"I'd love to help", he said. "Problem is, there's no way that I can get to you. The yard is buried under five feet of snow, and I don't know how I'll get to my car."

"Let me worry about that. Just be ready to work when we come to get you."

A girl spoke in the background, and Aguilar recognized the voice.

"Is that Scout Mourning?"

"Well, uh, she's over at my house right now."

"How in the world did she reach your house through all that snow?"

"You're breaking up, Aguilar. I can't hear what you're saying. Could you call back in a little while once the communication lines clear?"

Funny. It seemed like LeVar was avoiding her question. It was a simple one. How had Scout Mourning reached his house?

"Like I said, LeVar, just be ready when we come calling."

"I'll be ready."

∼

LeVar placed the phone down. He didn't know how to react. Aguilar had heard Scout in the background. How would he explain what the teenage girl was doing in his house in the middle of the storm? He wondered what Aguilar had meant about coming to get him. Even if they plowed a path down the lake road, there was no way to reach the driveway without snowshoes. Then there was the matter of clearing off his car. He tried to imagine the amount of snow sitting on his Chrysler Limited and shuddered. He didn't know how he would remove all that snow and help the sheriff's department.

"Who was that?" Scout asked.

"That was Aguilar. She wants me to come in. Would you be all right staying alone?" He shook his head. "What am I saying? Of course not. I can't leave you alone."

"But if you have a job to do—"

"Listen, the job isn't exactly police business. We won't be chasing criminals. My guess is the department needs help to clean the town. Getting people to safety, that's more of a volunteer thing. Maybe even a Wolf Lake Consulting thing."

"Or," she said, "an amateur investigation thing."

"Now you're talking."

"But how will you reach the department?"

"She says I'm supposed to sit here and wait. An answer is coming. I don't know if she means divine intervention. I'm guessing she sweet-talked some plow driver into clearing a path to the driveway. That won't save my car."

"How will you get to the car? Neither of us can walk through five feet of snow. We were barely able to open the door."

"Apparently, we'll find a way."

A second later, his phone rang. He looked down and saw Darren's name on the screen and answered.

"Future bro, what's going on?"

Darren scoffed. "You sound like your mother, LeVar."

"Not ready to tie the knot and commit to my sister?"

"Did I say that? Why is everybody pushing me to make decisions? There are things I need to do on my own time."

"Spoken like a true procrastinator."

"Now isn't the moment to make fun of me, LeVar. I'm about to save your bacon."

"How's that?"

"Raven and I are on our way over. We're going to clear a path so that you can get out."

"Appreciate that. Do you realize I'm stuck in the guest house? I can't make it to the road."

"Trust me, I have an idea. As long as Thomas doesn't mind a few tire tracks in his yard, we'll work this out."

"When is this daring rescue going to occur?"

"Give me ten minutes. Raven and I are on our way. And then it's a lot of hard work ahead of us. I'm talking all day. Maybe most of the night."

"Darren, I need to tell you something before you come."

"All right."

"Scout is with me; she has been all night."

"What?"

"Listen, she got trapped in the storm. It's no big deal. Her mother wanted it this way. Nothing happened; everything is fine. But it's unsafe for her to go home because there is an electrical wire hanging in the middle of the yard. There's another wire on Naomi's place."

"I see. So she's coming with you?"

"Darren, I think they both should. I'm worried about Naomi. She's alone in the house, and there's a wire hanging over the eaves. She doesn't have power. The heat is working, but she's trapped."

"I'll fix that. Give me ten minutes. Make sure they're ready when Raven and I show up."

"Will do."

LeVar recounted the conversation for Scout's sake. She perked up, knowing they were about to save the village. By the time they dressed in layers and put on their winter gear, the rumble of Darren's truck broke through the shrieking wind. As LeVar stared out the window in surprise, the state park ranger lowered the plow beside the road and carved a trail through Thomas's front yard and along the side of the house to Naomi's front door. The truck struggled to push through the banks, and quite a few times LeVar worried that Darren was about to get stuck. Somehow, he always figured out a way to keep the Silverado moving.

After Darren cleared a path to Naomi's front door, he reversed course and cut a new opening through the yard. Snow billowed to either side of the wide-mouth plow, and the truck motored forward, pushing through the fresh powder as if it weren't there. A tunnel opened like the parting of the Red Sea.

Scout looked on with slack-jawed amazement as LeVar snickered, wondering how Shep Dawg would react after he saw the tire tracks in his grass.

"Looks like the cavalry is here," he said. "Button your coat. It's going to be a cold one."

Even with Darren, Raven, Naomi, Scout, and LeVar working together, it took half an hour to clear the snow off his car. Once they did, the Chrysler Limited rebounded upward as the shocks lifted back into place.

He got to work by chipping ice off the windshield. Deputy Aguilar pulled up in the cruiser with Lambert.

"You guys ready?" Aguilar called out the window.

"Coming in a second."

Naomi joined Darren and Raven in his truck while Scout slid into the passenger seat of the Chrysler Limited. She relished the heat pouring out of the vents.

"What's our first stop?" LeVar asked.

"I just received a report of a non-responsive couple. Mr. And Mrs. Chadha. They're on the north side of Wolf Lake, and the plows are having a heck of a time clearing a path to their road."

"Can we get to the house?"

"We will. Between the two trucks working in the neighborhood, we'll clear a path. Darren and Raven, I'd hate to ask you again, but I need you to hit the village center so the emergency vehicles can access the major routes."

Darren nodded in agreement. In the passenger seat, Scout sifted through reports on her phone, rattling off numbers which seemed too incredible to be true. Seventy-one inches of snow in Cooperstown, sixty-eight in Oneonta. Wolf Lake was reporting sixty-two. But the worst number was yet to come. On the lofty peaks of Laurel Mountain, a storm spotter claimed he'd received seventy-nine inches of snow. LeVar blew out a breath, as if somebody had slugged him in the gut.

He was about to pick up his radio and contact Aguilar with the information when Scout stopped him.

"We have a problem. The National Weather Service just issued a snow squall warning. The storm is heading right at Wolf Lake. We can expect zero visibility when it strikes."

"How far away is it?"

"Half an hour."

LeVar pressed the gas pedal.

"Then we better get moving."

41

Though the silvery light shining through the barn slots told Thomas morning had arrived, he rested a little longer. He didn't wish to awaken Chelsey until he was sure she had recovered from hypothermia. She no longer shivered, but her eyes were closed as she snuggled against him. They curled on the uncomfortable barn floor, and he was happy to be beside her.

The fire kept them warm, though he needed to get up every half hour and throw fuel on the blaze. He was three quarters of the way through his supply. If they opted to stay longer, he would need to gather more branches and wood from the thicket.

Thomas didn't look forward to going out in the cold, yet he knew there was no choice. Either he gathered fuel or they got moving. It was a long walk to civilization, and he wasn't even sure where they were. What had become of his truck after the avalanche? Had the road succumbed and plunged the truck into the abyss of the gorge? It was just a possession, not flesh and bone. He could buy a new pickup if he needed to. Chelsey couldn't be replaced. She was everything, and he wouldn't move until he was certain she was all right.

Around mid-morning, she stirred, ruffled her hair, and turned toward him with glazed eyes.

"What time is it?" she asked.

"Almost eleven."

She bolted upright. "Then we need to go. We can't be stuck here for another day."

"Why can't we? It's warm inside the barn. There is an endless supply of fuel in the thicket."

"But you can't reach the thicket. It's still snowing outside."

"That's what I wanted to tell you about."

She gave him a quizzical look as he stretched his legs. From the corner, he gathered the makeshift snowshoes into his arms and carried them to her.

"Look at what I fashioned out of old boards and rope."

"Thomas, what are these? Did you make snowshoes?"

"That's exactly what I made."

"Do they work?"

"Like a charm. How do you think I reached the thicket and carried the fuel over?"

"That's ingenious. I never would have thought of it."

"Yes, you would have."

"Will these get us back to the township?"

"They'll help. With these, we won't have to worry about struggling through the snow. We'll walk on top of it."

"I need to ask you a question, and I need an honest answer. Do you know where we are?"

He scratched his head and looked away.

"Not exactly. I never should have left the river. That was a mistake. Following those footprints led us to the middle of nowhere."

"I wonder who those footprints belonged to? Who would be out in the middle of a storm?"

"I don't know, but I don't like it. It might have been a lost traveler like us, but my instinct tells me it was somebody who is up to no good."

"There you go, thinking like a sheriff."

"Well, who else could it be? What about you? How do you feel after resting?"

"Better. I'm not shivering anymore."

"We should stay another day to be sure."

"The longer we stay, the more we risk our lives. We need to leave, and I'm able to travel."

"Chelsey, you may feel more energetic, but that doesn't mean you're in good enough shape to walk through several feet of snow.

"With your snowshoes, I should be able to."

"It's still a workout. Exhaustion might not hit you in the first hour, but the longer we walk, it will."

"How will you know if we're heading in the right direction?"

"Honestly, I won't until this storm clears. There's no way for me to see the mountain and get a sense of direction. We'll just have to estimate where the sun is, even though it's behind the clouds."

She lifted her chin. "I'm ready, Thomas."

"You say that now but—"

"No, I'm ready. We don't have a choice. We're out of food."

"The human body can go several days without eating."

"Ah, your facts and figures again. Yes, the human body can survive, but not before strenuous activity. If you mean to walk to civilization, we'd better do it while there's still a little left in our stomachs."

"All right, but the minute you feel tired—"

"I know, I know. I'll tell you to stop."

They strapped on the snowshoes. Through the hole in the barn roof, Thomas could see the snow was still coming down. It might not have been falling as hard as yesterday, but the rates were still over an inch per hour.

The walk would become more dangerous and difficult the longer they waited. He hated pushing Chelsey, but she was right about the food situation. The lack of nourishment wasn't a problem yet. It would become a big one soon. With their snowshoes strapped on, they stepped out of the barn and into the frigid cold. He looked at her, wondering if she'd changed her mind, but she kept her eyes ahead, fixed on an unseen destination.

Around them, a blanket of snow covered the terrain. Everything looked the same, and that troubled Thomas more than the weather itself. She had been right to question him about his sense of direction. All they possessed was the vague light overhead and a belief they were heading somewhere toward the mountain and the township. Whichever they found first mattered not. They needed to reach civilization.

He monitored her as they traveled. Her pace equaled his, but her face was paler than usual. She was out of breath after the first half mile.

Chelsey gave him a pointed look, obviously perturbed that he was slowing down for her. What choice was there? If Chelsey Byrd had one thing in heaps, it was pride. By sheer determination, she would force herself through any situation no matter how grim, but doing so would get her in trouble this time.

After midday came and passed, they were no closer to finding Laurel Mountain Township or their cabin. Though it seemed crazy, he believed they were walking in circles. If that were the case, wouldn't they cross their tracks? Snow wet their faces and left his cheeks and nose numb. She was shivering again.

To make matters worse, he realized if they didn't find their way back to civilization soon, they would run out of daylight.

Like yesterday, they needed shelter, and there was none in sight. Would luck shine on them again and produce a barn in the middle of nowhere? Or would it grace them with a farmhouse and a kindly couple, who would take them in and call Sheriff Donner?

Through the swirling white, he swore he saw a dark shape rising in the distance. Was he imagining the mountain, or was it dead ahead as he expected? The snow left a curtain before his eyes, making it impossible to tell.

His anxiousness ramped up when the light faded from the sky. An animal howled in the distance, and the wind echoed its scream. They were in trouble. There was no barn to bail them out this time. They would have to make do.

"Chelsey, we're lost."

"As if that isn't obvious."

Her teeth were chattering. He feared the hypothermia was taking hold again. How hard had he pushed her today?

"We need to stop. If we don't, we'll die."

42

The beast that was Victor Bacchus wore the leer of a Cheshire Cat. Night blanketed the terrain, yet it seemed to pool deeper wherever he passed. Through the forest, the terrain climbed ever higher. He was unsure what he sought at the peak, only that he must get there.

Consciously, the cold didn't bother him, but in the back of his mind he realized escaping it was vital to survival. Ice encased his fingers, and the boots did little to keep the cold from reaching his toes. Now and then he heard the whoop of a sheriff's department cruiser below. They were looking for him. Let them come. He would chop them up as he had the couple and lay their bodies out for the animals to take. Nothing could stand in his way until he reached the peak of the mountain. That was his destiny. The more he killed, the more energy he gained.

As the snow blew past his face, he saw another light spilling through the trees. Fresh victims. Who lived in this house?

Whoever it was, they wouldn't see him coming until it was too late. He waited at the tree line and darted his eyes from side to side, wary this might be a trap. By now the deputies and police realized he was killing people on his way up the mountain. Would he burst inside and find the authorities waiting?

That would be foolish on their part. If they wanted to die, let them test him. From behind a stout, snow-covered tree, he spied movement in the windows. It was a man in his sixties or seventies, and he appeared to be alone. He wore a red flannel shirt, and the gray wispy hair barely covered the peak of his head.

Bacchus approached the house. Through the glass, he could see a fire burning in the woodstove. Warmth. This was the answer. The back of his mind whispered that he shouldn't knock this time. Too many knew about the murders and would be wary of anyone pounding on the door after sunset. He knew not what time it was, though he assumed it had to be after eight o'clock. The sun set early this time of year and made it easier for him to stalk his prey.

The inner voice that craved blood spoke to him now. It told him to smash the door to splinters as he had before. Trying not to laugh and give himself away, he hefted the ax, pulled it back, and let it fly. It struck the wooden door like Thor's hammer. Splinters rained upon the snow. An alarmed yell came from inside, and Bacchus kicked out, smashing the door. He could see the man holding a rifle and aiming it at the entryway. Yet that weapon trembled in the terrified man's hands. He couldn't hold the gun still.

With a demonic bellow, Bacchus leaped forward. The gun exploded, and the bullet whistled past his shoulder, taking out a section of the wall. That could have been his head, a part of him thought with a laugh. The old man's eyes widened as the ax rose again. The teeth of the bit slashed down on the victim's neck. Blood flew and wet the murderer's face. When the victim fell to one knee, Bacchus brought the ax up again. This time, he brought it down true, straight through the man's skull. He split the scalp in half. Blood poured into the floor slats.

Calmly, he set the ax aside, returned to the ruined door, and wrenched it shut, hoping no one had heard the gunshot. It wouldn't be easy for others to overhear the explosion so far up the mountain with the wind shrieking. To anyone, it might sound like a car backfiring. Still, he needed to remain alert. If the deputies had heard, they were coming for him now.

Though he was no longer hungry, he hobbled to the refrigerator with rote desire and yanked the door off its hinges. A pitcher of ice water sat on the top shelf. He pulled it out, bent his neck back, and drank until his stomach hurt. He couldn't recall the last time he'd consumed fluids. That was important for his survival, and he had to live, for he couldn't kill unless he survived the night.

He glanced back at the split skull of the elderly man. Without a word, he rummaged for food and found what appeared to be the last of a side of roast beef wrapped in plastic. Like an animal, he tore the plastic apart and ripped the meat with his teeth. He stood beside the woodstove and gnashed the flesh of some long-deceased being. When he was full, he spat the rest on the floor and kneeled to warm himself. The feeling returned to his hands and feet.

The stolen guard's jacket wasn't enough to keep him warm, so he wandered the house until he found the old man's bedroom. From the dresser, he removed a sweatshirt. It was a little tight on him but would serve a purpose. He also found a pair of wool socks. Removing his boots and tossing the wet socks aside, he replaced them with a new pair of cotton socks and yanked the others over them.

After searching through the drawers, he satisfied himself that he wouldn't find anything else to shield him from the elements. Bacchus didn't plan to stay long inside the house, but he took advantage of the resources available to him. He set the boots beside the woodstove and let them dry. In the closet, he discovered a ski hat and a new pair of gloves with fleece lining. These would help him reach the peak of the mountain. And once he climbed to the top, he would realize his destiny.

When the boots were warm, he pulled them over his feet and tied them off. Buttoning the jacket, he donned the hat and gloves. He was ready for the cold.

The storm greeted him with a high-pitched scream as he stalked outside. The terrain steepened ahead and told him he was closer to the peak. If he hurried, he might reach the top by tomorrow evening. But he knew that there would be more cabins and farmhouses between here and there, and they would satisfy his blood cravings.

43

Thomas knew leaving the barn had been a mistake. It was too much to ask Chelsey to travel after she'd recovered from hypothermia. She trembled more by the minute, and there was no sign of civilization. They'd walked all afternoon and through the evening, searching for residents—a barn, a sign of Laurel Mountain Township, or the mountain. They would have been a welcome sight.

Now they were lost, and the sun was almost below the horizon. Not that he could see it. Black boiling clouds masked the light and lent it an ethereal quality. With no shelter in sight, he searched for a forest to protect them from the gusting wind.

If he'd only waited one more day and allowed Chelsey to recover... They'd been safe inside the barn. Secure and warm. He could have kept the fire going for days or even weeks. Instead, they were somewhere on the outskirts of Aldridge County and wandering aimlessly.

The faint light disappearing below the horizon served as a compass. The mountain should have loomed straight ahead. Yet it didn't, or perhaps it hid behind the veil of flakes tumbling from the sky.

Close to six feet of new snow covered the ground. Were it not for the snowshoes, they never would have made it this far.

Her breath rasped, and her teeth rattled together.

"We'll find something soon, Chelsey. I swear."

"It's fine. I can keep going. You don't have to save my life."

"I'm not trying to play the hero. We both need shelter and a way to warm ourselves up. The cold will only get worse now that night is falling."

"Shouldn't the storm have stopped by now? How long can this go on?"

He didn't have an answer. Logic told him the storm should have ended last night. That the clouds continued to drop an inch of snow per hour boggled his mind. This was hell on earth.

As they descended into a shallow valley bowl, he spotted a thicket poking out of the white like hair standing on the back of a great beast.

"It's not much, but it will have to do," he said. "Can you make it? It's only another several hundred yards."

"I can make it; lead the way. I won't slow you down."

He was tempted to hook elbows with Chelsey and help her across the snow. But doing so would earn him a punch in the arm. She was stubborn and wanted to prove she could handle the cold and take care of herself. He couldn't convince her that this had nothing to do with him acting as her protector. He was freezing too. If he didn't escape the cold, he would die just as easily as she would.

Noises moved through the copse. It could have been the wind rattling the branches, an animal, or anything. He ensured his service weapon was still on his hip.

"That's what we need," he said, pointing into the center of the copse. "A hollowed-out tree. If we work fast, we can construct a shelter."

"Is it large enough for both of us?"

"It will have to be."

Amid the trees, he directed her to gather branches. He didn't think they could build a fire here. For one, it wasn't safe around so many trees, and second, the wind curling around the boughs would douse any fire.

The trees weren't thick enough to form a wall and stop the gusting wind. For that, they would need a proper shelter. Chelsey returned minutes later with her arms full of branches. He admired her work ethic. Despite being nearly frozen, she never complained as she set down the branches.

"What do we do next?"

He set his own collection of branches on the pile.

"We'll have to use the rope from the snowshoes. There's no other way."

"Does that mean we have to give up the snowshoes?"

"For now. Tomorrow morning, if we're both able to travel, we'll tie the rope around the snowshoes again."

"I promise I'll be able to travel tomorrow morning, Thomas."

"This isn't just about you. This is about me too. We're pushing our bodies too hard. If we don't stop, we'll invite death to our door."

He took the rope and securely tied the branches together, forming an arch.

"We need larger branches."

"What are we building next?"

"A wall. We need pieces twice as thick as what we found before."

She nodded in understanding and bounded into the thicket. He didn't like separating from her. Who knew if an animal stalked the woods? But they needed to build the shelter while daylight remained.

He found a bough that had fallen off a mature oak tree. She returned with two branches almost as thick as her thighs. He wondered how she'd summoned the strength to carry them. Using the remaining rope, they tied the branches together and formed a wall and roof over their heads.

At first, as they snuggled inside the shelter, the temperature seemed just as frigid as it was outside. Yet as the minutes passed, their body heat combined and the interior warmed. Her teeth continued to chatter. He rubbed her arms to force heat into her body. The temperature was dropping now that night had descended.

"Tell me about that tropical vacation again," she said. "Will there be sandy beaches, palm trees, and sunny skies?"

"I promise. You'll need to pack sunscreen because it will be in the 90s. By the time you get there, you'll wish it was winter again."

"Not likely, Thomas. Have you ever known me to complain about summer temperatures?"

He chuckled.

"Never. You got me there."

She snuggled against him, and he wrapped his arms protectively around her shoulders. Staying close increased the heat generated by their bodies. He couldn't say it was warm inside the shelter, yet it wasn't uncomfortably cold anymore. Given what little time they'd had, he was amazed by what they constructed.

Somewhere in the thicket, a branch snapped. Probably the wind. Yet as her eyes drifted shut, he wondered if somebody was out there.

Maybe the person who'd left the footprints in the snow.

44

The snow squalls struck in the dead of night. LeVar couldn't see a hand in front of his face as he stepped out of the Chrysler Limited and circled the vehicle to help Scout. If not for the whirling lights of the sheriff's cruiser, he wouldn't have known Aguilar and Lambert had arrived first. He was relieved they had gotten here. Had they arrived a minute later, the squall would have made it impossible to find the Chadas' house.

Aguilar blared her siren once. LeVar couldn't tell if it was for his benefit as a beacon, or if she was letting the couple know help had arrived. Either way, it had the same effect for LeVar and the stranded couple. A dim light shone at the window. It couldn't be electric. From the flicker, LeVar realized it was a candle. That raised his hopes that the couple was still alive. He didn't even see Aguilar until she grasped his arm and yelled over the shrieking wind.

"There's a power line down in the middle of the yard. That's why they lost power."

"Is it live?" LeVar asked.

"I don't know, and I don't want to find out the hard way. LeVar, Scout, I can't ask you to help. It's too dangerous."

"You can forget that. These people need help, and I intend to rescue them. Scout, wait in the car."

The girl shook her head. "It's safer if I'm with you. Imagine a plow coming down the street and not being able to see the car."

Aguilar released a frustrated breath, but there was no room for an argument. Desperate times called for desperate measures. The two deputies needed as much help as they could get.

Lambert carried a shovel, and LeVar grabbed his own from the backseat of the Chrysler. On Aguilar's advice, he'd taken it with him after clearing off his own car.

"Where's this power line?" he called over the wind.

"Dead ahead," Lambert said. "Follow me. We'll circumvent the hazard."

How Lambert and Aguilar knew where the wire hung was anybody's guess. LeVar couldn't see it. Nor could Scout, who gripped the back of his jacket as he led her forward. Their legs pushed through waist-high snow. Already, his brow had broken out in sweat from the effort, and that only made him colder. The whipping wind had teeth.

He heard the aluminum shovel chewing through the ice. As Lambert scraped through the massive drifts to reach the house, LeVar was close enough to spot two shadows at the window. The elderly couple waved their hands and pointed at the door. But LeVar knew the couple was blocked in. The wind had created a snowdrift so high that it reached the top of the door. There was no way Mr. or Mrs. Chada could push their way to freedom until the deputies and private investigators cleared a path. The couple would remain stuck inside their house.

The harder Lambert worked, the more LeVar pushed himself. It would have taken hours for one person to carve a path through the snow, but Lambert and LeVar were driven by a higher purpose. United, they tunneled through the drifts until he could see the porch steps. They were close to reaching the door now. And once they got there, they could take the couple to safety.

A sound like a whistling boomerang came from overhead. Then a snap and pop. LeVar looked up just in time to see the sparks raining alongside the snowflakes.

"Get away from the house!" Aguilar yelled.

LeVar tossed the shovel aside, grabbed Scout, and pulled her away just as the wire snapped and came down where they had been shoveling. Now there were two wires in the yard, and this one was definitely live. It stood between them and warned them backward like a strand of Medusa's hair. The wire hissed fire, which struck the snow and sizzled. How would they reach the door?

"Any ideas?" Lambert called to Aguilar.

"Not really. We have to get to them. I suppose we can go around and carve another path."

"I'm sorry, but my arms, back, and legs can't handle this a second time. Either we reach that doorway, or we smash the window and pull them out."

LeVar saw the couple was staring at the sparking wire now. They understood the implications. With the wire blocking the deputies' path, there was no longer an escape route. And the snow was just as deep on the other side of the house, where the back door stood.

LeVar called to them. "Stand back. I want to try something."

Aguilar warned him, "Don't get too close to the wire."

"I won't. I don't have a death wish."

He pulled the shovel back in his hands like a baseball bat and let it fly. It struck the wire with a hiss of sparks and knocked it further into the yard. There was no rescuing the shovel now that the power line was draped over the end, but at least they had made room to reach the door.

"Nice shooting, Tex," Lambert said.

"I'd say it was skill, but I think luck was on my side that time. The only problem is we all need to find another shovel."

Lambert laughed. "No worries. There isn't much left to do. I'll handle the rest."

Aguilar, Scout, and LeVar got on their knees and pushed the snow away with their gloved hands, while Lambert handled the grunt work with his shovel. After what seemed like forever, they reached the door.

"Aguilar," Lambert called. "Aim your flashlight into the yard so we can see where we're going."

The lead deputy nodded. Before Lambert could knock, Mr. Chada opened the door, having seen them remove the snowdrift from the entryway.

"My wife," the elderly man said. "Her speech is slurred. I think she might have hypothermia."

Behind the elderly man, the wife had dressed for the cold in a winter coat, hat and gloves. A scarf was wrapped around her neck. LeVar assumed she'd worn it all along to combat the frigid air inside the house.

"Your power line snapped in the yard," LeVar said.

Mr. Chada nodded. "We saw it."

"We'll take you around it safely," Aguilar said. "Follow our lead and hang on to each other."

The couple shuffled through the doorway behind the two deputies, hanging on to Lambert's jacket for dear life. Scout moved behind them, and LeVar took the rear, ensuring everyone was safe. They marched down the steps and struggled through the snow to the pathway, which was already covered as the wind blew drifts across the sidewalk.

The squall continued to rage, dropping snow at rates of three inches per hour. If the visibility had improved during their rescue, LeVar couldn't tell. He opened the door to the cruiser, and the Chada couple slid into the backseat. The engine was still running, and the heat was on. A relieved smile settled on the wife's face. LeVar closed the door and circled back to the Chrysler.

Lambert and Aguilar climbed into the cruiser. There would be many more who needed rescue tonight. LeVar only hoped they could reach all of them in time.

45

Thomas blinked in confusion when the pale light touched the backs of his eyelids. Was it really morning?

He shivered and realized Chelsey wasn't next to him. They must have parted in the middle of the night. He rolled over and saw that she was gone. He was alone inside their makeshift shelter. The outer wall had been nudged aside then put back in place. Scraping lines through the snow marked where she'd crawled outside.

"Chelsey!"

She didn't answer.

He rubbed the grit from the corners of his eyes, scrambled to his feet, and pushed the wall away, just in time to see her marching toward him with an arm full of what appeared to be tree bark.

"You scared the hell out of me. I woke and couldn't find you."

"I was only gone a minute. You sleep restlessly, Thomas. I thought I could leave without waking you, but fat chance."

"What's that in your arms? Do you want to stay another day and shore up the shelter?"

Snowflakes circled around her head, but they were lighter than before. Flurries. Had the storm finally stopped?

"I don't intend to stay a minute longer than we have to. As soon as we tear apart the shelter and put on our snowshoes, I want to get as far away from this place as possible."

"So what's with all the bark?"

"Breakfast."

"Breakfast?" he asked, his eyebrows shooting up.

"Thomas, you don't always have to be the one who saves me. I was in the Girl Scouts. I know a little about surviving in the wild."

"By consuming bark?"

"It's not pizza, but you can eat it."

"You can't be serious."

"The inner bark of pine trees is known as the cambium layer. It's full of sugar and calories."

"You can eat the pine tree bark?"

"Oh yes, except for yew trees. You can always tell a yew tree because it has red berries. Those are poisonous."

"So how am I supposed to eat this cambium layer? Do I just chew it up and swallow it?"

"It won't be in its most digestible form, not unless we can cook it. And I don't think you want to stick around and build a fire."

"No, I suppose not," he said.

"What we do is we scrape out the inner bark, chew it, and hope it agrees with our stomachs. It's the best we can do for now."

"Well, all I can say is *bon appétit*."

She handed him a piece of scraped-out bark. He stuck it in his mouth and twisted his lips. So much for the sugary taste. He might have been chewing on old tires. Its dry, fibrous form gnashed around in his mouth.

Thomas met her eyes before swallowing, and she nodded. He gulped it down, coughed, and for a second he thought he was about to vomit. But eating something poisonous wouldn't affect him that quickly. Besides, he trusted her. If she said the bark was safe to eat, he believed her.

"This is no substitute for a night out at a fine restaurant," he said, "but it will do."

She popped a palm full of bark past her lips, chewed, and gave him a mocking smile.

"Tasty. We need calories if we intend to make it to the cabin."

"And we will. This morning, if I have anything to say about it." He glanced around and raised his palms. "Am I correct in assuming the storm moved on?"

"The wind is still blowing, but not nearly as hard as it was before."

"Are you ready to travel?"

"As soon as you make those snowshoes again."

He pulled apart the fort, took the ropes, and tied them around the snowshoes. Once the shoes were fixed to their feet, they started off. Upon exiting the thicket, he was pleasantly surprised to see the faint glow of the sun hiding behind the clouds, which were gray instead of black.

"Wouldn't it be something if the sun came out today?"

"It would be a welcome change," she said. "The temperature rose."

"It's still freezing. It can't be warmer than the single digits."

"I'll take single digits at this point."

With each breath, they puffed out condensation clouds. The pale sunlight elevated his mood. He needed this. They both needed this. They had gone through hell over the past two days. Again, he wondered about his truck and if it lay at the bottom of the gorge, or if someone had found it abandoned on the road.

To think that Chelsey had survived an avalanche. If that

wasn't enough, she'd gone through two bouts of hypothermia in the last twenty-four hours and was still strong enough to trudge through the snow. She amazed him.

"Do you notice that?" he asked.

"What?"

"The terrain is rising."

"Is it the mountain?"

There was hope in her eyes for the first time since they'd gotten stuck in the storm.

"It might be. It's too hazy to tell for sure. But the north side of the mountain starts off gradually before it climbs toward the peak. That might be where we are. It would make sense considering how close we are to the gorge."

"Please tell me the cabin is somewhere ahead, Thomas. That's all I need."

"It might be, and if it's not, I deserve another punch in the arm."

He quickened his pace, emboldened by the thought that the cabin would appear on the horizon within the next hour. It had to. Even with the weather improving, they wouldn't survive for long. He couldn't ask her to build another shelter and sleep in the wild.

"Not too fast, Thomas."

"Sorry. I forgot that you couldn't keep up."

"I can keep up. I just don't want you to do something stupid and—"

Before the words were out of her mouth, the ground gave way. His leg plunged into a trench that the snow had made invisible. He cried out in agony as his knee twisted.

"Thomas, what happened?"

"My leg. I fell into a trench. Careful. You can't see it under your feet."

"Can you move?"

"I think so. Just give me a second to catch my breath."

He pushed himself up by his arms. His knee gave way, and he collapsed into the snow.

"You can't walk."

"I can. I'm in pain, but I don't think I tore a ligament or broke anything. I just need a little time to recover."

"What are we going to do? We can't stay here. The longer we sit in the snow, the colder we'll get."

"I know."

His head turned toward a tree poking out of the white.

"Grab me another branch. I don't need a shelter this time. I just need something that will serve as a walking stick or crutch."

"All right, don't move a muscle."

"Very funny. I'm not going anywhere."

As she hustled up the gentle hillside, he worried the ground would collapse under her feet as well. He needed to be more careful. She came back to him with a thick branch. Before she handed it over, she broke off the smaller limbs so it would be easier to hold.

"Thank you. This will do," he said. The walking stick was just a shade taller than Thomas. The perfect height. "You did well."

"As I told you, I was in Girl Scouts. You know, Thomas, it's okay if I save you for a change."

He felt his heart tighten.

"Chelsey, you saved me the day you returned to my life."

That left her speechless. Her mouth hung open for a moment, and then her eyes glistened with tears. Before he could raise an arm to protect himself, she punched him in the shoulder.

"What was that for?"

"Making me cry. Thomas, why do you always have to say the most beautiful things?"

"Because it's true."

"Are you ready to travel?"

"As long as you're by my side, I can survive anything."

He flinched, expecting another jab to the shoulder, but she shook her head and wiped away a tear. For the next hour, they struggled up the incline. The terrain steepened, and his hope burgeoned. This was Laurel Mountain. He was sure of it.

Trees thickened to either side, forming a natural tunnel through which they walked. With all the snow, it was impossible to recognize anything.

But as the flurries lessened, he spotted a bulk sticking out of the ground. Was that blue sky behind the structure? Yes. They'd reached the top of Laurel Mountain.

"Thomas, it's a cabin."

He was so happy he couldn't stop laughing.

"Not just any cabin, Chelsey. That's our cabin."

"Are you sure?"

"I'm positive. It's hard to tell with the snow covering everything, but that's our woodpile out back."

She hooted with joy.

"Thomas, we made it to the cabin."

"We did. We're safe."

As they hurried forward, no longer concerned for their safety, a voice called out in the distance.

"Ho there!"

Chelsey turned toward the sound. Thomas squinted into the brightening sunlight. Someone was marching up the hillside and waving one arm over his head. He was limping.

The stranger was a large man, and it appeared he was wearing an Aldridge County Sheriff's Department uniform.

Thomas nudged Chelsey with an elbow.

"I think our luck is finally changing."

46

The deputy struggled up the hillside. He was somehow able to traverse the snow. To Chelsey, he looked like a train off the tracks. Out of control. Thundering forward as he pushed the powder aside. As he moved toward them, it was clear the man was hurt by the way one leg dragged behind the other. There was something in his right hand. It might have been a walking stick like Thomas used.

"Hello there. Awfully cold, isn't it?"

Thomas lifted a hand.

"You must be one of Donner's deputies. How is my old friend?"

A confused look came over the deputy, and that made Chelsey prickle with apprehension. Who was this man? Yes, he dressed as a deputy. Surely that meant he was an officer of the law. So why didn't she trust him? And what was he hiding behind his back?

"Ah, Sheriff Donner. Yes, he's doing well, thank you very much. And who should I tell him said hello?"

"Believe it or not, Sheriff Thomas Shepherd. I'm from Nightshade County."

A strange look came over the deputy's face. It was there for only a flash before it disappeared. But Chelsey caught derision, anger, hatred. Maybe even bloodlust. What was that about?

"Is this your cabin?" the deputy asked.

"It's ours. We only reached it moments ago. We were trapped in the snowstorm."

Chelsey asked, "Are you injured?"

The man nodded.

"Hurt my ankle something fierce by falling in the snow. It's dangerous out here. Maybe it's warm inside your cabin. You could invite me in, and I can radio Sheriff Donner. He'll help us."

The deputy was closer. Now he was within steps of Thomas and Chelsey, and for the first time, she noticed blood on his uniform. Hadn't the man said he'd injured his ankle? There weren't just a few drops of blood. It sprayed across the front. And if she wasn't mistaken, a few drops crusted on his face. He looked like something out of a horror movie. The dead come to life.

Thomas didn't seem to notice. He was more concerned with helping the injured deputy, getting the man inside, and taking care of him. Chelsey took a step backward. She stood behind Thomas now, but she had no intention of forcing her future husband to defend her. She didn't trust this deputy. And if Thomas didn't see the truth, she would make him see it.

"What's that you're carrying?" Chelsey asked.

"Just something to help me walk. I wouldn't need it except for my leg."

"Why don't you radio Sheriff Donner right now? No sense waiting until we take you into the cabin."

"Now, now. That's no way to treat a fellow lawman. Let me warm up, then I'll radio the sheriff."

"Toss me your radio. I'll contact the sheriff for you. Then we'll get you inside."

Thomas gave Chelsey a curious look. Under his breath, he whispered, "What are you doing? He's a deputy, and he's injured."

"I don't trust him."

Thomas raised his voice. "What my fiancée meant to say is, the sooner we get Sheriff Donner up here, the sooner we can get that leg of yours looked after. No worries. We'll make a fire. That will keep you warm."

"The radio," Chelsey growled at the stranger.

Before anyone could react, the deputy revealed an ax crusted in blood. Just as he lifted the weapon, Chelsey spotted the gun on Thomas's hip.

She snatched it without thinking and fired two shots. The first blew through the deputy's shoulder, causing him to stumble back. The second missed his head by inches. With a guttural roar, the maniac righted himself and rushed at them with the bloodstained ax over his head. She shot again and missed.

"Inside!" Thomas yelled.

They retreated into the cabin moments before the ax slammed against the door. Wood splintered. It rained on the cabin floor.

"Give me the gun, Chelsey," Thomas said.

She had no problem shooting the man between his eyes if he broke in. But logic intervened. Thomas was the sheriff of Nightshade County. It was his duty to protect them.

Again, the ax slammed through the door. They could see the pretend deputy's face leering at them through a hole. He wouldn't stop until he found a way inside. The murderous man meant to kill them both.

With a thunderous blow, the door imploded. The insane beast stalked into the cabin, ax in hand. As he screamed with rage and raised the blade over his head, Thomas aimed and fired.

The bullets struck the man in the chest and drove him out the door, where he tumbled back and lay in the snow.

Bleeding into the endless white.

47

Thomas stood over the man in the deputy's uniform until he was certain he was dead. The psycho's eyes stared lifelessly at the clearing sky. The blue had spread from the horizon and rested over the cabin. Thomas might have been crazy, but he swore he heard the dripping of melting snow.

Chelsey wandered into the cold and hooked her arm with his.

"Who is he?"

"I don't know, but he's certainly not one of Donner's men. I've heard of people going crazy in extreme cold, but I don't believe this man ever worked for the law."

"Maybe this is the guy who left those footprints you were following."

Thomas had no way to confirm if her theory was true. But something deep inside told him the killer had left those prints. He'd been following death itself. The next question was, who was this man dressed as a deputy, and what was he doing in the middle of nowhere?

"There's nothing more to be done until Donner arrives. And I have no way of contacting him. Let's go inside and get warm."

He didn't have to ask her twice. In the cabin, Thomas located the old newspaper the ranger had left them. There was just a little left, but it was enough to start the fire. A few pieces of dried wood remained. That would keep them warm through the afternoon, but they would need more fuel to survive the rest of their stay.

He worried again what had become of his truck. Not over the monetary loss, but because without that truck they had no way off the mountain. If the weather warmed, they could use the snowshoes and hike to the township, but he was in no rush to put that much strain on their bodies.

Chelsey used the remaining kindling to build a teepee shape. She slid the newspaper into the fireplace, then used a match Darren had provided to ignite a flame. In no time, the fire roared to life, and Thomas loaded the larger pieces on top.

"That will do for now. Stay warm beside the fire. I'll go out and dig for more wood."

"Like hell you will. We work together, or we don't work at all."

He had no argument for her logic. Still bundled in their coats, Thomas and Chelsey stepped around the insane man and used the snowshoes to reach the woodpile. The snow was so deep, he assumed they must be standing on top of the fuel. It was enough to make him gasp. He wondered how much snow Wolf Lake had received.

"This is just a guess, but I think the pile is beneath our feet."

"Let's start digging."

Together they kneeled in the snow and shoveled the powder away with their hands. Even with gloves on, it took only seconds for the icy chill to bleed through the fabric and reach Thomas's fingers. A chill ran through his body. Ignoring the numbing pain, he kept working. The wood had to be under them. As he dug deeper, his fingers touched something solid. He'd reached the pile.

"It's here, Chelsey. Dig alongside me."

She helped, and within minutes they excavated three snow-crusted logs. Thomas didn't worry about the wood not burning. Although ice covered the exterior, the interior was well-seasoned and dry.

"All we need to do is set these pieces beside the fire," he said, "and let the heat take care of the rest."

They worked together, carrying wood back and forth to the cabin. As the fuel melted in front of the fireplace, it left puddles that would surely stain the floorboards, but he couldn't worry about that now. At last, when their work was complete, they peeled off their jackets, gloves, and hats and sat in front of the fireplace. The cabin was already more comfortable. Soon they could move about the interior and not feel a chill.

By Thomas's estimation, they had enough firewood to make it through two or three days. He would need to excavate more fuel from the snow if they were forced to stay longer. He hoped that wouldn't be the case. Either someone would rescue them, or they would use the snowshoes and hike down the mountain.

"How about some lunch?" she asked.

"Lunch? After that filling breakfast of tree bark? Surely you jest."

"We packed supplies. Even though our groceries are back in your truck, we have enough to eat."

She dug two energy bars out of her backpack and handed him one. He'd never been a fan of packaged health bars, but they looked like a four-course meal to him now.

"Remember what you said about saving me for a change? I owe you my life, Chelsey. I trusted that man and figured he was one of Donner's deputies. You were the one who knew the truth."

"I don't want to consider where he got that uniform from, Thomas. I'm sure he killed the deputy it belonged to."

Thomas pressed his lips together. He was certain she was right, but he didn't want to admit it aloud. Instead, he rubbed his hands beside the fire until he could feel his fingertips again. He was content to stay beside her. Yet the corpse outside their door was a chilling reminder of how close they'd come to dying.

"We have to do something about that door. Running a fire does us no good if the heat escapes outside."

"We don't have any way to patch the hole. Maybe we should look for another cabin."

He agreed, though he worried neither of them was fit to make it down that mountain. His knee throbbed, and she'd danced with hypothermia too many times since they'd become lost in the storm. At least they had warmth for the moment.

He was about to search outside for a way to patch the hole when a motor sounded in the distance.

48

Aguilar assessed the ragtag group of investigators and deputies she'd organized. The clouds were thinning, and the sun had risen, though the sky still spat flurries upon the village. They were all exhausted, none more so than her, yet she had a job to do, and she intended to keep the villagers and county residents safe from the storm.

Troubling reports trickled into the Nightshade County Sheriff's Department. It seemed there was a collapsed roof on every street corner. Several dozen villagers were homeless because of a caved-in roof or the loss of heat. The power company had no estimation of when the electricity would return, and she couldn't blame them. Lines needed to be restrung, and the utility vehicles would have a hell of a time getting down snow-covered streets.

In the corner, Scout Mourning and LeVar leaned together, shoulder to shoulder, fighting to keep their eyes open. They had worked all afternoon, evening, and through the night, and now neither had much strength remaining. Aguilar's junior deputies were also battling to keep their eyes open as they logged additional power outages into their computers, which were now running on a generator.

The door opened, and Lambert shuffled in bleary-eyed and with a slump to his shoulders. She'd never seen the deputy look so worse for wear. Then again, they were both working on an hour or two of sleep since the storm had begun.

"I just got back from the school. Thanks to the volunteers, we managed to pack over fifty people into the school. With the gymnasium unavailable, we divided them among several classrooms so the families could stay together. We're also using the cafeteria. The Senior High principal wasn't pleased about the arrangement. I don't think he wants all those people in classrooms where they can't be monitored."

"That principal can kiss my ass," Aguilar said. "He's been uncooperative since the beginning. I realize the gymnasium is unavailable, but he could have done more to help."

"Darren and Raven just finished plowing the north side of the village. Now that the snow has stopped, the crews can finally make headway. Let's hope the weather continues to clear. If it does, we should be able to get the utility workers out to repair those lines."

"Thank you for checking, Lambert."

"Have you been able to reach Thomas or Chelsey?"

Aguilar shook her head. "I spoke to Sheriff Donner an hour ago. He has two missing deputies and a detective he can't find. He's afraid they became lost in the storm. With all they're going through, he hasn't had a second to breathe. We really need Thomas leading our office."

Lambert shrugged. "It seems to me you're handling things just fine. Not that I don't love the sheriff, but we've been in good hands since he put you in charge."

Outside the window, a ray of sun split the clouds and painted the glass yellow and orange. Aguilar felt new hope burgeoning through her chest. Now that everyone was back at the station, she would put together a plan of attack and ensure the village got back to normal as soon as possible. Tarps could cover holes in roofs for the time being, and if anyone needed rescue, the school had room. Should the principal not like it, he could pound salt.

With Lambert's aid, Aguilar organized the team members into three groups, each led by herself or a deputy. As the flurries stopped and the sunshine increased, she drove off in a cruiser with Scout, LeVar, and Naomi, who a plow driver had transported to the station, while Lambert and two volunteers from the village drove to a senior living community to check on the occupants.

With Scout's help, Aguilar escorted a man in a wheelchair out of his house and into the cruiser. LeVar climbed the roof and covered the caved-in area with a tarp. She gritted her teeth, worried that the junior deputy would slip on the snow and ice and fall. But LeVar finished his work and tied off the covering. By lunch hour, they had rescued another two dozen people and driven them to the shelter.

But the most difficult work lay ahead.

49

Chelsey bounded to her feet and raced to the window. Standing beside her, Thomas spotted a snowcat bearing the Aldridge County logo. There were people inside, at least two, but he couldn't make out faces because of the glare across the windshield. The machine encountered no difficulty as it rode over the snow and ice.

As the snowcat churned across the wintry landscape, Chelsey rushed back for her jacket and gloves.

"Not so fast," Thomas said. "We don't know who's coming up the mountain."

"That's the Aldridge county logo on the snowcat. They're coming to rescue us."

"And I thought the deputy was on our side. Not that I expect another lunatic, but it pays to be cautious."

The machine grew larger the closer it came to the cabin. Thomas kept his gun at the ready, just in case. He wanted to believe they were finally safe, but after the events of the last two days, he trusted no one.

When the snowcat was just outside their door, Chelsey exited the cabin with Thomas trying to slow her down. Before either could react, two deputies in full uniform opened the doors and leaped down from the cab. They drew their service weapons and pointed them at Thomas and Chelsey.

"Show us your hands!"

"Drop the weapon!"

Thomas was unwilling to drop his gun in the snow. Instead, he lowered the weapon and let it hang at his side. There was alarm and panic in the deputies' eyes, and he worried they would shoot without asking questions first.

"Maybe you'd better do what they say," Chelsey said.

But Thomas wasn't about to give up their only means of defense. How was he to know these deputies were anymore legitimate than the psycho who'd attacked them with an ax? Tension hung in the air. The deputies shouted at Thomas to drop the weapon, but neither side was willing to give an inch. He worried this would end tragically. Should these be real deputies, he would never live with himself if he opened fire. Yet he would defend Chelsey until his last drop of blood. After all they'd gone through, things couldn't end like this.

"Show me some identification," Thomas said. "If you work for Donner and Aldridge County, prove you're real deputies."

"We heard gunfire. If you don't drop the weapon, we'll have no choice but to remove you as a threat."

The two deputies eyed the fallen man in the snow. Blood girded the killer, and the deputies couldn't take their eyes off the Aldridge County Sheriff's Department uniform on the corpse.

"It's not what you think it is," Thomas said. "He's not a real deputy."

"He's wearing one of our uniforms."

Thomas realized what this was about. The deputies had heard gunshots and arrived to find someone dressed as one of their own dead in the snow. How would he turn this around? He noticed a third figure inside the snowcat who hadn't moved.

Then the door opened, and an aging man with a grizzled face jumped down from the cab. All at once, Thomas recognized his fellow sheriff. Taking his free hand, the one that didn't hold the service weapon, he waved to Sheriff Donner. Blinded by the sun, Donner shielded his eyes and said, "Sheriff Thomas Shepherd, is that really you?"

Chelsey wrapped her arm around Thomas and gave him a squeeze. Cooler heads were finally prevailing.

"It's me, Donner. This man attacked us. He's dressed as one of yours, but I'm certain he isn't. His nametag reads Barton."

Donner turned to his team members. "Lower your weapons, dammit. He's one of us. Thomas, I've been looking all over for you. Were you at the cabin the whole time, because we found your truck two miles from here."

"Was it in the gorge? We left my vehicle to help a stranded driver, and the side of the road collapsed in an avalanche."

Showing his deputies there was nothing to fear, Donner walked forward and clasped Thomas on the shoulder. He wore a grin which suggested he harbored good news about the truck, but there was something else, a haunted desperation that lurked behind his eyes.

"Your truck is fine, Thomas. When last we saw it, it was under five feet of snow. But don't worry, we'll dig it out."

"Donner, this is my fiancée Chelsey Byrd."

Donner tipped his hat at Chelsey.

"There's something wrong, Donner, isn't there?"

The Aldridge County Sheriff kneeled for a better look at the dead man lying at Thomas's feet. With a powerful yank, he tore the badge and nametag off the uniform. He stood.

"Congratulations, Sheriff Shepherd. You did what we failed to do and caught Victor Bacchus, the escaped convict who killed three guards and multiple officers."

"Bacchus," Chelsey said. "Should we know that name?"

"He's the leader of a crime syndicate out of Rochester. It seems he went a little crazy in the storm and started killing anyone who crossed his path, including a detective and two of my deputies. Deputy Barton was one of his victims."

"I'm sorry, Sheriff," Thomas said.

"Don't be. Were it not for you, Bacchus would still be out there and killing people. I don't want to guess what the body count is up to, but I fear he killed at least ten during the storm."

Chelsey hissed. "Ten?"

"At least." Donner turned to Thomas. "Now for the million-dollar question. I don't suppose you wish to remain in the cabin and enjoy the rest of your vacation. I'm happy to leave the two of you alone if you think you can survive up here for the next several days, but I'd just as soon bring you back to your truck and get you on your way. Nightshade County took it hard, Wolf Lake especially. You have a mess waiting for you at home, Sheriff."

"I think I can speak for my fiancée when I say we'll be happy to accept your generous offer. If you would be so kind to take us back to my truck and help me remove all that snow, I'll get back to my people and see what I can do."

Donner nodded and ordered his deputies to search Bacchus. They would have to transport the corpse back to the township, a thought that left Thomas troubled. Neither he nor Chelsey wanted to share a ride with the deceased maniac. It took them less than ten minutes to gather their belongings, douse the fire, and exit the cabin. Donner helped Chelsey into the cab, and Thomas limped up behind her.

"What happened to your leg?" Donner asked.

"Just my idiocy. I fell in the snow and twisted my knee. I'll be fine if I stay off it for a few days, but I don't suppose that will be possible given the circumstances in Wolf Lake."

With a boost from Donner, Thomas climbed into the snowcat. The motor whirred as the machine turned around and climbed over the snow. He shared a look with Chelsey, one of gratitude that they'd survived and were going home.

Yet he worried about what he would find when they got there.

50

Even after the plow driver cleared a path to his truck, it still took Thomas, Chelsey, Donner and the two deputies over an hour to remove the snow from the pickup. They shoveled the powder and ice into the gorge so as not to leave it in the road, where it would block the way for other drivers. Thomas was surprised by the clear road. The tractor trailer was gone, and the plows had opened up enough room for single-file traffic to pass through.

When they were done, there was still the minor matter of seeing if the pickup would start. The keys hung in the ignition where Thomas had left them after they'd attempted to save the tractor-trailer driver. With Chelsey in the passenger's seat, Thomas cranked the engine and felt relief when the motor purred to life. Somehow the truck still had power after all that cold and snow.

Donner knocked on the window and tipped his hat to bid them farewell. Thomas squeezed down the tunnel forged by the plows and wondered what he would do if another vehicle came from the opposite direction. There was only room for the pickup, and the white walls of ice closed around the vehicle, nearly scraping the doors. He kept a close eye on the dashboard whenever the traction control engaged. Snow tires were one thing, but they were driving on an ice-skating rink.

"How about some music?"

Chelsey nodded without saying a word. She was too fixated on the road to pull her eyes away. Normally Thomas avoided the news talk channels and the controversy they loved to drum up, but he wanted to know what was going on around the region and how the surrounding counties and municipalities were dealing with the storm. The usual national dialogue had shifted to local reports about the blizzard. Reporters interviewed emergency managers, police officers, mayors, and even the governor of the state. All were working together to return a sense of normality to Upstate New York. After this storm, Thomas suspected it would be a long time before anything felt the same. He'd witnessed harsh winters before, but nothing close to the way this one was starting, and according to the calendar, the solstice was still days away.

So he could concentrate on the road, Thomas turned down the radio until it became little more than white noise in the background. As before, Chelsey gripped the door handle. He couldn't blame her, not after they'd become lost in the storm and the hell they've gone through to reach the cabin.

In his mind, he pictured the insane leer of Victor Bacchus wielding the ax and stalking them. Was it true he'd shot the most notorious crime lord in Western New York? A man who'd killed ten or more people since the storm began? Thomas didn't feel like a hero. He was just lucky. Had it not been for Chelsey, Bacchus would have split his skull in two with that vile ax, and he would be dead in the snow. Thomas and Chelsey needed each other; they accomplished more together than they ever did apart, and that was just one reason he wanted to spend eternity by her side.

The road never improved. Even after driving fifty miles, the conditions only worsened. Though the plow drivers had been hard at work, there was only so much they could do. Every time the wind blew, it drove fresh drifts across the road and created hazardous speed bumps, which Thomas kept an eye out for. Several times, he felt the truck sliding and turned into the spin to avoid wrecking the pickup. All he wanted was to get them home in one piece.

His heart beat a little faster when he spied the road sign for Wolf Lake. Just eight miles away. He glanced over at Chelsey, but she pressed her lips together, gritted her teeth, and watched the snow and ice, expecting the worst. They were so close to home. After being lost in the wilderness in sub-zero temperatures, it seemed like a dream that the village was just ahead. Yet he feared his first view of Wolf Lake would be nothing more than a nightmare.

A few miles later, when the finish line was just over the horizon, a barricade of snow and ice appeared on the road. Thomas pulsed the brakes, and the truck continued sliding. His heart was in his throat before the pickup came to rest. It seemed Mother Nature didn't want them to reach their destination. A massive snowdrift blocked their way. It occurred to him they had nothing in the vehicle to move it with. His only shovel was at home. He kept ice scrapers in the cab, but they were little help.

"If we backtrack," Thomas said, "we'll have to drive another ten miles before we find another route to Wolf Lake. And even then, there is no guarantee the passage will be open."

"We've faced larger obstacles than this over the past two days."

"What do you propose?"

"If we have to dig our way to Wolf Lake, that's what we'll do. I'm not letting this stand in our way."

Seeing no other choice, Thomas and Chelsey climbed down

from the cab and left the truck running. In front of the vehicle, they dug their gloved hands through the drift and shoveled it away, bit by bit. Yet the snow stood taller than Thomas's head. All the determination in the world wouldn't help them move this pile. How had the plows missed the humongous obstruction?

Despite the chilly temperatures, sweat trickled down Chelsey's face as she pushed and pulled at the pile. They were getting nowhere. At this rate, it would take until tomorrow before they cleared a path. Thomas was already short of breath, and Chelsey looked on the verge of collapse. Maybe it made sense to turn around and find a different route to Wolf Lake, no matter how long the drive took.

Just then, a rumble sounded in the distance. Chelsey pointed, and Thomas turned his head toward a tractor grinding up the road. The man inside waved to them. When the tractor stopped behind the pickup, Thomas recognized the driver. Mr. Lenderman, Sheriff Gray's neighbor.

"Looks like you have a wall blocking your way, Sheriff."

"Mr. Lenderman, is there any chance that tractor of yours can move this pile?"

The man grinned. "If you get that truck out of the way, it sure can. There ain't much of a shoulder, but if you can make enough room for me to squeeze past, I'll knock this bad boy on its backside and get you out of here."

"Right away, sir."

The farmer finished and climbed down. Chelsey, smiling for the first time since they'd found the cabin, threw her arms around Mr. Lenderman's shoulders and kissed the farmer on the cheek. His face blushed, and he stammered, searching for a reply. Then he cleared his throat and climbed onto the tractor. Thomas and Chelsey retreated to the truck, and he backed down the road, giving Lenderman enough space to pass.

The tractor thundered forward with determination. It scooped the snow and deposited it along the roadside, accomplishing in minutes what would have taken two humans more than a day. Ten minutes later, the tractor had cleared the road.

He honked the horn twice and waved to Lenderman as they passed. A happy butterfly fluttered in his chest. This was how Wolf Lake and Nightshade County did business. People helped each other, and no one got left in the cold.

Though the road remained icy and treacherous, Thomas encountered no more blockages in their path. All at once, the village appeared on the horizon, as if it had risen from the earth.

But what hell awaited them inside?

51

The village of Wolf Lake came into view as though a curtain had opened on a tragic play. Around Thomas and Chelsey, trees lay on their sides, well-built houses had holes in their roofs, and snow drifts blocked access and escape from entryways. No lights shone, only the flicker of candles through the windows. Thomas's heart clenched. This wasn't just his municipality; it was his home. Throughout his life, he'd seen summer and winter storms ravage parts of the community, but never its entirety. It was as if an angry giant had stomped down on the village and flattened everything, leaving all of it encased in ice.

He didn't need to say anything to Chelsey. Her eyes misted with new tears, and she glanced from one street to the next in frantic desperation. The work required to rebuild the village seemed overwhelming, yet he knew Wolf Lake would rise from this graveyard of snow and ice if it believed in its future. The streets were clean, in much better shape than the roads had been between Aldridge County and Wolf Lake. In the distance, a Silverado motored past, and for a fleeting second, he swore Darren was behind the wheel. That pickup lowered its plow and scraped the macadam clean. Behind it, a truck sprayed salt in all directions.

"This is overwhelming," he said. "I don't know where to start. Should we drive straight to the station and see what we can do, or should we search for a cruiser? Surely the deputies are working in the field and doing everything they can to help."

He was too stunned to think of using his radio. Chelsey shook her head and stared at the destruction through the windshield. Snow piled several feet high in people's yards, blocking off sidewalks, forming impenetrable walls in front of garages and tunnels along the sides of the roads, which gave Thomas a feeling of claustrophobia.

He started down Fourth Street, intending to drive straight to the station, when he saw a cruiser with flashing lights stopped beside the road. He recognized Deputy Aguilar as she led an elderly man bundled in a winter coat and parka out the door and toward her cruiser. Stopping his pickup in front of the house, he was surprised to see LeVar and Scout leading three dogs on leashes to the cruiser as well. No sooner did he shift into park than Chelsey climbed out of the truck and raced to help. While Aguilar situated the man in the back seat of the cruiser, with the dogs packed beside him, Thomas shuffled on the icy concrete to meet his lead deputy. Aguilar didn't notice him until he reached them, and her eyes widened in surprise and worry upon seeing the sheriff.

"Thomas, you're safe."

"Sheriff Donner told me you called, concerned about our safety. I appreciate the concern. I'm only relieved we made it back in one piece."

While the man and his dogs waited inside the heated cruiser, Aguilar ran a hand through her hair and stammered.

"I'm so sorry, Sheriff. We did everything we could to keep up, but I'm afraid I left you with a mess. The power is out everywhere, the emergency shelter at the school wasn't available, and we had to stick families in cafeterias and classrooms. Several residents suffered from hypothermia, and the hospitals are overwhelmed now that the roads are open."

"Stop right there. You honestly believe I'm angry with you? Tell me something, Aguilar. How many did we lose?"

"How many did we lose? I'm not sure I understand."

Thomas met her eyes. "It's a simple question. How many residents of Wolf Lake perished in the storm?"

"Well, none. At least I don't think anyone died in the storm. The communications systems are touch and go, and I'm still working to ensure everyone who lost power has heat. I don't worry about the freezers and refrigerators. People can keep perishables safe by setting them outside. Of course there are always worries about attracting hungry animals, but it's the best I could think of under the circumstances."

"Am I to understand the village received over six feet of snow with little or no warning, all of Wolf Lake lost power, and nobody died? Not even the people who depend on electric heat?"

"As far as I know."

Thomas had always been proud of his lead deputy, but never more so than at this moment. He drew Aguilar into a hug. She appeared uncomfortable at first, then returned the embrace.

"You saved so many lives, Aguilar. Without you, we would have lost dozens to the storm." He gestured at the destruction. "None of this is your doing. What could any of us have done to prevent the damage from the storm? Do you think I expected you to drive from street to street, catching every flake and tossing it skyward? Under this much snow, destruction was inevitable. So too were casualties, yet we had none. The work you accomplished should be considered nothing short of miraculous."

Aguilar shuffled her feet. "I didn't work alone. Deputy

Lambert and I have been up for the last two days, making sure we had a place for the evacuees. We had two deputies out sick with the flu, but the junior staff stepped forward in a big way and proved themselves. And that's not to mention the Wolf Lake Consulting crew."

"She must be talking about me, Shep."

Thomas spun around to a smiling LeVar.

"I should have known I could depend on Chelsey's crew, especially you and Scout."

Scout leaned into the cruiser and checked that the old man was buckled in properly. One dog, a slobbering Great Dane, was licking her face as she tried to work. The teenage girl looked exhausted and ready to drop, and so did LeVar and Aguilar. To Thomas's surprise, Naomi was in the cruiser and helping too.

"All of you have worked long enough," said Thomas. "You are to go home and sleep as soon as you take this man and his pets to the shelter. And give the same order to Lambert. Chelsey and I are here to serve, and I'll check on the sick deputies and see if they're ready to return to work. There's a long road of rebuilding ahead, and I'll need all of you fresh and able to help."

Aguilar appeared ready to argue, but she didn't. The cruiser drove off, and Thomas turned to Chelsey in wonder.

"Did I hear correctly?" Chelsey asked. "Nobody died in the storm?"

Thomas shook his head in wonder. There was so much to do. He saw tarps covering holes in roofs and figured that must be LeVar's work. They would need to get the power running soon. That was the priority. As soon as they did, people could return to their homes, freeing up space at the school.

Despite the apocalyptic setting that was Wolf Lake, Thomas felt nothing but hope. Up and down the street, neighbors worked together, snow blowing driveways, clearing walkways, and pounding on doors to check on each other. Two men and a woman drove in a pickup truck; roofing materials filled the back. These people intended to begin the rebuilding process today. Nobody was waiting for the temperatures to become comfortable, nor did anyone expect compensation. The village was coming together like never before.

Just as he'd believed it would.

52

A week after the storm struck, one would hardly recognize the village of Wolf Lake. It looked different from before, but Thomas could only describe the village in one word: better. He found it difficult to believe the worst winter storm in a century had struck this village seven days ago. The only evidence of its passage was the bone-deep fatigue that made him want to rest through the next year. He wasn't alone. Every deputy, every citizen, and the members of the Wolf Lake Consulting team, not to mention Serena Hopkins, Darren, and Buck Benson, had lent their help and brought the village back from the brink.

Christmas music played through village speakers set on light poles. Christmas decorations adorned storefronts, houses, and even the Nightshade County Sheriff's Department. The twinkling lights made the village appear festive. After the last week, he would never take electricity for granted. The utility companies had worked day and night to restore the electrical grid in Wolf Lake, restringing lines, erecting poles where others had snapped from the strength of the wind and ensuring every street and every corner had working power. Thomas's A-frame hadn't received power until two days ago. Yet he considered himself one of the lucky ones. Many people couldn't turn on the lights or operate their electric heating systems until yesterday morning. Those people had remained stuck at the school.

People from the village filled the square and crowded the streets, which were cordoned off by police roadblocks. On the promenade, the village had erected a stand and a podium. The mayor of Wolf Lake was about to address his people.

With just days remaining until Christmas, the village was celebrating early. Everyone deserved it. There was to be a grand festival with food, music, dancing, games for the children, and a fireworks display. The village was never this busy except during the springtime Magnolia Dance.

Thomas waited beside the steps, nervous because he knew the mayor wanted him to speak. In the crowd, he spotted Darren and Raven beside Serena and Buck. Scout and her friend Liz Yarwood were here with their mothers, and LeVar had found his way to the front, probably to heckle Thomas when he began his speech. The junior deputy lifted his chin at Thomas.

"Shep Dawg, I hear you're about to drop knowledge on the village. That true?"

"I am, but with no help from you, LeVar. If you try to make me laugh while I'm up there, I promise to show up next year at Kane Grove while you're taking exams and make faces into the classroom."

"Now why would I do something like that to my best buddy?" Thomas smirked. LeVar hadn't promised he wouldn't heckle Thomas. And besides, the deputy's best buddy was Scout, not him.

Someone cut off the music to the speakers, and the mayor waddled up to the podium and tapped the microphone to ensure it was working. Feedback screeched, causing several people in the crowd to chuckle. The mayor cleared his throat and adjusted his tie. He spoke for a few minutes, praising the villagers for helping one another and saving Wolf Lake from disaster. But as the talk continued, he thanked Thomas for saving so many people and ensuring no one died. Everyone looked at Thomas, smiling and nodding their heads in appreciation. The attention made him uncomfortable, and not just because of all the staring at him. He wasn't the one who had saved the village. Aguilar, Lambert, the deputies, and the Wolf Lake Consulting team had saved the day. Aguilar seemed not to notice, because she patted Thomas on the shoulder and held pride in her gaze.

Time passed too quickly before the mayor called Thomas to speak. It was as if someone had released a swarm of butterflies in his chest. He approached the podium with trepidation, adjusted the microphone height, and looked out at the villagers packed in the square. Above them, blinking lights formed Santa's sleigh and reindeer, complete with Rudolph at the front with a flashing red light for a nose. Wide-eyed children pointed at the Christmas decorations as parents prompted them to be polite and pay attention to the sheriff.

Thomas set his hands on the podium and leaned forward.

"What happened here was nothing short of a Christmas miracle. I have never been prouder to be a member of the Nightshade County Sheriff's Department."

A cheer rose from the crowd.

"But I'm not the one who deserves thanks for rebuilding Wolf Lake and saving lives. As some of you know, I was on vacation with my fiancée when the storm struck. Before I left, I put the department in Deputy Aguilar's hands. Veronica Aguilar is a gem. By all rights, she should be sheriff of this county or any of her choosing. She possesses all the qualities of a born leader, and if it weren't for her quick thinking, many people would have lost their lives. Together with Deputy Tristan Lambert and a bare-bones staff of deputies who were filling in for their ill workmates, they saved people from homes, transported people to hospitals, and even provided escorts to the shelters. It was their organizational skills that started the spirit of cooperation in this village and across Nightshade County.

"So many volunteered to help others. If I had a month to speak, I couldn't name every one of you, but you know who you are. From the selfless members of Wolf Lake Consulting to the volunteers, to the plow services who worked for free to clear the streets, and the residents who rebuilt their neighbors' houses, patched roofs, and made sure everyone had heat and food, I thank you all. Let everyone remember this day as a celebration of everything that is right about Wolf Lake and this beautiful state. This is my home, and whether or not I'm your sheriff, I will always serve you to the best of my ability. I only ask that you remember the less fortunate this Christmas. There is no greater gift than making a stranger smile. Before I get long-winded, I'll stop. Please enjoy tonight's festivities because you all deserve it. This isn't a celebration of us, it is a celebration of you."

All was silent as Thomas stepped away from the microphone. For a second, he thought he had offended them. Then a roar of approval deafened his ears. Someone tossed confetti into the air, while another tooted on a bugle at the back of the crowd.

Chelsey and LeVar were the first to meet him when he descended the steps. He shared embraces with them, but he saved the biggest hugs for Aguilar and Lambert.

It seemed his family grew in size every day. And so did his heart.

Ready for the next thriller and mystery in the Thomas Shepherd series? Find book five on Amazon today.

GET A FREE BOOK!

I'm a pretty nice guy once you look past the grisly images in my head. Most of all, I love connecting with awesome readers like you.

Join my VIP Reader Group and get a FREE serial killer thriller for your Kindle.

Get My Free Book

www.danpadavona.com/thriller-readers-vip-group/

SUPPORT YOUR FAVORITE AUTHORS

Did you enjoy this book? If so, please let other thriller fans know by leaving a short review. Positive reviews help spread the word about independent authors and their novels. Thank you.

Copyright Information

Published by Dan Padavona

Visit my website at www.danpadavona.com

Copyright © 2023 by Dan Padavona

Artwork copyright © 2023 by Dan Padavona

Cover Design by Caroline Teagle Johnson

All Rights Reserved

Although some of the locations in this book are actual places, the characters and setting are wholly of the author's imagination. Any resemblance between the people in this book and people in the real world is purely coincidental and unintended.

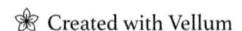

✻ Created with Vellum

ACKNOWLEDGMENTS

No writer journeys alone. Special thanks are in order to my editor, C.B. Moore, for providing invaluable feedback, catching errors, and making my story shine. I also wish to thank my brilliant cover designer, Caroline Teagle Johnson. Your artwork never ceases to amaze me. I owe so much of my success to your hard work. Shout outs to my advance reader Marcia Campbell for catching those final pesky typos and plot holes. Most of all, thank you to my readers for your loyalty and support. You changed my life, and I am forever grateful.

ABOUT THE AUTHOR

Dan Padavona is the author of The Wolf Lake series, The Thomas Shepherd series, The Logan and Scarlett series, The Darkwater Cove series, The Scarlett Bell thriller series, *Her Shallow Grave*, and The Dark Vanishings series. He lives in upstate New York with his beautiful wife, Terri, and their children, Joe, and Julia. Dan is a meteorologist with NOAA's National Weather Service. Besides writing, he enjoys visiting amusement parks, beach vacations, Renaissance fairs, gardening, playing with the family dogs, and eating too much ice cream.

Visit Dan at: www.danpadavona.com

Printed in Great Britain
by Amazon

Booklover's Death

Sandrine Perrot - Brittany Mystery Series
Book 4

Christophe Villain

Copyright © 2023 by Christophe Villain

All rights reserved.

No part of this book may be reproduced in any form or by any electronic or mechanical means, including information storage and retrieval systems, without written permission from the author, except for the use of brief quotations in a book review.

Christophe Villain
Pettenkoferstr. 2
45470 Muelheim
Germany
author@christophe-villain.com

Coverdesign by Giusy Amé
Translation by Rose Bodenheimer
Copy editing and proofreading by Elizabeth Ward

La Cité du Livre

Sandrine and her friend Rosalie Simonas ambled through Bécherel, a picturesque little town in the heart of Brittany, just 45 minutes away from Cancale. The whole region had been suffering under a heatwave for more than a week, and the grey-brown stone houses surrounding the village square threw long shadows over the plaster. A cat lay under a chair and looked at them with practiced boredom. Flowers were drooping their heads, and brown spots sprinkled the leaves. It was about time for a liberating thunderstorm. Sandrine looked towards the horizon, but the brilliant blue sky was without even a wisp of cloud.

"How nice that you could take some days off and come here with me," Rosalie said, and linked her arm with Sandrine's. She grinned at Sandrine as if they were on a secret mission. She had refused to give her a hint as to what exactly it was that brought them into this small town. It did not seem to have anything setting it apart from the other towns in Brittany. *Apart from all the bookshops.* Sandrine looked around. Even in the village square, she could count half a dozen.

"A little trip is just what I need. Especially with some nice company and without another murder to solve. The investigation in Le Mont-Saint-Michel was exhausting. I'm more than happy to leave the paperwork to my colleagues in Avranches."

The last case had led her into Normandy, at least a little bit, to the tidal island with its famous gothic cathedral jutting out of the bay. If the weather was good, she could see it from her garden in Cancale. She would have preferred to visit the place as a tourist only.

"Then this holiday is just what you need." Rosalie sounded cheerful, but it was not enough to hide her worry. Commissaire Matisse had suggested a time-out to Sandrine until the prosecutor, Antoine de Chezac, dropped the accusations towards her. She had agreed, though hesitantly. It was hard for her to stand at the sideline and watch everyone else solve cases. The trip to Bécherel was a welcome distraction. It was a lot more pleasant to walk here than to sit at home and wonder what was going on in the commissariat.

"I have to go to the bookshop Farz Gwad. Just over there." Rosalie pointed at the opposite side of the square. "Margritte Violinet, the owner, is already waiting for me." She led Sandrine to a multi-storey stone house with dark red painted window frames. An awning of the same colour shadowed a narrow wooden deck built against the building. Only one of the four tables was occupied. Not surprising on a Wednesday afternoon. Most of the tourists had been lured to the sea and were enjoying the nice weather.

"She also runs a café, and her cake is heavenly," Rosalie gushed. "Everything is homemade, using traditional recipes that barely anyone knows nowadays."

"That's why there are so many cooking and baking books on display."

"Exactly. There are two shops inside. The ground floor houses the café and Margritte's bookshop, and on the two floors above is a well-stocked antique shop."

"Did you write another cookbook, or is there some other reason for our trip?"

"I wanted to spend some time with my friend and landlord, have a chat and enjoy some good cake. Isn't that enough? You work so much that we barely see each other anymore."

"It must be a very good cake to justify 45 minutes in the car. At least you have a convertible."

"It will be worth it, trust me. And yes, just by coincidence I have written another cookbook. A Breton one, this time. In between all the thrillers, I have to do something pleasant from time to time that doesn't constantly remind me what dark corners lurk in the minds of ordinary people."

Sandrine smiled. Rosalie loved to come up with thrillers stuffed with unforeseen twists and turns and a big splash of eroticism. However, cooking and baking were also part of her passions. *And I'm the beneficiary.* She herself was a rather mediocre-to-poor cook, and so she enjoyed the invitations whenever Rosalie tried a new recipe and needed someone to taste it. Maybe she just wanted to keep Sandrine alive and offer her a treat once in a while as she knew how empty Sandrine's kitchen normally was.

"Let's stay outside. It's nice in the shadow under the awning," Sandrine suggested.

She chose a table on the terrace which offered a view through the window and inside the bookshop.

"Now, out with it. Something strange must be going on in the commissariat if a workaholic like you suddenly gets a week off," Rosalie stated.

"I'm that easy to read?"

"Like an open book. One just needs to know how to read the language. That's what friends are for."

"I'm not entirely sure what's going on, but it's nothing good. Matisse suggested that I take a week off."

"The commissaire? Why? Is it that prosecutor again? He already tried to get you kicked out of the force back in Paris."

"De Chezac. He senses the chance to be more successful this time."

A boy, most likely still a school student, in an apron the same shade of red as the window frames, took their order and hurried back inside.

"They did a raid in the Équinoxe," Sandrine said.

"That's Léon's club, isn't it? A pleasant, handsome guy." Rosalie had been doing her best to find a man for a stable relationship for Sandrine, and Léon was the best choice for her. Sandrine had forgotten to tell her that they had spent the night together last week in Le Mont-Saint-Michel. She was still unsure where all of this would lead, and it made her current position with the commissariat difficult.

"Yes," she answered tartly.

"And?" Rosalie scooted closer, curious to hear the news.

"One of the brigadiers found drugs in his office. A whole bunch of pills."

"He never seemed like a drug dealer to me."

"To me neither. He denies owning them or to have known of their existence."

"You believe him?" Rosalie watched her intently.

The waiter was a welcome distraction, as he gave Sandrine time to think while he placed two cups of Café Crème on the table. She ripped open one of the sugar packages and stirred the small crystals into her coffee.

"I think he's telling the truth. My gut tells me that he wouldn't lie to me."

"How did the drugs get in his office? Someone must have planted them there."

"He has no idea. On that evening he wasn't in Cancale but with me and he vouches for Simone who was taking care of the club in his absence. He's known her since he opened up the Équinoxe and trusts her."

"What's your theory? I'm sure you have been thinking despite your holiday."

"I don't know if he has any personal enemies that would go so far. I don't know him well enough for that. But I can come up with one or two people who wouldn't hesitate to use him just to get to me."

"To make you the girlfriend of a drug dealer would be a real blow to your career."

"My career isn't the most important issue in this." She was surprised how relaxed she felt while saying this, and that she actually meant it. It had taken a few years in the police force for this revelation to sink in. Every further promotion would bring her closer to a desk job. She would hate not being able to investigate in the field. Besides, protecting Léon from a fabricated accusation was her top priority at the moment.

"Come on now. You're in your mid-thirties and have a brilliant clearance rate. You could make it to Madame le Commissaire, maybe even in Saint-Malo. We need more women in leading positions."

"Not for me. I came to the police with the idealistic view that it was all about catching criminals. Nothing has changed about that. I never wanted to be stuck behind a desk. That's something for someone like Commissaire Matisse. I would just crumble there. The constant paperwork and all the politics do nothing for me."

"Where's the problem, Capitaine Perrot?" she asked and grinned as if she understood Sandrine perfectly.

"Apart from that Léon could lose the license for the club and go to jail?"

"Yes, apart from that. I like him a lot, but at the moment I'm more interested in you." Rosalie took Sandrine's hand and gave it a squeeze.

It was good to have a true friend to open up to and get some advice. "As I said, this time-out was not my wish. Commissaire Matisse made me take it to get some distance between me and the commissariat. Most likely something else in which de Chezac has his fingers in. They want to keep me away from Léon and the evidence. Adel told me that the coroner was dropping hints. He said that I had been in cahoots with Léon and had warned him about raids."

"That's ridiculous," Rosalie scoffed.

"Of course it is. Since I started work in Saint-Malo there hasn't been a single raid, neither at the Équinoxe nor any other club. Léon told me a few times that his club was clean so why should I have warned him about anything? And I always keep private life and work separated." That was not 100% accurate. From time to time, she got some tips from Léon as he knew what was going on in Saint-Malo.

"In any case, I have long been *persona non grata* with certain influential people. Should they find out what de Chezac wants to stick to me I'll have the media on my heels. That would be a godsend for some of the reporters." Deborah Binet popped into her head. If she was to learn of the story, she would bite her teeth into it like a terrier biting into a trouser leg. A sigh threatened to spill from her lips, but she swallowed it down as to not burden her friend.

"Then we will have a nice week and stay out of the way of any of these vultures from the press."

Rosalie would stand by her side. Even though Sandrine had never questioned her loyalty, she felt a weight drop from her shoulders. Suddenly the future did look a bit brighter.

"Ah, Rosalie, how nice of you to take the time to come over."

A woman, most likely in her mid-fifties, with short wavy

hair and an open smile made her way over to their table. She balanced two plates in her hands. "I saw you through the window. You're just in time to try the cake."

She placed the plates in front of them and sat down.

"Margritte," she introduced herself.

"Sandrine." She shook the offered hand.

"Margritte is a very good friend. Bookseller, author, excellent baker and the soul of this café, all in one person." Rosalie leaned over the table and gave the woman a big hug.

"Rosalie exaggerates." Margritte waved the compliments away. "My last publication lies years in the past, and I'm only baking for the guests of the café. Leanne, my daughter, is running it now. There's not much left to do here. Basically, I'm enjoying retirement." She winked at Rosalie. "At least I can organise a reading or book signing for good friends."

"Don't believe her, she's understating terribly," Rosalie said. "She's part of the active posts in Bécherel, the Cité du Livre."

"The city of the book?" Sandrine looked around. "I already noticed all the bookshops."

"Oh, yes. In 1989, the Savenn Douar Association created the Book City in our town. We were the first in France and after Hay-on-Wye in Wales and Redu in Belgium the third in all of Europe. By now there are seven more in France. Someone should try saying again that the book is dead, and that people only sit in front of the television." Pure joy sparkled in her eyes, and the words spilled from her lips with the pride at what had been created here.

"There are more than a dozen bookshops here at the moment," Rosalie explained. "And that's with less than 700 inhabitants."

"Bookshops, but also exquisite antique shops, like the Rabelais on the upper floor. Bookbinders, illustrators and calligraphers have made their home here. Bibliophiles can find everything in Bécherel to make their hearts beat faster. And delicious cake in my café on top."

"It looks fabulous." Rosalie pierced her fork into the delicate Breton apple cake.

"Nothing special, but I hope you like it."

"I'm sure of it."

Loud voices sounded from the top floor of the house down to them. Sandrine lifted her eyes, but the awning did not let her see anything.

"You can't do this to me!" a man shouted.

"And what should stop me?"

A window slammed shut and locked out any listeners.

"Meeting of the local book club," Margritte explained and looked at Sandrine as if to excuse the upset man.

"They meet in Rabelais. From time to time, it gets a bit emotional. Most likely they're comparing glue binding and thread binding again." She threw a look into the bookshop. The fight seemed to make her nervous.

"Or someone dared to say the word 'E-book'." Rosalie tried to lighten the mood.

"No, definitely not. If that had happened, we would have heard shots and be caring for the injured now." Margritte took up Rosalie's joke.

The steps of the ancient-looking staircase creaked, and the hard heels of a man's leather shoes banged on the wood. With quick steps he crossed the bookshop. The waiter retreated with his full tray behind the counter and shook his head at the man.

"Monsieur Savier, is everything alright?" Margritte asked with worry in her voice.

Without answering the question or even acknowledging her, a heavily built man with an imposing moustache stormed past them. Shortly thereafter, he disappeared down a side street.

"Frédéric Savier is a notary public and chairman of the book club. He's a calm and friendly booklover. I have never seen him this upset and rude," Margritte explained. The confusion was written plainly on her face.

"Capitaine Perrot. Bonjour, what a pleasant surprise." Someone addressed Sandrine from behind her back. Sandrine turned in surprise. A man dressed in the uniform of the gendarmerie stood in front of her.

"Capitaine... Ah... Commandant Jenaud, how nice to see you again and congratulations on your promotion. You earned it."

"Thank you very much. The quick success in our case certainly contributed to it. But you also left your mark in the short time you have been with us."

"Is that so?" Sandrine wondered what he was getting at. Had the rumours already spread over the borders of Saint-Malo?

"I met le juge d'instruction Bonnard by coincidence the other day. You solved the case in Le Mont-Saint-Michel with her? That was excellent work. Congratulations."

"Thank you. It was a treat to work together with Madame Bonnard and the Gendarmerie Nationale."

"I like to hear that, as I don't hear it a lot." Jenaud winked at her. Normally the tensions were high between Police Nationale and Gendarmerie Nationale.

"And what brings you to this peaceful little village?" she asked. The policeman was in uniform, so it was more than just a personal venture.

"I'm here for the next book market. We'll post some staff, and I want to look around. It is always an advantage to know one's surroundings in case something unforeseen comes to pass. Of course, we do not expect anything to happen."

"I hope you are just talking about illegal parking," Margritte chimed in. "We have never had anything more serious than that.

Bécherel is a quiet town with people who like their peace and follow the law."

"If we kill someone, it is only on paper," Rosalie added.

"Of course," Jenaud appeased. "We are expecting a harmonious and peaceful event. There is no reason to worry." An affirming smile spread over his lips with the goal of calming the bookseller.

Sandrine remembered the policemen with their machine-guns in front of the gates of Le Mont-Saint-Michel. She did not doubt for a second that Jenaud was ready for chasing a book thief or more. She had come to know the man as a thorough and strategic cop.

"Come round on Sunday. I'm signing my books here in Bécherel." Rosalie pointed to the shop behind her. "I'll also bring a few of my crime novels for you."

"Thank you very much for the invitation. I'll see if my time allows me the pleasure of collecting new reading material," said the policeman.

"I'd be delighted to see you," said Rosalie. "Sandrine will come too, of course."

Sandrine had not known any of this, but by now it was clear that her Sunday afternoon had been booked. Rosalie would not accept no for an answer. The cake was excellent, so that was a good argument to accompany her. She also did not have any other plans. She would meet Léon in the evening during training. He had decided it would be bad if people saw them together. Sandrine thought it was ridiculous to act like the rumours were true, but he was worried about her.

"Then I'll get back to work. If there is time I will see you on Sunday." Commandant Jenaud said his goodbyes and made his way towards the police car parked at the edge of the square.

"Let's go inside and prepare a corner for the book presentation," said Margritte. "It will get a bit tight in the shop. Monsieur Savier has also reserved a room, but I think he wants to use it for the book club. It's nicer down here with me than upstairs in the antique shop, and the stairs are really steep and not the newest."

"From what I have seen from your bookshop so far it looks very welcoming."

"It won't take long. If you want you can go on a little walk before we drive home," Rosalie suggested.

"I'm not done with my cake. Here on the terrace in the shadow is the perfect place to enjoy the weather and do some thinking."

"Bernard will get you a second coffee then," Margritte decided. "And another piece of cake. No one should leave my café without having tasted the Tarte au Chocolat."

A broad-shouldered man with a belly that hung well past his threadbare corduroy trousers, straggly hair, and a shirt with dark stains under the armpits stepped out of the door. The floorboards of the terrace groaned in protest under his weight, and he flicked the ashes of a self-rolled cigarette onto the floor.

"Bonjour, Monsieur Neville. It's quite lively today." Margritte was clearly trying to get a clue as to what had happened during the argument upstairs.

He stopped for a moment and threw a gaze her way as if he wanted to reprimand her for eavesdropping, but then he forced himself to smile thinly.

"Yes, emotions run high with every enthusiast. What to do?" He managed to simultaneously shrug his shoulders and sigh.

"Enthusiast?" Rosalie asked. Her eyes wandered over the untidy man and her eyebrows drew together ever so slightly.

"The higher arts, of course." Monsieur Neville smiled condescendingly. "Unfortunately, I have to go. Alfonse is upstairs keeping an eye on the shop. Would you be so kind and send a can of coffee up his way? Our machine has finally given up completely."

"No problem," said Margritte.

The lover of the higher arts grabbed his belt, pulled up his trousers and went on his way. The shop couldn't be running too well if the employee needed coffee to stay awake. Sandrine suppressed a grin.

A very interesting little town.

A Booklover

Sandrine sat at her kitchen table and coated the tip of her croissant with butter and strawberry jam. Léon had come over late in the afternoon and had stayed the night.

"Would you like a fried egg or an omelette? With bacon, onions and some Gruyère?" he asked and rummaged through one of the kitchen drawers trying to find a suitable pan.

"As if I would have the ingredients for that. You should know the minimalism of my kitchen by now," she said with a mixture of sarcasm and a pinch of guilt for being a terrible hostess.

"Minimalism. I didn't know that was your philosophy. And here I was thinking it was because you hate to go grocery shopping."

"That too."

"On the way here, I picked up some things. I wouldn't come over unprepared. I've seen mice leaving this place because they were scared of starving to death."

"Make yourself at home," she said in a succinct tone that suggested an indifference she did not feel. On the one hand she loved waking up with him and having breakfast in the open kitchen, but on the other hand she needed her freedom. *Most likely I'm already too old for a real relationship in a shared household.*

"I think I feel more like something sweet." She refused his offer. "I'll stay with my croissant. Rosalie made the jam and brought it over yesterday."

The landline phone rang.

Léon took it from the charging station and handed it to her. "Probably someone from work. It's better they don't know who has breakfast with you."

"What I do in my free time is no one's business," she retorted, even though she knew it would be better to follow his advice.

"Perrot," she answered.

She held her hand over the speaker. "It's Inès," she informed him. Léon knew the young office manager, who had visited his club several times, from the commissariat.

Sandrine listened for a while, nodded and said goodbye.

"So much for my holiday," she said. "I have to go to Saint-Malo." She avoided mentioning the commissariat. They had not told her to go there. Her bosses were still doing their best to keep her away from her place of work. *But what do they want from me?*

"They're dragging you all the way there? What does that mean? Are you exonerated, or did they decide to kick you out for being friends with me?"

"Commissaire Matisse wants to talk to me. Alone. That makes the likelihood of them kicking me out rather slim. That would be a day of celebration for de Chezac, and he would never let the chance of watching my defeat slip through his fingers. We will see what worries plague him."

She bit into the croissant and licked the rest of the sticky jam from her fingers.

"I'll go and get dressed. I can't let them *drag* me there like this, to phrase it like you did."

"Looks sexy to me," he said and looked her up and down with a boyish grin which made her heart beat faster. She only wore panties and a long t-shirt. It was a fitting outfit for a lazy morning alongside her lover.

She stepped close to him and wrapped her arms around his neck. "Do you really want me to visit another man half-naked?" she whispered in his ear.

"Definitely not." He pulled her closer and held her tight against his chest. Sandrine rested her forehead against his shoulder. In this moment she enjoyed not having to be tough and just being held.

"How urgent is it?" Léon asked. His gaze towards the kitchen clock did not slip past her.

"A tempting thought," she whispered and kissed his cheek. "But he didn't give me enough time for that."

"Will I see you tonight? The club is closed on Thursdays. We... I could cook something nice for us, and afterwards we can hang on the couch together and watch a movie like an old couple."

"Another tempting idea." She let go of him and stepped back. "I would be happy to, but as long as I don't know what they want from me I can't promise anything. Maybe they just need someone to do an overnight observation. It's the holidays and not many are working." *Or the news is so bad that my mood afterwards will be terrible.* "Let me call you."

"I'm sure they listen to your telephone."

His objection sounded like a joke, but his eyes showed no trace of humour. That he thought it possible that her own people were listening to her conversations felt like a punch to her stomach, and she needed all her discipline to force a smile. *No, that's impossible*, she told herself.

"I can call you from Rosalie's phone if you'd feel better about that."

"It's not about me," he replied. Léon was one of those people who always thought they could cope with their problems alone. Because of that he cared all the more about his close friends. And she was obviously a part of his circle now. She gave him a soft kiss on the lips.

"Thank you."

"I..." he began but did not finish his sentence. Sandrine knew what he wanted to say, but for sentences that included the word *love* she was not ready. He knew that.

"I'll manage," she said. "As soon as I'm back I'll call you."

Sandrine took a long shower and got dressed for her drive to Saint-Malo. She found Léon sitting at the table eating his breakfast. He exuded all the calm in the world. The smell of fried mushrooms and ham made her regret that she had refused the offered eggs. She sat down next to him and fumbled the knee protectors into the pockets of the sturdy jeans she had bought for motorcycling.

"Looks good and it's practical." She stretched her leg and gave the protector a few slaps. They sat perfectly. "It's too hot for the leather outfit."

"You look hot in everything," he said and watched her with a smile. "Now you only need the right weaponry."

"The gun is in the commissariat."

"In case you have some surprising free time, what do you say to a little trip along the coast? Cape Fréhel?"

"Car or motorbike?"

"Your choice."

"I'll let you know." Sandrine fastened a necktie around her

neck, took her helmet and gloves. "Maybe I can find out something about the raid."

Léon placed his cutlery on the plate and pushed it aside.

"You will do no such thing," he said in, for him, an unusually serious tone. "They're just waiting for you to get involved with the investigation. It will only prove to your colleagues that you have given me information about the raids. I don't want that."

"Maybe the accusations aren't about you at all and it's just someone trying to get to me. You might only be a means to an end here. To learn as much as possible about the raids might become vital for both our survival."

"That may very well be, but it's still mostly my problem. They found the drugs in my office. If you don't get involved whoever is responsible for this will realise that they can't get to their goal this way and leave me alone."

"You believe that?"

"We will see."

"Do you have an idea who could have planted the stuff with you?"

"Not the slightest. I searched around a bit and requested a few favours, but no one knows anything."

She looked at him thoughtfully. Léon was perfectly networked in Saint-Malo, much better than the police. If his contacts didn't lead to anything, things would become more and more mysterious.

"My money's on Albert Chauvin," she said. "The guy's in for people smuggling. I caught him and now he's trying to damage my credibility as a witness. I wouldn't put it past his lawyer, that Lianne Roche, to pull a trick like that."

"I've spoken to him. He assured me he had nothing to do with it." To her surprise, Léon seemed to trust the man.

"The guy lies as soon as he opens his mouth."

"He usually does, but this time I believe him. We've known each other for years. He wouldn't pull a stunt like that on me, he's too clever for that. He knows I'd find out sooner or later. Besides, he wouldn't gain anything from it. The police have enough evidence against him. What good would it do him to ruin your reputation? The prosecutor could keep you out of the trial completely and the evidence would still be overwhelming."

"And assaulting a policewoman? That could earn him some time in jail."

Léon shook his head. "His thug, Jacques Chopard, is going to jail for that. He doesn't mind, it's like his second home. Chauvin didn't touch you after you waved the gun around. He is not given a long sentence for this."

"You're probably right." She kissed him goodbye and went outside. What she had not told Léon was where her boss wanted to meet her. Somewhere that had her stomach twisting with worry.

* * *

Sandrine decided on the route along the coast. The drive with one turn after the other distracted her brain from the conversation about to happen. Still, it did not take long for her to reach Saint-Malo. She recognised Commissaire Matisse from far away. There were not many people who would sit in a conservative suit above the Plage du Sillon, especially when the temperature had already climbed above 20 degrees.

She parked her black and yellow BMW at the side of the road. Her boss turned towards her and nodded. The smile he threw her way was laced with uncertainty, and maybe even guilt. He had definitely not stood by her side like he should have done, and that knowledge draped a heavy weight around her shoulders. The situation must be more serious than she thought. She stuffed her gloves inside the helmet and placed it on the seat. No one would steal anything in front of her eyes. If they did, they would quickly regret it. Her built-up frustration was just waiting for an outlet. *I have to get training again. Best with Lilou.*

"Monsieur le Commissaire," she greeted her boss.

"Ah, Capitaine Perrot. You were nearly faster from Cancale to here than me from the office." He passed her one of the two coffee cups.

"Thank you." She sat down next to him and took a sip. It was strong but not terribly hot anymore.

"It's a wonderful place to take a little break from the commissariat." He started the talk which she knew could be about anything, but definitely not a break from work. He had cancelled her time-out and called her over for a private meeting. It could only be related to her work for the police.

She let her eyes wander over the beach and took a few breaths in and out until her pulse calmed down. The sea had retreated and the tidal islands of Petit and Grand Bé were dryshod. A group of small children jumped over the rocks in search of fishes and crabs in the tidal pools. The holidays were coming up. The beach would fill up further, and the chances of finding a vacant bench would drop considerably.

"Why are we meeting here and not in your office?" Sandrine went straight to the point. If he preferred to meet her here it must be utter chaos in the office.

"No one will interrupt us here, and no one needs to know what we are talking about. Should someone be watching us we are just two colleagues having a coffee together."

"The raid and drugs?"

"Obviously."

"I have nothing to do with either of those things."

"I am aware. Apart from a few, no one believes that in the commissariat."

"Let me guess: Brigadier Poutin?" Sandrine retorted.

"He never liked you."

"I can't blame him for that. I feel the same way about him."

"He used to be a good policeman."

"Must have been a long time ago."

She had only met him as a bitter man who tried to get away from work and stomped on everyone who came too close to him. Dubois, his partner, took over most of the work and kept Poutin's back free.

"However, that's not your main problem."

"I know that. De Chezac wants my head. I can't think of any reason to justify that. I'm not guilty of anything. Being friends with someone under investigation is not a misdemeanour, otherwise half of the Paris police force would have to be fired."

"The man is not stupid. He knows." A seagull landed in front of them, and Matisse ripped a piece from his baguette. "The prosecutor wants to get you for corruption. He is convinced that you inform Monsieur Martinau about all upcoming raids."

"That's ridiculous. I have never had anything to do with those things. It's Dubois' and Poutin's job to organise raids. I also doubt that there was a single raid planned at the Équinoxe in all the time I have been working here."

"Inès is checking as we speak."

"Can I have a look at the evidence?" she asked, without much hope.

"Of course not. Or are you keen to add suspicion of evidence tampering into the mix? Before you ask, Brigadier Azarou will be staying away from this as well. This is exclusively the case of Poutin and Dubois. The more inconspicuously you behave, the faster the spook will be over."

Maybe for me, but Léon won't get off the hook that easily. I have to take care of him too. He's only in this because of me.

"We could have discussed all of this over the phone. There's something else that you have hidden."

"You met Commandant Jenaud in Bécherel yesterday." He suddenly changed the topic.

"Yes, by coincidence. Is that of any importance?"

"He felt like you might not be needed in Saint-Malo and asked if you could help him with an investigation. The holidays are about to begin, and the Gendarmerie is short-staffed, just like us."

"He didn't mention anything yesterday. Neither that there was a crime nor that he wanted me in his team."

"Back then there was no case."

"So, that's it with my holiday? You're sending me back to the front?"

"You'll get along well with Jenaud. Drive over, help him a bit and by the time you are back the waters here should have cleared. I'm sure it will be good for you."

"You want to get me as far away from the commissariat as possible, right? Is that a goodbye forever?"

"I hope not," Matisse replied without any hesitation. It sounded like the truth. "I like working with you. You're very efficient and have a good feeling for people. At the moment it will be better, though, if the prosecutor sees as little of you as possible. Same for the media."

"And I will be safer with Jenaud somewhere in the countryside?"

"A happy coincidence."

"What are we dealing with?" *Most likely some tiny thing. Just an excuse to get me out of Saint-Malo.*

"The man has a corpse. It was an unnatural death, that's all I know."

Sandrine looked at him in surprise. She had been miles off with her guess. It sounded like a real case.

"Where do I have to go?"

"Bécherel, where you met Commandant Jenaud."

"La Cité du Livre. What a coincidence."

"One of my people will wait for you on the village square and show you to a Mansion owned by a Monsieur Savier."

The name Savier rang a bell. She was sure she had come across the name somewhere recently.

"Then I'll be on my way. I have my police badge and will pick up my weapon in a few days."

"Not necessary. I have it here." He handed her a yellow tote bag with the logo of a bakery from town. "Brigadier Azarou has the second key to your drawer and was so kind as to unlock it for me."

"Sure. He has to get at my notes and things when I'm not there. He's my partner and I trust him."

Sandrine stood up and packed the weapon in her motorbike. Yesterday, it had taken them roughly 40 minutes with Rosalie's car. She would be faster today. Most of the road led in four-lanes towards Rennes.

She put the helmet on, nodded at her boss and started the motorbike. With a little crack the first gear engaged. She drove off and zipped into the tight traffic. The commissaire vanished in her mirror, and she wondered under what circumstances she would meet him next time.

* * *

In front of the café which she had visited with Rosalie yesterday, was parked a police car. A policeman in uniform sat at one of the small tables, drinking a glass of water.

That should be the man waiting for me.

Sandrine stopped behind the car and got off her motorbike. She was careful to not let the side stander slip between the old cobblestones. She pulled off her helmet and nodded towards him. According to his badges he was a major, the highest non-commissioned officer rank in the Gendarmerie. *That fits.* She guessed the grey-haired man with the angular profile to be somewhere in his fifties. If Jenaud had chosen him to work together with her he had to have experience and be decent at his job. The commandant would not pretend to dedicate less than his best man to joint investigations with the Police Nationale, and especially with her.

"Capitaine Perrot?"

He rose and gave her an appraising look. There must be a few things from his side that spoke against working in a team with her. She was part of the Police Nationale, had the reputation of being arrogant, wore normal, everyday clothes, drove a motorbike and, on top of that, was a woman with a higher rank than him. From his facial expressions she could not gain any clues as to what he was really thinking. The man clearly had himself under control. At least he had recognised her. Either Commandant Jenaud had told him of her love for motorbikes, or Commissaire Matisse had announced her as being on the way.

"Yes."

"Major Destin," he introduced himself.

"Nice to meet you. I assume that we will be working the case together?"

"We will get along with each other," he answered tartly but did not sound too optimistic. She was wondering what Commandant Jenaud had told him about her.

"I was informed that you had an unnatural cause of death. That's all I know at the moment."

"Correct. Please, follow me to the crime scene." Major Destin had apparently decided that she should get her own impression of the scene without any information which might lead her eye. He stood up and went to his car. In a bowl on the table lay the bill and some change. He must have paid before she arrived.

At least he leaves a tip. Good sign.

She followed the police car out of town. Just past the sign, they turned onto a path lined with plane trees. It led to a detached house, more a manor or estate. Sandrine took her time judging the two-storey building. Two floors with regularly arranged windows sat on the square basic form. The stone façade was covered by climbing Virginia creepers, which the owner had been careful not to let reach the slate roof, which was broken by tall chimneys and dormer windows. The property looked lovingly cared for. Apparently, the victim was not one of the area's poorer people.

In front of the house was parked an ambulance, three police cars, a van, most likely from forensics, several private cars and a hearse. The forensic technicians came from Rennes, the capital, as well as from the arrondissement in which Bécherel was located in, and the department of Ille-et-Vilaine. A gendarme sat on the wide steps, smoking. When he noticed Destin he squashed the cigarette, threw it on the gravel path, and stood up.

"Come with me," the major told Sandrine. "And you, clean up your mess. We are policemen and do not stub out cigarettes on other people's steps," he barked at the brigadier and marched past him. She wondered if it was really important for him that all his subordinates behaved correctly or if he wanted to show that he also expected such perfect behaviour from her. *Most likely both. He can have that.*

She left her helmet and jacket with the motorbike and followed the major who was waiting for her at the wide, open double door.

"The corpse was found in the library. He is Monsieur

Savier, the local notary," he informed her on the way through the foyer. He opened an intricately carved oak door and let her go first. Several men in disposable overalls were placing evidence in clear bags, one was taking photos of the crime scene, and a forensic scientist was taking fingerprints. The dead man sat in a brocaded armchair, his head tilted to one side. A wound was not visible from the door but drops of clotted blood clung to the chair, and a pool of blood was spread out on the polished parquet floor below. A musty smell of dust and old furniture hung in the air, as if the library was not aired a lot. Sandrine concentrated on the corpse, barely paying attention to the rest of the room.

"May I?"

Major Destin looked at one of the forensic technicians who gave her an approving nod and handed her gloves and covers for her shoes.

"We are finished. Please, touch as little as possible," Destin reminded her.

He can't possibly take me for a beginner, so why the comment? Another attempt to show me who's in charge of the investigation? She had no intention of being intimidated by the man, but here was definitely not the right place to discuss their partnership. She pulled on the gloves and shoe-covers and went to the corpse.

"There are nicer things to see." A man who must have been well past his retiring age stepped next to her.

"Xavier Duchamps," he introduced himself. "I am the town's physician. The housekeeper called me, but when I arrived there was nothing I could do. An ugly wound."

"Capitaine Sandrine Perrot," she replied. "Nothing I haven't seen before. This side of the job is not very nice."

"There are nice sides?" the man mumbled and looked at her with one eyebrow raised.

Careful not to step in the blood, she looked at the victim. He rested heavily against the back of the armchair, and his head was bent to lie on his right shoulder. A deep wound gaped out between his blood-clotted hair. His face was pale, and his cheeks were sunken down. The physician must have closed his eyes, but she still recognised him. Now she knew where she had heard the name Savier before. It was the corpse of the chairman of Bécherel's book club. She had seen him only yesterday when he had left the antique shop Rabelais, after an argument with the owner, Monsieur Neville. *A first clue.*

"I assume the time of death to have been between 10:00 p.m. and midnight. Definitely not any later than that. We have full rigor mortis. The colleagues from forensics will be able to tell you more details. It is unlikely that they will find anything else though. It is not very complicated."

"Thank you."

Normally, doctors were reluctant to give any information and she was used to having to laboriously extract the details from them. Monsieur Duchamps was a welcome deviation from the norm and seemed confident in his skills.

"He was struck down with a blunt instrument. Most likely he was dead instantly. It was lucky he didn't suffer."

Sandrine leaned forward and studied the wound.

"The perpetrator must have hit him with quite some force."

"You could say that," the physician agreed. "The wound is deep and bled a lot. Look here." He pointed at the space between the hairline and the collar of the blood-soaked shirt.

"It looks smeared," Sandrine mumbled and looked closer at the blood stain.

"I think that someone grabbed him there after his death while the blood was still running. I wonder for what reason?"

"Maybe the perpetrator did not want his victim to fall forward onto the floor and kept a hold of him."

"A lot of consideration for someone who just beat the man's brains out," the physician huffed. "It would have been easier to just grab his shirt."

"You're correct." *Though one could have phrased it slightly less drastically.* He was right though, it was unusual for a murderer to touch his victim after death, especially when there was a lot of blood. Most people she had met tried not to get in contact with blood. There would be traces of it on the perpetrator's clothes if the forensic technicians managed to find any.

"Was the murder weapon found?" she asked.

"Yes, a bust of Voltaire. We found lots of blood, hair and pieces of skin on it. Unfortunately, no fingerprints." The forensic technician looked towards the writing desk. A clear evidence bag lay on top. The bust inside seemed to be roughly the size of a big fist and made of bronze, most likely a paperweight. The bust's face was covered with red dots. She did not doubt that this was indeed the murder weapon.

"Audubon," corrected Duchamps.

"Excuse me?"

"The bust. It is John Audubon, the ornithologist, and not Voltaire," he repeated. The man from forensics did not seem to be as well-read as the doctor. Certainly not a bad starting point for investigations in this little town, where everything seemed to revolve around books.

"Who found the corpse?" she asked Major Destin, who had been silent, observing her. *I hope he's satisfied with me,* she thought and suppressed a smile. It would not be proper to smile at a crime scene. Especially not as she was under the watchful eyes of the major.

"His housekeeper, Madame Fleur Garaine. She was in the house around the time of the murder. The victim's wife, Isabelle Savier, is on holiday visiting her sister in Provence. Her husband was supposed to join her in the upcoming weeks. No idea why they travelled separately."

"There might be many reasons, but in this case, I think it might be because he was the president of a book club, and on Sunday there is a book market in town. He probably didn't want to miss it." Sandrine remembered that he had rented a room from Margritte.

"These markets are once every month. If you've been to one, you've been to them all," Destin said dismissively.

"Will the autopsy be conducted in Rennes?" she asked. Doctor Morvan from Saint-Malo would have been much more to her taste.

"Certainly. We are in the arrondissement Rennes," he answered.

She knew where they were, but that just meant that she had to find her place in a new team once again. At least not Normans, as in the last case, but Bretons, Inès Boni would have commented.

Sandrine stood up and looked around. For a private library the room was a comfortable size. Through two windows on the long side and one more on the head side of the room fell daylight on two high reading chairs. They were placed with a view of the garden. Within easy reach was an open globe that someone had converted into a well-stocked bar. A thin-walled China cup, a thermos and a half-full milk jug sat on a round side-table made of fine-grained cherry wood. A half-eaten cookie and a lump of sugar were on the saucer, along with some blood splatters. A book lay beside it with a bookmark sticking out. The man had apparently almost finished the story when death caught up with him. He would never get to know the end.

"What do you make of this?" Major Destin was looking at a huge bookshelf spanning nearly the entire long side of the room. Books, most of them antique-looking with gold imprinted leather spines, squeezed against each other on the shelves. More expensive volumes were protected from dust behind glass plates. A couple of dozen just lay on the floor. They were open with bent edges. Rosalie would not have been able to cope with the massacre in front of her without trying to help the books.

"Someone was searching through the shelf and was very short on time," Sandrine said. "Monsieur Savier would never have treated his books this way surely."

"Any idea what could have happened?"

Most of it was obvious. *Does he want to test me?*

"Signs of burglary?" she asked.

"None."

"Was a second cup found?"

"In the kitchen. The perpetrator must have really been busy. We found a badly rinsed cup next to the sink. It still has stains which look like coffee. There are also lipstick marks and fingerprints."

"I think I've seen enough. Let's get some air."

The man did not complain and followed her into the garden.

Sandrine sat down at one of the cast iron tables, shadowed by the branches of a tall oak. The garden, more of a park, led in a gentle slope down to a lake which a couple of ducks had made their home. In the middle of the lake throned a small island with a duck house. High bushes surrounded the property and protected it from any curious passers-by. It was a very nice place to live.

"It's just a little mind game at this point. We don't have sufficient facts," she began.

"Of course."

"Monsieur Savier must have known the perpetrator and let them in himself. It's possible that he was even awaiting them."

"Because of no signs of burglary? A cunning burglar does not leave many signs," Destin replied.

"That might be true, but the windows on the ground floor have censors, and in the hallway, we have a control unit for an alarm system. It wasn't turned on." It had not been a very complicated one. Back when she was a teenager it would not have cost her much time to switch it off, but for an unpractised burglar it might have been a proper obstacle. "Either the victim switched it off when he let in the visitor, or he was murdered before he could activate it. Both are possible."

"The coffee cup?"

"Savier invited his murderer for a coffee. That's why I assume they knew each other, and the visit was planned. The man's death was not planned though. The offence was committed in the heat of passion. Something must have led to an argument which got out of hand."

"I'm thinking the same thing," the policeman agreed. "A bust like that is not a weapon I would carry around if I planned on murdering someone. And the housekeeper has confirmed that it belonged to the victim and would normally stand on the writing desk in the library. Just close enough to grab."

"There was no fight. The room is too clean for that. Savier was hit from behind. He must have trusted the other person enough to have his back to him or her. It's not too daring to assume that the perpetrator was someone from the victim's circle of acquaintances. That narrows the number of suspects. A failed burglary which ran out of hand, can be placed to the files, as far as I can see."

"It didn't look very clean to me. The books on the floor could have fallen down during a fight."

"Possible but unlikely. One was lying in the blood on the

floor. Even with a wound bleeding a lot it would take a while for such a pool to form under the chair. The book was only thrown from the shelf after its formation. My guess is that Monsieur Savier was already dead and did not have to witness how his treasures were being mistreated."

"It could have been like that, but what was the perpetrator looking for?" Major Destin stroked his pointer finger over the bridge of his nose while thinking.

"No idea. Files, documents, photographs hidden between book pages, or rare collector's pieces," answered Sandrine.

"The valuable pieces are kept behind glass to protect them from dust and curious hands. Most of them were locked in."

"Then we can exclude an expensive first edition as the reason for the murder. At least for now."

"I agree. Who would get into a fight resulting in murder just because of an old book?"

"Bibliophiles, collectors. I could imagine a few, especially in a place like this."

"These bookworms do not murder people." His condescending tone left little doubt as to what he thought about people who cared for books. He seemed to her more like someone who always felt like he was on duty, and who liked to spend his little free time in nature. *Most likely he hunts bears which he wrestles down with his bare hands.* She could not hide a grin. To her luck, the policeman's phone rang.

"Excuse me," he said before he took the call.

"We are on the way," was his only comment.

"We have to go. There was a break-in," Destin informed her and put his phone away.

"You can go. I'll use the time to check the victim's acquaintances." She had not waved goodbye to her holiday to deal with simple break-ins.

"Someone broke into the victim's office. Last night. Most likely after the murder."

"That means the perpetrator didn't find what they were looking for in the house." Everything else could wait. "Drive ahead, I follow you."

* * *

The chancellery was located on the first floor in one of the typical Breton houses of Bécherel's centre. A policeman stood in front of the broken door and greeted Major Destin. Sandrine knelt on the floor and studied the dented doorframe. Wood fragments and parts of the doorframe had been ripped off.

"This strengthens our theory that Savier let his murderer inside. It doesn't look like a professional did this," she said.

"More like a total beginner. I would guess at a crowbar. The door is destroyed."

"That should have made a lot of noise."

"The shop downstairs had been closed for hours already, and the people renting the apartment above are on holiday," said the policeman. "So far, we haven't found anyone who witnessed the break-in. It will be difficult, I fear. No one's around at night in this village. I grew up in a town close by and know every nook and cranny here. My people are checking if there are any cameras around. We should find something."

"I would have parked further away and walked here on foot to avoid cameras in the vicinity of the crime scene," Sandrine declared. "But the person must have been in a hurry. First the fight at the estate and afterwards the break-in at the chancellery. There wouldn't have been much time. Maybe we'll be lucky and they were careless enough to park nearby."

"Or maybe it was the other way around. First, they broke in here and then drove to the Saviers' estate."

"If I'm correct and the murder of Savier was an affect action, they would have come here afterwards. Otherwise, they would have carried a fitting weapon and not just used a random bust."

"Sounds logical, if it was spontaneous," Destin agreed.

"Most likely they were looking for the key to the chancellery but couldn't find it in the library, and they couldn't ask the victim anymore."

"Who discovered the break-in?" Destin turned to the policeman who had been watching them.

"His secretary, Madame Descours. She had the morning off. As soon as she saw the broken door, she tried to contact her boss but obviously without success. Only afterwards did she call us."

"Has the victim's phone been found?"

"Not yet. My people are searching the house, but we assume the perpetrator took it. It would be interesting to find out with whom he talked yesterday. Without the phone it will take several days to get the data from his provider."

"Let's look around his office." Sandrine went ahead into the notary's rooms which took up the entire floor. The furnishing was dignified but old-fashioned. Everything felt like it was covered with a layer of patina. Even the pictures on the walls were black and white, most of them photographs of the village. Red-brown wood panelling covered the walls, and the bookshelves were stocked with folders and law books.

Sandrine entered Savier's office. A wide mahogany desk ruled the room. Most likely the wooden monstrosity was supposed to intimidate his clients or show his success as a notary. It left her with the feeling of an uneasy man who used to hide behind all this wood. The drawers had been broken open and their contents were scattered across the hardwood floor. Large format books lay in between. Judging by the gaps, they came from the shelf that ran along the width of the office.

"For someone from the Cité du Livre, the perpetrator treats

books quite contemptuously," Destin remarked. Sandrine looked over at him and wondered if she had detected a spark of humour in his statement. Somehow, she doubted it.

"If they were looking for a specific book it would be enough to simply check the spine. Most likely they are after something hidden inside a book."

"Documents, letters, photographs. It could be nearly anything."

"Or a box disguised as a book. People invent marvellous things if they want to hide something."

"I wish we had an idea who we are dealing with," he muttered, turning away from the shelves.

"We will get there."

"Monsieur Savier..."

Sandrine turned. A woman, around her forties, stood in the doorframe. She wore a dark blue dress that seemed to have been washed way too many times.

"They say he... isn't alive anymore." Her voice trembled and she stopped. She wiped her face with a crumpled tissue. Sandrine was amazed that she had kept a hold of herself until the end of the sentence. She went over to the woman and pressed her hand.

"I'm sorry. Monsieur Savier was the victim of a burglary."

"Did he...?"

"It was over very quickly. He didn't suffer."

"A small consolation."

"You were the one who discovered the break-in?" Sandrine asked, despite already knowing the answer. She wanted to make the woman talk to distract her from her boss' demise.

"Yes, half an hour ago."

"So, just after 10:00 a.m. Pretty late in the morning. Was there a special reason that the office was closed earlier?"

"Fréderic... Monsieur Savier wanted to visit a few clients,

and Madame Cassian is in court. I used the time to get some things done."

"Madame Cassian?"

"His partner. Only in business, don't get me wrong." A blush crept up her cheeks and Sandrine questioned why. It couldn't just be because of one wrongly phrased sentence. She had called her boss by his first name. Most likely that was the reason for her embarrassment. Were they closer than it appeared at first glance?

"Then you were expecting your boss around midday?"

"No, not at all. This afternoon, the Treasure Hunters are meeting."

"The Treasure Hunters?" Destin looked at her with curiosity.

"Some of Bécherel's inhabitants have devoted their time to the search and restoration of old books. Monsieur Savier was president of the club."

Sandrine nodded. Margritte had mentioned something about that yesterday after Savier had bolted past them.

"Are the treasure hunters connected to the antique shop Rabelais?" she asked.

"Yes, of course. They meet in Monsieur Neville's rooms to display their discoveries. I really don't understand why. The owner is a scruffy guy. And his temp gives you such a weird look. Kind of creepy. Surely, they could find a more comfortable place."

"You are also part of these treasure hunters?" Destin asked.

"What?" She shook her head vehemently. "Not me. In these musty libraries and book shops my dust allergy would kill me. I don't even want to think about the overrun flea markets. No, I prefer to be a solitary reader."

"It seems your boss was a very well-read man." *Maybe she can find some comfort in that,* Sandrine hoped.

The woman took courage and entered the room. The broken drawers caught her eye and she sighed deeply when she beheld the chaos on the floor.

"Thinking about it, not really. I fear that he valued books more for their material wealth than their content."

"How may I understand that?"

"For the members of the club it's not so much about the written word in the book, but more about finding an especially rare and coveted book to then display it. Like a hunter showing off his trophies on the living room wall."

She bent down and picked up one of the books on the floor.

"Please, do not touch anything." Major Destin stepped towards her. "Our colleagues from forensics have to do their job first. Once they are done you are free to clean if you want."

"Having something to do would distract me."

"Have you already informed Madame Cassian about her business partner's death?"

"She's in a meeting and her phone is switched off. I left her a message."

"In case she contacts you could you please let her know that we want to talk to her?"

"Of course."

"Had Monsieur Savier been acting any differently recently?" Sandrine asked.

"I didn't notice anything. Just before the monthly book market he was always a bit more tense. It's when collectors from all over France come here, and a few valuable books change owners."

"Were there any rivalries or quarrels between the collectors or in the book club?"

"No, at least nothing serious as far as I know. They are notable citizens: the pharmacist, a lawyer, several doctors, and a few local businessmen. None of them would break in here, or commit a murder." Her voice broke again. "I have to sit down," she mumbled and sank onto one of the chairs. From her jacket pocket she took a perfumed tissue and wiped over her hands.

"We'll give you some time. A brigadier will take your statement. Should we have any further questions, we know where to find you," Major Destin concluded.

A rumbling on the stairs made him stop. Voices were approaching quickly. The colleagues from forensics had finished their work at Monsieur Savier's house and were ready to continue here.

Sandrine followed the major outside.

"Let the technicians do their work. We'll only be in the way," Destin said. "I'll drive to the office in Rennes to start with Savier's background."

"Have you notified the victim's wife?"

"So far, I haven't been able to reach her. The housekeeper informed me that she spoke with the wife and told her about the incident."

"I can't really help you in Rennes. I will stay here and question Madame Garaine for myself. Maybe she'll remember a detail that can help us."

"Do that. We'll talk later. It is likely that the responsible prosecutor will want to talk to us soon."

"Sure."

They left the building together and Major Destin drove off. She looked after him until the police car disappeared from view.

It was approaching noon, and her breakfast had ended abruptly with Inès Boni's call. *Maybe I can kill two birds with one stone.* The notary's office was only a few minutes' walk away from the bookshop Farz Gwad. She hoped to not only get something nice to eat, but also some information about the victim from

Margritte. People knew each other in Bécherel, especially those connected through books it seemed. On top of that, Monsieur Neville, the owner of the antique shop Rabelais, stood high on the list of people she wanted to question. She was keenly interested in what Fréderic Savier and the antiquarian had argued about yesterday.

In the fenced village square, the flags hung limp on their poles and the park benches stood deserted. Locals preferred to stay inside their homes and in the cool during the midday heat. Only two tourists sat at the red and green tables in front of the Neiges d'Antan bookshop and were leafing through a large-format photo book.

Sandrine was also the only guest of the Farz Gwad who chose a seat outside under the awning. She looked through the window into the shop. The tables inside, which were close together, all seemed to be occupied. She was fine with being alone. It was easier to think when no one was on the phone or arguing loudly at the next table.

"Ah, Sandrine, what a surprise. I didn't expect you back so quickly. We thought you would be back on Sunday with Rosalie," Margritte greeted her.

"This time I'm in Bécherel on business."

"You work for the police, right?"

"Yes, in Saint-Malo, but at the moment there's a lot of free time, and my boss has lent me to the police department here."

"That doesn't sound very nice," she said and sat down next to Sandrine. "But I'm sure they're glad to have your help."

"We will see, but first I would like a bite to eat. Otherwise, my stomach will keep interrupting the questions."

Margritte smiled and the thin lines around her blue eyes deepened.

"I was wondering yesterday, what does Farz Gwad actually

mean? I know it's Breton, but that's it." She shrugged her shoulders.

"How should you know as a Parisienne? Farz or Far is the Breton word for a type of egg-cake. Next to Galettes and Kouign amann, Far is definitely one of the most well-known specialities of Brittany." Margritte's smile brightened even more. "The other day a British tourist asked for pudding-cake. It took me a moment to understand that he was talking about a Far. On the other hand, it makes sense – some say the Far is the predecessor of the English plum-pudding. Far was originally nothing more than a wheat porridge which the buccaneers of Saint-Malo refined with vanilla, rum and plums. Today, almost every village has its own recipe and there is a heated argument as to whether plums belong in it or not. The very daring not only use plums soaked in rum, but even bacon, potatoes and raisins, as in Farz Oaled, which is also called Kamin-Far. Farz Gwad is just another local variety. One from the Île d'Ouessant, where my family is from."

"A fitting name for a bookshop specialising in cooking and baking books."

"I thought so too, but here I sit talking your ear off while you're hungry. What can I get you?"

"Now I feel like a Far Breton."

"I'm sorry, but at the moment we don't have any. This evening there will be a traditional Farz Gwad for the treasure hunters. They meet upstairs in the antique shop." She stopped. "If there's a meeting at all. The poor man. I'm truly sorry for what happened to him. That's why you have come to Bécherel, isn't it?"

"Unfortunately, yes. I wish there was a nicer reason for my being here."

"What a terrible thing to happen. We saw him only

yesterday and now he's dead as a doornail." She shook her head and cast her eyes to the ground. "The poor man," she repeated.

"I hoped you could tell me more about him. We're still at the beginning of the investigation, and I want to get a clearer picture."

"He was a quiet man. I don't have much to say about him really. His grandfather was an entrepreneur who retired here. Fréderic spent his entire life in Bécherel. He even drove from here to university in Rennes. Now he owns the only chancellery in the area and is a valued part of the community."

"The office must run really well to support such an estate." The town did not exactly give the impression of being the centre of any major business or real estate transactions which would fetch a tidy sum for a notary. The cost of the property had to be significant though.

"I don't know how his business was going, obviously, but I know that he inherited the house from his parents."

"And books were his passion?" Sandrine asked.

"Definitely. He was president of the treasure hunters and rummaged through every antique fair from here to Montolieu, the only Cité du Livre in the south of France. It's close to Carcassonne."

"Successfully?"

"Well, he always boasted of his discoveries. But what do I know? Those guys are like fishermen. With every glass of Pastis, the caught fish gets bigger and the bought book rarer and more precious."

"Was it a hobby or was there some money involved?"

"You should ask Louis Neville, the owner of the Rabelais. It's through him that they sell their loot to other collectors." A disapproving tone had crept into her voice, which made Sandrine take notice. The treasure hunters of Bécherel did not seem to receive much goodwill. Madame Descours, the secretary from the chancellery, had made similarly derogatory remarks. Could this be the reason for the dispute between Savier and his murderer?

"You didn't appreciate what the members of the club were doing?" she asked for clarification.

"There has always been trade with books. I mean, I do the same thing in my shop, but for those people it's all just about the price they can get for their pieces. It's only a competition. They don't see the real worth most of the time. Louis Neville also sells lots of books abroad. I believe that important French pieces should stay in the country."

"I didn't think that there was an international market for French classics." Life, especially in Brittany, kept surprising Sandrine. "That will be an interesting talk with Monsieur Neville."

"The whole bunch will meet up there later in the afternoon." She gestured towards the upper floors of the building. "But now I will get you something to eat. Sweet or savoury?"

"I would prefer something savoury."

"I can recommend a galette. Quick to make and always good."

"I will have one then. With a Cidre, please."

"Brut or doux?"

"I'm from Paris, so doux."

Margritte laughed and returned to her shop.

Sandrine quickly checked her phone as she had switched it on silent. Since this morning a couple of dozen messages had amassed. Most of them were from reporters who wanted a statement from her. Especially stubborn once again was Deborah Binet, not much of a surprise. Word had gotten around Saint-Malo that there was a rumour of Sandrine being corrupt, and that the new juge d'instruction was considering investigating. It was not hard to guess how the rumours had trickled through:

Antoine de Chezac himself. It still amazed her that he had not objected to his transfer to Saint-Malo. He called it the boring province after all, and it was far from a career in the Home Office. The man had excellent connections which would have surely allowed him to stay in Paris if he so wished. But now he was in Brittany and had to show successes, otherwise this place would become a dead end for him. There was nothing that brought one more quickly into the newspapers than accusing a policewoman. Whether he was able to prove his accusations in the end was not important at the moment. The investigation would eventually fizzle out and be shelved, but her reputation would be ruined forever. As it turned out, the man could only win, and she could only lose. She felt helpless at the thought of de Chezac, lurking like a spider in his web, spinning his threads while she crouched far from Saint-Malo. *Oh no, I won't make it easy for him.* He had nearly managed once before to push her out of the police force in Paris. She had turned her back on Paris and moved to Cancale. She had written her termination and nearly sent it. Since then, lots had changed. By now she felt at home in Brittany, had a job and found friends which she would not give up without a fight. The hand that had been dealt to her was bad, but she would play it as best as she could.

Sandrine considered going to a shop to get a newspaper, but it was still too early. As the journalists were desperate to get a hold of her the story would be printed tomorrow. Today she might only find something online. She hoped no one from her family would see anything. The Perrots had always doubted that she would enjoy a happy life as a policewoman. Uncle Thomas had broken down in tears when she had told him that she was joining the police. She remembered all too well how he sobbed something about *wasted talent* into his tissue. A grin stole onto her lips. Despite his fears, she had not let her talent dwindle, still practicing the old tricks. Her uncle had taught her everything she needed to know about professional burglary as a young child, and Sandrine had proved to be a perfect pupil. A door lock was no obstacle for her, and most alarm systems only stopped her briefly. From this point of view, nothing spoke against a return to the bosom of the family. Her uncle would love to take her on his nightly outings again.

Sandrine pierced the egg yolk on top of her galette and watched it drip around the ham and potato pieces and dissolve into the crème fraiche. Next to the dark buckwheat crepe a few salad leaves with some drops of vinaigrette had been arranged to make the whole composition look a bit healthier.

Her phone vibrated, but she ignored it. No matter who it was, she would enjoy her meal in peace. To wolf down the galette while being on the phone would be a sacrilege. Only when she pushed the empty plate away did she check who had tried to call her. There was a message from Major Destin. He had organised a desk for her at the police station in Bécherel. The long, one-storey stone building opposite the mayor's office had already caught her eye on the drive here. It was a gloomy building which did nothing to help her look forward to sitting at a desk. She liked it much better on the terrace of the bookstore. *Maybe I will set up my temporary office here.*

She also had several messages from Deborah Binet, the journalist for the *Ouest-France*. She went through the list and deleted one message after the other, until she came across one from Inès Boni. She pressed call back.

"How nice that you're finally answering your calls," the woman greeted her with a slightly annoyed edge to her voice. Sandrine had never heard Inès get cross about anything. "I was starting to worry."

"Worry about me? I feel flattered even though it's not necessary."

"Yes, about you. Don't claim that there isn't a reason."

She could tell that the door of the office was closed on the other side of the line. Inès was making sure that no one could hear them. Now Sandrine felt uncomfortable.

"The prosecutor is constantly snooping around wasting the commissaire's time, and probably stealing his last nerve," she explained.

"There isn't the slightest truth in what the man accuses me of," Sandrine said before the question could arise.

"I know that, as well as everyone else here. But that doesn't help us. We have to get you out of this before it gets even worse."

"*You* don't have to do anything," Sandrine replied, maybe a bit too harshly. It was enough that her career was on the line. She had to avoid Inès and Adel also getting caught in the prosecutor's line of fire. "This is my own business."

"I won't just abandon you. Even if you don't want any help."

She heard the office manager's serious tone and gave up. The young woman was at least as stubborn as she was.

"Alright, but be careful. De Chezac is not to be trifled with."

"Neither am I," retorted Inès Boni. There was no trace of humour in her voice.

"What's your plan?"

"Nothing that I want to talk about on the phone. Adel has taken the afternoon off because of his overtime. I think he wanted to search for some old thrillers, so old that you can't buy them in normal bookshops."

"He might be able to find them in Bécherel. What a coincidence."

"No idea, but I wouldn't be surprised. Where better to find some antiques than there?"

Sandrine checked her watch. "I want to have a look at the crime scene again. Maybe I can find a clue that slipped past us. By now the forensic technicians will be gone, and I'll have the place to myself."

"Savier? The notary?"

"How do you know about this?"

"On my last training for office managers, I met a few nice colleagues. Susanne works for the office in Bécherel and Sophie in Rennes. Isn't that another coincidence?"

"Unbelievable." Sarcasm dripped from the word. Inès Boni was the most connected woman she had ever worked with.

"We'll talk later, now I have to work." Inès hurried to hang up. Sandrine assumed that someone was making his way to Inès' office. Someone with whom the young woman did not want to share information with. Poutin was the first one that came to mind.

Sandrine placed the money and the bill on the small plastic plate and stood up. Her motorbike was parked on the opposite side of the square, close to the chancellery. From here, it was only a few minutes on foot to the Savier's estate. She would have enough time to look around before Adel made an appearance.

A familiar, sleek sports car passed and squealed to a halt in front of her. A blonde woman in beige chinos and a white blouse jumped out and stepped in her way. Sandrine sighed. The journalist had sniffed her out. *Was to be expected. Maybe it's not the best strategy to have my office on the bookshop's terrace. It's too easy to find.*

"Capitaine Perrot, how lucky to find you here." Deborah Binet acted as if she was auditioning for a role in a small-town-theatre play.

"Madame Binet. How's work for the *Ouest-France*?"

"Something new every day. The perfect job for me. As we happen to cross ways, I have a few questions. You have a few minutes, don't you?"

"Firstly, no comment. Secondly, no." She tried to squeeze past her, but the journalist shifted into her way again.

"Do you really want the newspaper to print what I was told

by my sources without having had the chance to defend yourself and correct them?"

"I can very well imagine what sources those are."

"Maybe you're wrong."

"I'll take my chances on that."

"Do you expect me to disclose my informants? That won't happen."

"There are a handful of people who want to see me stumble and fall, some want to avoid going to jail, others don't like the fact that there are women in the police force who refuse to be pushed around, and who have higher ambitions than making coffee for their colleagues." Sandrine refrained from mentioning female lawyers who did everything they could to protect their clients. There was no reason to set her on that path. Even the devil would hide from a team comprised of Deborah Binet and Lianne Roche.

The journalist grimaced and nodded her head. "Sounds like a fitting description. What do you say to the accusations?"

"I don't know the accusations so I cannot give a comment." She checked her watch. It should take Adel around 45 minutes to get from Saint-Malo to here with his calm driving style. She did not have to hurry, but still did not want to waste her time with the journalist.

"I have to visit a crime scene and I have to hurry. Come with me to my motorbike and I'll answer what I'm able to on the way."

Deborah Binet beamed at her as if she had already won. She loved to be one step ahead of her rivals. Quickly she pulled out her phone and started a recording.

"Are you having an affair with a well-known club owner from Saint-Malo?"

"No comment, that's my private life."

"The receptionist of the Auberge Saint-Michel confirms

that you both spent a night there and had breakfast together the following morning. One double room." She clearly stressed *one* double room.

"No comment."

The woman's eyebrows drew together in dismay.

"Did you warn your friend about the raids at the Équinoxe and send him other official information? There are claims you stopped check-ups at his club."

Sandrine walked around the sportscar and over to her motorbike.

"The planning and execution of raids is not part of my area of work, so I don't have any knowledge of it to pass on. It might be worth checking with the commissariat's press office to see if any raids had been planned in the time of my employment. I started working here about four months ago. To my knowledge there weren't. The previous coroner, Lagarde, wasn't a big fan of raids because they hurt tourism. De Chezac has been in office for less than two weeks. During that time, I was working a case in Normandy and was rarely in the Saint-Malo office."

"I will have that checked. Lagarde is working in Rennes."

"Please do. You will see that there was no police operation I could have warned anyone about."

"Have you misappropriated drugs and passed them on to Léon Martinau for sale?"

She stopped in her tracks. Even for Deborah Binet, this accusation was grotesque.

"Do you really believe this garbage?"

"It's not about what I believe, but simply about what you are being accused of," she deflected. It wasn't any different for her than for de Chezac. They both had to make it on the front page to seal their careers. Just like the prosecutor, the woman was happy to use all means possible.

"Of course not. How could I? I have no business with drug-related cases. The only option would be to steal something from the evidence room, and it's very well-secured. Inputs and outputs are strictly logged, and I have no knowledge of anything missing. In addition, Club Équinoxe has not yet been linked to drug trafficking."

"So, you assume that someone is feeding false information to the prosecutor to discredit you?"

"There are a few people who would like that. There's no doubt. I cannot say what the prosecutor thinks or will do, but I'm very sure that he will be open to an interview."

"He already gave me an interview." She sounded like she was very pleased to have already talked to de Chezac. Sandrine could not suppress a smile. Most likely the man had waited in front of the phone until the media called. By now he must also know that Deborah Binet and Sandrine had fought through their own conflicts. *Does he count her among his allies? Quite possibly. Certainly, as one of the assets in his crusade against me.*

"That's it then." She unlocked the steering wheel of her motorbike and pulled the helmet and jacket from the side cases.

"If more questions arise, how can I contact you?"

Sandrine pulled her helmet on and mounted the BMW.

"You're good at your job. You will find me without any trouble."

"Here in Bécherel, where you've been transferred as a punishment, like back in Paris? Do they want to keep you away from the commissariat in Saint-Malo? Does your boss think you might tamper with evidence otherwise?" She used the last opportunity to fire her questions like arrows.

"Not at all. Normally people call this vacation replacement. A routine procedure for which I was requested." She managed not to sound insolent, or so she hoped. She pushed the starter and the engine roared to life.

"See you around," she said, engaged the first gear and

drove off. In the rear mirror she saw the woman turn around and call someone. Most likely she was passing changes and additions to her editors. That was if she had decided to implement any.

* * *

The wind shook her helmet and the trees at the side of the road whizzed past her. The road led in long curves through the green landscape of Brittany, past fields, isolated farms or hamlets. The anger about the journalist's allegations had to be released and she accelerated as hard as the winding road allowed. It took her less than five minutes to get to the Savier's estate, near the Caradeuc park. There was no sign of the police cars except for tyre tracks on the gravel driveway.

She rang the doorbell. Steps sounded from inside the house shortly after. A woman in a dark, straight cut dress opened the door. Sandrine guessed her to be roughly the same age as her, so around her mid-thirties. Her blond hair was brushed back tightly which only made her pale face look thin and pointy. She eyed Sandrine over her rimless glasses.

"Capitaine Perrot." Sandrine pulled out her police ID and showed it to the woman who had to be Savier's housekeeper. She pushed her glasses up the bridge of her nose and leaned forward to study the ID.

"Police? Your colleagues have already left." Her eyes wandered over Sandrine and stuck to the jeans which bulged at the knees.

"Protectors, for riding a motorbike," Sandrine explained and slightly lifted her right leg at an angle.

"I didn't know such things existed," the woman murmured pensively. "Come inside."

"We haven't met yet. You are the Savier's housekeeper?"

"Fleur Garaine," she introduced herself. "I have been running the household for three months now."

"My colleagues already questioned you, but I would also like to talk to you if you feel able to answer some questions. Finding a corpse is a shock for most people."

"I'll be okay. I already talked to a Major Destin this morning. Not the most delicate person."

Sandrine nodded. The man did not care if people thought he was coarse and impolite. *In our profession, aesthetes and philosophers have a hard time. We see too many atrocities.*

"Unfortunately, we will have to disturb you a few times during the upcoming days."

"If it helps to catch the perpetrator, I am happy to assist. Please, come in." The woman stepped aside and let Sandrine enter. She seemed very composed for someone who had found her boss' bloody corpse in the library not too long ago.

"Was Monsieur Savier a good boss?"

"I cannot complain. They treated me very respectfully, and what they were demanding was nothing out of the ordinary."

"What exactly were the demands?"

"Monsieur Savier's? He was rather humble. The man was happy if the house was clean, the garden cared for and dinner was on the table on time. Otherwise, he asked for little more than small errands in town, mostly taking books to the antique shop or picking them up."

"That sounds like a lot of work to me. The house is big, and the garden is more like a park."

Madame Garaine had kept silent about the demands made by the lady of the house. They were probably significantly harder to fulfil than the ones her husband had posed.

"Most of it is only organising. The Saviers have a cleaning lady who comes over three times a week, and Arnault from town cares for the garden. The man loves lawnmowers and leaf blow-ers. Basically, everything that makes a lot of noise. But I digress. You did not come here to listen to me gossip."

"Every detail is important to get a clear picture of what happened here yesterday." In fact, it was the gossip that was interesting to Sandrine. Nobody knew more than the employees working in the house, who were always present and had to live with the quirks of their employers.

"I assume you want look in here?" Fleur Garaine stopped in front of the door to the library. "It has been sealed. I assume you have the authority to enter the lib... the crime scene."

"Yes, I have."

Sandrine pulled a knife from her pocket, flicked it open and cut through the seal which spanned the doorframe. She opened the door and let Madame Garaine go first.

"When did you find Monsieur Savier?"

"Around 8:00 a.m. He did not come for breakfast which was very unusual for him. Normally he was extremely punctual."

"You searched for him?"

"Not really. I thought he must have worked late into the night. Madame Cassian was here for a business meeting."

"When did she arrive?"

"Around 7:00 p.m. I opened the door for her, and Monsieur Savier greeted her in the library like usual."

"She came here a lot?"

"From time to time, maybe once a month. What I meant to say was that Monsieur Savier normally greeted all his guests in the library. It is like the salon of the house. Madame Savier does not enter the room a lot."

"Did you bring them coffee or any other drinks?"

"He was a man with a passion for coffee. There was always a can of coffee, warm milk and a few cups in the library. The small bar was only for guests. He rarely touched alcohol."

"He must have offered a cup of coffee to Madame Cassian and later returned it to the kitchen."

"I would be surprised by that," replied the woman.

"Why?"

"He never moved used dishes. He always left them over there. It was one of my tasks to clean." She nodded in the direction of the bar. Behind it stood a small table, on it a tray with clean cups and glasses. "Also, the woman loves tea. I have never seen her drink anything else but tea or water."

"We found a cup with coffee stains in the sink. There was lipstick on the edge."

"I could be wrong, of course." Judging from her tone of voice it did not sound like she thought she was, and Sandrine was inclined to believe her.

"When did you last collect the cups?"

"In the early evening. When the lawyer arrived, there were no used cups in the sink. I switched on the dishwasher before retiring to my room. I would definitely have noticed dirty dishes."

"Then he must have had another female visitor after Madame Cassian left." *Or she did decide to have coffee and return the cup to the kitchen on the way out? Forensics found some fingerprints on the cup. They will know if it was used by her.* "Do you know when Madame Cassian left the house?"

"I cannot say. After she arrived, I was in my room and only left this morning to prepare breakfast."

"Did you notice anything of what transpired here? Maybe an argument?" She looked at the books on the floor. "The way it looks, someone searched the room. That would have been quite noisy, you must have heard something."

"I fear not. To relax after a long day, I like to read while listening to music. I always wear headphones, so even if there had been a shooting going on I would not have heard anything."

Her hand twitched to her mouth as if to hold back the words. "That was probably a rather inappropriate remark."

"No, that way I can get a clear picture of everything going on in the house." She smiled at the housekeeper with encouragement. "If you weren't searching for your boss, why did you go into the library this morning?"

"To bring back some books I had borrowed. With Monsieur Savier's permission, of course."

"You enjoy reading?"

"Oh, yes. After I began working here, I joined a reading group in Bécherel." She turned towards Sandrine and scrutinised her closely, as if she was trying to gauge her as an avid reader or one of the other people.

"You joined the treasure hunters like your boss?"

"No, no, their members are not readers."

Madame Garaine took a few more steps into the room and stopped. Her eyes travelled over the shelves.

"Monsieur Savier owns an exceptional library, but I am sure that I have read more of his books in the last month than he has in his lifetime."

"He must have known a lot about books and their value. Otherwise, he would not have been such a successful treasure hunter."

"I cannot say anything about that," answered the woman in a tone that made it clear that she could have filled books on the topic but was deciding to stay quiet. Maybe it was out of deference to her deceased client, but maybe also for reasons that Sandrine could not yet know.

"These are the books I wanted to return. You probably understand that with everything that transpired I was not able to sort them properly." The woman looked in the direction of the writing desk. On the upholstered chair towered a pile of four or five leather-bound books. "Do you still require my assistance? Work does not do itself around here."

"When do you expect Madame Savier's return?" Sandrine asked, ignoring the question.

"I informed her of her husband's death. She wanted to leave immediately. She is currently staying with her sister near Nice. It is a long drive, and I am expecting her late at night, unless she decides to stay overnight somewhere on the way, which I have strongly advised her to do."

"Please let me know once she arrives. We have to talk to her."

Sandrine handed over a business card which the woman took hesitantly.

"I will inform Madame Savier of your wish."

A nicely worded rejection. She clearly found it inappropriate to notify the police of Madame Savier's arrival and would leave it to her employer to do so at her own discretion.

"How was the relationship between the two?"

"I cannot say anything about the Savier's marriage. I never noticed anything unusual."

Another topic she danced away from. She was either very discreet about the Savier's private life, or the marriage had not been great.

Madame Garaine's gaze wandered through the room. Her eyes locked on the bloodstain under the chair for a moment before moving on over the books on the floor. She sighed quietly and shook her head. Sandrine wondered if the death of Fréderic Savier or the contemptuous handling of the books was harder for her.

"When am I allowed to clean?"

"The forensic technicians have taken all evidence. As soon as I have had a look around you are free to enter and clean the library." She began to suspect that her sympathy lay more with the mistreated books than with the victim.

"In the meantime, I have to prepare the house for Madame Savier. Do you have any idea when the body will be released?" She seemed to push away the thought of the murder and concentrate on the tasks ahead of her.

"At the moment, the body is with forensics in Rennes. As soon as I learn more, I can let you know."

"That would make my life a lot easier." The woman's gaze returned to the chair the man had died in. The blood had clotted entirely by now.

"That cannot be saved," she mumbled. "And the parquet has to go too." Her voice was cool and down to business. Sandrine had seen countless times how people tried to distract themselves with everyday tasks to avoid constantly thinking of the crime which had invaded their lives one way or another.

"I really have to get back to work." The woman clearly did not want to stay in the room any longer.

"Of course, I will get along just fine."

"Then I hope you have a nice day and a successful investigation." She spoke fast, turned on her heels and left the library with fast steps. It almost looked like she was fleeing the scene.

Sandrine leaned down and pulled a white garden rose from under one of the books. She could imagine the fragrance more than she could smell it and placed the rose aside. The book's pages were stuck together in waves. She ran her fingers over the carpet. It was still wet. Someone must have pushed over the vase and the flowers. Was it clumsiness or was there a specific reason for it? Had the perpetrator needed the vase for something?

The dark red leather couch creaked quietly when she sat down. Sandrine observed the room and tried to visualise the events of yesterday evening. At the moment, Madame Cassian was the last person who had seen Monsieur Savier alive. Either they had gotten into a fight, and she had struck him down, or he had welcomed another female visitor after she had left. At that time, the housekeeper had already been in her room listening to music. Who would someone like Savier greet at the door and not send away but invite into the library and offer them coffee? It must be someone he knew personally, maybe even very well. That would also explain why he had not cared about turning his back towards the murderer. The blow had been treacherously struck from behind and killed him instantly. Most likely he had had no idea what was coming for him.

So far, she had assumed that it was an affect action, but how did that fit with the victim sitting and relaxing in his chair and facing away from the visitor? *In an argument I would always look at the person I was talking to, and never turn my back on him or her. Maybe my guess is wrong, and the attack was calculated and planned.* She scanned the top of the writing desk. The bust of Audubon had disappeared and was surely by now in the lab in Rennes. It would take a few days until they could confirm that it was indeed Fréderic Savier's blood on it. She did not doubt that it was his, and neither did Major Destin.

The perpetrator dealt the blow, Savier died instantly, and then? Sandrine rose and stepped behind the victim's chair. The writing desk was out of reach. The perpetrator must have had the bust in hand already. *But why? I would have used a letter opener or a knife or even one of the big bottles.* The drinks-globe was well-stocked and wide open. *It's much easier to grab a bottle by the neck. Still, the perpetrator decided to go for the bust. Does it hold a special meaning?*

After Savier's death, his visitor had ransacked the shelf. *No, first they knocked the vase over.* The books were lying on the flowers so they must have already been on the floor. *So, they were standing here with the vase in hand.*

What could have been the reason for this? Sandrine remembered the smeared blood on the victim's neck. In one hand the vase, the other holding the victim's neck. Did the perpetrator want to make sure that he was dead and search for the pulse? Maybe hit him again with the vase? Why? They had the bust which was definitely much better than a porcelain vase. Lost in thought, she shook her head. It did not make any sense. Not yet at least. The vase clearly played an important role, but so far, she had no idea which one.

The desk's drawers were closed. She pulled on them, but they were locked. The perpetrator had not gone to the pain of breaking them open as they had in the chancellery. They had either lacked the right tools, or had known that what they were searching for was not contained within. They definitely had not found what they had been looking for. The break-in at the chancellery had followed.

Sandrine pulled a few books from the shelf. The thick layer of dust which covered the tops showed her that they had stood here a long time without ever having been read or moved. On the one hand, she could agree with the housekeeper. Monsieur Savier clearly had not been an avid reader. On the other, he had a few thousand books on his shelves and most of them French classics. *With the little time I have to read it would take me several lifetimes to finish this library.* Rosalie liked to talk of her pile of to-be-read-books; this here was more like a library of to-be-read-books.

Her phone vibrated and she took the call.

"Hello, Adel. I hear you're off and having a good time."

"You could say that. My thriller collection is missing a few older editions, and I think I can find them in Bécherel."

"What a coincidence. I'm also in Bécherel. I will be at the crime scene for another half hour. It's quite a mess," she said and tried not to sound ironic. Of course, Adel knew very well where she was, but she played along and pretended to be surprised. Did he really assume that her phone was being monitored? Even Léon seemed sure of it. *They're watching too many thrillers on TV*.

"Don't work too much, it's holiday season."

"I'm trying." She hung up and let the phone glide back into her pocket when her gaze was drawn to the writing desk again. The tip of a piece of paper poked out from under the desk pad which was made from the same red leather as the armchair's upholstery. She pulled it out carefully. It was a yellow post-it, looking new and still sticky. *How did that get there? It looks like Savier tried to hide it before his visitor came.*

'JJLFA' was written on it in capitals, with several exclamation marks behind it. She had no idea what the abbreviation could stand for. It seemed way too long to be the initials of a name. Maybe it was a note for his work, and the abbreviation for a filing process. She would ask Madame Descours the secretary, or even better Madame Cassian. She checked the list of calls on her phone. The lawyer had not contacted her yet. Another visit at the chancellery would be necessary as soon as Destin was back from Rennes.

Sandrine heard a car pull up in front of the building, and tyres crunched on the gravel. Shortly after, steps sounded from the foyer and Adel appeared in the doorframe. He had chosen a pink polo-shirt to his beige chinos.

"The door was open, and I let myself in. I hope that was okay?" He smiled at her as if it had been weeks since the two of them had last met, even though only a few days had passed.

"In theory you have no business being here as this is not your crime scene," she said, but was glad to see him again.

"Maybe not, but it's my partner's. Commissaire Matisse lent you to the gendarmerie to get you out of the line of fire?"

"Looks like it. It didn't work though. The Binet has already found me. It's only a matter of time until the rest flocks here too."

"The woman is unpleasant, but very efficient at her job."

"You shouldn't get involved in this. It could end badly for you," she warned him, even though she knew it was futile. There was no way he would be dissuaded from helping her. Exactly like Inès.

"We miss you at the commissariat."

"You're a terrible liar."

"My parents raised me to be an honest man. I would never disappoint them," he replied and made his way over towards the writing desk. He looked around the room. Like a scanner, the trained police officer recorded all the details that could be of importance for the investigation.

"You're becoming a reader? I didn't think you had enough inner quiet for that. Rosalie always complains how long it takes you to finish one of her thrillers." He tapped on the pile of books on the chair.

"I wish I had more time to read. The housekeeper brought them back. Unfortunately for us, the only person who was in the house at the time of the murder spent the night in bed with books and headphones and heard nothing of what transpired." Maybe lucky for her. *Otherwise, there might be two corpses.*

Adel picked up one of the books. "*Nana* by Emile Zola." He put it back and checked the others. "Nabokov. Miller. *Lady Chatterley's Lover* by Lawrence. Interesting mixture. But then this should be..." He leaned down and pulled out a thin book from the pile. "Anaïs Nin. Her books could hardly be missing from such a collection. Lots of classics with a decent portion of eroticism. At least for the time in which they were written."

"No wonder that she didn't notice anything." Sandrine had not expected this selection from the cold woman, but she had learned long ago that looks were sometimes deceiving. "Let's get out of here. I have seen enough blood for one day."

"Gladly."

They sat down at the table at which she had already rested with Major Destin. She looked up at the sky. There was not a single cloud to be found. A man in green dungarees walked through the garden and threw a curious glance their way.

"Hello, Arnault," Sandrine greeted him.

The man stopped and looked at her. "Do we know each other?"

"Madame Garaine mentioned an employee named Arnault who takes care of the park. You look like a gardener to me."

"Let me guess, she also mentioned that I strain her nerves with all the noise I produce?" A friendly smile spread over his face. "It's hard to please that woman. The lawn always has to look perfect, but I'm not allowed to mow it because that makes too much noise? How shall that work, I ask you."

"I think she spoke about a lawnmower or a leaf blower."

"Most likely both. She hates noise and dirt." He glanced in the direction of the house, but nothing was moving behind the windows. "You must be from the police. Terrible thing that happened here."

"Did you know Monsieur Savier well?"

"I didn't know him at all. He barely ever used the garden, and my tasks were given to me by Madame Garaine. Sometimes Madame Savier told me what to do, but I wouldn't even call that a conversation." He looked at his watch. "I have to go now. Another client is waiting for me."

"One more question – were you in the garden yesterday?"

"In the afternoon."

"Did you notice anything out of the ordinary? Maybe someone on the grounds who had no business being here?"

"I was alone, at least I didn't notice anyone. The house seemed quite abandoned. Madame Garaine was out buying groceries and Madame Savier is, as far as I know, somewhere in Provence. I took the time and quickly cut the hedges."

"Thank you, that's everything. Should you remember anything else, please give me a call." She gave the man her card. He tucked it into the breast pocket of his chequered shirt without so much as a glance.

Sandrine looked after him until he disappeared behind the house.

"You think they bugged my phone?" she asked Adel.

"Inès was the one who got me thinking. I'm not sure if they have, but better to be careful."

"That's ridiculous. On what basis would such a request be approved?"

"I've always admired your infallible instincts, but here you're wrong. You should be careful."

"Okay, I will remember that," she promised half-heartedly.

"What will the Binet write about you?"

"If I understood it correctly, de Chezac hasn't only accused me of supplying Léon with information, but also with drugs. Investigations against corrupt policewomen give extra points on the career ladder."

"And justify phone surveillance." Adel's fingertips stroked over the stubble on his chin while he pondered the problem. "As I said, you should better be prepared for everything. That way you can't regret anything."

"Perhaps the investigation against me will sweeten de Chezac's transfer to Brittany. He must hate it here."

"I don't think so," Adel answered and threw her a surprised look. "Inès knows someone who knows someone and so on. It looks like our prosecutor worked hard to be transferred to Saint-Malo. He definitely came of his own accord."

Sandrine whistled. That changed the whole situation. The assumptions she had made so far fell in on each other like a house of cards.

"Does Inès' source know the background to all of this?"

"It's a mystery for everyone. The man was just about to be promoted."

"De Chezac willingly refusing a career-changing event? That doesn't sound like him."

"We can agree on that."

"What could have brought him here? Revenge on me because of the trifles from our past is definitely not enough. The snob despises us common police far too much for that. There must be something more serious behind it. Destroying my career is probably just a little candy on top."

"Maybe even prison."

"Unlikely. He can't prove any of his accusations."

"Poutin has become his page boy help. Who knows what they want to frame you for? Then we have statement against statement. Something always sticks to you. That's inevitable."

"I can very well imagine how happy he will be once he's rid of me."

"Poutin doesn't make it a big secret."

"What do the others say?"

"You're much more popular in the commissariat than you think. Jean-Claude Mazet threw Poutin out of his lab just yesterday, and Inès lost his expense report from last month."

"Messing with Inès is a really bad idea," she said. "But back to my problem. What did you find out?"

"Not much, and what I found isn't very good. They discovered drugs in Léon's safe during the raid. One plastic bag with 500g ecstasy. At least that's the rumour circulating the office."

"He swears he never owned or dealt any drugs."

"You trust him?"

"Yes. He wouldn't lie to me."

"Then I will believe him too. Your knowledge of human nature has always been reliable."

She was happy to hear that. The evidence against him was so crushing that she herself had harboured doubts.

"But the drugs exist," she said. The facts could not be ignored. "Someone must have deposited them and then informed de Chezac of their whereabouts. I can't imagine anything else."

"Let's summarise what they actually have. You have a relationship with Léon Martinau who owns the Club Équinoxe."

"Even the press knows that by now." That damned woman had bribed the receptionist of the Auberge Saint-Michel to get the information that Léon had spent the night with her. It would be written in her article tomorrow. She could imagine it in bold letters in some overblown sentence: Policewoman Falls for Dubious Club Owner and gets Involved in Criminal Activities. Or something equally far-fetched. A deep sigh escaped her. If her mother saw that, she would jump in the car and drive over to protect her daughter. Something that she definitely had to prevent.

"Shall I cut the articles out for you?" Adel asked, sarcasm swinging in his voice. "You can frame them later."

"It's okay. Rosalie will do that for me, and if not, I will get the online version and save it."

"Alright, so, they found drugs. They should by now be in the evidence locker, but I can't get to them without causing a ruckus. I'll have to depend on hearsay, at the moment, to find out what kind of drugs and how much was confiscated."

"An analysis must have been commissioned when they came in. Can you go through the lab report? Or we wait until the report goes through Inès. Maybe we can track them and find out where they came from."

"The analysis was commissioned directly by the prosecutor. It's possible that no copy will come to the commissariat. I'm honestly surprised that the stuff is with us at all. If I was him, I would place little trust in the colleagues here and would send the drugs to Rennes."

"That would have made sense, but don't underestimate de Chezac. He doesn't do anything without a motive."

"Maybe you overestimate him?"

"No, I definitely don't. What would I do in such a case?" Suddenly, she snapped her fingers. "Stay away from the evidence locker. It's a trap. It must be. Either the man really thinks that I'm dealing drugs and hopes that my accomplices will destroy them, or he wants to pull everyone who helps me down with me. The more people he accuses the more dust he throws up."

"You think he's surveying us?"

"I assume that there's some form of mini transmitter in the bag, but at least video surveillance of the evidence. Anyone who gets close to the box will be recorded."

"Good to know." He nodded in agreement. "I'll stay away from the stuff."

"And from the prosecutor."

"As you wish. What can I do to help you?"

"Léon didn't think so, but I can imagine that Albert Chauvin is behind everything. He's about to face his trial for human trafficking. He would like it if I had to drop out as a witness. He could claim I tampered with the evidence. Maybe that would help him."

"It would give him a lenient prosecutor. The enemies of my enemies are my friends."

"And there's also..." She stopped. "But I will take care of that myself."

"You're thinking of Lianne Roche, aren't you?" He had interpreted her pause correctly.

Adel and the lawyer had a shared past. They had been in a relationship, and the separation was still hard on the brigadier. The normally calm and collected man lost his composure as soon as she was around, which the lawyer used to her advantage.

"What would she gain from that?"

"She's representing Chauvin and would do anything to keep him out of jail. It would even be enough of a reason to pay you back for the losses she had to deal with because of you. The woman is a psychopath. Unfortunately, I found that out too late."

"She's definitely like poison to you. Keep your distance from her."

"I'm done with that, and back in a stable relationship. Lianne won't manage to pull me under again," he assured her.

"Geneviève is a real treasure. You deserve to be happy. Another reason to leave Lianne to me and not get on de Chezac's wrong side."

"Okay," he agreed, though hesitantly. "But Chauvin I will take care of."

"Check him out. I want to know where he was on the day of the raid. It's more than just likely that he has connections to drug dealers. Maybe we can find out from whom he bought the drugs. This much ecstasy should have cost quite a bit, and you can't buy it at every street corner. Inès can check Simone, Léon's deputy general manager. But everything under the table. Not even Matisse can know anything. I don't want to drag him into this."

"Makes sense. No one will notice. We can work very discreetly."

"Is there anything else strange happening in the commissariat? Something I don't know of?"

"I don't think so. Only that Dubois is off on sick leave."

"If that's the worst..."

"I've been here for five years, and every single day Dubois has sat at his desk. Not a single absence."

"Sooner or later even the best people get ill. Don't tell him that I wish him well. He doesn't have to know that we have had any contact."

"Sure. But I will definitely talk to him once he's back. He's been Poutin's partner for decades. They even go together to Pétanque. If someone noticed anything, it's Dubois."

"Okay, but be careful."

"The guy likes you, despite you being a bit brusque from time to time."

"Nice to hear that." She checked her watch. "I'm expected in town."

"I've got to go too. Where shall we meet next?"

"I drive home in the evenings. You're very welcome to come over for dinner. Whenever you have time."

"Will Rosalie cook?"

"Would you show up sooner then?"

"Cooking isn't one of your special talents." He avoided the rhetorical question. She knew that he thought she was a complete disaster in the kitchen. His parents ran one of the most prestigious Moroccan restaurants in the region, and one of his big sisters was working towards her first Michelin star. Sandrine was not a lousy cook. Adel was simply spoiled.

"I'll ask her. You will have to pay in new ideas for her next thriller."

"Oh, no problem."

They walked together outside.

"Adel," she called after him.

The car door already in hand, he turned back to her.

"Thank you for your help."

"Of course. We're partners and you would do the same for me."

"I still appreciate it a lot."

"We will get you out of this mess. I promise."

She wished she was as optimistic as Adel. In contrast to her partner, she knew de Chezac a lot better. Once she had underestimated the man, and she would never make that mistake again.

"Take care of yourself," she repeated.

"I will. And Inès has my back." He smiled once more at her, got in his car and drove off.

Sandrine turned around. On the top floor, the curtain of a closed window moved. *Madame Garaine is waiting for me to leave so she can get her peace back.*

She pulled her things from the motorbike's cases and put them on. She kept an eye on the front of the house, but nothing was moving. One could have thought the house was abandoned.

Slowly she drove to the exit and listened to the gravel crunch under the wheels. The perpetrator must have come the same way last night, but the tyres of the police cars had destroyed any older tracks.

Sandrine stopped at the office of the gendarmerie. It was on the town's main road, and straight opposite the town council. It was a one-storey dark stone building with barred windows that looked anything but inviting. Major Destin sat behind a writing desk covered in scratches and cigarette burns. It must have been an heirloom from generations of police officers.

"You went back to the crime scene? Find anything else?"

"I had a short chat with Madame Garaine, the housekeeper,

though I have to admit that it didn't lead to any new insights. At the time of the crime the woman was in her room and claims to have heard nothing of what happened in the library. As to the relationships of the Saviers, she's closed up like an oyster."

"Pretty tough and cold as a fish, that woman. You should have seen how she commanded the gardener. I would not want to be married to her." He rolled his eyes. The housekeeper must have impressed the man, though he was not very sensitive when commanding his own people. She remembered the pile of books Madame Garaine had brought back to the library. Her cold demeanour seemed to be a façade. The question was, who did she want to protect herself from and what did she have to hide? She was a woman with secrets, and Sandrine needed to find out what they were.

"In my case too, she gave nothing but criticism in Arnault's direction. I'm wondering why she hasn't fired him yet."

"Do you think she would be more pleased with the next employee? Unlikely."

"Did forensics find anything interesting?" She returned to the investigation at hand. They would have lots of time for gossip as soon as an observation came along. After sitting together in a car for hours on end one normally knew more of one's colleague than one would have liked.

Destin placed a thin personal planner on the table and pushed it towards her.

"The fingerprints have been taken and run through the database. It could take a while longer. I bet we will only find the victim's. At least we have the fingerprints of the Saviers. Someone broke into the house last winter."

"A break-in." That piqued her interest. It could be a coincidence, but maybe it was not. Fréderic Savier's murderer had searched for something in the library and the notary's office. Maybe not for the first time.

"What was stolen?" she asked.

"An older laptop and some jewellery. Stuff of no value."

"Can I see the file?"

"Of course. I will get someone to find it. You will not be able to find much in it though. Just some fingerprints from the burglar which we could not assign to anyone. The perpetrators were not in the system."

She took the personal planner and turned the pages to today's date.

"J. Robine, or something like it. The man had terrible handwriting. With three exclamation marks. 'Today at 4:00 p.m.,'" she read.

"Unfortunately for us, it does not say where the meeting point is. It makes it a lot harder to track down this Robine. It could be anywhere, in his house, the chancellery, or any café or restaurant. Maybe it is not even in Bécherel." He leaned back in his chair and crossed his hands behind his neck. "The victims never make it easy."

"At least not in the beginning of an investigation. Sooner or later all the evidence begins to link, and a clear picture is created. But we aren't that far yet."

"We have no trace of this J. Robine. He is not in the phone book. We found only one person with that name in a village roughly 30km from here. The guy is over 80 and his daughter cares for him. That does not make him a very likely candidate."

"Definitely not someone who would have anything to do with Savier and deserve three exclamation marks." She sat down. "The letter J could be for a woman or a man. We shouldn't jump to any conclusions here."

"Sure, but we could not find a Josephine, Julie, Jeanette or any other Madame Robine."

"Maybe it isn't a person."

"A company? Maybe a lucrative job or a client in the law firm? A lot is possible here."

"Who knows?"

"Madame Descours did not know a man of that name. I sent an officer there. Should there be a visitor at 4:00 p.m. he will hold him there and we will be notified," said Destin. "There was only this one appointment in the calendar for today. Nothing else. Also, for most other days there were barely any entries. I assume the calendar was for private purposes. The secretary had her own calendar for the business. I bet the visitor was expected at his private house."

"Very possible. If I was going with my gut feeling, I would keep an eye on the antique shop. This afternoon at 4:00 p.m., the book club is meeting there. He was their president. I don't think he would miss that. Maybe J. Robine was a new member, and the note is completely harmless."

"Or he wanted to keep the meeting with J. Robine a secret from the other members and made it for a time when everyone would be busy and in the antique shop. He could have excused himself for professional reasons. Pierre Salazar would have been happy to take over the meeting."

"Also possible. Until we find the mysterious visitor we're searching in the dark."

"Then let us separate," the major suggested. "I keep an eye on the estate, and you blend in with the bookworms in Neville's junk room."

"Have you been to the antique shop Rabelais before?" Sandrine asked in surprise.

Destin opened his bag and took out a file which he handed her.

"I got his police records for you. The man has been repeatedly accused of dealing in counterfeit antiques or stolen goods. However, we could never prove anything. Either he was warned in time, or he actually has a clean slate. We do not have any specialists in the office who could quickly check the authenticity of any of these dusty finds."

"I'll have a look around. Maybe I'll notice something," she offered.

"You know about books?"

"Just a bit." She played down her experience. Her father had an exclusive lifestyle at the Côte d'Azur which was financed by making copies of paintings, which her uncle Thomas occasionally exchanged with the originals behind closed doors. Everything she knew about art, counterfeits, break-ins and the sale of stolen goods she had learned in the circle of her family. You learn for life, her uncle always said, and he was right. She had caught a handful of burglars because she knew exactly how they worked and where they would sell their loot.

"Then let's go. I will call you if something happens at the estate," Destin said.

"Sounds like a plan."

* * *

On the way to his desk, Inès Boni caught Adel by his arm and pulled him into her office.

"You met her, right?" she asked before she had barely closed the door.

"Of course. What did you think I was doing in Bécherel?"

"How is she?" Since the allegations had been made the office manager had not seen Sandrine, only spoken with her on the phone. The worry about Sandrine was plain to hear in her voice, and Adel was tempted to calm her. However, Inès did not deserve to be lied to.

"Not very well, as you can imagine. She tries her best to

seem as cool and collected as always. As expected, she tried to stop me from interfering with the investigation."

"And you refused."

"She gave a few good arguments, but of course I will get her out of this mess. We're partners and I know she's innocent."

"We will get her out of this." Inès stayed adamant.

"Think about it. It could cost you your job."

"Are you really afraid that I can't get anything better than this here?"

"No," Adel said. He thought Inès was extremely competent and was convinced that she could always get a more lucrative position. He strongly doubted though that she would love it as much as her current job.

"So, what's our plan?" Her voice was unusually hoarse and trembled slightly from suppressed tension. It had always been her deepest wish to get more involved in investigative work than just doing the paperwork. Now was her chance to prove that she had a real cop inside her, and she was determined to not screw it up.

"She trusts Léon," Adel said. "Her gut feeling has always been right, and so I assume that he really isn't dealing."

"Me too. He's a nice guy, and I never noticed any drugs in the Équinoxe. At least none which people didn't bring from home."

"Then we will remove him from the suspect list. I will stop by him anyway."

"I can't think of any other suspects," she said with an underlying sigh of frustration. Adel guessed that she had already been wracking her brains for days to find who could have been the one to blame Sandrine.

"She thinks Albert Chauvin capable of having smuggled the drugs into the office," said Adel. "I will talk to him this afternoon."

"Won't they notice? Poutin is keeping a watchful eye on anyone who's interested in the investigation. We should tread carefully."

"We got Chauvin for human trafficking, and that's still my case. No one will think anything of it if I question the man again."

"If you talk to Chauvin you will have to go through Lianne." She sounded worried and scrutinised him.

"I'm over her. I told Sandrine the same. The times in which I fell for her tricks are over."

"Good," she said, but there was still a wisp of doubt in her voice. She knew him too well. "And what shall I do?"

"Check the files. We need to find out who was part of the raid and who discovered the drugs. Sandrine doesn't believe that one of our own could be behind this, but I don't have that much trust."

"De Chezac and Poutin. That's easy. No one else in the commissariat knew about the raid or worked on it. Not even Commissaire Matisse."

"Can you access the files about the drugs? What type of ecstasy it was and where it came from? There's talk it was taken from our evidence locker. We need to check that."

"Sure. It won't be easy to find an excuse, but I will do my best."

"That's always enough," Adel nodded. He had known Inès for years. If she did not manage to get to the documents, no one would.

"Dubois is still off sick for the next few days," Inès said and looked in the direction of his neat and tidy desk. It looked like the owner had taken all personal belongings and did not plan on ever returning.

"You also think that's strange?"

"The man has never been ill, which I know as I'm the one taking the attendance lists."

"Let's wait. If he doesn't come back, we'll visit him."

"They will notice. You aren't exactly the best of friends."

"It's a risk I'm willing to take. If someone noticed anything off about the way Poutin was acting it would be Dubois. The two of them are always together. I'll be on my way to Chauvin, then. He's probably in a container on the junkyard."

"I will take care of all the things here."

Adel turned to leave, but she held him back by his sleeve.

"If we need something from the technicians, Marie is off this morning. She and Jean-Luc are on our side. The man has been grumpy for days, which is unusual for him."

"Sandrine didn't believe that she has a bunch of support from friends in the commissariat. I hope she will open her eyes before she gives up altogether."

"She will need a thick skin tomorrow. Her name will be all over the newspapers."

"She knows. The Binet already found her in Bécherel. Sandrine's prepared," Adel said. He was aware that it was impossible to be fully prepared for the wave of public prejudice about to sweep over her. It would always hit her heart. However, for Sandrine it would push her to prove her innocence. At least, that was what he hoped.

Adel parked his car in front of the container which housed Albert Chauvin's office and got out. He straightened the light blue polo shirt he had just changed into before leaving the office. He always kept some freshly ironed and folded shirts in his locker. With the heatwave tormenting Brittany, he went through his reserves rather quickly. To turn up to a questioning in a sweat-soaked outfit was not an option for the brigadier. Style had always been important to him, and even for someone like Albert Chauvin who had his office in a junkyard and oversaw the yard, and his less-than-legal business, he did not make an exception. Like a spider in its web, he sat in the container. The windows were barred and marbled with corrosion which blistered through the formerly white paint. The air-conditioning was rattling loudly in the fight against the unusual heat.

Two men in towing company overalls got out of the container and held the door open for him. The air inside was sweltering with an overpowering lemon-zest-air-freshener scent that did little to mask the smell of sweat and cigarette smoke.

"Ah, our guardian of law and order," Chauvin greeted him with a tone that dripped sarcasm like a kebab skewer dripped fat on a grill. The secretary reached for a half-full cigarette pack and stood up. Without another word she left the office. Adel assumed that the woman had worked with Chauvin long enough to know when it was time for a smoking break. A visit from the police was clearly one of them. Perhaps she had seen her boss being questioned by the police so many times that by now she was simply bored. The cheap plastic door slammed against the frame behind her, not latching. The man pointed at the chair in front of his desk.

"No idea if it's worth it. I don't have much to say, but feel free to sit down."

"It won't take long." The chair's upholstery was dusty, and in some places so thin that crumbs of foam padding spilled out. Adel preferred to stay standing.

"What's this about? If you want to talk about that human trafficking you want to blame on me, you should call my lawyer. She forbids me to say anything to you or your colleague." His eyes travelled over the brigadier and a snide grin spread over his face. He then coughed and spat in his handkerchief. Most likely not a sign of particular respect towards the police.

Adel suppressed his anger. People who took care of their looks and who cared about manners seemed to be unfavourable to the man.

"Blame? We have enough evidence to guarantee your conviction. This time you won't get away with a warning."

"My lawyer would disagree with you," he answered and wiped a piece of cloth over his face. A bit of fluff got stuck to his sweaty skin and looked like a pus-filled pimple. "She's pretty clever. But who am I telling this to? You know her better than I do." He threw a blow at the relationship which Adel and Lianne Roche, the lawyer, had had.

"That's long ago. Many things have changed since then."

"Ah," Chauvin waved his objection aside. "People don't change. At most the whitewash. Underneath we always remain the same. You're no match for Lianne Roche. It's not an insult, but the woman knows what she's doing."

"We will see," Adel answered and hoped that it sounded like more than just an empty threat.

"So, why are you harassing me?"

"When did you last visit the Club Équinoxe?"

"Oh dear, the questions you ask." He scratched his chin and blew air through his lips. "It must have been a few months ago. I'm too old for bars like that. It's too loud, too many little boys and the music is crap."

"Are you sure?"

"The owner is Léon Martinau. He will confirm to not having seen me in a long time."

"I'll ask him."

Chauvin leaned forward until he rested his forearms on the desk. His sardonic grin deepened. "Must be hard to be ordered around by a woman. Especially for someone from your background. There women jump when the men snap their fingers."

Adel fought with himself not to tell the guy, his belly

protruding between shirt and trousers, anything of his *background*. He was born in Beziers and had grown up in Brittany. It would not help. Either Chauvin really was as much of a racist as he seemed to be, or he just wanted to throw him off balance. *Most likely both.*

"They found drugs on your boss' lover, they say." Chauvin pulled a half-full glass of water towards him, took a bottle of Pastis from a drawer and poured. "Must've been pretty embarrassing for her. To hop in the sheets with a criminal." He shook his head. "The things you hear. On the other hand, the way she acts I shouldn't have been surprised."

"What do you know about the drugs?"

"Me?" His chair gave a tortured squeal as he straightened, hands open like a minister on a pulpit. "For a while your colleagues have been trying to blame me for all kinds of things, but drugs and stuff like that is new." He let his gaze wander theatrically. "Or does this place look like a meth-lab to you?"

The door opened and Adel turned around. The sight of Lianne Roche hit him like a punch in the stomach. *What is she doing here?*

"How nice. I was just on the way to my client." Her intonation was sharp like a razorblade and the threat was obvious. "No one questions him without my presence. I thought I had made myself clear in that regard."

"It's not about the human trafficking," Adel answered, and hoped his voice sounded more confident than he felt.

"Is that so?"

She sauntered past him in her carefully chosen business-suit and stood next to Albert Chauvin, who had crossed his arms in front of his chest. It looked like he had not changed his clothes in days.

"They want to frame me. They say I had something to do

with the drugs found in Léon's place," he said and looked up at her.

"Did you?" the lawyer asked without looking at the man. Her eyes were trained on Adel. She was first class in not having to blink.

"I've no idea where they got that idea from," Chauvin answered.

"I can explain it to you. His boss got involved with Léon Martinau's criminal business. Now that they have been discovered they are looking for a scapegoat. As there is a case running against you, Capitaine Perrot must have thought it would be easy to throw drug dealing on the pile."

"That's not true," Adel blurted out, and at the same time he was annoyed that the woman could provoke him into overreacting that quickly.

"Really, Brigadier. What good would it do my client to slip drugs to Léon Martinau? It would just cost him a lot of money and amount to nothing."

"What about revenge on the woman who finally managed to send him to court?"

"That's a very unconvincing reason, and a lot of people would qualify for seeking revenge," replied Lianne Roche.

"It would serve your client well if the investigator's reputation was compromised."

Chauvin looked up at the woman with questioning eyes. She placed her hand on his shoulder like a schoolteacher with an elementary school student.

"Her credibility would be destroyed," she translated for him.

"Why doesn't he say so?"

"Drugs are not needed to question her value as an investigator," the lawyer continued. "In Paris disciplinary proceedings were running against Capitaine Perrot. She was demoted and suspended from duty for some time. She was only able to avoid being expelled from the police force by agreeing to be transferred to Saint-Malo. The woman is no shining example of a devout policewoman." She looked at Adel and triumph flashed in her eyes. "Please, correct me if I am wrong, Brigadier Chief de Police Adel Azarou." She stressed every single syllable to underline her point. Adel knew she felt like she was his intellectual superior, but now was not the time to provoke an argument. Especially because she was not totally wrong, if one presented the facts in such a manipulative way.

"Then I will note that Albert Chauvin claims to have nothing to do with the drugs."

"I'm innocent," the man confirmed again, while she only looked at Adel like a reptile might look at its prey.

"We will meet in court." Adel stood up and left the container. In front of the door, he waited for a lorry with car-wrecks to drive past. On the opposite side, the secretary sat on a bench in the shadow of some high, dusty bushes with drooping branches. He nodded her way and opened his car.

"You're here for the drugs from the club, right?" she asked, taking him by surprise.

"Correct. Can you tell me something about them?"

"Albert isn't a very nice person and has done a few things not quite on the legal side."

"I would call that an understatement," he had to comment.

"No drugs though. He's got nothing to do with that."

"Why are you so sure?"

"He hates drugs like the plague. His mother died of an overdose under a bridge in Rennes. He was young, so it burned into his memory. Albert doesn't touch or deal with the stuff. That's just not an option." She pressed the cigarette butt on the wooden bench and threw the filter on the ground to join some others. The secretary did not acknowledge him again, just stood up and returned to the container.

Adel looked after her. He thought the man capable of every crime, but something in the woman's voice convinced him that Chauvin was not the culprit in this case.

Sandrine parked her motorbike in front of the antique shop and looked at her watch. The book club's members should have assembled by now. She entered the bookshop and came across Margritte carrying a tray with cake.

"Is that for the treasure hunters?"

"Oh yes, the shop isn't only named after Rabelais. The bookworms eat so much that Gargantua and Pantagruel would have been proud."

A look at the cake tray seemed to confirm that. Everyone knew the two ravenous giants from Rabelais' stories. They had even made it into everyday language. If someone spoke of a *pantagruelian* appetite or a *gargantuan* meal everyone knew what one was talking about.

"Art makes you hungry," Sandrine said. "I have to go upstairs anyway. Shall I take this up for you?" She reached for the tray.

"That's nice of you. I will bring up some bottles of Cidre too."

Sandrine climbed the tight stairs. They creaked so loudly, it put any modern alarm system to shame. A glimpse into the small corridors between the stuffed shelves made it clear that the shop did not need any protection from burglars. Well-read paperbacks with yellowed pages piled high on wobbly tables. It reminded her more of the home of a compulsive hoarder than of an antique shop. The air smelled stale, and barely any sunlight filtered through the dusty windows. The place had not been touched by fresh air in what felt like a century. At the end of the room, behind several tables with vinyl records, sat roughly a dozen men on cheap folding chairs.

"Ah, there's the food. Madame Violinet must've made something especially nice for us." Monsieur Neville, the shop's owner, rose and had to save his greasy corduroy pants from falling to the floor with a courageous grip. With more skill than she had given him credit for, he unfolded an aluminium camping table. Sandrine looked around for a rag with which to wipe away the greasy layer of dust, but the man did not bother with such trifles, simply grabbing the cake tray and putting it on the table.

"Thank you very much. Are you Margritte's new helper?"

"No, she definitely isn't." The thin voice rose a pitch with each word until it stopped just before breaking into panic.

I know that one. She turned towards the members of the book club. He sat in the first row.

"Monsieur Salazar, what a surprise to see you again."

The petite man's mouth twisted as if she had readied the drill for a dental procedure. His joy at seeing her was definitely limited, which she could understand. In the case of the murder of Aimée Villette, they had put the unsuccessful thriller writer through the wringer, and on top of that he had lost his publisher. She doubted that he had found a new one.

"That's not a waitress but a policewoman from Saint-Malo. Lieutenant Perrot, if I remember correctly," he informed the other members.

"You are correct, Monsieur Salazar. Though by now I'm Capitaine."

"Then you must be here because of the awful thing with Fréderic." The antiquarian jumped into the conversation, holding a breadknife next to the cake tray. "I'm Albert Neville, the owner of the Rabelais."

"You are assuming correctly."

"We have nothing to do with his death, nothing at all," Pierre Salazar stuttered and swallowed up whole syllables.

"It's okay, Pierre. No one will assume that. We are book lovers, not barbarians and definitely not criminals." Neville tried to calm him.

"I'm not here to accuse anyone. I just want to learn more about Fréderic Savier. He was a member of your book club, wasn't he?"

"Not only that," Neville said, "he was the president, the soul of the treasure hunters."

A murmur of agreement filled the room.

"You can stay here. I just have a few questions, and then will let you get on with your business," she called after a man who had slipped from his folding chair and was sneaking towards the stairs.

"Will be back in a sec. Nature's calling."

"Then I will take your name now."

"Why?" The man straightened and looked at her with widened eyes.

"Simple routine. Nothing else."

"That's Marcel, our bookbinder," Neville introduced him. "A true artist who can make old treasures sparkle again."

The man threw a thankful look at Neville before turning and climbing down the stairs.

"After Fréderic's sudden end, Pierre is now our new president," Neville determined.

Salazar pressed his back so hard into the chair that he grew a few centimetres and looked around as if waiting for applause.

"We have several authors, an illustrator, Jacques the calligraphist, our pharmacist, a few craftsmen and businessmen in our club. All of them bibliophiles." The men nodded when Neville looked at them or mentioned their professions.

"And you are?" Sandrine asked a man in the last row who

fitted into the group like a flamingo in between blackbirds. He was dressed with taste and with an ease that required money and time in front of the mirror. In contrast to the others the revelation of her being a policewoman did not seem to have startled him. The man felt like the infamous wolf among sheep. *What brought him here?*

"Alain Ducasse," he answered nonchalantly. "But I'm no member of this club. You could say that coincidence brought me here."

"What coincidence?"

"I was looking for a well-preserved first edition, and this antique shop was recommended to me."

"From a specific author?"

He chuckled. "You got me. I'm a businessman and need presents for clients who show more passion for reading than I. That's why I count on the expertise of Monsieur Neville."

The stairs creaked and announced Margritte balancing a tray with four jugs of Cidre and an array of glasses.

"Something to drink is on the way," she called.

"Thank you for your attention, Madame Violinet," Neville called back with more theatrics than necessary. Exactly the sort of fuss he probably figured might distract Sandrine from his guest.

"A traditional Farz Gwad from the Farz Gwad's kitchen," Margritte said and smiled happily.

"Then let's eat." The antiquarian cut a few pieces resembling squares from the cake and distributed them on the plates. The Far was four to five centimetres high and had a strong deep colour. Sandrine easily spotted the plums at the bottom. Nothing held the bibliophiles on their chairs anymore, and they jumped up to get pieces as big as possible. When order returned and everyone went back to their chairs, Monsieur Ducasse had disappeared. Sandrine was annoyed that she had let him slip past her, but she was convinced that she would see him again. His reason for being there seemed plausible, but her gut feeling told her that there might be more to it than that.

"May I also offer you a piece?" The antiquarian offered a plate to her. Cold cigarette smoke wafted off him and she took a step back.

"Maybe a small one," Margritte pushed between them, "the plums are pitted with rum, of course, and not just a little. After a big piece of Far no one should ride a motorbike."

"Then I will postpone it to Sunday. Rosalie will most likely drive me to the book presentation. I'm looking forward to it." Sandrine turned to Neville. "How does your shop participate in the book market?"

"Well, we're open on a Sunday, isn't that something?"

"Well." Margritte wiped her hands on her apron. "A booth outside with a bit of fresh air wouldn't hurt."

"Humidity, heat and sunlight aren't good for my books. Some are very rare." He pointed at an open display case filled with leather bound books. "Feel free to touch one. The covers are of such a high quality you can't find anymore, and don't even get me started on the drawings."

"Thank you." Sandrine took one and leafed through a few chapters.

"Aren't those ornaments breathtaking? And the figurative representations, clearly Renaissance. And yet extremely well-preserved, as if they had been painted yesterday."

"Very pretty," she answered.

"Pretty?" He yanked the book from her. "They're more than pretty. It's art, priceless art."

"Sandrine didn't mean it that way." As if by coincidence, Margritte moved again between Sandrine and the angry man.

"I'm sorry," she apologised. "I don't have much knowledge concerning books."

"Well, they won't ask for it in your job." He put the book back and mumbled, "Standards are slipping."

"I have work downstairs." Margritte said her goodbyes.

Pierre Salazar joined them. His curiosity seemed to win over his desire to stay away from her.

"Were you expecting Monsieur Savier today?"

"Of course," answered the author and pushed up on his toes to look Sandrine straight in the eye. "He was the president of the treasure hunters."

"The members of the club share the passion of finding rare books?"

"We save them from decay. You have no idea what treasures are rotting in shabby flea markets or in underappreciated inheritances."

"What do you do once you find a book?"

"We give them new life." Neville took over the conversation again. "In Bécherel you will find all the skills you need: bookbinders, calligraphers, painters and of course dealers and customers who still appreciate such works."

"So, it's about selling the books?" She threw the bait.

"Definitely not!" Salazar snapped at it. "It's all about the love for the written word."

"Our friend Pierre is a true idealist." Neville winked at Sandrine. "Who's also joined us book dealers."

She threw a questioning look at Salazar. The last time they had spoken he had been a teacher at a gymnasium in a grammar school, in Saint-Malo. She doubted that his students were shedding tears over his absence.

"The job of a teacher wasn't enough for me anymore. Interest in literature is waning at a worrying speed."

"Still, a bookshop?"

"My passion: thrillers. I have specialised in crime literature. Novels that stand out from the dreary crowd."

"To answer your question, selling the books is my department." The antiquarian could not bear to listen to the conversation any longer without being the centre of attention. "Skilful restoration of old works is a costly undertaking. Every now and then we have to part with some treasures with a heavy heart in order to be prepared for further discoveries."

"Is there a market for books like that?"

"Yes, of course, but you need to know the right people."

"And you do?"

"Of course," he assured her, his chest swelling with pride. "The Rabelais couldn't survive from tourists and the book markets alone. The situation is different, of course, in the bookstores that offer trivial literature, women's stuff and useless odds and ends." He could apparently not resist a dig at Margritte's shop, which specialised in what he probably understood to be *women's stuff*.

"We found an entry in Monsieur Savier's calendar: J. Robine, 4:00 p.m. As this is the time when the book club meets, I assumed that it must have some connection to the club."

"Robine, you say? No, that doesn't ring a bell. We don't have a member with that name. Maybe he was expecting a visitor from outside and forgot to let us know."

A trained investigator like Sandrine did not miss the short hesitation and the twitch of the eye towards Salazar. Both of them knew something about the name, but they would not admit it. She decided to keep the men in the belief that she trusted their ignorance.

"I need a list with the names of all the members."

"No problem, Alfonse will write a list for you." He looked at a young man in a suit way too large for him. He exuded funeral vibes. His blond hair stood in spikes away from his head, and Sandrine wondered if it was a style decision or more out of disinterest in his appearance.

"Is there any other way we can help you? If not, we would like to start our meeting. After the tragic death of Fréderic we have lots to discuss." Neville tried to end her visit.

"For now, I'm happy. Just one more thing. On Monsieur Savier's desk we found the abbreviation JJLFA on a bit of paper. It looked like he wanted to hide it. Have you come across it before?"

"JJ and after?" Salazar asked.

"LFA."

"No, sorry. Those letters don't mean anything to me. Maybe it's something from his work?"

"I agree," Louis Neville chimed in. "You should ask at the office."

"I will. Thank you for your help."

She said goodbye and made her way to the steps. There was not a lot that she had actually learned from the meeting, but there were many things she had to think about. Neville and Salazar had heard the name Robine before, and she had to find out more about that. She also wanted to learn more about Alain Ducasse. Maybe he had been the man with whom Savier had planned to meet. He definitely did not fit to the otherwise drab group she had just encountered in the Rabelais.

"Capitaine Perrot?"

She turned around. Pierre Salazar stood a few steps above her on the stairs.

"Can I help you with something?"

"You know," he stepped closer, and his voice dropped to a whisper, "the little mishap with my last novel..." His voice broke and he looked at her pitifully. To speak of the 'mishap' was bold. The man had stolen an entire novel and passed it off as his own work.

"I don't know how this is connected to the case at hand, or why you would bring this up now."

"Thank you very much," he stammered, turned and rushed back up the stairs.

Sandrine nearly overlooked the little group as she was about to leave the shop. Half-hidden behind a shelf, sat Margritte Violinet with half a dozen women at one of the café's tables. Sandrine just wanted to nod as a goodbye, when her eyes locked on Madame Garaine, the victim's housekeeper. She stopped and gave the group a closer inspection. *And there's also Madame Descours, the secretary.* She had to find out what connected the women.

"Mesdames, what a coincidence to meet you all here."

A soft blush shot into Fleur Garaine's cheeks as if Sandrine had caught them doing something forbidden. Jocelyn Descours on the other hand did not go to too much trouble to mask her dismissive gaze. Sandrine did not know who the other women were.

"Sandrine, come sit with us," Margritte invited her. It was slightly too loud and fast to seem genuine. She was interrupting their circle. That was obvious.

"I don't want to interrupt your meeting."

"Ah, so what." The bookseller pulled a chair close and smiled at her. She had caught herself quickly while Madame Garaine avoided direct eye contact. "We all indulge in the same hobby and meet here once a week for coffee, cake and to talk about the book we are currently reading in our little circle."

"Like the treasure hunters up there." Sandrine pointed her finger at the ceiling.

"No, not really," a woman with dark skin and curly, black hair replied. "The men up there are collectors, but definitely not readers." The assembled women nodded their agreement. Between the two book clubs there seemed to be little sympathy.

"I can't judge that." Sandrine gripped the chair's backrest and leaned on it.

"I'm Florence Cassian, by the way," the woman introduced herself. She could not be older than her early forties. Her wavy hair fell down to her shoulders and framed a slim face with dark eyes that managed to look at Sandrine with curiosity while keeping their distance.

"Fréderic Savier's partner?"

"Only in business. What happened to him is terrible. We just met last night."

"You did?"

"Oh yes. I wanted to cancel. After an exhausting day at court, I didn't want to go, but the man was a little obsessive with his appointments. He insisted and so I drove over." She looked at Madame Garaine. "Fleur let me in. That should have been around 7:00 p.m."

"I already told you that," Madame Garaine interjected.

"I wanted to keep the meeting short. The man can be a bit difficult."

"In what way?"

"In the way that he tried to bore one to death with his monologues. There wasn't anything in the world he loved more than rambling on about something that rarely deserved that much attention."

"That's very true," Madame Descours agreed. "Sometimes I hid from him when there was other work to be done that could not wait."

"So you had a quick chat with him, had a coffee and drove off again?" Sandrine watched intently how she would react.

"That devil's potion from his library?" She looked at Madame Garaine. "I'm sorry, Fleur. I know it's not your fault."

"He gave strict instructions as to how the coffee was to be prepared," the housekeeper defended herself.

"No, I don't drink coffee, and Fréderic never had an acceptable tea. Those discounter teabags aren't for me."

The outrage about the drinks at Monsieur Savier's was harsh but seemed genuine. *He therefore received another visitor who did not shy away from his coffee. So, he was still alive when she left.*

"That makes you the last person who saw him alive," said Sandrine.

"Except the murderer, of course," replied the lawyer routinely. She must have used this sentence many times in court.

"We found an entry in his calendar for today at 4:00 p.m. J. Robine." Sandrine watched the two women from the chancellery who were sitting next to each other. "Have you heard the name before?"

"Robine," Madame Cassian repeated and looked away. Finally, she shook her head. "Never heard of it. And you?" She turned to the secretary.

"That cannot be one of our clients. I am sure of it. I already told this major the same thing," she said in a tone that was a tad too harsh for the occasion, which Sandrine might have missed had she not deliberately thrown out that bait to see the women's reactions.

"Shame." *It would have been too easy.* "Then we have to keep searching."

"Were the men upstairs able to help you?" Margritte asked. All the women turned their heads in Sandrine's direction as if it was now their turn to analyse her reaction.

"No, unfortunately not." *But Louis Neville and Pierre Salazar reacted to the name. And I am sure you know more than you are willing to share with me.* She did not even try to ask about the abbreviation on the post-it. The women would deny having heard of it. First, she had to find out more and then question each individual member of the reading group. The women definitely knew more than they let on. The question was: what were they trying to hide?

"Then I'm on my way back to Cancale. I'm sure we will meet again during the upcoming days. Investigations have just started." She did not try to hide the undercurrent of a threat in her voice. It could be useful to ruffle some feathers in the reading group.

"The latest at Rosalie's book presentation," said Margritte. "We will not miss out on a famous author visiting."

Sandrine said goodbye and left the bookshop. A couple of new messages showed on her phone. One was from Léon who wanted to see her. She typed her answer and let the phone slip back in her pocket.

"Madame Capitaine," someone called after her.

She stopped and turned around, already holding her helmet. It was the pale, young man from the antique shop. His name was Alfonse if she remembered correctly.

"Monsieur Neville asked me to give you the list of members."

She looked at the sheet. The names of 30 to 40 people had been listed, including addresses, and printed. *Must have been from a spreadsheet.*

"He threatened a handwritten list," she joked.

"Of course we have a computer. Monsieur Neville is always very suspicious towards any changes. What he doesn't like he ignores." The man looked back over his shoulder as if he feared his boss was towering behind him.

"Thank you very much."

"I didn't eavesdrop," he started but then stopped as if bravery had deserted him.

"I didn't think so, but we must have been loud enough for you to hear. We weren't discussing anything secret."

"True," he quickly agreed. "There's no member with the name of Robine. I also couldn't find anyone of that name in our client and merchant database, but I remember that Monsieur Savier took a call Monday afternoon in the antique shop. Monsieur Neville doesn't like that at all. I heard him mention that name. I assumed it was one of his business partners. But of course, I can't be certain."

"What phone did he use?"

"His mobile phone."

"Thank you. That really helps." Now she just had to wait for Savier's phone provider to give them the information and go through the numbers.

"Should you need anything else you should directly come to me. I'm on the top floor."

"Sounds good. Should you remember any more about this Robine, you can call me anytime." She pulled a business card from her jacket and handed it over to him.

"I definitely will," he promised, turned and went back to the house.

Sandrine swung onto her motorbike and slowly drove off. In her rear-view mirror she saw Alfonse stand at one of the bookshop's windows as if he wanted to make sure that she really left Bécherel.

* * *

Sandrine pulled into the driveway and parked her motorbike next to the garage in which the Citroën 2CV was parked. She had inherited the car from her aunt. Léon's car was parked in front of her apartment in the outbuilding. It had been a former sheep stable into which she had moved during spring. The main house had been rented to Rosalie for a couple of years now.

Sandrine did not have the time or money to care for the big building.

Connected to the outbuilding was a lawn, slanting down to the garden wall. The Brittany Coastal Path ran just behind her property, a hiking trail that circled all of Brittany. One day she would take enough time for the hike. When there was no murder to be investigated. Behind the hiking trail, the coast broke off steeply towards the sea. On a clear day, her view stretched across the bay all the way to Mont-Saint-Michel and the Normandy coast. Leaving Paris and settling in Cancale on the Emerald Coast was a decision she had not come to regret. However, that could soon change as her problems from Paris caught up with her. Maybe I will have to leave all of this, she thought, and a feeling of wistfulness swelled up in her. *But I won't give up that easily.*

She circled the house and found Léon on a sunbed in the garden.

"I'm sorry, it took a bit longer." She leaned forward and kissed his cheek.

"I don't mind waiting for this view." His eyes travelled over her, and a happy smile made his eyes sparkle.

"You must mean the bay."

"Or the dangerous woman I want to kiss."

She was holding the shoulder holster with her gun which she had kept locked up in her motorbike's case all day. When they had first met, he had also called her a dangerous woman.

"How dangerous it is to know me is something you are experiencing yourself at the moment. It looks like I've already dragged you into trouble." She put the gun and her helmet on the small garden table and shrugged out of her jacket. It must still be way over 20 °C. With a little sigh she let herself drop onto the second sunbed. He handed her a bottle of lukewarm water.

"The good stuff is inside." He pointed with his thumb at the small house. "So, you have to be content with what I have to offer."

Quickly she thought about giving him a key but decided against it. They did not know each other well enough yet. She was used to living alone and not ready for another human to come and go as he pleased.

"Water is just what I need." The bottle cap clicked when she opened it, and she took a big gulp.

"You still think someone is actually targeting you?"

"You assured me that you had no idea where the drugs came from."

He wanted to reply, but she waved him to stay quiet.

"It's okay, I believe you."

"Thank you," he said.

"You also think your manager is innocent."

"I would put my hand into an open flame for Simone. She's been with me since the founding of the club. I can always count on her."

"Then who's left? Someone slipped you the drugs."

"It's not as easy as it sounds. Your colleagues claim to have found the drugs in my safe. No one knows the code apart from Simone and me."

"Claim?"

"As you know well, I wasn't in the club that evening."

Sandrine smiled. It had been the first night they had spent together in the little hotel on Mont-Saint-Michel. His manager's call had reached him late in the night. When the raid had happened, he had been an hour's drive away from the Équinoxe.

"You think they're lying?"

"All I want to say is that I didn't come across any drugs when I was getting new change for the bar in the afternoon. Apart from Simone, no one was in my office. Tell me how they got inside if it wasn't your colleagues who brought them?"

She leaned back into the soft cushions of the sunbed and looked into the clear sky. She did not have a good answer.

"It's hard for me to imagine that a member of the police slipped you drugs."

"Your partner visited me today. He didn't seem as adverse to the thought as you. Especially after he talked to Chauvin," Léon commented.

"Brigadier Poutin, the one who found the drugs, doesn't like me. But what we're accusing him of would cost his job and maybe even send him to prison. I can't imagine that I'm worth taking such a risk."

"Think of the prosecutor. Another one who doesn't like you. It's possible your colleague thinks he's safe because he has someone to keep his back covered from above."

"If he was discovered, de Chezac would stand to lose a lot more than Poutin." Her throat felt tight and dry. She drank the rest of the water. "A warning about some little thing, maybe driving too fast or something. I wouldn't put that past him, but jeopardising his career to throw me out of the police force is overkill. The man is a careerist who thinks rationally, not one who lets himself be guided by desire for revenge or offended vanity. No, that doesn't go together."

"Maybe there's another motive that you have overlooked so far."

"I can't think of anything."

She stood up and went into the house. There was a bottle of white wine in the fridge which she took. The temperature was pleasant and fresh, and she poured them two glasses.

"Thank you." Léon took the offered drink.

"I'll still check out Albert Chauvin and his lawyer. Those two would stop at nothing to put a spoke in my wheel."

He put the untouched glass on the garden table and looked at her.

"Out with it," she demanded. "You look like you have something to tell me."

"You're a fantastic policewoman."

"One who doesn't like fake compliments at the moment."

"I mean it. But you're right, I have something to tell you."

She sipped on the wine and held the glass up. "Is that enough or should I take a big swig before you tell me?"

"Wouldn't hurt," he said with a calm and pensive inflection.

"This morning I stood next to a man whose brains swelled from his wounds without throwing up. I'm sure I will manage your news."

"Good, if you see it like that. You know my situation. It has taken the club years to get to where we are now. An entire team depends on my decisions, and they will lose their jobs if my license is revoked." He took a deep breath.

"It's okay. I know what you're getting at."

"Really?"

"Either you want to stop seeing me because you think you can get a deal with de Chezac or you hired Lianne Roche as your lawyer."

"I would never leave you," he said without a moment of hesitation.

"So, it's the lawyer." Now Sandrine took a big gulp from the wine.

"You were the one recommending her to me," he defended himself.

"That's not entirely true. You asked who the biggest bitch was with whom I had the displeasure of working. That's Lianne Roche, quite ahead of anyone else."

"From a policewoman's mouth that's a clear recommendation."

Despite knowing better, she could not withstand his grin.

"It's okay. The woman knows what she's doing. It will make de Chezac's life as hard as possible. But be careful, she can't be trusted. For a more lucrative deal she will drop you like a hot iron. She might even send you to prison because she knows that we're in a relationship."

"Do we have a relationship?" Léon straightened up and looked at her.

"Didn't you listen to me? You can't trust that woman."

"Yes, of course I listened to you. You said relationship, didn't you?"

"We're sleeping together after all," she retorted, annoyed. The word had slipped past when she wasn't paying attention.

"That's something different to a relationship." He stayed adamant.

She moved to sit next to him.

"I'm not much of a family person. I'm independent, like living alone and need a lot of freedom. My work hours are terrible..."

"And you lie across the whole bed."

"That too."

"Doesn't scare me."

"I can't cook."

"I cook. No problem."

She leaned her back against his chest and Léon wrapped her tenderly in his arms.

"Let's just see how it goes. I don't know if it's the right time at the moment."

"Every moment is perfect," he said gently. "But I don't want to push you."

For a while they sat together on the sunbed and enjoyed the warmth of the day, the silence, and the view over the bay.

The Rabelais

Her shoulder-length hair still wet from showering, Sandrine stood in front of her wardrobe and searched for the things she would need for her day. Léon had driven home after dinner and had spent the night at his. It was always busy in the Équinoxe on Friday nights, and they closed early in the morning hours. She found a message from him on her phone. He would come over in the afternoon if that worked for her. *Who knows where I will be.* It was complicated to manage and organise a life with her job. Her being sent to Bécherel was a perfect example. Her weekend would definitely be ruined. His work hours might be more regular, but equally relationship-destroying. When she came home from work on normal days, he was getting ready to drive to the club. Though she did not want to admit it to herself, she did not give what, with a lot of good will, could be called a budding relationship much of a chance of survival.

With enough time I'll go to the studio. Let's meet there, she texted back. They both trained at the same martial arts studio in Saint-Malo. It would be good to torture herself until her muscles hurt.

She pulled on a dark t-shirt and strapped on the shoulder holster. Her phone vibrated; it was Rosalie. *What does she want this early in the morning?*

"Good morning," she greeted her friend.

"Come over for breakfast." The surprising command fitted more to Major Destin than Rosalie. Sandrine looked through the window and over to the house. She was curious and wondered if there was anything out of the ordinary.

"Why? What's happened?"

"Just come over. I've put the kettle on." She ended the call, and Sandrine looked at her phone in surprise. Normally Rosalie was extremely polite. Sandrine had never experienced her that uncommunicative. *Strange.* To refuse an invitation for food was not an option, anyway. She had no food at home and had planned on buying a baguette on the way.

Sandrine took her gun from the safe, put it in the holster and was on her way to the main house. The helmet she hung over her motorbike's mirror and threw the jacket over the seat. A little tour with the Citroën 2CV was very tempting, especially with the open roof. However, the motorbike fitted her slightly irritated state a lot better.

She found Rosalie in the kitchen. The table had already been laid out. Next to the vase filled with flowers from the garden stood a breadbasket with fresh croissants, baguette and a few Chaussons aux Pommes, made with exactly the type of apple she liked best. The foam layer on top of the café au lait looked thick and stable, perfect to dip a croissant into.

"What's happened? Is there bad news, and you want to cheer me up?"

"Whether it's bad or not can be seen either way." Rosalie evaded the question. "I think first you should have a nice breakfast with a good friend. Afterwards, the world always looks better."

"Tell me!"

"No idea what you're talking about. Try a croissant, they're still warm." She pushed the breadbasket towards her.

Sandrine surveyed the room, and her eyes locked on a bunch of folded newspapers on a shelf. Before Rosalie could stop her, she grabbed the top one.

"Surely that nonsense can wait until after breakfast. It won't run away." Rosalie reached for the papers, but Sandrine quickly pulled them aside and her friend only caught empty air.

"Okay," Rosalie sighed in resignation. "But don't take it to heart."

Sandrine sat at the table and held one of the newspapers in her left hand. With the right she sipped from the coffee bowl and licked the foam from her upper lip.

"Very good." She dunked the tip of a croissant into the café au lait and took a bite while scanning over the newspaper's headlines.

"'Policewoman exposed as drug dealer's lover'," she read. "Fat and at the top of the front page."

"Leave that trash for later!"

"It's from the Binet. I didn't know we still had a score to settle. She's clearly doing that now. She's received more than one good tip from me in the past. Apparently, she's not a very grateful person."

"The woman is a careerist. She would sell her children for a front-page article. No one believes a word of what she writes."

"Unfortunately, the people do believe her. As soon as it's in the paper it's true, right? To doubt that would be stupid." *My career will be over with this. This uproar will be heard all the way to Paris.*

"And tomorrow they'll have forgotten all about it."

Sandrine kept reading and bit into her croissant from time to time.

"This is good: 'Capitaine Perrot has previously been accused of criminal offenses in Paris, which were swept under the carpet by the police after she agreed to be transferred to Saint-Malo. Our city deserves better than corrupt metropolitan cops.'"

She put the newspaper on the table. Now she knew why she had been invited for breakfast. Rosalie had tried to avoid her getting her hands on the articles without a friend around to cheer her up.

"In a few days no one will care anymore," Rosalie said. "You didn't do anything wrong, and they can't prove anything else." Her voice was heavy, and tears sparkled in the corners of her eyes.

"It was the same back in Paris. This time it won't be enough to just do nothing. Either I can clearly prove Léon's and my innocence, or that's my end in the police force."

It had only been a few months ago that she had written her notice. But that had been her own decision. She hated being forced to do something. It would be a personal defeat. They did not just want to get rid of her, they wanted to destroy her reputation and disgrace her. That wasn't something she would accept without a fight. She would not do de Chezac that favour. Maybe it was exactly what the prosecutor wanted, a fight which would show him as the superior. He had a clear advantage, and the man loved nothing more than winning a fight, especially when he could humiliate his opponent.

"Don't do anything stupid," Rosalie implored.

"Don't worry. To get out of this in one piece I can't make any emotional decisions. I have to think clearer than ever before."

"You have people supporting you."

Sandrine stood up and gave her a hug. For a few long breaths she kept her close.

"It helps to have you as a friend." She looked at the full table. "Thanks for the breakfast, even if I've lost my appetite over the news."

Rosalie managed a trembling smile and nodded without saying anything. Most likely she was unsure if her voice would obey her.

"Can you save the newspapers for me? Maybe I'll have time to read them later."

"I would prefer to throw them away or burn them."

"Better not. I need to know who I can trust in the future and who has connections to whom."

"What do you mean?"

"Well, some journalists are halfway cautious, while others are very imaginative with the accusations against me. Binet has written some stuff that sounds a lot like insider information from de Chezac. Maybe Adel is wrong, and the guy is deeper into all of this than he has assumed."

"You need to tread carefully. The guy has influential friends, and you don't."

"At least none in politics."

She put the rest of the croissant in her mouth and said her goodbyes. It was time to drive to Bécherel. There was work to be done.

On the way to the garage her phone rang. *Damn.* The loud ringing woke a bad premonition.

"Perrot."

"It's Major Destin."

"A call at this hour doesn't mean anything good. Or am I wrong?"

"I cannot deny it. A second corpse was found. We will meet in the bookshop..." His voice broke off. Most likely he was searching through his files for the name. "Farz Gwad?"

"Margritte Violinet? Is it her?"

"The owner? No. She was the one who called us. The corpse is supposed to be upstairs in the antique shop."

"Who is it?"

"She could not say for certain."

"Is it a stranger, or is the body too damaged to tell?"

"She spoke of two legs sticking out from under a pile of books and a heavy oak bookshelf. That is all that can be seen of the body. I am on my way and should be there in a few minutes. Doctor Duchamps has been notified."

"Depending on the traffic, I should be there in half an hour."

"No problem. Corpses do not run away, and forensics also needs time to get here from Rennes. We also have to talk about something else."

"What?"

"Not on the phone. It would be best with a Pastis or something stronger."

"Sounds mysterious. I'm curious."

She hung up and put her phone in one of the pockets of her motorbike jacket. Even though he made a secret of it, she was expecting it to be about the situation in Saint-Malo. The man must have read one of the daily newspapers or de Chezac had informed him. What else might the prosecutor have come up with to make her stumble?

Sandrine put on the helmet with the integrated Bluetooth speakers and loaded a playlist of old rock songs onto her cell phone. Her bad mood called for strong basses and smoky voices. She drove up the driveway and shortly after turned onto the Route départemental, which would take her straight to Bécherel. Matching a fast guitar solo from Guns N' Roses, she accelerated the BMW, and the fields and small wooded areas flew past her.

***

A good half hour, various speeding violations, and risky overtaking manoeuvres later, Sandrine stopped in front of the Farz Gwad. Alfonse was sitting on the terrace looking even paler than usual. He ignored the cup of coffee on the table and just stared straight ahead. The young man was obviously in shock.

I can rule him out as a suspect.

Margritte went to the door. Unlike Alfonse, the bookseller had not missed her arrival.

"How terrible. Something like this in my house," spilled from her. "At least he's still alive. I thought he was dead as a doornail."

"Who's still alive?"

Major Destin had spoken of a corpse, but Sandrine was relieved. She had seen more than enough dead people in her life.

"Louis. He's inside and complaining that he has to wait until he can go into his shop. At the moment, the police are sealing off everything. And you can see Alfonse. The poor boy found him this morning when he was opening up the shop. Of course, he had to assume that his boss had been murdered as well. It was hard on him, but he will be okay. I'll sit with him for a bit."

"That's very nice of you."

"It's the least I can do. We help each other here. Especially book-people."

"He will appreciate it." She looked over at the young man whose eyes stared at nothing. He barely seemed to realise what was happening around him.

"I have to go up to the antique shop now." Sandrine had nearly said *crime scene*, but it was unclear if it had been a crime or just an accident. It happened that people found themselves under a falling shelf and got hurt. Shelves and books were rarely used as weapons in violent crime, and the Rabelais did not take safety very seriously, so she assumed it was an accident.

The physician came her way with his leather bag in hand.
"How's Neville?"
"If stubbornness was an indication for health, he would be perfect." He looked over his shoulder back to the bookshop. "Someone gave him a proper hit with a round object, maybe a baseball bat, and he must have passed out instantly. He refuses to go to the hospital, so I had little choice but to stitch up the wound and leave him with some painkillers."
"Will you check on him again later?"
"Of course. The stubborn guy should at least have a good concussion if he has enough brains for that."
"I'll go inside and talk to him," she said to the doctor and went into the café part of the bookshop.
The antiquarian sat on a dainty chair and stared at her as if she had smacked him over the head herself.
"Good morning, Monsieur Neville. How are you?" Without asking him for permission she sat down at the table with him.
"Better than that quack thinks," he spat out. With his right hand he pressed a bag with ice cubes against the back of his head. That must have been where he had been hit.
"Can you tell me what happened?"
"I have already chewed through it with that rough block of a cop. But if I have to..."
"Unfortunately, yes. Maybe you noticed or remembered something in the meantime."

"On Sunday it's the book market and I have lots to prepare so I went to the Rabelais very early before we opened, to take care of the customers. Everything was how it always was. On the way to the office, I heard a noise and went to check."

"A burglar?"

"I didn't even go that far. My enemies are normally mice. The little beasts ruin my books in the shortest of times." He threw a look in the direction of the kitchen. "They are lured into this house. Madame Violinet should know better."

"And then?"

"It's an old building, and it has been refurbished several times. The light switches are on the opposite wall, so I had to feel my way forward in the dark. I remember that I stood between two shelves. Afterwards everything went black, and I woke up when someone yanked at my legs."

"Did you see the intruder?"

"No, they must have sneaked up on me and..." he clapped his flat hand on the table, "I was beaten down."

"Any idea why someone would break into an antique shop?"

His angry expression morphed into confusion and perplexity.

"Not the slightest. In the evening we clean out the till. Apart from a handful of change no burglar would find anything valuable. Unless he had an interest in books. But most of them are hard to sell without the right contacts."

"Have any been stolen?"

"How should I know?" he snapped at her. "Margritte and Alfonse pulled me out from under the books and then doctored me here in the café. Afterwards your colleague showed up and forbid me to enter my own shop."

"Forensics will be here soon, and we don't want to change anything on the crime scene."

"I have a couple of very expensive books up there. Can I at least check if they are undamaged?"

"I will talk to Major Destin."

"I don't want to file a complaint. Take your co-worker and have a nice day, and I can take my time cleaning up the mess."

He wants to get rid of us. He either has a problem with the police or he's hiding something up there he doesn't want us to find.

She would tell the people from forensics to be very thorough in their search. However, should it really be about a valuable book, the chances of finding it were very slim. The best hiding place for a tree was in a forest after all, was what her father always said. He was definitely right about that. There were thousands of books on shelves, on tables and stacked on the floor up there. To find a particular one would be nearly impossible for a stranger. On top of that, no forensic technician would be able to accurately guess the value or confirm the authenticity.

"It's not that easy. This is an assault case that could be related to a murder investigation. We are forced to investigate, even against your will."

"If you have to," he growled, "but be quick about it."

"We will do our best."

Louis Neville snorted in displeasure. He did not seem to have a lot of trust in their work.

"Do you have any enemies that could have done this to you?"

"I'm a bookseller, not a secret agent or hitman. I don't have enemies who would resort to physical harm."

"Then I'm wondering why someone would break into the Rabelais."

"Certainly not to kill me like poor Fréderic."

"I'm assuming the same thing. The perpetrator managed to

kill Savier. Apparently, you weren't important enough to kill, so it was enough to knock you out."

"Ah," he waved her argument away. "It must have been about the inventory. There are a couple of well-preserved first editions and expensive books up there. Most of them are in the display cases which I keep locked. You saw them yesterday."

"I'll check if the doors of the cabinets have been damaged."

"You will?" He did not sound like it was actually the books he was worried about. It must be something else that occupied his mind.

"Did Monsieur Savier maybe give you something for safe-keeping?"

He straightened up with a jerk. The hand with the icepack sank down, and he stared at her in surprise. She had beaten around the bush and apparently hit something. She wondered what.

"No, w-why do you think that?" He stumbled over his words.

"The bookshelves in his house and his office had been searched. Now a break-in here in your shop. Doesn't it seem obvious that the perpetrator is looking for a book or something similar?"

"Yes." He stretched out the word as if he wanted to win time to think. "That seems logical but wrong. Fréderic constantly gave me books which I sold on for him, but during the last couple of weeks he hadn't been successful in his hunts."

"Was just a thought. We have to follow every track."

Someone was walking briskly across the wooden floor of the antique shop upstairs. Neville looked up and his gaze seemed to follow the footsteps. He placed the ice pack on his thigh and wiped his forehead with a handkerchief. Sandrine took it as an opportunity to say goodbye and to look at the crime scene herself.

. . .

She found Major Destin in front of a pile of books, covered by two overturned shelves wedged together. They must have been the ones burying Neville. She wondered how Margritte and Alfonse had pulled the heavy man out from underneath. Alfonse did not look like he would be of much help.

"You were quick. It's a way from Saint-Malo to here." Major Destin sounded impressed.

"From Cancale to be precise. I live there."

"Not much closer."

"As it's an official mission I assume that the gendarmerie will take care of my speeding tickets," she tried to joke, but her humour bounced off the man ineffectively.

"I am sorry, but it is impossible to do any such thing. After all it was not a car chase. We informed you that we assumed to have a corpse. Corpses do not run away, and the perpetrator had been gone for hours."

To explain it was a joke felt too tedious, and she switched over to the case at hand.

"Neville thinks he was struck down by a stranger."

"Same as Savier. From the back with a blunt object. The physician suspects something round like a baseball bat or an iron rod. Unfortunately, Neville refuses to have his wound further examined. He didn't even want to file a complaint. Unbelievable. Instead, the man keeps nagging that we should leave." Destin seemed to waver between dislike and contempt for the antiquarian. "The way he is acting I would not be surprised if he had too much to drink and toppled the shelf over by accident."

"So, no weapon was found. Would have been too easy."

"As you can see. There were no useful fingerprints on the bust from Savier's house. What forensics was able to tell was that the bust had been wiped clean after the act. Parts of the blood had been smeared. In the trashcan behind the house a tissue with traces of blood was found. Results from a DNA comparison are still a long way off, but whose would it be if not Savier's? In any case, the cook denies having cut herself while cooking, and Madame Garaine claims that it did not come from her."

"Leaves the gardener."

"He is on my list for today," Destin replied.

"In any case, it solidifies our suspicion of an act in affect. Otherwise, the killer would have been wearing gloves, and they wouldn't have left the bloodstained cloth so carelessly. Not to mention the cup in the sink."

"I agree," the major said.

Sandrine turned and went over to one of the massive, standing shelves. She grabbed the boards with both hands and shook it. It moved slightly but was far from falling over.

"It feels like we can exclude an accident. A shelf like this wouldn't suddenly drop because he pulled out a book too fast or grabbed it while intoxicated. Someone helped a lot here."

"The intruder strikes him down from the back and drags the unconscious man into the hallway. Only then does he or she topple over the shelf." Major Destin stood next to one of the oak shelves. "If you lean against it with your back and lock your legs, it is easy to do. Even for a woman. However, you'd need a lot of strength to pull the bookseller. I estimate the guy to be at least 120 kilos. And most of it is not muscle," he added snidely.

"Are there any signs of forced entry?"

Destin pointed at the door. "It was broken open, just like in the chancellery. A crowbar could also have caused the man's wound."

"A failed break-in. The burglar couldn't know that Neville

would show up early in the morning. If I were them, I would simply have bolted."

"Neville would have called for help. At least that's what I think he would have done. He's not a man of action," Destin noted.

"But honestly, who would be awake at such a time in Bécherel and come to his aid?"

"No one."

"They didn't run but hid in the dark, let the bookseller walk past and then struck him down in cold blood."

"Why would they take that unnecessary risk?" The policeman looked around and shrugged his shoulders as if he wanted to suggest that none of this bric-a-brac was worth being stolen in the first place. Most likely he was completely correct.

"First, they searched for something at Savier's house, then in the office. Apparently, it was without success. Last night they tried their luck here. Judging from that, they clearly haven't found what they're looking for. I'm wondering if the perpetrator kept searching with all the calm in the world after knocking out the antiquarian."

"Then they would have to be very desperate or very greedy," commented Sandrine.

"And without any regrets. They didn't want to kill Neville but would have accepted it if it happened." Destin kicked the tip of his toes against one of the massive oak shelves. "They would have smashed his skull if they had hit him properly."

"So, attempted murder?"

"The prosecutor will have to decide that. I think the perpetrator did not give a damn whether Neville died or not."

"How's the juge d'instruction from Rennes?" Compared to de Chezac he could only be amazing. At least that was what she hoped.

"You can experience him in person soon. He's on the way

over." Destin did not sound like he had a particularly good opinion of him, but did not want her to hold any prejudices.

"Now I'm really curious. Before he shows up, we should try to gather some more information."

"My people will keep searching for any private security cameras. The ones we found so far were useless. Maybe we'll be lucky and can find one that actually recorded the perpetrator."

"How far are we with Savier's phone records?"

"They say they are on the way. I would not expect them before Monday. Due to the holidays, there are not many people working in Rennes."

"The perfect time for a crime."

"If I was planning one, I would choose July or August. At least if I wasn't hoping to get away by car. That would only end in a traffic jam."

"I'm interested in the shop's finances."

"We won't get a search warrant for that. The man is not a suspect."

"I fear so too," Sandrine agreed.

"Did you notice anything when you visited yesterday?"

"Neville showed me one of his showpieces. I'm not an expert, but I think it was a fake. The thickness of each individual page felt different to the last."

"Those are pretty old tomes. I'm sure that can happen."

"Counterfeits rise and fall depending on the ink and the paper. This is the easiest way to determine authenticity. I have heard of people buying up worthless books from an identical period of time to find blank pages in the book block. The text of the book they want to fake is then written or printed on it. The age and composition of the paper match the information provided by the seller. For a not too detailed analysis, the fake would pass as genuine."

"You seem to know a lot about it." A trace of admiration had crept into his voice.

"Back in the day I had a lot of work with counterfeiters and forgers." That those people had been family and close friends she did not need to tell him. The major would not show any compassion when it came to her past. At least this detail had not been carried to the newspapers. *Just a matter of time.*

"Could you also check this Alain Ducasse?" Sandrine asked. "The man didn't fit the picture, and I want to know what he was doing here."

"I already did. He's from Paris. Old money and lots of it. He is collecting art in as grand a way as possible, which brought him to Bécherel..." He shrugged his shoulders.

"It can only be about a book owned by Savier."

"That is why libraries and bookshops are being ransacked?"

"It's a first assumption, but what else could it be about in the Cité du Livre?"

"Even in the city of books there are the usual motives such as greed, love and jealousy. People are not that different here."

"You could be right about that. I still think we will find the perpetrator in the circle of bibliophiles though."

"Then I will get this book club to assemble this evening," decided the major. "It is time we got some answers."

"Don't forget Ducasse."

"My people are checking where the man is staying. There aren't many hotels someone like him would consider decent. I don't think it will take long."

Sandrine went over to the pile of books and knelt down. She picked up one of them and wiped dust from the cracked cover.

"The perpetrator hid behind the shelf. Neville had to feel his way through the room in the dark and didn't see them. The light switch is over there, far away from the door." With the book still in hand she pointed at the counter. "The perpetrator seemed to have known that. I guess they are one of the regulars here."

"Forensics will turn the whole place upside down," Destin assured her.

Sandrine looked around. Every centimetre was covered in books, magazines, posters, vinyl-records and souvenirs from better days. The people from forensics were not to be envied. Fingerprints would be no use in this place. There were simply too many people coming and going. The weapon, the perpetrator would have taken with them. With Savier it might have been an affect action, but here it had clearly been calculated and planned. *Was it the same perp or do we have two?*

"It's getting more and more mysterious," she said thoughtfully. "I don't believe Neville just came here in the early morning for the book market. The man doesn't even put up a table to sell his things. There must have been a more important reason. Maybe he owns the ominous book and wanted to sell it to Ducasse or another collector? Someone found out about it and tried to use it to their advantage. The question remains if the book has really changed owners."

"We will know once we check Ducasse's and Neville's backgrounds." Destin looked at her. "For now, all we can do is wait for forensics and try not to destroy any evidence."

"Let's go downstairs," she suggested and placed the book she had been holding on the shelf.

"Stay at the door and do not allow anyone to enter the crime scene. Understood?" Destin commanded one of the policemen.

Sandrine's gaze fell outside the window. In front of the bookshop, a black van and two cars had stopped. "That must be them."

"Then we'll let them work in peace." Destin climbed down the stairs, and she followed him. Neville was still sulking at the small table, but Pierre Salazar had joined him and they were talking. *Another one with whom I need to talk. I bet he knows more than he's admitting. The man is an opportunist and will certainly be waiting for a chance to get a piece of the cake.*

The forensic team donned their disposable coveralls at the van and were briefed by Major Destin. Meanwhile, Sandrine sat down at a table on the terrace and watched them. The man gave clear instructions on what to look out for. He knew his work, but she still missed her partner, Adel. Even though they had only been working together for a few months, she had gotten used to his calm and polite manner.

"They're on to it." Destin sat down with her and stretched his legs as far as the small terrace allowed.

"You wanted to talk to me? I assume it's about the article in the newspaper."

"You are famous. Some politicians are jealous of the attention you are receiving from the public."

"I could do without that. There's some slander going around, but if you decide you want to end our working engagement, I understand." She offered her resignation. Now it was up to the man to decide how to proceed with the investigation.

"Nonsense," he refused briskly. "Those media people always need to find someone to throw dirt on. Sometimes they find the right one, but more often than not it's the wrong one, just like you."

"You can't know that. We've only known each other for a day."

"And so far, you have done excellent work. I am convinced you will continue to do so until the case is closed."

"Thank you."

"Commandant Jenaud recommended you. That means a lot in this area. The man is well-respected."

"He's an excellent policeman."

"He thinks the same of you." Destin allowed himself one of

his rare but sincere smiles. "And you have another benefactor whose word also has weight."

"Who would that be?"

"Commandant Renouf."

She had solved the murder in Le Mont-Saint-Michel with the man. The starting position had been quite confused. A team from Normandy, one from Brittany, Malouins to be precise, and she: a Parisienne. But they had managed to put arguments aside and focus on the case, in which Commandant Renouf had played a not inconsiderable part.

"Give him my best wishes the next time you play Pétanque."

"He will be happy to hear from you."

"Please get to the point. What do you want to discuss?"

"There is nothing to discuss. It is basically just some information I want to share with you." He scanned their surroundings for a second, a precaution that struck her as odd from the confident man. "This morning, I received a call from an agent in the prefect's office."

"From Rennes?"

"Of course. Do we have another one?"

"The sub-prefect responsible for me from Saint-Malo."

"That one does not really count. They were asking for you. In the end they wanted to know if you are a trustworthy policewoman."

"Or a corrupt one who sleeps with a criminal."

His face twisted. "He did not phrase it quite like that, but simplified, yes. The prefecture will not have a lot of time before the press demands a statement."

"Thank you for letting me know."

"Do you want to know what I told them?"

She thought about it a moment and then shook her head.

"No. You're an astute observer and will have made a clear picture of me for yourself. I trust you."

Major Destin watched Sandrine closely. She held his gaze until he nodded.

"I hope it will soon untangle itself."

"Me too, and I promise that it will not interfere with our investigations."

"I assumed that. You are a professional after all."

"I'm happy you see it that way."

"Sure. What do you suggest, how shall we proceed?" Major Destin asked.

"You know the team, so it makes sense for you to take care of the background checks and the results from forensics. In the meantime, I will have a closer look at the two reading clubs: the treasure hunters and the women's reading group."

"Then I'll drive to the office here in town now."

"And I'll talk to Alfonse. Maybe he noticed something unusual when he came to the shop this morning. Sometimes it takes a moment for memory to resurface."

Before the policeman could say goodbye, Margritte stepped to their table.

"After all this excitement you must be ready for a small Breton delicacy."

"Well, that depends on what the café has to offer today." The policeman did not seem opposed to a second breakfast.

"I still have some pieces of the Farz Gwad which I baked for the treasure hunters."

Destin straightened on his wobbly chair and nodded his approval.

"A traditional Farz Gwad?" he asked.

"After a family recipe from the Île d'Oussant," Margritte asserted.

"How could I refuse such an offer?"

"And you, Sandrine? A piece for you too?"

"To try the local specialties is part of becoming a proper Breton. Only a small one though."

"There's always room for a Farz. Back in a sec."

"That's a rare offer these days. Those old traditional recipes are slowly going extinct. I remember my grandmother pulling all types of treats from her oven." By his standards, the major's tone was almost sentimental. So, he was a man whose roots ran deep in the soil of Brittany.

Pierre Salazar came out of the bookshop. With his eyes fixed on the ground, he tried to avoid the police officers' attention. Like a weasel, he weaved his way between some tourists and had almost reached the square when a shout from Sandrine stopped him.

"I would like to talk to you, Monsieur Salazar. If your time allows."

He froze, turned slowly and looked at his watch defiantly.

"I have to prepare for the book market. If it..."

"It will not take long. If you prefer, I can have someone drive me over in one of the police cars," she offered.

His scrawny face froze with the prospect of having police in his shop, scaring his clients away and fuelling the rumour mill. Fréderic Savier's death and Louis Neville's assault must be the ruling topic in Bécherel.

"I can carve out a few minutes." His voice moved between condescension and fear which made for a strange mixture.

"Would you like a piece, too?" Margritte called through the open window.

"Please. Just a small one. I had too many yesterday."

Pierre Salazar sat down with them.

"What can you tell me about Fréderic Savier?" Sandrine asked as soon as he had pulled his chair closer to the table.

"I fear I can't tell you anything you don't already know." He was clearly trying to get around answering.

"From a thriller author, that's not a very satisfying answer. An excellent observer like you must have noticed more than the other members of your club. You know what interests us police officers."

"When you phrase it like that, then maybe."

She had hit the mark. The vain man felt flattered and could not resist sharing his observations.

"Fréderic won nearly all the competitions, which for someone with hardly any feel for books was astonishing."

"What competitions?" Destin asked.

"At the end of each month, we bring our discoveries to the antique shop. Louis Neville evaluates them and whoever has acquired the most valuable piece is declared the winner."

"And that was Fréderic Savier."

"Nearly always. That's also why he was made the president of the club. But the man was an outright scammer."

"What do you mean?" Sandrine could guess where this was going, but she did not want to put any words into his mouth.

"You found him in his pompous library. Those are all books he inherited from his grandfather."

"And?"

"If he couldn't find anything good enough, he simply took something from his shelves. There were always plenty of treasures close at hand, and he barely read anyway." She could see from his pursed lips how the president's deceitfulness had gnawed on him. *Probably because of his vanity. He wanted to win himself. When it comes to honesty, he doesn't take it very seriously either.*

"I noticed it," he said and swelled his thin chest. "He liked to show off his estate and lead us poor beggars through it as if he had worked years for it. No, he inherited it."

"Had he acted out of the ordinary during the last few days?"

Salazar moved closer to the table and leaned forward. "You could say that," he whispered conspiratorially. "He wanted to present his newest find on Sunday. He claimed it was something extraordinary. Something so big that Bécherel had never seen anything like it."

"Who knew of that?"

"Only me. No one else."

"Are you sure?" Sandrine asked.

"Of course. He trusts me. I'm his deputy in the club after all."

"Good to know that. Your information helps us a lot." Sandrine saw her suspicion confirmed, as to what lured an art collector like Alain Ducasse to Bécherel. Definitely not a stack of dusty detective stories. Savier must indeed have discovered something of significant value. *And that cost him his life*.

"Your order," Margritte said, and Salazar jumped in his chair.

"Do you need to sneak up on us like that?" he hissed at her.

"With three plates, cutlery and a cup of coffee no one can sneak up on anyone," she corrected him. "You should simply stop daydreaming, Pierre."

He muttered something incoherent and took the plate she offered him.

"Did you remember anything about J. Robine?" she asked Salazar.

He avoided her gaze and pierced his cake with a fork. "No, not at all," he mumbled with his mouth full.

"And you, Margritte?"

"J. Robine?" She shook her head thoughtfully. "I racked my brains about it, but the name doesn't ring a bell. It's definitely no one from the area or my clientele."

"Then we will stop asking and enjoy the Far. It looks a bit darker than usual," remarked Sandrine.

"Do you know the secret ingredient?" Destin could hardly keep himself from blurting out.

"The plums pitted in rum?" Sandrine guessed.

The policeman looked at Margritte who gave him a satisfied nod.

"Gwad is Breton and means blood."

"That relates to the darker colour?" She could not quite follow him. "How does that happen?"

"Is it not obvious? It is through a cup of ox's blood which is added to the dough." Destin grinned happily as he saw her eyes widen in surprise. But he misunderstood. Something she had pondered for a long time last night suddenly became clear to her. She quickly grabbed Pierre Salazar's slender wrist and held it tight.

"Hey, what are you doing?" The gaunt man tried to wriggle from her grip, but she kept a hold on him.

"Not another bite!" Sandrine ordered.

"Are you okay? It's nothing strange, just think of black pudding." Margritte looked at her in surprise, and Sandrine wondered if she was an excellent actor or really had no idea what she was suspecting.

"Would you mind if I have a look around your kitchen?" she asked the bookseller. "Officially, as a policewoman."

"My kitchen?" she repeated, confused. "No, no problem at all, but what do you think you will find there?"

"Come with me, Destin." She got up and heard the scraping of the chair on the wooden decking as her colleague got up to follow her. Out of the corner of her eye she noticed the shrug with which he answered Margritte's questioning look.

She stopped in the doorway. The kitchen was small but furnished modern. The stainless-steel surfaces reflected the shine from the ceiling lights, and the scent of coffee and freshly baked cake filled the room.

"Where's the cup with the blood?"

"Where it should be, in the dishwasher. I don't leave dirty dishes around. Especially not from yesterday."

"Is the dishwasher finished?"

"Yes, I was just about to take everything out."

Damn. She had been too late. Still, she put on her gloves, went into the kitchen and opened the cupboards. As she had expected she found tidily stacked plates, glasses, cups, pots and pans. She had nearly given up when she decided to unfold a small stepladder to get to the thin top-shelves.

"There's only old stuff up there which we rarely use," Margritte said.

In between a dented metal sieve and measuring cups of different sizes stood a white porcelain vase. She grabbed the vase and pulled it out from the shelf.

"Is this your vase?"

Margritte stepped closer and searched for her glasses in her apron.

"I have never seen it before. No idea how it got here."

Sandrine climbed down the ladder and went over to the window. Red stains showed on the porcelain's edges.

"What did you find?" Destin asked from the door.

"I assume it's blood. Forensics should have Luminol. Then we can check directly."

"Inside the vase?" the bookseller stammered in disbelief.

"And what do you assume?" Major Destin leaned forward and looked over the red stains.

"That it is the blood of Fréderic Savier."

"But how would this thing have gotten here and what does it mean?" Margritte's eyes darted from Sandrine to the policeman and back.

"It means that the special ingredient in this Farz Gwad was no oxblood," she answered.

"Instead?" Destin could not believe what she was getting at.

"Blood from Fréderic Savier, I would assume," she said, as calmly as she could manage.

"What?" Salazar, who had followed them, choked out. "We ate Fréderic yesterday?" The blood drained from his face and his eyes bulged. The man turned on his heels and ran off. The sound which shortly emanated from the toilet was unmistakable. He had not kept the remains of his president with him.

"That can't be," Margritte disagreed. "The butcher brought over the cup with oxblood just yesterday. You can ask him."

Destin waved at a woman from forensics. She took out a clear plastic bag and offered it to Sandrine.

"Pack in the rest of the cake too. It's out on the terrace." She looked in the direction of the toilets. "I don't think Monsieur Salazar will finish his."

"No problem. I will collect it and bring everything to the lab." The woman turned to Margritte. "How long was the Far in the oven?" she asked.

"Around 45 minutes."

"180 degrees?"

The bookseller nodded.

"The blood on the vase is no problem. In the cake it will be denatured due to the baking temperature and thus unusable for analysis. With any luck we might find a few areas where there is an acceptable sample for DNA comparison, but I don't want to get hopes up too much."

"Do your best," Destin commanded, and the woman left the kitchen. "We need the blood type for a first check as fast as possible."

Margritte slumped on a chair and breathed heavily.

"I have no idea how that stuff got here." She made eye contact with Sandrine. "You believe me, don't you?"

"There's a chance I'm wrong and it's just some fruit juice," she lied. "We will find that out soon." She did not think that the woman was a murderer, but she was sure that it was blood. It was the only logical explanation for the smeared patch on Frédéric Savier's neck. His blood must have an important meaning for someone, though she had no idea what that could be.

"Am I under arrest now?" Budding panic made Margritte's voice shrill.

"Not at all," said Major Destin with, for him, unusual empathy. "We do not know yet what the liquid really is. As Capitaine Perrot said, it could be anything. I still have to ask you to come to the gendarmerie this afternoon to give a statement, though."

"Of course, if it means solving this thing quicker."

"No one believes that you're a murderer," Sandrine assured her. *But someone's trying to make us think that. Otherwise, the vase would not have been in this kitchen.*

Sandrine and Major Destin left Margritte in the kitchen. Salazar had disappeared.

"How did you think of that?"

"Sudden inspiration. The flowers were on the floor, water had soaked in the book pages and the vase was nowhere to be found. There was also the smeared spot on the man's neck just under the wound. After the perpetrator hit, they didn't want to waste the blood. Apart from the vase on the writing desk, they didn't have any other vessel in the heat of the moment. So, they took it, poured out the water and flowers and held it under the wound to catch some of the blood."

"But how did it get here?"

"No idea, to be honest. Maybe Margritte really struck him down with her cake recipe in mind. It's possible that someone wants to divert our suspicion and focus it on her. It would certainly throw us off the right course and send a message to the treasure hunter's book club. The blood must have some meaning, but which one I can't tell yet."

"You think the murderer is crazy? What person of sane mind would collect their victim's blood?"

"Quite the opposite. They're acting very cold and calculated. Through this find, we've progressed quite a bit."

"In what way?" Destin asked.

"Only one person from Margritte's immediate surroundings knew that she wanted to bake a Farz Gwad for the treasure hunters. That person would also have had entry to the bookshop to swap the blood unnoticed. Someone who wouldn't arouse suspicion being seen in the kitchen. That limits the circle of suspects."

"There are still quite a lot," Destin said, and did not sound overly optimistic.

"I'll go upstairs and talk to Alfonse."

"Then I will see you later in the gendarmerie."

The forensic technicians had finished their work on the first floor. Louis Neville stood in front of the book-pile which had buried him last night and seemed to be fighting back tears. Two policemen pushed a few books aside with their feet to find enough room to stand, grabbed one of the shelves and lifted it up. Judging from their contorted faces it was not an easy feat. Neville had had a lucky day. On most others he would not have gotten out of this without heavy injuries.

Sandrine climbed up the stairs to the top floor. The windows were open, and a refreshing breeze swept through the room. Insulation seemed quite a foreign word in this old house. 10:00 a.m. was approaching, and in a couple of hours it would be sweltering up here. The sloping ceilings were low and made it difficult to set up shelves. Books, especially large format illustrated books and antique odds and ends, crowded together on long wooden tables, or were stacked on the floor.

At the end of the room, Alfonse sat at what looked like an old kitchen table with a computer with two screens in front of him. The creaking of the stairs was impossible to ignore, and he looked at her tensely.

She rested her hands on the backrest of one of the chairs. "May I?"

"Of course."

"How are you? It must have been quite the shock to find Monsieur Neville under the books."

"Better by now. When I first saw him, I thought he was dead like poor Monsieur Savier. Only his unmoving feet were sticking out of the pile. It was like I was paralyzed for a moment. I just couldn't move." The man took a couple of deep breaths. His lower lip trembled, and his fingers thrummed a quick rhythm on the scratched surface of the table. "I must've screamed even though I don't remember it. Madame Violinet showed up suddenly. Together with her and Bernard the temp we pulled out Monsieur Neville." He looked at her. "Who would do such a terrible thing?"

"We don't know yet, but it's my job to find out."

He placed his right hand on the computer's mouse and moved it as if it was calming him down. The cursor whizzed over the two screens without doing anything.

"I didn't expect such modern equipment in an antique shop."

"Before I started, Monsieur Neville did everything by hand and with paper. It was quite the task to convince him to change his system." Alfonse's voice regained some stability and the twitching cursor slowed. To talk about his work seemed to give him some confidence.

"By now we do the bookkeeping, accounting and the management of the inventory on the computer. The record cards he used to use are mothballed. Monsieur Neville couldn't bring himself to throw them away." He clicked on a button and the website of Rabelais opened on the screen. "The site is ready and online. We even have a newsletter." His sentences gained liveliness and he turned to her. "Maybe you want to sign up. It's still in its beginnings, but on Sunday I will put flyers out. Hopefully we will gain some new customers."

"I wish I had more time to read, but the job doesn't leave me much." *And if I do find the time, I have to give my comments on Rosalie's thrillers.*

"That's a shame. Reading is like dreaming. The world outside is bad enough, so..." he stopped. He must have realised what Sandrine had to deal with on a daily basis. "In theory I can't complain."

"The antique shop must run well if Monsieur Neville can invest and have an employee."

"He's fulfilling one of my dreams. All day I'm surrounded by books, and I can read whatever I want. Salary isn't important to me. I don't need much." The haircut that looked like he had done it himself and the washed-out t-shirt he wore confirmed his frugality. The young man did not seem to be interested in money or vanity.

"How does the Rabelais sustain itself?" She came to the point that really interested her.

"Bécherel attracts lots of tourists, especially during the holidays when it's really quite busy. Though most prefer looking and taking photographs to buying something. Add to that the monthly book markets and the book festival around Easter."

"That's enough to survive?"

He turned the screen to Sandrine so she could read through the columns of numbers.

"Most turnover comes from the trade with collectors. It was always like this, but by now we have a proper online shop. That way it's a lot more professional."

Alfonse clicked on another button and a new page opened.

"Here you can search if we have a book and directly order it without shipping fees."

"Are there that many collectors?"

"Oh, yes." He nodded a few times like a pigeon picking up seeds. "Over the Rabelais' website the treasure hunters sell all the works they find. That adds up quickly."

Sandrine pulled out the paper with all the member's names which Alfonse had printed out for her yesterday. She let her eyes wander over the list.

"And you have the overview over the separate members?"

He patted the black case of the computer which stood next to him on the floor. Three blue rings were shining at the front and the fans hummed quietly.

"If you wanted to know how much money the Rabelais made from one particular treasure hunter could you find that out?"

"No problem. They go under the commission business division, and the name of the respective seller."

"How does it look for example with Pierre Salazar?"

Alfonse smiled softly. "I fear you picked the wrong one. The man rarely finds something valuable. If he does, he keeps it for himself."

"And Monsieur Savier?" She had gotten the young man to talk about the customers of the antique shop. Salazar had just been bait. Savier was the fish that really interested her.

"That looks totally different. Monsieur Savier had the real talent of a treasure hunter."

His fingers flew over the keyboard. A table opened with numbers running long.

"Impressive," she said.

"In just his first quarter he sold books worth nearly 50,000 euro."

"I didn't expect that. I thought it was only a hobby that costs more than it brings in."

"Not for him. He had a good feeling for where he could find something."

"And the Rabelais makes money with that too?"

"For every sale we get commission."

"And your system could print me a list of Monsieur Savier's transactions?"

"Without any problem, but I don't know if that's allowed."

"It's a murder investigation," she replied even though that did not change the situation. What she needed was a legal search warrant. Maybe she would receive one from the prosecutor in Rennes Major Destin had mentioned.

"True. We all want Savier's murderer to be found."

His fingers flew over the keyboard once again. The expensive-looking laser-printer whirred to life shortly after and pushed out two sheets of paper. Alfonse handed them to her.

"And you could do that for all members?"

"Yes, but for everyone alive I would ask Monsieur Neville's permission."

"Are the ladies of the reading group also customers?"

"No, those are bookworms. They don't care about the prices. They also don't like the treasure hunters much. It's mutual."

"I got the same impression." She scanned through the member's list. "Who's Monsieur Montfort?"

"The man owns a painting business with a few employees here in town. He has an exceptionally fine touch for first editions by Victor Hugo. Always amazing."

"And Monsieur Decoste?"

"A lawyer, as far as I know. Shall I check?"

"No, it's fine. I will talk to everyone as the day progresses."

"If there's anything I can do to help the police, you just need to ask."

"Not much of what happens in the Rabelais passes by you, does it?"

"I know my way around the shop, but not around town. I'm not the most sociable person. I prefer being alone and up here."

"Had Monsieur Savier been acting strangely?"

Alfonse let go of the mouse and pushed it aside.

"Now that you mention it, the last few days it looked like he was very excited about something. He marched through the antique shop as if he had discovered an especially rare find."

"Why do you think that?"

"He couldn't help himself and constantly dropped comments saying our eyes would grow wide soon. He also had an argument with my boss."

"And you know about what?"

"Normally, the treasure hunters present and display their discoveries during the book market in the Rabelais. However, this Sunday, Monsieur Savier rented a room in the Farz Gwad. It really seemed like he had found something remarkable."

She nodded. This was consistent with Salazar's testimony and Ducasse's appearance.

"Any idea what it might have been?"

"No. He always treated me like a piece of inventory with which one didn't have to talk. Was fine with me."

"Just for clarification, where were you last night?"

"You think..."

"No. These are just routine questions. No one is suspecting you of anything."

"That's reassuring." He leaned down and rummaged through a backpack under the table.

"There we go," he mumbled and placed a bus ticket and a receipt from a bicycle shop in front of Sandrine. "I visited my family in Nantes, bought a few things and took the first bus this morning. Is that enough?"

"Definitely." She pocketed the ticket. "Thank you very much. You've really helped a lot."

"Always. Should you have more questions, you know where to find me."

She said goodbye and climbed back down the stairs. After everything she had heard it really looked like the victim had made a significant discovery. Valuable enough to lure a collector like Ducasse to Brittany. But he had not been able to keep his mouth shut. Salazar, Alfonse, Neville and Margritte had known of his plans to present his discovery on Sunday, even though he had not told them what he had found. To all of this came Ducasse who had to know more details. *Hopefully we will find the man soon. He should be able to tell us what book all of this is about.*

On the way to the chancellery, she typed a message to Inès. Although her office manager was not officially involved in the investigation, she worked efficiently and usually dealt with Sandrine's inquiries immediately.

* * *

Inès sat down at Adel's desk and pushed a couple of sheets his way.

"My expense report. Is something wrong?"

"It's a good reason for me coming over without anyone noticing."

As inconspicuously as he could manage, he looked over at

Poutin who did not seem to care about anything. The brigadier looked at her with a frown.

Adel took the top sheet and pretended to read it.

"Any news?"

"I couldn't get a hold of the report, but reliable sources told me that it really was the same type of drug which they found in the car of that Paris gangster. The contents are identical."

"Charles Carnas."

Sandrine had discovered the drug dealer's corpse in the boot of his Firebird Trans Am. The car had also been well-stocked with drugs.

"Good to know," he said and handed the sheet back to her.

"What's our next step?"

"I'll go through the names of people who had access to that crime scene or had anything to do with the car. Maybe someone noticed something that can help us."

"The forensic technician took care of the drugs. Jean-Claude swears that everything is in the evidence locker."

"I'll check it anyway. They must have come from somewhere after all."

"Do that. I'll hold the fort here." She leaned forward. "Matisse received a call from the prefecture in Rennes."

"Do you know what it was about?"

"No, but I would bet my entire salary that it was about Sandrine."

"Then we don't have a lot of time."

She stood up and placed her hand on his shoulder before returning to her office.

* * *

Madame Descours opened the door of the chancellery for Sandrine.

"Oh." It slipped past her lips, and she sounded disappointed. She had clearly not expected her. Most likely she had been waiting for someone she wanted to impress. Her blouse looked new, and the grey roots of her hair had vanished. She had treated herself to some shopping and a visit to the hairdresser. *For whom is she dressing up?*

"I would like to speak to Madame Cassian."

"Let me see if she has time."

"Please do."

Sandrine sat down on the narrow couch in the waiting area. Before she could even check the messages on her phone, the secretary returned.

"Unfortunately, Madame Cassian has a lot of work at the moment. Could you come back tomorrow?" She did not even try to make the excuse sound believable.

"No problem. Please tell your boss to come to the office tomorrow while we search the chancellery." She pointedly checked her watch. "The prosecutor from Rennes should arrive in Bécherel soon. He will certainly sign the search warrant. Until then I will post one or two policemen in front of the house to make sure no evidence vanishes."

The woman's chin had dropped a finger's width while she stared at Sandrine.

"You can't do that."

"What would stop me? It's a murder investigation and my patience with this town's residents is depleted by now." She stood up. The secretary's eyes were glued to her weapon which she always wore to be visible under her jacket. "On the other hand, we can also resolve everything in a matter of minutes."

"As I said…"

Sandrine went for the exit. "I will see you tomorrow."

"Capitaine Perrot," a familiar woman's voice called. "Before you carry out your threat, I will interrupt my work, even though

I have nothing to add to your investigation. You are wasting your time here. Unfortunately, mine too." The lawyer stood at the door leading to her office.

"I'm sure I will learn something helpful from you. Isn't it in our mutual interest to catch whoever killed your business partner?"

The corners of Madame Cassian's mouth gave a quick twitch before she regained her composure. She clearly was not too disturbed by Savier's death.

"Come in."

After Sandrine had entered, the lawyer stayed at the door and closed it to lock out any curious listeners.

Her shelves were as filled as her partner's had been. Most of the books were law-related works which looked very new.

"You're also a passionate reader?" Sandrine asked.

"Of course. You saw me attend the reading group." The woman stepped next to Sandrine.

"Here you will only find business-related literature. In contrast to Fréderic, I keep business and pleasure strictly separate."

"He didn't?"

"You searched his office. It was more an antique store than a notary's working space. At least it was not as shabby as the Rabelais."

"You don't like Monsieur Neville?"

"Am I that easy to read?" Her voice was soft but soaked in sarcasm. "Neville is a disgrace to the world of literature."

"Why?"

"You should make your own picture of the man. As a part of the police that's your job after all."

"Do you detest him for selling counterfeit works?" She dropped the bomb in the middle of the room and waited for the lawyer's reaction.

Madame Cassian turned her back towards Sandrine and sat down at her desk. The sarcasm she had wielded like a weapon left her face and was replaced by unconcealed surprise.

"You have been here for one day and found out what the police have not been able to prove for years. You have my deepest respect."

"It's only an assumption and my personal experience. Nothing that would count as evidence in front of a court."

"Then you should get investigations rolling," the woman requested. "The man is like a rotten apple who wants to poison everyone who comes too close to him. It's bad for the town's reputation."

"My cases are the murder of Fréderic Savier and the attack on Louis Neville. Everything else will be dealt with by the gendarmerie as soon as we catch the perpetrator."

"Neville was attacked?"

"Last night in his shop."

"What happened? Was anything stolen?" She sat ramrod-straight on the chair with her hands clamped around the armrest as if she was ready to jump up any second. What was making her so uncomfortable?

"He claims nothing was stolen."

"Maybe he's lying."

"Humans tend to lie. However, in this case it seems unlikely. If the burglar had found what they were looking for there would have been no reason to attack Neville. The toppled shelf must have been so loud that they ran off afterwards."

The woman's shoulders dropped a bit, but Sandrine still felt like she was very agitated.

"Do you know of anything Neville might be keeping that would justify a break-in?" she asked to clarify.

"No, there is nothing in that shop that anyone could want."

"Your business partner seemed to have made an important discovery. What do you know of that?"

"Why me?"

"You work together. People talk about more than just business."

"We had different views on most aspects in life."

"Also about the worth of a book?"

"Among others." Madame Cassian shrugged.

"More than one witness told me that he was planning on presenting his newest find at the book market this Sunday. He reserved a complete room from Madame Violinet."

"So you know that too."

"Part of my job."

"Alright. The man strutted up and down like a rooster and boasted about putting Bécherel in the spotlight of literature on Sunday. Whatever that was supposed to mean."

"Do you know what book it was?" Sandrine leaned forward and looked the lawyer straight in the eyes. "It is very important."

"He made a big secret out of it, and I did not want to sweettalk him into telling me."

"Pity."

"I would have found out during the book market anyway, so why hurry?"

"One person was in more of a hurry than you. His private library had been searched, just like his office here. Someone broke into the Rabelais yesterday. I don't know how to interpret it any other way. They thought that the book was worth killing for."

"Poor Fréderic," Madame Cassian said, unusually gently. "His heart's desire to be known in the art collecting world finally comes true, and then someone breaks his skull before he can shout his discovery from the rooftops. Tragic."

"You had an appointment with him on that evening."

"True, but I already told you that."

"Somehow, I'm having trouble imagining you two wanting to spend a cosy evening together. What was the reason for the meeting?"

She halted before answering.

"Fréderic planned to retire from the firm and wanted to sell his shares."

"To you?"

"I have a right of first refusal. To my surprise, he set the purchase price very moderately. And yes, I would have agreed."

"He didn't like you very much. Why would he offer you a reasonable price which made you agree quickly?"

"Maybe I completely underestimated the man, and he actually found a treasure that would bring in so much that he would not need the money from the sale. Or he wanted to avoid lengthy negotiations with other interested parties. In any case, he wanted to close the deal quickly. Unfortunately, we can no longer ask him."

"And what will happen to his shares now?"

"They fall to me under the death clause of our law firm contract. I have to transfer a fixed amount to his wife, but the actual value now far exceeds this compensation."

"His death was lucky for you then?"

"That's a harsh assumption."

"Murder is a harsh profession."

For a few moments they judged each other until Madame Cassian looked to the side and sighed.

"It may look like it, but I did not wish this end on him. The man was annoying but basically harmless."

"I'd like to believe that."

"I am wondering if his wife knew of his plans," the lawyer said in thought. "Maybe that was why he refused to postpone the meeting. He wanted to keep it a secret from his wife."

"For what reason? Are there problems in the marriage?"

"For that you'd have to ask Madame Savier."

"I will as soon as she gets back," Sandrine said.

"She's here. At least I saw her car roughly an hour ago in the city."

She didn't think it necessary to report to the police, so I will pay her a little visit.

"Where could Monsieur Savier have kept such a valuable book? Do you have any idea?"

"If not in his house, then here in his office. He had a safe."

"The safe was open and empty when we arrived."

"Then the burglars must have gotten it," Madame Cassian surmised.

"Unlikely."

"It seems very plausible to me."

"If I was to break in somewhere and search for something valuable the safe would be my first choice. As it was open, it must have been empty. Why else would the burglar have gone through the shelves afterwards? No, I'm convinced the book wasn't in his office. We also have the break-in into the Rabelais shortly after. The perpetrator was also searching there."

"Fréderic might not have been the brightest candle on the cake, but neither was he naïve enough to give Louis Neville anything of value. He knew his views on morality and honesty quite well."

"Then the perpetrator must be quite desperate by now. They haven't found the object they murdered for."

"I'm sorry that I can't be more helpful," the lawyer said, and this time Sandrine believed her.

"Please come to the gendarmerie in the next few days to give your statement for the record."

"Can we start using Fréderic's room again?"

"Forensics should be okay with that. I will send over a man to remove the seal."

She said her goodbyes and left the office.

Back on the street Sandrine took out her phone. There was no news from Inès. She decided to call Rosalie.

"Hey, it's me."

"Hey, Sandrine. How's the case going?"

"I can't really get anywhere, but maybe you have an idea as it's all about literature."

"Tell me. You've piqued my curiosity."

"The victim had a note in his calendar: J. Robine. There's no one in the area with that name. It must have a connection with a very valuable book."

"Maybe it's not a person."

"I'm open for suggestions."

"Off the cuff, I have no idea, but I'm cooking which always helps me think."

"It would really help me. As well as the abbreviation JJLFA."

"I'm meeting Hugo later. Maybe he has an idea what could be behind it." Hugo Delacroix was the protagonist of Rosalie's successful thrillers. She always spoke of him as if he was a real person.

"I would be forever indebted to the commissaire."

"He will be happy to hear that. Just one more thing, how's your victim's handwriting?"

"The man could have been a GP. Very hard to read."

"I'll call you." Rosalie hung up.

* * *

Inès Boni walked down the stairs to the forensic department. Her steps were light and feathery.

"Hello, Jean-Claude," she greeted the boss, who sat at his desk sorting through papers.

"What leads you down here to the lowlands of the working people?"

"Marie and I want to go to the beach during our lunch-break." She lifted a paper bag. "I got us some sushi and she's getting the drinks. The water will be amazing.."

Jean-Claude Mazet's face pulled into a grimace.

"Raw fish is not really my thing. Especially in this heat. It's way too easy to get all wonderful kinds of things from it. Just the other day, a friend of mine..."

"You won't spoil my appetite. Be quiet." She lifted her pointer finger in warning. The man lifted his hands in an apologetic gesture, and Inès sat down on the opposite side of his writing desk.

"Any interesting work?"

"Just routine stuff. When Sandrine's on holiday the murderers seem to take a break too."

"She will be back before you get too bored."

He studied Inès carefully.

"All hell broke loose up there, didn't it?"

"What do you mean?" she asked, even though it was obvious what he was getting at. Instead of an answer he pulled out today's newspaper and put it on the table.

"You don't believe it, do you?" Inès asked.

"What exactly should I question? That your boss works with rather unusual methods and finds unorthodox ways to get to her goal as soon as she's convinced it's necessary? I don't have to believe that. That's a fact."

"But..."

"That Sandrine is corrupt and passes on official secrets? That's the biggest nonsense I ever had to read."

"I agree."

"What do you really want from me? A quarter of an hour ago, Marie demolished a baguette that would have been big enough for two. Meeting her for lunch can only be an excuse to snoop around here."

"You got me," she admitted. "I want to find out what and who is behind the accusations."

"Sandrine's always welcome in my department. She does an excellent job, doesn't stomp through the crime scenes, and respects our work. That's much more than many others do. So, what can I do for you?"

"Her boyfriend claims to not have had any drugs in his safe, and she believes him. I'm wondering where they came from."

"I didn't get to see them, but there's rumours that the prosecutor accuses her of having stolen the stuff from the evidence room."

"Just by coincidence, I happened to stumble across the inventory lists. We barely have any drugs here at the moment."

"True, and everything that went in is accounted for in the inventory. Nothing is missing. I checked just to be sure, so they can't accuse us of not doing our job correctly," Mazet stated.

"Where did the stuff come from then?"

"Everything we found recently has been properly accounted for and stored. It can't have come from us."

He pulled a list from his papers and handed it to Inès. "Most of it was in the car from the case of the corpse on the Brittany Coastal Path. Apart from that, only small amounts came in from other sources."

"And all of it is in the evidence room?"

"Down to the last pill. Everything documented and accounted for."

"Then they couldn't have been stolen from our storage, which means that there's nothing to the accusation."

"Definitely not. And from the way she looked when we found her at that burning barn, I highly doubt she used the opportunity to pocket some drugs."

"How did the prosecutor get the idea that the drugs are from us?"

"That's above my paygrade. Maybe the pills' composition was similar? Why don't you ask Poutin? He was the one who discovered them, after all."

"It's better he doesn't know what I'm interested in."

"I see. You assume that he's somehow connected to all of this."

"He never liked Sandrine. Maybe he used the opportunity to show her who's boss. Especially if de Chezac was there to keep his back covered."

The boss of the forensic department leaned back and pensively scratched his cheek.

"I don't know. That would be pretty extreme. Even for someone like Poutin. What does Dubois say to all of this? The two are like Siamese twins."

"Called in sick. He's out for the whole week."

"The man has never been ill before. Strange. But for Dubois, I would walk over burning coals. He's an honest man. I could never understand how the two of them are friends in the first place."

"I hope he turns up again soon."

"He will. In the meantime, I'll ask around here. Maybe I'll notice something that I missed. I'll let you know."

"Thank you very much. I'll start searching for Marie. The sushi wants to be eaten," Inès lied and went back towards her office.

***

Sandrine's phone rang. She did not recognise the number, and her first impulse was to ignore the call. Still, in the end she decided to answer. Maybe it was a witness calling.

"Capitaine Perrot."

"Hello, it's Arianne."

The voice sounded familiar, but it took her a moment until she matched the name to a person.

"Arianne Briand from the local radio station?" she asked to make sure.

"Yes, Sandrine, you owe me an interview."

The journalist and the rest of her crew were in their mid-twenties, and the thought of not being on a first name basis with everyone did not even cross their minds.

"Right now, it's a bit inconvenient. My calendar has been booked by the press."

The woman chuckled, her voice scratchy as if she had partied through the night. Arianne Briand was hard but fair. Sandrine wondered what news might have been spread about her on the local radio.

"They have you on the hook, and a shitstorm is raving through Saint-Malo," the journalist summed up Sandrine's situation. "Is that why they *deported* you all the way to Bécherel?"

"I wouldn't call it that. My holiday was interrupted so I could work on a murder investigation... but to be fair, they probably also got me out of their way."

Her superiors would probably phrase it as *get-out-of-the-line-of-fire*, which did not really mean anything else, just sounded nicer.

"I happen to be in the area. We should have a chat," Arianne suggested.

"I'm not sure if that's a good idea."

"If you want to save your ass you should come over. I will be in the Park des Château de Caradeuc in 15 minutes. It's less than five minutes away from the closest bookshop in Bécherel."

Her phone beeped. The woman had hung up. She had made her message clear. *In contrast to Deborah Binet, she can focus on the important points. I have the choice.*

She checked her watch. She still had enough time until she had to be at the gendarmerie. *It can't get any worse, right?*

Sandrine pulled into the makeshift parking lot opposite the entrance and stowed her helmet and jacket in the motorcycle's bags. She put the gun in as well and locked it.

Arianne Briand was easy to recognise from afar. The bright red hair, shaved a millimetre short, was hard to miss. She sat on a park bench and typed something on her cell phone. Sandrine assumed that most people would have played games or found other ways of killing time, but the journalist struck her as a workaholic.

"Hey, Sandrine. Nice that you could find the time." She put her phone in her trouser pocket, stood up and pulled up the sleeves of her t-shirt. Colourful tattoos with Asian motifs covered her arms.

"New haircut?"

Arianne stroked over her head. "Only the sidecut. It's super practical. After I take a shower, it dries before I even get a towel."

"Maybe I should consider it."

"You're not the type, if you will accept my fashion advice." She laughed. "Let's walk a bit. I've already sat in more than enough cars and conference rooms today."

. . .

The castle lay stretched out before them. It had been built in the 18th century and resembled an estate more than an actual castle. It was a three-storey property whose linear symmetry was broken only by an attached tower. As far as Sandrine knew, it was still inhabited by the original founder's family and was not open to the public.

They strolled down the gravel-covered path and stayed in the shadows of the trees.

"What are they saying in Saint-Malo?" Sandrine asked after a while.

"There're those who only read the newspaper and believe everything they read. Those who want to see you in prison."

"Yes. There's nothing more satisfying than a criminal policewoman who receives a just punishment."

"The others who know you better are irritated by what is going on in the police station and the administration. Léon Martinau has run the Équinoxe for years, and there has never been any trouble. It's hard to imagine that he suddenly turned drug dealer."

"He didn't."

"But they found the stuff with him, and no one can deny that."

"The question is, how did it get there, and how did they discover it?"

"You think they want to get to you through him?" Arianne asked.

"It seems to be worth a lot to someone to push me out of the force."

"De Chezac? That prosecutor?"

For a couple steps Sandrine walked in silence. *Can I trust her? Doesn't matter. What do I have to lose?*

"For a long time, I couldn't believe that one of us could be behind all of this, but by now all evidence points at it. He ordered the raid, kept it secret in the police station and specifically chose the one brigadier who can't stand me. It all fits together."

"Any concrete proof?"

"None. So far, I only have puzzle pieces which fit together perfectly."

"I will help you wherever I can," the woman promised.

"Thank you. It would already be enough if I wasn't crucified on the local radio. Of the rest, I have to take care of it by myself."

"One step after another. De Chezac is holding a press conference tomorrow afternoon at 4:00 p.m., just in time for the front pages of the Sunday newspapers."

A quiet groan sounded from Sandrine's throat. "So, he's reached the last metres of his crusade to destroy me. I have a little over 24 hours to exonerate myself, which in itself is far too short, but I also have a case here and I can't get away. I have no choice but to watch helplessly as my career and reputation are dismantled."

"Don't give up. You have many people on your side."

"They would be a lot smarter if they stayed out of this."

"I shouldn't hope for that. You have a talent in finding new friends."

"I'll go back to work. Maybe I can catch a murderer before they throw me out on the street."

"I have to get back, too. If we find anything interesting on de Chezac or Poutin, I will let you know."

"Give my greetings to Inès. Tell her to be careful," Sandrine said.

"How do you know we're talking?"

"How else would you know where I am?"

"I will tell her, as well as your other ally."

"Another one?"

"The Binet called and offered her help."

"The same woman who tried to murder me in her article? That's hard to believe."

"Exactly that one," Arianne confirmed.

"But why? The investigations against me bring her stories to the front page. That's her goal."

"She might be cold as a fish but she's also pretty smart."

"Then she should realise that the chances are not on my side. Normally, she joins the victor's side."

"I don't think you can expect her to defend you or offer a lot of help, but she will hold back with prejudice in her articles for a few days. That's something..."

Sandrine took the woman's arm and pulled her between two densely grown trees.

"What's up?"

"Be quiet for a second."

On the path running parallel to them walked a couple. *I didn't expect them to be here.*

"You know them?"

"Yes."

The click of a camera made her twitch. Arianne had used the moment and taken several pictures.

"They mustn't notice us."

"Are you scared that they might mistake us for a couple or are those suspects?"

She did not even answer the rhetorical question. Fleur Garaine and Arnault Gaudry, the gardener, were strolling through the park together. They weren't touching, but were definitely walking closer than usual for two people who apparently did not like each other.

Sandrine and Arianne stayed in the cover of the trees until the two were out of sight. Only then did they leave the park.

* * *

Sandrine stopped in front of the Savier's estate. A red sports car was already parked in front. Arnault came towards her.

"If you're looking for Madame Savier, she's in the garden." He gestured towards the backside of the house.

"Thank you. Have you seen Madame Garaine today?"

"She hasn't come out yet to complain about something I've done. I have not seen her today."

"There isn't much love between the two of you." Sandrine did her best to put as much feeling as possible into the sentence.

"Ah," he waved her comment away. "I'm just happy the woman lets me do my work." He checked his watch. "I have to go. Other clients are waiting."

He marched to a huge pickup truck and got in.

Why was he lying to her? She had seen the two of them in the park together, and now he claimed to not have seen her.

Sandrine found Isabelle Savier in the garden in the shadow of the oak tree. A bottle of Rosé and a half-full glass stood on the table in front of her. One could see that she had stayed in Provence. Her even tan definitely did not come from Brittany. She was tall, slim, just at the border of being considered too skinny, and wore a white summer dress. Her straight, blonde hair fell down low between her shoulder blades. She was way too attractive to be imagined with a man like Fréderic Savier.

"Capitaine Perrot," Sandrine introduced herself. "My condolences."

"Thank you. Please, sit with me."

"Thanks. I'm sorry if it's not the best time, but I have a few questions for you."

"May I offer you a glass of wine?" She pointed at the bottle, a layer of condensation already forming on the glass.

"I'm working and have to drive back," she refused.

"To drink alone is very sad," Isabelle mumbled and filled her glass.

"You arrived this morning?"

"After Fleur told me of Fréderic's death I jumped in the car and drove here. Just before Rennes I couldn't keep my eyes open anymore and stayed in a hotel for the night. I have only been here for a few hours."

"When did you last talk to your husband?"

"On Tuesday. In the afternoon."

"Did you notice anything unusual about him? Did he sound different, or mention that he had had an argument with someone or was threatened?"

"Not at all. He seemed the same as always. Fréderic didn't like telephone calls and always kept them very short."

His secretary had said something else. She had hidden to escape his chitchat. Did she not know her husband very well, or was he less talkative with her? That would not cast a good light on their marriage.

"What did you talk about?"

"Nothing special. We were planning a trip to Nice, after this ridiculous book-circus was over."

"You don't join in your husband's hobby?"

"Not at all," she said and sipped from the glass. "A boring pastime that cost him little but didn't bring in a dime. Fréderic avoided spending money on useless things. He was a frugal person."

Her husband seemed to be a stranger to Isabelle Savier. The numbers which Sandrine had received from Alfonse showed a totally different story. Apparently, Savier had not shared his financial successes with his wife. Or Pierre Salazar had been correct, and the man was slowly selling off his family's library and putting the money to the side. Had he been preparing for a divorce and trying to keep his money safe?

"He hated using the car and always wanted to take the train," she continued. "The journey leads through Paris where he wanted to meet an old friend from his studies. We wanted to spend the rest of the summer with my family in Nice, but then... Why did someone murder him? Fréderic was a peaceful man who wouldn't have hurt a fly."

"We don't know yet. At the moment, we're assuming that your husband was in possession of a very valuable book which the perpetrator was targeting."

"The whole library is teeming with precious old books which are hard to find anywhere, or so he liked to say. I have my doubts. The stuff is just taking up space."

"It must be a book surpassing all the others."

The woman's eyebrows twitched up. Her surprise felt genuine to Sandrine.

"I don't know anything about that."

"Your husband didn't mention anything?"

"Not a word."

"Nothing in the last phone call?"

"Maybe he wanted to surprise me." Suppressed sarcasm flashed out between the words, and a suspicion seemed to rise up in her, freezing her features for a moment.

"Did he mention a certain Alain Ducasse?" Sandrine asked.

"No. I've never heard that name. Who's that? Should I know him?"

"He's a well-known and respected art collector from Paris. He wanted to meet your husband."

"Rich?" she said as if in disbelief and stretched the word. *Most likely she didn't believe what I told her about the book.*

"You're sure that he didn't drop a hint on what book it was?"

"He didn't. Though I have to admit that I didn't always pay attention when he rambled on about his hobby."

She must regret that now.

"Do you think this book is still in our house?" Isabelle put her glass down and leaned forward tensely. The prospect of wealth seemed to eclipse the grief for her husband with amazing speed. The tip of her tongue slid over her upper lip. Like a snake, Sandrine thought.

"We assume that the perpetrator hasn't found it yet. We don't know where it is."

"Should I stumble over it I will let the police know instantly," she promised and leaned back. "The name is Alain Ducasse?"

"Yes. It would be good if you could inform us immediately should the man try to get in contact with you."

"You think he's the murderer?"

"Not at the moment."

"Good to know," she said in a thoughtful tone. In her mind, she was probably already negotiating with the collector about the sale of the book which she was clearly hoping to find in the house.

"I still have a few routine questions I need to ask you." Sandrine liked using the phrase once the questioning turned more intimate.

"No problem. I want nothing more than to see that guy behind bars."

"Would you call your marriage a happy one?"

"Of course. Fréderic was a wonderful husband." It bubbled out of her as if she practiced the sentence and had just been waiting to use it.

"You wanted to move away from here together?"

"Why…why would you think that?" The question had caught her off guard.

"Your husband was planning on selling his shares from the chancellery to Madame Cassian. For a very reasonable price."

"Ah, that's what you mean. He mentioned it, but I'm not very involved in his business decisions." She had caught her composure very fast.

"You own an exceptionally beautiful estate. What do you plan to do with it?"

"As you know, we don't have any children. I can't endure the thought of living in the house Fréderic was murdered in. I will most likely sell it and move somewhere else. Try to get over the loss. I don't know how I will manage," she said, her voice breaking. She shook her head and looked at the ground.

Too much theatre. Madame Savier's grief was not very believable. She suspected that the woman could not wait to sell the estate and move back to Provence.

"Then I won't take up any more of your time," Sandrine said as her goodbye. "There will surely be more questions during the next couple of days."

"I will be here. Where else would I be?"

She stood up and left the woman in the garden. *Most likely she can't wait for me to leave so she can research Alain Ducasse on the internet. But now Destin and the prosecutor are waiting for me.*

* * *

A policeman led Sandrine to the only conference room in the gendarmerie of Bécherel. The major stood with a man she did not know in front of one of the pinboards. Both turned towards her as soon as she entered the room. *That must be the prosecutor from Rennes. I wouldn't have thought that at first glance.* He looked like he was dressed for sport, with light, casual trousers, fashionable slip-ons without socks and a polo shirt that matched the colours of the outfit. His blond hair nearly skimmed his shoulders. A barely perceptible touch of makeup highlighted his sun-tanned skin, and a thin eyeliner accented his black lashes. He would have passed as the star of a local theatre group.

"So, you're the investigator from Saint-Malo." He stepped

towards her and offered his hand. "Pleasure to meet you. I'm Sébastian Hermé, the responsible prosecutor." His voice sounded soft and melodious without losing its masculine touch. He radiated an internalised self-confidence that was needed to gain respect from police officers.

"The pleasure is all mine," she said. Judging from his firm handshake he did not just spend his days behind a desk.

"I have heard a lot about you and am curious to work this case with you."

"It's rather difficult not to hear anything about me at the moment," she replied and watched him intently. His reaction would give a clue as to what she was to expect of him.

"Oh, yes. You very much stepped into a wasps' nest, and I have been warned sufficiently."

"You're an honest and open person. That's hard to find." *He must have received a call from the prefect as well.*

"It's a shame actually. We're one team with one goal. If one of us fails, everyone suffers."

"I don't plan on failing," Sandrine retorted.

The man looked into her eyes and did not break contact for a moment.

"I'm convinced by that. Your reputation precedes you, and I don't mean that graffiti in the newspapers, but the cases you have solved. Your success speaks for itself. I hope we can continue like this here in Bécherel."

"Then we should start."

"Yes, but I need a coffee first. I went to sleep too late and got up way too early." He turned and left the conference room.

"What do you think of him?" Major Destin asked immediately.

"He's not a typical prosecutor, judging from the ones I have worked with in the past. I'm ready for a surprise."

"He is quite headstrong, you are right. If you take him as he is, you can get along with him."

Sébastian Hermé returned, holding a tray with three mugs, sachets of sugar and some plastic jars of coffee creamer. The man was more atypical than she had assumed. De Chezac would never have considered bringing anything other than his own coffee. Surely, he would have sent someone to fetch it for him as well.

"I didn't know how you like your coffee, so I brought sugar and milk. Unfortunately, I couldn't find any snacks." He placed the tray on the table and sat down on a chair which he turned to face the pinboard.

Sandrine took one of the magnets and stuck a picture of the victim onto the board.

"Fréderic Savier. He was murdered in his estate just outside of Bécherel on Wednesday between 10:00 p.m. and midnight. He was struck with a bronze bust of Audubon on the back of the head."

"Audubon?" Hermé asked. "Those are quite rare. Most people think of him as an American even though he was raised in Nantes which was part of Brittany back then. My partner is an admirer of his nature illustrations. This Savier must have had excellent taste."

"I fear not," Sandrine replied. "The library and the furniture were inherited from his grandfather."

"What else is there to know about him?"

"He's married to Isabelle Savier. I talked to her this morning."

"How's the marriage? Love and jealousy are often motives."

"Hard to say, but I didn't get the impression that it was a love marriage. At least not from her side. The woman is a lot younger and more attractive than her husband. She doesn't think much of his passion for books and spends the summer separate from him in Provence."

"Financial motives?" Hermé asked.

"More like it. I suspect the marriage was indeed not at its best, and Savier intended to separate from his wife."

"Why do you think that?"

"He offered the shares in his law firm to his partner without informing his wife. He also seemed to be selling books from his library for a long time, again without her knowledge. We are still clarifying to which account the amounts were transferred to, and who was authorised to access them."

"She might have found out. A fight started and her temperament got the better of her."

"At the time of death, the woman was with her family in Nice."

"Was her alibi checked?" Hermé asked Major Destin.

"We're on it. It's proving hard to get a hold of the sister with whom she stayed."

"Savier was a notary and president of a book club. The members are known as the 'Treasure Hunters'," Sandrine continued.

"I've heard of them."

"A man with little confidence who was greedy for the acceptance of his fellow people. Most likely he cheated in the monthly competition by passing off books from the private collections as finds from his treasure hunt in order to win regularly."

"But this time he must have stumbled over something extraordinary," Hermé said.

"From what do you draw that conclusion?" Major Destin asked.

"I saw the reports. Someone struck him down, searched his library and his office, and it seems highly likely that Alain Ducasse was here because of his find. An esteemed collector wouldn't come all the way into the provinces for some mouldy writings by Voltaire. Savier must have caught a big fish."

Sandrine nodded in agreement. The man was clever and had drawn the right conclusions.

"As I said, being recognised by his fellow men was very important to him. He couldn't stop himself from telling everyone that he would present his treasure at the book market in the Farz Gwad bookshop."

"Then we can assume that all of Bécherel knows about it."

"Without any doubt," Major Destin agreed with the prosecutor.

"We have the murder weapon as well as the motive: greed. But who had the opportunity to get close enough to the victim to kill him with his own bust?" Hermé leaned back in his chair and watched Sandrine who pinned more pictures on the pinboard.

"Only he, his wife Isabelle and Fleur Garaine the housekeeper live on the grounds," said Destin. "A cleaning lady and the gardener come and go. According to a consistent statement, they were not in the house or at the property on Wednesday."

Sandrine thought about revealing her discovery in the park but decided against it. She wanted to find out more about the relationship between the two. *Maybe it's completely harmless.*

"That leaves Madame Garaine," Hermé said.

"At the time of the crime she was in the house," continued Destin. "Her room is on the top floor in the west wing. She claims to have let in Madame Cassian and then gone to bed. She says she did not hear a fight or any late visitors."

"Is that believable?"

"I looked around. Her room is far enough away for her to be undisturbed. The walls in that old building are thick. If she told the truth and was reading and listening to music, it is highly likely that she did not hear a thing."

"What do you think, Capitaine Perrot?" the prosecutor

turned to her.

"I agree with Major Destin. It's possible. At least, we can't prove her statement false."

"I took from the report that the victim's blood was caught in some form of vessel. Can you imagine that the woman would be capable of such an act?"

"I have been in the police force long enough to picture everything. The day after Savier's death, Madame Garaine attended her reading circle at the bookshop. She could have left the vase with the blood in the kitchen without attracting attention. She claims that her car is in the workshop and that she has no keys for Monsieur Savier's. It wouldn't be impossible, but rather difficult for her to commit the crime and break into the notary's office shortly thereafter."

Destin took out a notepad. "We checked. The car is in a workshop. She drives a diesel, and an injector is defective. The parts arrived yesterday. We found the key to Savier's Mercedes in a locked drawer. Forensics say they have never seen a cleaner car. Either the man rarely drove, or someone cleaned it very thoroughly."

"Then it's very probable that she didn't drive it?"

"The evaluation of a security camera of a private house didn't show anything. She would have had to drive past to get to the chancellery. Apart from two pedestrians and a cyclist it was quiet. We identified the two pedestrians, and neither could be the perpetrator."

"What do you suggest?" Hermé addressed her.

"I would like to find out more about Madame Garaine. How did she find work in the Savier's household, and where did she work before? And if there are any criminal records and relationships to other members of Savier's family."

"Good idea. Does she stay on the pinboard as a suspect?"

Sandrine took the woman's picture and moved it to the

upper corner.

"Then we have Madame Cassian, the business partner. She came to a meeting at around 7:00 p.m. The housekeeper invited her in and led her to the library. She is currently the last person who saw the victim alive. She claims she tried to reschedule the appointment, but Savier insisted on seeing her."

"Judging from his phone records that could be true. She called him late in the afternoon," Destin said. "The call did not last longer than two minutes. That does not point at a fight."

"She claims that this was the evening he offered her his shares on the chancellery, for a very good price which he kept a secret from his wife."

"What advantage would she gain from the man's death?" the prosecutor asked.

"Through the death clause in the contract, she receives the shares at a significantly lower price. The severance payment she has to pay the widow is rather small. We should look at the files just to be safe." Sandrine looked at Hermé, who nodded.

"Either the lawyer will give us a copy of the contract, or you'll receive a search warrant."

"Maybe she wanted to kill two birds with one stone. Frédéric Savier was a talkative guy, and she knew of his discovery. She, like all the other members of the reading group, detested the ways in which the treasure hunters worked. Maybe she was acting on ideals and wanted to protect the book from being sold, or she wanted the money for herself." She stroked her cheek in thought. "I'm not sure yet what to think of her."

"At least she admitted to profiting from his death."

"Why wouldn't she? We would have found out anyway. To play with open cards makes her less suspicious. The woman is clever and knows her way around police work."

"You could say that," Hermé confirmed. "I have met her in a few cases. She has a hard core in a pleasant wrapping."

"Then we have Margritte Violinet. The vase was found in her kitchen, and it seems to be the missing one from Savier's library." She turned to Major Destin. "Are there already findings from forensics?"

"Only a few. The red stains are definitely human blood. The blood group is also identical to Frédéric Savier's. A complete DNA analysis will take a while longer though. The Farz is also being examined. With a bit of luck, we can find useful samples, but that will also take time."

"Is Madame Violinet a suspect, or was the vase planted with her by someone else?" Hermé looked at her questioningly.

"I don't think the woman is a murderer. Why would Savier have invited her into his house late in the evening and offered her a cup of coffee? That wouldn't be his style."

"But why all that nonsense with the cake?" Destin shook his head.

"I see it more like a type of punishment or humiliation," said the prosecutor. "The bookstore in which the so-called treasure hunters meet is named Rabelais, isn't it?"

"Correct," confirmed Destin.

"Rabelais is known through his tales of the two giants he created, Pantagruel and Gargantua. Gargantua is an insatiable drunkard and glutton. He consumes food like these treasure hunters consume books, greedily and with no true love for literature. Our killer must despise these people because he made them consume, or simply put, eat their own president. What an irony."

The major exhaled loudly between his lips and looked at Hermé in disbelief, while Sandrine thought she caught a brief flash of respect for the perpetrator in the prosecutor's eyes.

"That's sick." Destin grimaced, revolted. Most likely he was remembering the piece of Far which he had eaten on the bookshop's terrace.

"Or maybe a fitting punishment and humiliation in the eyes of our murderer," retorted Hermé.

"Nothing to argue with there. The women in the reading group don't have a lot of sympathy for the men in the Rabelais," Sandrine agreed with him.

"What's your impression of the ladies?"

"Fleur Garaine, Margritte Violinet, Florence Cassian and Jocelyn Descours form the core. Each one of them spoke with disdain about the treasure hunters, and none of them has an alibi for the time of death."

"My men are already checking the women," said Destin. "So far, we have not come across anything out of the ordinary."

"We shouldn't forget the cup in the sink," Sandrine continued. "The cup wasn't used by Madame Cassian. She only drinks tea and uses a darker lipstick."

"That means he must have welcomed another female visitor. The murderess?" He looked at Sandrine who held a flashcard with a question mark.

"It looks like it. Our priority must be to identify that person quickly."

"We found fingerprints. If they are in the system, we will know very soon."

"Then we also have Alain Ducasse." Sébastian Hermé wrote the name on a piece of paper and personally stuck it onto the pinboard. "He seems to be the only one who knew what Savier wanted to sell. I know the man. He's not made from the right material to plan and commit a murder. We still have to find him, though. I want to know what we're dealing with."

"He is staying at a hotel in the area. According to the receptionist he's in his room and reserved a table at the restaurant for this evening." Major Destin looked up from his notes. "For two people."

"It would be interesting to know who the second person is," said Sandrine.

"Then we will find him and ask. I'm sure it will be quite informative."

Destin checked his watch. "We'll let the members of Monsieur Savier's book club assemble in the antique shop. They should be there in 30 minutes. Will you be there?" he asked Hermé.

"Do you need me?"

"Not necessarily. You know Monsieur Ducasse personally, so you'd better take care of him. He will be more likely to tell the truth if a prosecutor is present and not just two unimportant police officers. It's better if you talk to him, and we deal with the guys from the book club," Sandrine suggested. Also, she preferred to go to the Rabelais without Hermé. She would have enough opportunity to question the art collector later now that she knew where he was staying.

"Whatever you think is best," he agreed.

"On top of that, I wouldn't like to directly roll out the big guns."

"That's a nice compliment." Hermé chuckled. "But you're right. If the two of you get stuck, you can still threaten them with a bone-hard prosecutor from Rennes who will make their lives difficult."

"That was my plan. How far am I allowed to go?" asked Sandrine.

"Don't lean out of the window too far. It's easy to lose balance. However, a bit of theatre is never amiss."

She looked at Major Destin. "What do you prefer, to keep checking the suspects' backgrounds or to question a bunch of bookworms?"

"Without us adding some pressure, forensics will take weeks until they send us the results. I prefer to stay in close contact with them and drive to Rennes. I am sure you can deal with some people in a stuffy bookshop."

"I'll manage. Though I don't think I will be able to shine new light on anything interesting." She played down her task.

Sandrine finished the rest of her coffee. Midday had passed and hunger was creeping up on her. She preferred not to eat at Margritte's café. Not because of the unfortunate incident with the Farz Gwad, but because Margritte was now one of the suspects in the murder case. To go to the Rabelais without her colleagues fitted into her plan. Hermé could take care of the art collector, even though she was convinced that the man would stay quiet until his lawyer showed up. At least, that would be her strategy in a murder investigation. She would find Ducasse as soon as she discovered his weakness.

* * *

Roughly a dozen men were waiting for Sandrine in the Rabelais. When she entered, they fell silent. Suspicious, but also scared glances followed her on her way to the counter in front of which Louis Neville sat on a chair. The chair was dwarfed and barely visible under the massive man.

She leaned against the counter and directed her attention to the people present. The tension seemed palpable in the air. It felt obvious to her that these self-proclaimed treasure hunters were hiding something from her and were now scared that she had uncovered their secret. *I don't want to disappoint them.*

"Thank you for accepting my invitation," she greeted the men.

"We didn't have much choice. What were you thinking, ordering us to come here on an afternoon in the middle of a workweek? As if we had nothing else to do. We are businessmen and craftsmen who pay their taxes," one of them began.

From which I'm paid. But he didn't dare to say it or isn't angry enough yet.

The man wore a white overall covered in dried paint-splatters. She remembered; the owner of a painting shop had been on the member list. He must have come directly from a building site.

"My name is Capitaine Perrot from the Police Nationale. I am here to investigate the murder of your club's president, Fréderic Savier." Casually, she adjusted her shoulder holster. It was a reminder that they were dealing with the police, and not with a mere trifle but a murder. "Of course, each one of you is free to go. No one is accused of having committed the crime. At least not yet."

"What's that supposed to mean? Not yet?" the man reared up again.

"Exactly what I said." She assessed the man who looked around nervously as if searching for support. The other members stayed silent. *They hope to stay under the police's radar.*

"You're Monsieur Montfort, aren't you?"

"Yes. How do you know that?"

She did not answer the question and ignored the man which seemed to make him nervous as he began to move back and forth on his chair as if the wood had become highly uncomfortable.

"Fréderic Savier was struck dead in his house. Everyone should know that by now."

A murmur of agreement and nodding filled the room. Pierre Salazar, who had secured a front row seat as befitted the club's future president, wiped his eyes with a handkerchief and sobbed just loud enough to be heard.

"The poor man," whispered Louis Neville. "What a loss for Bécherel."

And for your business.

"We want to know if he had been acting out of the ordinary during the last couple of days or if he talked about any threats he might have received?"

"He was like he always was, I would say." Monsieur Montfort tried again to stand out as the leader of the group.

"I hadn't seen him since the last meeting," someone in a dark suit called from the last row. "Because of that I would like to leave. There's a lot of work waiting for me at the chancellery."

"There will be more," mumbled Sandrine. The painter and Salazar understood her and looked at each other with raised eyebrows.

"Your president wasn't a very discreet person. As far as we know, he told a couple of people that he had made an exceptional find, a very special book, which he wanted to present this Sunday. He rented the necessary room from Madame Violinet."

"Is it true that the old witch murdered him, mixed his blood into the Far and served it to us?" someone shouted.

"Investigations are still running. At the moment, she's a suspect just like most of the people present."

"What kind of accusation is that?" The man with the dark suit jumped up. "I'm a prosecutor, and I will complain about you."

"We'll find out if the blood in the Far really was Fréderic Savier's, and how it got there in the first place, only once the samples have been examined in the laboratory."

"We ate a part of Fréderic?" Louis Neville turned pale and swallowed heavily.

Apparently, Salazar had not informed him.

Sandrine waited until order returned before addressing the prosecutor.

"Everyone here is free to complain about me and the investigation. The gendarmerie will be happy to record it and initiate any further steps."

"We will, you can be sure of that," the painter shouted. "To claim that we had anything to do with Fréderic's death is just unbelievable. The love of books brought us together. We would never harm each other."

"Is that so?" She pushed away from the counter and took a step towards Montfort. The man shuffled back with his chair as she approached.

"Your business leaves you plenty of time to peruse book markets on the weekend?"

"I don't have lots of free time, that's true," he evaded the question. "But everyone has some form of hobby."

"What was your most significant find last year?"

"What? I don't understand," he stammered, and his eyes darted towards the antiquarian, searching for help.

"What's hard to understand? Which was the most valuable book you found and presented at your monthly meetings?" she said and stressed every single syllable.

"A first edition by Victor Hugo, if I remember correctly." Neville jumped to his help.

"Yes, exactly. The book was in pretty bad shape, but we polished it up a bit."

"I love books too. May I see the first edition?"

"We already sold it." Neville rose and stepped to the painter's side. "It didn't bring a fortune, but it was worth it."

"How much? I bet something between 1500 to 2000 euro."

"That might very well be. What are you getting at?" the painter asked suspiciously.

"Isn't it an obligation to report purchases of artworks in this area since the last amendment to the Money Laundering Act?"

"I'm not an expert in this," Monsieur Montfort threw in. "Everything on the business side goes through the antique shop."

"An all-inclusive service," she said and smiled at the man.

Neville could not have liked how quickly Montfort pushed the responsibility for the transactions onto him.

"There isn't much to that. Everything is completely legal." The lawyer seemed to deem it necessary to make another comment, but this time it was missing sharpness.

"Most likely not." Sandrine went back to the counter and leaned against it once more. She crossed her arms in front of her chest and let her gaze travel over the members. The budding fear and confusion in their eyes were hard to miss.

"A few craftsmen, a lawyer... Sorry, two lawyers, the owner of a repair shop, and so on. Normally people pay with cash, don't they?"

No one answered, and she had not expected them to.

"One works until late into the night, and then the tax office comes along and takes a huge chunk from the hard-earned profit. I would be annoyed by that."

Sandrine paused to let her words sink in. No one was chatting with their neighbour or playing on their phone. She had the full attention of the treasure hunters.

"Sometimes clients pay cash and don't want a receipt. Then you're faced with the dilemma of whether to throw it down the throat of the tax office or keep it secret. After all, the state spends most of the taxes on nonsensical things or subsidises the lazybones to lead a comfortable life. But what do you do with black money? It's difficult to deposit into an account, and there's always a high risk of a pile of cash lying under the mattress being discovered and stolen."

"We're only here because we love literature." Montfort tried to distract her.

"As soon as you can give me a quote from Jean Jacques Rousseau, I will leave you alone."

"Okay, okay..." he stammered.

"So, I take my untaxed money and buy, maybe even here in

the bookshop, a historical book with a value just below what has to be reported to the tax office. A nice investment."

"But then the money is gone," Salazar mumbled and earned a look of pity from his neighbours. It seemed like he was the only one who had no idea what was going on in the Rabelais.

"True. The sum was transferred to a foreign collector. Maybe to a master painter from Lyon. Just by coincidence, and with a lot of luck, one finds a small book treasure in one of the flea markets. Monsieur Neville manages to sell the find to another trader or collector. Roughly in the same price-range. The proceeds are transferred from the buyer to the seller's bank account, and you suddenly have clean money with an origin to be verified. Since they are individual private sales and not commercial trade by the members, no income tax is due." She turned to the antiquarian. "A small commission to Monsieur Neville at most. I'm guessing ten percent. Significantly below the tax rate, but seen across the book club as a whole, a lucrative sum for him. So, one collector sells to the next, and that one to the next, and so on. I'm not even convinced that the books which have been in circulation actually exist, they are just fantasy bookings. A nice money laundering scheme, especially if enough booksellers or collectors get involved. Not suitable for large amounts, but I suspect there are no drug dealers or pimps among you."

Neville returned towards his chair and sank down into it. The tortured creak sounded through the silence which had fallen over the room.

"What's your plan?" the lawyer asked. Nothing seemed left of his fighting spirit. His shoulders slumped forward, and fear flickered in his eyes. Surely the men had viewed it as a minor offence or thought they were clever enough to not be traceable. Who would find a book club in the Cité du Livre unusual? They probably would have gotten away with it for a long time, but Savier's murder had attracted too much attention.

"Good question. Normally it's my job to catch criminals and bring them to justice."

"Criminals?" Monsieur Montfort surged to the front. "We aren't criminals."

"If tax evasion and commercial fraud are criminal offences, you are welcome to discuss that with a competent judge. I assume the lawyers in your ranks can give you an initial assessment."

"You said 'normally'." The lawyer stood up and looked at her. "What options are you offering us?"

"You will have to take responsibility for what you have done here. That's for certain. My objective is catching the murderer of Fréderic Savier. If you have enough reason to stop with your lies and excuses and give me the information I require I might be too busy to initiate an investigation into tax evasion until... let's say until the end of next week." She had reached the point which had made it necessary for her to come to this meeting alone. Major Destin would never have agreed to her methods, and she had not wanted to get the prosecutor into a dilemma.

"We're screwed anyway," complained the painter.

"Shut up, Montfort. I will explain later," the lawyer snapped at him.

The man had understood what she offered them. As long as no official investigations had been initiated, all those involved had the option of reporting themselves. They would pay back taxes and get hefty fines, but no one would go to jail. Except for Neville. She saw dark times ahead of him.

Maybe he'll be lucky and there'll be a vacancy in the prison library.

"I will tell what I know," said the lawyer, "but it isn't much."

"I'm listening."

"Fréderic was already hard to bear on a normal day, but lately he had been strutting around with his chest puffed up like a bullfrog's. If he had exploded no one would have been surprised."

"Would have been better. Then the police wouldn't be all over us," Montfort mumbled under his breath.

"He showed off terribly, claimed he had found the treasure of the century. When this rich collector from Paris showed up, he completely lost it. Instead of quietly selling his find and getting rid of it, he craved the admiration of the literary world. What an idiot."

"You knew that he planned on presenting it in the bookshop?"

"Of course. All Bécherel probably knew. The man couldn't keep anything to himself. I wouldn't be surprised if he told the wrong person. Someone who wouldn't let an opportunity like that slip through his or her fingers."

"What book was it?" Sandrine came to the interesting point, but the man shrugged his shoulders.

"That was the only thing which he didn't tell anyone. This Ducasse must know. Otherwise, he wouldn't have come into this boring Province all the way from Paris. Ask him."

"We certainly will." With a bit of luck, Sébastian Hermé would reveal the secret after a talk with the art collector. "Does the name J. Robine ring any bells?"

"Never heard of it. Honestly." The lawyer sat back down. She did not expect anything else from him. She looked at Neville, but he had his eyes fixed on the ground, looking defeated.

"I want you all to write down where you were at the time the crime was committed. The papers you will hand to..." He stood half-hidden behind one of the shelves. "Alfonse will collect them. I will pick them up later."

The likelihood that she would find anything was close to zero. The men were shaken by the vague possibility of going to jail for tax evasion or losing their license to practice law. None of them had the cold blood it took to break into and search a victim's office after a murder. Let alone paying a late-night visit to the antiquarian bookshop one day later.

She left the Rabelais. She had not found out much but had expected nothing else. A storm of voices rose behind her. The treasure hunters would have many things to discuss today.

On the way out, her phone rang. The number was unknown to her.

"Capitaine Perrot."

"Sébastian Hermé. Did you find out anything interesting?"

"Nothing connected to Fréderic Savier that we didn't already know or suspected. No one knows what book he found or where it came from. Let alone where he might have hidden it. Could you find out more with Ducasse?"

"Unfortunately not. The man clamped shut like an oyster. Without his lawyer he won't say a word. I'm convinced he could help us."

"Shame, I had counted on your charisma." Silence answered from the other side. *Damn.* The comment had slipped out. "Am I allowed to try a bit more of a direct approach?" she added.

"As my charisma didn't lead to a result, I give you free roam. Maybe with you he'll be a bit more forthcoming." He had caught himself fast. She hoped that he did not hold the little joke against her.

"Then I will see you tomorrow in the gendarmerie," Sandrine said as a goodbye and put her phone back. She looked at her watch. She should be back in Saint-Malo just in time for the training. *At least a light at the end of the tunnel.*

. . .

Sandrine's punches banged against the two pads which Léon held in his hands. The clapping echoed loudly through the gym.

"Take a break," he invited her and took a step back.

"Are you already tired?"

She leaned forward and braced her hands on her thighs. The muscles in her arms burned from exhaustion, and her shirt stuck wet to her back.

"That was very much necessary." She looked up and smiled at him.

"Are you stuck with the case?"

"That's not it. My instinct tells me that we're close."

"What then? Your prosecutor?"

She turned her head and smelled her shirt.

"I need a shower."

"You just started and want to stop again?" A slender woman, maybe a head taller than Sandrine, leaned against the ropes of the ring.

"Still have to work, Lilou. New colour?"

Lilou Lanvers stroked her hair. The strong red had changed into a platinum blond with violet stars.

"Yes, my students like to be entertained by the coolest teacher."

Sandrine nodded. The woman, who had already given her a couple of bruises in the ring, taught history at the Saint-Malo high school and was an enthusiastic follower of experimental archaeology. She remembered the lump of iron she had shown her: the end product of a Celtic kiln that she had built and operated with her students.

"I bet they do," she agreed with her. The woman was definitely a better teacher than someone like Pierre Salazar who must see his students as either idiots or enemies.

"You're famous now. At least your picture is all over the newspapers."

"Yes, there's lots of rubbish."

"I don't believe anything of that shit." She looked at Léon, and a wide grin spread over her face. "And you're a drug dealer now, hm?"

Léon slipped out of the protectors and went to the ropes. Sandrine followed him and sank down on the ring's floor.

"You believe that?" he asked.

"You would make a terrible drug dealer. You're much too soft-hearted. You would be bust in a day," replied Lilou. "Who framed you?"

"I don't know." He put the protectors on the floor and shook out his arms. They had finished half an hour of box-training, and he had withstood a lot.

"I have an idea," Sandrine said.

"Really?"

"You will know when it's time."

"Then you'd better hurry up. Otherwise, you will only see the commissariat from the outside or a cell from the inside."

"I won't let it get that far."

"If I can help, you know where to find me," Lilou said. Normally she was not overly liberal with offering help.

"You talked with Arianne. That was enough help."

"She's a good journalist. Not one of those who only repeat nonsense. She also likes you. No idea why. You barely have anything in common."

"Neither do we, and you still love me."

"Ah," Lilou waved him away, "don't get all emotional. I just tried to avoid losing an acceptable sparring partner. That's it."

"Then I will do my best to get out of this thing unscathed. Ultimately you have to defend a title as Brittany's champion in kick-boxing and need my support."

"Hurry up. They say the noose is tightening."

"We'll get through this together," said Léon.

"I didn't expect anything else." The woman picked up a couple of leather training gloves from the floor. "Now piss off. I need the ring."

Sandrine laughed and stood up. He lifted one of the ropes and ducked under it.

"Don't think I'm going to hug you to wish you luck or anything. You're sweaty and stink." Lilou ignored the open arms and climbed into the ring. Laughing, Sandrine walked in the direction of the showers.

"Any plans for this evening?" Léon asked and followed her.

"Have to work, unfortunately. A nightshift."

"How long?"

"At midnight I should be home the latest. By then you'll have been in the club for a few hours. I would come over for a beer, but at the moment it's better I'm not seen at the Équinoxe. I'm certain that some journalist would be waiting to pounce."

"Would you mind if I come along?"

"Why?" she asked, surprised. "Most likely I'll spend most of the time in the car waiting until something happens that's worth the effort."

"We can make out in the car like teenagers," he joked.

"I have work to do, and your club doesn't run itself."

"Simone can manage. I wanted to give her more responsibility anyway."

"Why?" Sandrine tried to keep her suspicion from her eyes but judging by the way he looked at her she had failed.

"Don't look so scared. I'm not assuming I'll go to jail."

"I hope not." In fact, her guess was that he wanted to squeeze out more time for the two of them. She was happy with how things were going between them at the moment. She had always avoided a steady relationship and was not sure if she was ready for one.

"You're here with the motorbike, and a thunderstorm is

coming. It's not a good idea to drive into town during the night. You will be soaked before you get there. Let's take my car, and I promise to stay in it while you risk your neck."

"Promise?"

"Pinky promise." He lifted his hand as if to swear, but she did not believe a word. Léon knew that she could take care of herself, but he still wanted to protect her. It would be hard to keep him in the car should he become concerned for her safety.

* * *

Léon's SUV rolled along the long-stretched driveway which was bordered by trees. The drive ended in front of a sprawling château housing a hotel. Judging from the cars parked in front, it was on the expensive side. *Where else would someone like Ducasse stay?*

"What's your plan here?" he asked. "Do you want to go for dinner before? The restaurant is surely excellent."

"Just a quick chat, nothing else."

"Shall I come in with you? Maybe they happen to have a free table..."

"Nice try. I'm here for work, and you're not a policeman but a suspect in a drug case. It's probably better I do this alone. A bodyguard won't be necessary, the man I want to talk to isn't dangerous."

"Your choice. I'm just your driver and can wait out here in the dark."

"We went to the studio early, and it's just before eight. The sun's just going down. You have another hour until it gets dark."

"But..." he began when her phone buzzed.

"Hey, Rosalie." Sandrine took the call.

"Where are you? I was waiting for you."

"I was in Saint-Malo to train and now back in Bécherel. Lots of work to be done. Did I miss something? Were we supposed to meet today?"

"We weren't, but I could explode from how proud I am. I wanted to tell you face to face and show off properly, of course."

"It doesn't sound like it can wait until breakfast."

"Hey, Rosalie," Léon called in between.

"Oh, you have company. How nice! So much for work. Have a nice evening, you two."

"I'm helping as deputy."

"As driver," Sandrine corrected him. Rosalie's laugh sounded from the phone.

"I finished a chapter of Hugo Delacroix's case. He was forced to fight through the files of a doctor in Nantes. The guy had terrible handwriting which made it hard for the commissaire to get through."

"That sounds very interesting, and I'm looking forward to reading it soon, but now I have to go, or I run the danger of missing my suspect."

"I'm an author and need a bit of drama so you must wait."

"Okay. Five minutes and then I hand you over to Léon, so he doesn't get bored in the parking lot. He loves thrillers." The look he shot her said something else.

"So, the doctor had terrible handwriting, like most, that's why I asked after Savier's handwriting."

"Yes, the man very much scribbled."

"Is it possible that it's not Robine but Rabine?"

"It's possible," she said, trying to remember the note.

For the next couple minutes, she listened intently to Rosalie. She nodded several times before she finished the talk and sat unmoving for a moment. Léon did not ask. He could see she needed time to think and figure out what to do with the received information. She did not have any doubts that her friend might be incorrect. Everything fitted together too perfectly for that.

"I have to go. It won't be long."

Sandrine got out of the car. A gust of wind whipped up sand and swirled it through her hair. Dark clouds towered on the horizon, and the first lightning flashed through the sky. After the unusually hot and dry weeks a thunderstorm would do wonders.

"Capitaine Perrot," she introduced herself to the man at reception and placed her police badge in front of him. "I want to talk to Monsieur Ducasse."

The receptionist typed something on the keyboard and checked the screen.

"Monsieur Ducasse reserved a table at the restaurant. I can fetch him for you if you want."

"A table for how many?"

"Only for two, as far as I can see."

"Has his guest already arrived?"

"Half an hour ago."

"I won't interrupt them for long." She turned and marched towards the restaurant.

"You can't just..." he called after her, but she did not intend on being stopped by a hotel employee.

She stepped through the door and directly to the table. The man recognised her instantly, and his companion sat with her back to her.

"Monsieur Ducasse, I'm Capitaine Perrot, and I have to talk to you."

Sandrine pulled over a chair from the neighbouring table and sat down before he could refuse.

"What do you think you're doing? We're having dinner."

She did not pay any attention to his objections and instead turned to the woman.

"Good evening, Madame Savier. What a surprise to see you

again so soon. Didn't you say you had never heard of a Monsieur Ducasse?" Had she found the man, or had he contacted her to finish the deal?

The woman's cheeks darkened, and she wiped the napkin over her mouth to gain some time to think.

"We ran into each other in a bookshop and got talking. You know, bookworms among themselves." He jumped to her help. His outrage had given way to a tone that was as jovial as it was mendacious. She was sure that he hated having been surprised in his endeavour of having dinner with Fréderic Savier's widow and was now trying his best to hide it.

"Exactly," she chuckled nervously. "We have more than enough of those in Bécherel."

"You discovered your love for old books since the last time we talked? Your late husband would have been overjoyed." Sandrine did not hold back the irony. She was certain the woman had never entered a bookshop in her life.

"As you have now been informed of everything that's going on, you might understand that we would like to enjoy our evening. I already talked to your boss, Hermé, the prosecutor. I will not offer any other information without my lawyer present." He waved at a waiter. "You will be shown outside."

"As you wish," Sandrine agreed but stayed in her chair unmoving. Alain Ducasse gave her a look that snobs like himself would probably describe as indignant. She had met more than enough of that sort of man in her father's galleries.

"Monsieur Savier is dead, and yet you stayed in the area. Judging from that, you must still hope of somehow getting your hands on the book. Do you expect to buy it from his widow?"

"How...?" he snapped at her.

"It took me a while to figure out what it was, but in the end it was obvious."

"I don't understand what you're getting at." To belie his words, he motioned to the waiter not to interfere.

"One of my friends writes thrillers. Quite successful ones, I might add. Anyway, the last one was set in Nantes."

"A very nice city." His tone was too casual to feel genuine. His posture was losing its nonchalance. The man was tense. He must still be hoping that she'd jumped to the wrong conclusions, but doubts clearly were rising up in him.

"John James Audubon grew up there, didn't he?"

Ducasse exhaled deeply. The hope to keep his intentions secret had just evaporated.

"The naturalist who liked to draw birds?" Isabelle Savier asked in a desperate attempt to seem ignorant.

"Your late husband must have had a special passion for Audubon. He had his bust on his writing desk. You don't see something like that a lot. And then to be struck down with one is very tragic, isn't it?"

"Fréderic inherited the whole house, including the library and the bust, from his grandfather. I have no idea if he even knew who the bust depicted. He definitely wasn't the type of person who stood up early to watch some dumb birds."

"I can't imagine that either," Sandrine agreed with the widow.

"What has this inherited bust, which just happened to be standing around when he surprised a burglar, got to do with his death?"

"Isn't it obvious? In his calendar was an entry with J. Rabine. Audubon grew up in Nantes with his mother's name as Jean Rabine. More than just a coincidence, hm?"

"What does that have to do with me?" Ducasse carefully folded his napkin and placed it next to his plate. He grabbed his champagne glass and took a sip.

Again, he's playing for more time.

"We met you at the given date and time. I wouldn't expect to find a well-known art collector in a town like this unless it's for an important piece of work."

"I have to admit, Monsieur Savier contacted me and made big promises. Unfortunately, he died before we could meet. I can't say what exactly he wanted to offer." He lied in a way that suggested he had been practicing a lot.

"An appointment about Jean Rabine, and a note with the initials JJLFA. The name he took when he emigrated to North America: John James La Forest Audubon. As a dramatic end he was struck down with Audubon's bust. You really want to make me believe everything is just a coincidence?"

"Who knows?" A smug grin spread over his lips.

"I assume that you met him the night of his death to close the deal."

"That's not true."

"Did you get into a fight about prices?"

His smile crumbled and made way for a nervous twitch. "Not at all," he hissed.

"It must be about an important piece: *Birds of America*. What would something like this be worth nowadays?"

"A nice sum. At least if one receives a well-preserved first edition. However, a work like this does enter the market very rarely."

"I heard that the last edition changed hands for around nine million at an auction."

Surprise light Isabelle Savier's eyes. Most likely Ducasse had tried to use her lack of knowledge and offered her much less.

"That was luck," he appeased. "Such auctions are famous for firing up the bidders' temperaments. I wouldn't bet on getting an amount anywhere near that high." The comment had been directed more at Savier's widow than at Sandrine.

And also, an admittance to what business they were talking about.

Mentally she thanked Rosalie who had given her the decisive clue mere minutes ago. The murderer must have had excellent insight into Fréderic Savier's life or must have gleaned from his boasting what the man had discovered. He was either well-educated or an admirer of the naturalist. The perpetrator must have considered it stylish or appropriate to hit his victim with the bust of the artist whose book he was trying to steal.

"A very nice story, but nothing of it is true. It's the first time I'm hearing about a first edition of Audubon's *Birds of America* here in Bécherel. That would be sensational. What he actually found, and if it has any value, we will most likely never find out." He shrugged his shoulders.

"We will, no worries. I came here with the goal of warning you. The book already cost one man his life. Even though you don't have your hands on it yet, the murderer will expect you to have made a downpayment. Which endangers you." She looked at Isabelle Savier. "Both of you. Be careful. Should the book be in your possession it would be wise to hand it over to the police."

"I neither have a suitcase with cash with me, nor do I fear a cowardly burglar who attacks their victims from behind their backs," Ducasse replied while Isabelle evaded her gaze.

The first thing might be correct, even though she doubted it, but the second was simply stupid. She actually feared those who ambushed her more than those she saw coming.

"Now, I would be glad if you would spare us your presence and further insinuations. We intend to enjoy our dinner in peace."

"It was my duty to warn you. How you handle it is up to you." Sandrine rose and pushed the chair back to the table. She gave a quick nod as a goodbye and left the two of them in the restaurant. They must have lots to discuss. Ducasse could not be happy that she had appeared and meddled with his business. Most likely, the price of the book would increase significantly during the dinner.

***

Léon parked in the shadow of the trees lining the alley. He had switched off the headlights as soon as they had passed the entrance. The estate lay dark in front of them. Only one window had a soft glow.

"Isabelle Savier is still out for dinner which means this must be the housekeeper's room."

"And you want to pay her a visit?"

"That's exactly my plan."

"I assume you won't just ring the bell and wait until she lets you in."

"You're exactly right. It's the woman's evening off. Why would I annoy her?"

"What are we doing here then?" he asked, perplexed.

"I just want to check really quickly with whom she spends her free time." *With her books like she told us or in another way? I have to know if she is keeping secrets from us to protect a third party.*

"Are you going to pull out your lockpicks and open the backdoor?"

"Why do you think that? That would be illegal." She played being shocked and grinned at him happily. "Won't take long."

She got out of the car and approached the house. She had noticed a ladder behind the garden hut when she had been here on Thursday and hoped it was still there. If Arnault Gaudry had taken it with him, or locked it away, she would have to revert to her alternative plan which included the lockpicks in her trouser pocket.

Lucky. She pushed some hip-high nettles to the side with her boots and grabbed the wooden ladder. Quiet music sounded from the sightly open window.

Chances were high that Fleur Garaine was in the room. Sandrine leaned the ladder against the ivy-covered wall and checked her surroundings. Apart from a bat which darted through the sky to catch insects, everything was quiet. The SUV's silhouette was swallowed up by the increasing darkness. The wind was picking up, and deep thunder announced the coming thunderstorm. She had to hurry up.

Sandrine stepped on one of the lowest steps and rocked slightly. The ladder did not look very stable but seemed to hold her weight. Slowly and soundlessly, she climbed up until she reached Fleur Garain's room. To her luck, the woman had not fully drawn the curtains. Carefully she lifted her head, glimpsed inside and grinned. Her suspicion had just been confirmed.

A lightning bolt lit up the sky, and she twitched away from the window. Deafening thunder swallowed any sounds of descent. She had to be gone before Fleur Garaine thought of closing the window. A few thick raindrops hit her head and back. She jumped from the last step, grabbed the ladder and carried it back behind the shed. Ducking low in the shadow she watched the house. The housekeeper came to the window, closed it and pulled the curtains shut.

She stood up and wiped her wet forehead. The rain was pouring from the sky by now and pushed like a veil between her and the car. Cold water hit her face and soaked through her clothes in seconds.

Léon opened the door from the inside, and she slipped in. He handed her a towel, and she rubbed her hair until it was dry enough to no longer drip on the seat. With skill, she climbed on the backseat and got out of her wet clothes.

"What's your plan?"

"I don't want to get a cold."

"Shall I keep you warm?" he asked and smiled back at her.

"Later," she mumbled and pulled a clean sweatsuit from her sport's bag which she had deposited in his car after the training.

"Did you see what you were after?"

"Don't make me sound like a voyeur. That was for work."

"I assume the housekeeper had a visitor and both are reading a good book as is proper in this town."

She threw her trousers and shirt on the rubber mat and rolled her slip and bra into the wet towel. The cotton of her sweatpants felt luxuriously dry and soft.

"Look at the street," she admonished Léon.

"Normally you're not this coy."

"Normally I'm not working."

"And when is your nightshift over?"

"As soon as you drop me off in Cancale." She slipped into the hoodie and climbed over the passenger seat.

"Thank you for driving me." She leaned over and kissed his cheek.

"Of course. In this weather I could never let you take the motorbike."

"I was referring to the pleasant company. Maybe we have enough time for a hot coffee or something else at my place before you have to leave for the club."

"I'll take the *something else*." He started the motor, engaged reverse gear and turned. The rubber of the wipers squeaked across the windshield. They rolled along the avenue at walking pace until they reached the main street. It would take them more than 40 minutes to get to Cancale, given the weather. Plenty of time to reflect on what she had learned tonight. She turned on the radio and swivelled the seat back until she was comfortably seated, almost lying down.

An Uncovered Lie

More thunderstorms had been announced for the day, and Sandrine had decided to free the Citroën 2CV from the garage. She had driven comfortably to Bécherel and stopped in front of a small hardware shop. The shop seemed to run better than she had assumed. The hall in which the equipment was kept was not very big, but it looked new. Arnault Gaudry was in the process of driving a ride-on lawnmower up the ramp of his heavy pick-up truck. He looked up and waved at her.

She got out. The gardener jumped off the truck bed and came towards her. Judging by his lively walk, he was in the best of moods and looking forward to the day with anticipation. She thought about what he might be up to and smiled.

"The woman from the police. How can I help you?"

"You seem to be in high spirits," she greeted him.

"I am. The rain was just in time for the gardens. If it had come any later, everything would have withered away."

"Where are you off to today?"

"To the Savier's."

"To mow the lawn and make lots of noise?"

He chuckled. "I can't help it."

"Madame Garaine won't like that, will she?"

"I just avoid her. That's always best."

"You didn't manage very well last night."

He halted and his smile dropped.

"What do you mean?"

"Did you not meet Fleur Garaine after you met in the park of Château de Caradeuc?" Sandrine asked.

"How...?"

"Madame Savier wasn't at home. Who could blame you for using the situation for a romantic meeting?"

"Fleur... Madame Garaine and I only had a... talk about the garden. Nothing else." The man tried to save himself.

"Naked and in her bed? Is that a normal business meeting for you?"

"You...?" Gaudry fell silent and stared at her in surprise.

"Yes, and I'm sorry about it. I borrowed the ladder from behind the shed. That might not have been 100% correct, but..." She shrugged her shoulders in apology. "After I saw you in the park, I was curious to see how well you actually knew each other. It's a murder investigation after all."

"This has nothing to do with the murder of Monsieur Savier," bubbled out of him.

"And you? Do you have anything to do with the death? It would be easy for you to get into the house."

"Me?" He stared at her with his mouth hanging open. He looked like he could not believe what she was accusing him of. "I wouldn't kill anyone."

"How long has the relationship with Fleur Garaine been going on?" Her attack had thrown the man off balance. She could not let him off now.

He opened the door of the truck and sat sideways on the passenger seat.

"She'll be sacked if Madame Savier finds out that she lets me into the house at night."

"She'll sack her anyway," Sandrine retorted in a harsh tone.

"Why? No one knows anything about our relationship. Apart from you." He threw her a begging look as if to beseech her to not tell anyone.

"The woman hates living in Brittany. She'll sell the estate as fast as possible and move back to Provence. There she won't need a housekeeper. You'll be made to beautify the garden quickly before the first interested parties appear. So, it doesn't matter what you tell me. Your friend will definitely lose her job."

He took a deep breath and wiped his sleeve over his forehead.

"Alright. What do you want to know?"

"Madame Garaine stated to have been in her room at the time of the murder. Was she alone?" She looked at him questioningly.

"No. I was visiting her."

"For how long?"

"I was working in the garden when Florence Cassian arrived. Shortly after I went to Fleur and only left after midnight."

"And Madame Garaine can confirm that?"

"Of course."

"Did you notice anything strange? An argument, noise, a car driving off late in the night?"

The man hesitated. "I didn't pay attention to that."

"Every little detail could be of importance," she pressed.

"Very well, we heard a car's engine. Fleur's a bit skittish and directly thought of burglars, and so I stood up and went to the window to check. I only saw a car driving off. It was quite fast considering the terrible condition the driveway is in if you ask me."

"Did you see the driver?"

"No, but I'm pretty sure that it was the red sportscar of Madame Savier. The car has a dent on the left side on the back. She got it while backing up against the garden shed a while ago. She was probably in a bit of a hurry or had one glass of rosé too many."

"Are you sure?" she asked. *The woman claims to have been with her relatives in Provence at the time. That's why we can't find the sister. She doesn't want to lie to the police.*

"Yes."

"When was that?"

"It must have been just before midnight. Afterwards, I drove home."

"Why didn't you tell us earlier?"

"Fleur asked me to stay quiet. She didn't think that her boss could have anything to do with the murder, and she feared for her job. It's not easy to find a good position in the area."

"She wants to stay in Bécherel?"

"We're in love. Of course she wants to stay in the area."

Thinking about Fleur Garaine brightened his expression. She hoped it was the same for the woman.

"Anything else that you didn't tell us?"

"No idea if it's important, but on the way back to Bécherel, I nearly ran over a cyclist. The guy was driving without the lights on. At that hour! He should be able to confirm if you can find him."

"I will let the gendarmerie know," she promised, though she did not question his report. *The two definitely have a waterproof alibi. I can take Fleur's picture off the pinboard.*

"What's your plan?" The worry of having gotten his girlfriend into trouble was written all over his face.

"I will check with Fleur and see if she confirms your report." *And after that, talk to the grieving widow.*

"She will. 100%."

"I think so too. Now, I don't want to keep you from work any longer."

Sandrine went back to her Citroën 2CV, slipped in the driver's seat and called Major Destin.

"I questioned the gardener again. Guess who he saw in front of the house the night of the murder."

"Madame Savier," the man answered.

"I'm surprised. Who told you?"

"Forensics. The results came in a few minutes ago. The fingerprints on the cup which we found in the sink were from her."

"Then she wasn't just in front of the house but also inside."

"I don't see another possibility. We asked the colleagues in Nice to check her alibi again. Her sister cannot hide from us forever. Sooner or later, she has to come to work."

"Then we should really talk to Isabelle Savier."

"I'm in Rennes with the prosecutor. Do you want to wait for us or question her alone?"

"I would prefer having you here, but the longer we wait the likelier it becomes that she'll hear what's going on and come up with some story. The gardener is in a relationship with Fleur Garaine and will definitely gossip about it. Then it's only a matter of time before the housekeeper tells Madame Savier."

"Drive over and confront the woman so long as she has no idea that we are coming. We'll jump in the car and should be there in 30 minutes."

"Then I will see you at the Saviers' estate."

She nodded at the gardener who sat with his shoulders

slumped on the passenger seat of his truck and drove off. At the exit she hesitated. *If she found the book it's likely she is with Ducasse.* The hotel lay in the opposite direction. *I will try my luck at the house.* She pressed the gas and steered the Citroën 2CV towards the estate of the Saviers.

The entrance door stood open. No one seemed to be around, and Sandrine stepped into the hallway. Isabelle Savier's irritated voice sounded from the library. She was giving instructions to someone.

Sandrine stopped at the door. Madame Savier sat on the floor, piles of books on either side of her. The glass doors of the showcases were open, and there were wide gaps in the shelves where books had been. Mountains of books were stacked up behind the desk. She had systematically searched the entire inventory of her deceased husband. Thinking of the dead man, Sandrine looked at where he had been murdered. Someone had removed the armchair and a carpet covered the area where the blood had seeped into the parquet floor. Madame Garaine stood on a stepladder clearing one of the top shelves while her boss watched impatiently. Sandrine knocked on the door frame, and the women's heads immediately turned to her.

"What are you doing here?" Isabelle Savier threw an annoyed glance her way.

"The door was open, and I was so free to enter." She took another step into the library. "Is this not a good time?"

"I have to take care of my husband's legacy." She pointed at the mountains of books. "That doesn't leave much time for anything else. I already told you everything. What else do you want?"

"I assume you offered the book for sale to Alain Ducasse last night. He will have given you a nice sum."

"I wouldn't know why that's any of your business!" she replied tartly and stood up from the floor. She patted some dust from her trousers and sat down again on the narrow, brocaded sofa. "What I do with my inheritance is my responsibility. No one has the right to interfere."

"It's a murder investigation. The police have to interfere in everything."

She turned to address Fleur Garaine who was still up the ladder.

"Feel free to come down and have a break. We will talk later."

"It won't take long," Isabelle Savier interjected. "You can stay here." She obviously planned on getting rid of Sandrine as fast as possible and continuing her search. The sale was her ticket to the luxurious lifestyle she had probably always envisioned for herself. She had not found it in her marriage.

"We'll see how long it takes," Sandrine retorted.

"Alright. What do you want?" The woman sighed and gestured for her to hurry.

"Did Alain Ducasse make you an offer?"

"Of course, that's why the man is here."

"A generous one, I assume."

"You can assume that."

"He's obsessed with owning it. Buying without risking an auction where a competitor might raise the price is certainly worth a premium to him. I assume we're talking about an amount in the high millions. Maybe even double digits."

"You can assume whatever you want."

"The book has already cost your husband's life. You should be careful."

"I am. You don't have to be worried about me."

"Many people are ready to kill for such a sum."

"It's mine now. Fréderic wanted to sell it, and I'm simply closing the deal. I'm following his wishes."

"And then?"

"We will see." At least she had enough sensitivity to avoid mentioning the impending termination in front of her employee. She probably did not want to lose her only helper in the search.

"How was your marriage?" Sandrine changed the topic.

"Very good," the woman answered shortly. "As I told you before."

"After all, your husband didn't inform you of his find and the negotiations."

"He must have wanted to surprise me."

"You think he also wanted to surprise you with selling books from his library, hoarding the money in his bank account and with offering Madame Cassian his shares of the chancellery?"

"He did what?" She straightened and anger flashed in her eyes.

"I assume he was planning a divorce and was saving his finances."

"Nonsense." She fended off the statement. "He loved me."

Sandrine threw a glance at Fleur Garaine, but she was just looking at the ground. Clearly, she neither wanted to lie to the police nor enrage her boss any further.

"Our marriage is none of your business, and I don't know what that would have to do with his death. As you know, I was with my sister in Nice."

"Unfortunately, we are unable to contact your sister. It's like she disappeared into a black hole."

"She will have taken a few days off. Who knows? She's a spontaneous woman."

"We will find her, it's just a matter of time."

"Do that." The shadow of a smile ghosted over the woman's

lips. She knew where her sister was hiding and was convinced that the police would not find her.

"You said on protocol that Madame Garaine informed you of your husband's death Thursday morning. Do you want to make any changes to this statement?"

"Of course not." She looked at her housekeeper.

"I called Madame Savier directly after I found him here." Her eyes drifted towards the place where the chair had stood.

"But she already knew that her husband had died, right?"

"How could she have known?" Fleur Garaine stammered.

"That's a malicious insinuation." Isabelle Savier jumped up from the sofa. "Get out of my house!"

"I can, but I'll come back with an arrest warrant. Then the police will take over your search for the book. Our forensic technicians are very good at finding certain objects."

"You wouldn't dare." The anger in her voice gave way to panic.

She doesn't trust anyone. There's no chance she will leave the library of her own accord.

"Let's start again from the beginning. Where were you the Wednesday evening your husband died?" She avoided saying *murdered*. That way it sounded less like an accusation.

"At my sister's. Where else?"

"Your car was seen by more than one witness close to the house."

"There's lots of cars of that type," she answered but hesitantly.

"The witnesses mentioned a certain dent. Your car's parked in front of the house. Shall we have a look?"

"The people must be mistaken."

"We found a cup in the sink with your fingerprints and lipstick on it."

"That's impossible." She stayed adamant.

"We can easily check if you were in the car. A transponder for the motorway toll is stuck to your windscreen. It is a routine matter for us to receive the data. Then the misunderstanding will be cleared up."

Isabelle Savier stared at her, fuming. Finally, she exhaled violently. She was trapped and she knew it.

"Alright. You win. I drove here on Wednesday."

"You admit having been in the house the evening of the murder?"

"I came back earlier, that's true. But Fréderic was already dead when I arrived."

"When was that?"

"Eleven, maybe half past. I didn't check my watch."

"And then?"

"I came in through the backdoor. There was light in the library, and that's where I found him."

"You didn't want to inform the police?"

"No, he couldn't be saved. He was definitely dead... all the blood." She shook from disgust. "I panicked and ran off."

"Where to?"

"To Rennes. I stayed in a hotel to calm down." She looked at Sandrine. "You have to believe me. I have nothing to do with his death."

"I believe that you panicked. Otherwise, you would have properly cleaned the cup and put it away."

"What cup?"

"Let's start again. It's quite a distance from Nice to Bécherel, not a little trip. And don't tell me you came because you missed your husband."

"Definitely not." She went to the writing desk, opened her Louis Vuitton handbag, and took out a plane ticket. She let it drop on the desktop with distaste.

"He wanted to leave?"

"I was supposed to wait for him in Nice. The liar was never going to meet me. He wanted to piss off and leave me behind with this decrepit house and the debt."

"You have debt?"

"How much do you think it takes to maintain this property? The inheritance has been used up, and the law firm isn't making enough money for a decent living. He wasted most of it on his book collection." With one angry movement she wiped a stack of papers from the table. "One time this idiot is lucky, and all he does is keep his mouth shut and plan his escape."

"Was there another woman in your husband's life?" Sandrine asked directly.

"Yes, but I don't know who it is."

"How did you find out?"

"As a wife, you know. Working hours grew steadily longer, and trips to his seedy flea markets expanded. Surely, she was there with him."

"Do you have any suspicions?"

"No, but I wanted to find out."

"And how did you imagine that would work?"

"I received a message which stated that he would meet this other woman here on Wednesday. That's why I jumped into the car and rushed over."

"You wanted to catch him cheating?"

"You can be sure of that. I arrived here and shot into the house, and there he was in the library in this damned chair. He was dead when I found him, I swear it," Isabelle Savier said firmly.

"You know who sent you the message?"

"No idea. The number was unknown to me. I tried to call back but without success."

"Instead of calling the police you fled."

"It was stupid, but I had to get out of here. Everyone would have assumed that it was me who cracked the bust over his skull."

A car pulled up outside. A moment later, footsteps approached. Destin and Hermé entered the library.

"My colleagues will take you with them."

"Am I under arrest?" Her eyes darted from the men to Sandrine and back.

"First, you have to put your details on record, then we decide what to do with you."

"I can't go to prison before I find the book. It must be here somewhere."

"We will post a policeman here who will keep watch over the room until you are released," the prosecutor assured her.

"It's important. No one's allowed to enter the library until I'm back."

"I promise."

Reluctantly, she went with him. She kept glancing at the half-empty shelves as if hoping to discover the treasure at the last second. Destin led her out.

"I should leave too," said Fleur Garaine.

"Not before you have answered some of our questions."

"If it's necessary," she agreed hesitantly.

"I'll come to the office," Sandrine said to Hermé.

"We'll hold off the questioning until you arrive."

"It shouldn't take long."

The prosecutor said goodbye and went outside. Shortly after, she heard the car drive off.

"May I have a look around your room?" Sandrine asked the housekeeper.

"Why? There's nothing special up there."

"The location is interesting to me. An experienced lawyer

will ask if I have been inside, and he will try to shed doubt as to whether it is believable that you didn't hear anything of the fight between the couple."

"I was wearing headphones."

"It's easier to confirm that if I have inspected the premises thoroughly." *A nightly glimpse through the window won't be enough in this case.*

"Do you not need a search warrant?"

"Only if you refuse me entry, but why would you do that?"

The woman's forehead creased, and she bit her lower lip.

"The case is solved."

"Looks like it. One can only be certain after Madame Savier has been convicted, although I have little doubt about that."

"I have nothing to hide. Follow me," she agreed.

Sandrine trailed after her through the hallway and up the stairs to the top floor. At the end of a long, door-lined hallway was the room.

"The library is in the opposite wing of the estate," Fleur explained to Sandrine.

The door scratched softly on the wavy floorboards when they opened it. Incomplete stucco framed the ceiling, and cracked red-and-gold fabric wallpaper covered the walls. A wide, high-poster bed with an embroidered bedspread sat at the head of the room. It left just enough space for an antique wardrobe. The pictures were thrown together as if someone had been looking for a place to hang everything that was a nuisance in other rooms. Nothing seemed to have changed here since the house was built.

"Cosy," she mumbled.

Sandrine opened the window and leaned over the sill. The jutting, covered entryway made it impossible to see the opposite wing.

"Are you happy?" the housekeeper asked.

"Absolutely. From here it would be hard to hear what's going on in the library even without headphones."

"Then we can…"

The phone vibrating on the nightstand interrupted her. The woman reached for it, but Sandrine stopped her with a wave of her hand.

"It's not necessary to take the call. I can tell you who it is and what he wants to tell you."

"What do you mean?"

"It's Arnault Gaudry trying to reach you. I assume he already left several messages."

"The gardener?" Madame Garaine pulled her hand back. "Then it cannot be very important. I will see him later once he has finished the lawn. It must be about his work plan."

"More like the plans after a long day's work."

"What are you getting at?"

"How long have you and Monsieur Gaudry been in a relationship?"

"What relationship?" she replied in a weak attempt to appear ignorant.

"Coincidentally, I saw you together in the park of the Château de Caradeuc."

"I… It was a business meeting."

"You seemed quite close."

"You are mistaken," she continued, acting upset. "That would be ridiculous."

"That's what I thought in the beginning, but curiosity is one of those symptoms that come with my work, and I played spy."

"That's unheard of!" Outrage and fear mixed in her voice and made it crack.

"I came past the estate last night."

The woman pressed her lips together and stared at Sandrine without moving a muscle.

"There's an old ladder behind the shed. It's long enough to reach your window. It was open a crack, and I couldn't resist curiosity and took a look inside."

"You did..." she began but decided to fall silent. A soft blush crept into her cheeks.

"Arnault Gaudry seems like a nice guy. Why are you hiding your relationship?"

Sandrine went to the small table on which a handful of books had been stacked. At the top lay a copy of the *Kama Sutra* elaborately bound in ochre leather. She ran her fingertips along the embossed cover. If the books came from the library, which she had no doubt of, Frédéric Savier's grandfather must have had a taste exceedingly frivolous for his time, and which his grandson probably did not share.

"I'm sorry to have invaded your privacy like this," Sandrine apologised. "However, it was necessary to check some alibis."

"You should be ashamed of yourself," the woman whispered with her eyes lowered to the floor.

"In my job this type of shame doesn't last very long. So again, for how long have you and Monsieur Gaudry been together?"

"Only for a short time, maybe two weeks. We kept it secret. Madame Savier would not approve if she found out."

"Are we still living in times like that?" Sandrine shook her head in disbelief. "When did you let him in on Wednesday evening?"

"After I led Madame Cassian into the library. Monsieur Gaudry... Arnault was waiting for me at the back entrance."

"He visited a lot?"

Madame Garaine stayed silent and nodded.

"Then he knew his way around the house?"

"He never stepped foot into the library if that's what you want to know. Arnault is not the type who reads."

"Did he know of Monsieur Savier's discovery?"

She shook her head. "Definitely not. Most likely he has never heard of Audubon."

"And who told you?"

"You saw what we were doing when you came in. I mean Madame Savier and I. She has no idea where her husband could have hidden it and is now searching the whole house."

"The woman seems to not trust anyone. How come she trusts you enough to tell you which book it is?" Sandrine queried.

"She hasn't told me, but I'm not stupid. Her husband had been patting Audubon's bust lately, and she has me looking for a large-scale work with drawings of birds. It is not difficult to piece together what we are searching for: *Birds of America*. The greed is written all over her face. The joy of leaving everything behind and finally being able to live in the luxury she was hoping for alternates with the panic of not finding it. I guess she told that art collector that she had it."

"I thought so. Do you have any idea where Monsieur Savier could have hidden it?"

"Not at all. His wife keeps asking me at least once per minute. We were not very close. I was only working here, and that was it."

"Back to your visitor. Could he have snuck out during the night?"

"He was here for the entire time. I can swear on that. Arnault only left around midnight. I watched him drive off from my window," Madame Garaine confirmed.

"Did he tell you that he thought he saw Madame Savier's car in front of the house?"

"Yes, he did. But I thought he was mistaken. The woman was in Nice with her family, after all. She hated it here. Why would she interrupt her holiday? Definitely not out of love for her husband."

"You listened to us in the library. He was planning to divorce her."

"I am not terribly surprised by that," replied Fleur.

"An unidentified person informed her of her husband having an affair. She jumped in the car and drove here to catch him in the act, so to speak."

She wiped her hand over her cheek and nodded slowly. "That sounds like her. I think she never loved him and was unhappy in the relationship, but if someone was to end the marriage it should not have been her husband. She is one of those women who are never left. She is the one who leaves men behind, and not the other way around."

Sandrine was convinced that in that case, the long way from Nice to Bécherel would be worth the drive.

"Are you suspecting me?" she asked quietly.

"Oh, no. You and Arnault Gaudry have a waterproof alibi."

"Thank you."

"Did you see someone arriving on a bike by any chance?"

Fleur Garaine's head jerked in her direction, and she straightened up. The question had hit its mark.

"A cyclist?"

"Arnault Gaudry nearly ran one over when he left. A little later, a person on a bike showed up on the footage of the security camera. He drove in the direction of the chancellery."

"You don't think that Madame Savier is the murderer?"

"Everything points to her, but I have to follow every sign to close the case."

"I understand. No, I did not notice anyone on a bike."

"You are the one taking care of the washing in the house, aren't you?"

"It is part of my duties."

"Lots was going on the last couple of days, so it would make sense if you hadn't had time to switch on the washing machine."

"I am a bit behind."

"May I have a look?"

"I cannot imagine that Madame Savier would approve of that."

"At this very moment she's sitting in an interrogation room in the gendarmerie under the strong suspicion of having killed her husband."

"As you wish," the housekeeper answered and gave up the last bit of defiance. "I will show you where we keep everything."

A washing machine and a dryer stood in the basement. Dirty washing spilled from a basket. Sandrine lifted a couple of pieces.

"Do these trousers belong to Madame Savier?"

"Yes, she wears them a lot."

Sandrine took a closer look at a stain on the leg. *Looks like blood*. She must have tried to wipe it off but had only managed to smear it.

"I have to take this with me."

"Are you allowed to do that?"

"Yes. Do you have a garbage bag I could use?"

"Only a big one."

"Give me two of those."

Fleur Garaine held open the bags for her while Sandrine stuffed the washing inside.

"You want to take everything?"

"Yes. The colleagues in forensics will sort through them. The ones with no results we will send back the next day."

"I will let Madame Savier know," she answered.

"I will take care of that."

The housekeeper took one bag, Sandrine the other and they carried them up the stairs and into the hallway.

"What surprises me is that the woman put her cup in the sink but didn't rinse it properly."

"I imagine she was upset and forgot. Madame Savier isn't used to putting anything away or even washing up. That's my job."

"That might explain it."

Fleur Garaine followed her to the car and handed the bag to Sandrine who put them on the backseat.

"Was Monsieur Savier having an affair?" She tried to catch the housekeeper off-guard. She clearly did not like talking about her employers' private lives.

"He didn't mention anything to me." She evaded giving an answer.

"You live with the man under one roof. One notices a lot."

"That might be true, but he is very discreet with his private life."

"He won't have any issues with that anymore, and it could help us to find a murderer."

Madame Garaine sighed and reached into her trouser pocket. A squished packet was produced, and she pulled out one cigarette.

"An evil vice," she said. "But I rarely smoke."

She lit one and took a deep breath.

"I don't know anything for certain. Recently, he had been coming home later than usual, and Jocelyn Descours called more often. She said it was for business, but he always closed the door of the library. He never used to do that."

Sandrine had not expected that. The secretary had not really sung high praises of her boss. On the other hand, neither had Fleur Garaine about Arnault Gaudry.

"Thank you. That helps me a lot."

"I might be completely wrong."

"That's where my job comes in."

Sandrine got into the car, send a text message to the prosecutor, and drove to Bécherel. It was time to talk to Madame Descours.

Sandrine had barely made it to the main street when her phone rang. She stopped at the side of the road and took the call.

"Major Destin here," she heard her colleague's distinctive voice say.

"I'm on the way to speak to Madame Descours. The interrogation can wait another 30 minutes, I'm sure."

"Of course it can, but we had a call that might interest you."

"From whom?"

"Your friend, Alain Ducasse."

"Let me guess, he was robbed."

"You surprise me once again. You hit the mark. He requested you on the case. He seems to like you."

"Since when can investigators be chosen?"

"People who play golf with the prefect in Rennes enjoy certain advantages, although nobody likes to admit it."

"Understood." Only a few days ago, his colleagues had asked Destin and the prosecutor if she was corrupt. *Things can change quickly.* "The theft was in the hotel?"

"Someone broke into his room and stole his travel-bag. Hermé is already on the way and will meet you there."

"My plan was to talk to Madame Descours, but she won't run away. I'll see you later in the gendarmerie."

Fréderic Savier's plane ticket was not dated until the middle of next week. If the woman really was his secret lover, they must have planned to disappear together. Now that he was dead, she would stay in Bécherel in order not to appear guilty. If the book was in her possession, she would first have to settle the deal with Alain Ducasse to finance her new life. That would take some time. She did not trust Jocelyn Descours to know many potential buyers, so surely she would stick with him.

Let's go. She was curious to hear the art collector's story.

The news was still blaring from the radio when she stopped on the parking lot of the Château. She parked her Citroën 2CV between a Jaguar and a fat Bentley.

"Madame?" An older man in a grey suit barred her way in the foyer. Most likely he was the manager. She pulled her police ID from her bag and held it in front of him.

"Capitaine Perrot," was all she said.

"Albert Senlis, the manager. I would be obliged if we could handle this unwelcome matter as discreetly as possible. We have never had such an incident at the hotel."

"Where can I find Monsieur Ducasse? My discretion will vary depending on what he tells me."

"Our guest is awaiting you in the greenhouse. One of your colleagues has already arrived. Please follow me."

The man led the way and crossed through the dining room which was just being prepared for lunch. The eyes of the employees followed them. *So much for discretion. I bet we won't find a single employee who hasn't already heard of the theft.*

The greenhouse was situated on the backside of the castle and had been built over two storeys. It was much bigger than she had expected. A stream of coloured blossoms flowed down from hanging baskets and bright awnings protected the guests from the blazing sun. At the moment, only Ducasse and Hermé were present, occupying a seating area surrounded by lemon trees.

"Monsieur Ducasse, what a surprise to see you again this quickly." Sandrine greeted the prosecutor with a simple nod.

Her attention stayed fixed on the art collector. His lips were pressed together into a thin line. *Most likely he doesn't want to remember our talk from yesterday. I did warn him though.* She did not like to have been proven right, but her pity for the condescending man had its limits.

"Have a seat," Hermé asked her. "We waited for you."

The seat's cushions made her sink in deeply, and she scooted forward until she was sitting on the front edge.

"What happened?" she asked Ducasse. She wanted him to tell the whole story from the beginning.

"I was robbed. You should know that much by now," he answered in his pretentious tone.

"That's a very small part of all the things that have happened in this place during the last couple of days. Someone was murdered, another one assaulted and you are in all of this up to your ears. The time for petty secrecy is over, once and for all." *And your connections with the prefect won't protect you from that either.*

The eyes of the snobby man widened in surprise. Clearly, he had not expected anyone to talk to him like this. He turned towards Sébastian Hermé, most likely to search for some respect and support, but he was ignored.

"Murder is always a terrible thing," the prosecutor murmured and stirred his espresso in his nonchalant way. He would not let Ducasse get to him either.

"You don't want to catch the thief?"

"We are waiting for results from forensics," replied Hermé.

"When did Monsieur Savier last contact you?" she continued. She did not want the man to relax for a second before she had learned all the details of the planned transaction.

"Someone steals my money and disappears with it. Who knows where they are now? Most likely he's already gone, and you sit here and do nothing."

"Yesterday you claimed that you don't carry a lot of money with you."

"I might not have been entirely honest there."

"If it is only about money, the burglar is already in a café on the Champs-Élysées in Paris and enjoying his coup. But the potential loot he's eyeing is many times more valuable, so our man is probably still around, and your money with him," she replied.

"I fully agree with my colleague. It's all about this book."

Ducasse gave a resigned sigh. He seemed to understand that it was not him who commanded the police.

"A few weeks ago, the man called me. First, I assumed he was an imposter. How would someone like that get his hands on a valuable book like this one? But then he sent me photos that looked genuine. Professor Connesson, an Audubon expert from Nantes, was of the same impression. Of course, there needs to be a thorough examination before he can give his final opinion."

"Savier wanted a deposit?"

"250, 000 euro. In cash. And a preliminary contract for the remaining sum which would be due as soon as my surveyor confirmed the authenticity."

"When did he want to hand it over to you?"

"The man was a vain poser. First, he wanted to present it in some bookshop in this hovel." He exhaled. "All the things that might have happened to the book there!" He turned back to Sandrine. "To imagine children's sticky fingers touching the unique prints is a haunting thought, but the man couldn't be dissuaded from his absurd plan."

"And another collector might have learned of his find. Did Savier try to hike up the price?" Hermé asked.

"I don't think so. The contract was signed. In theory, the book was already mine."

"He would have probably gotten more at an auction. Why did he turn to you?"

"I don't want to be too self-regarding," Ducasse lied, "but in the art community I have an excellent reputation."

"That wasn't an option for him," Sandrine interjected. "He planned on leaving his wife without having to give her a part of the sum. How would he have kept an auction a secret from her? That's also why he wanted to sell while she was in Provence."

"I agree with you." Hermé placed his espresso cup back on the table. "Who knew you were storing a quarter of a million euro in your room?"

"Only Fréderic Savier, no one else. In contrast to that man, I am never someone to brag. The money was also supposed to change owners on Thursday."

"There must be a safe in the hotel. A sum like this would have been a lot better there. Someone must have found out, and breaking into your room probably isn't difficult."

"Maybe it wasn't about the money," Sandrine said thoughtfully.

"That would be a bit much of a coincidence. Someone breaks into my room and finds the money by luck?" Ducasse replied.

"Maybe the burglar was looking for the other, much more valuable loot. Savier's murderer searched the library but couldn't find the book. They also couldn't locate it in the chancellery or the antique shop. What other options are there? Savier might have left it with the future owner."

"Then the quarter million was only a consolation price," Hermé joined in with her theory. "However, the question remains, where's the book?"

"Madame Savier assured me it was in her possession." Ducasse looked at her questioningly. Doubts about the woman's statement were clear in his gaze.

"I can't say that for certain, but we will ask her," promised Sandrine, even though she knew very well that Isabelle Savier had no idea where her husband had hidden it. *A lost book and a murder committed for it makes a thrilling story. That should hike up the price even more if the book is ever found.*

"How did the burglar get in?" she asked the prosecutor.

"There were no signs of forced entry on the door. The window is also undamaged, but Monsieur Senlis reported to have had a master key stolen from the staff locker room. One of the cleaners noticed it missing this morning."

"Madame Savier insisted on meeting me during the day. I opened the bag roughly an hour ago. You can imagine my shock to find only an old pillow which the burglar had stuffed inside."

"When did you last see the money?"

"Last night before I went out for dinner. I wanted to make sure that everything was ready in case the woman had the book with her and wanted the money. That wasn't the case, of course."

"That means it must have been stolen during the dinner. Either the perpetrator didn't want to cause a ruckus, or you were extremely lucky."

Alain Ducasse stared at her, perplexed. His mouth dropped open sightly, and the colour drained from his face when he understood what she was getting at.

"You think they would have... like Savier?" His voice was barely more than a whisper.

"They killed once. Why would they hesitate with you?" She was only a little ashamed of herself. The arrogant man deserved to have his feathers ruffled a bit. The murder of the notary still seemed like an emotional act to her, and not at all planned. With Neville, the perpetrator had been content to knock him down when the latter surprised them. She assumed that the time of the crime had been carefully chosen yesterday. The thief had made sure Ducasse was not in the room before searching it.

"Let's look inside," Hermé suggested.

They left the greenhouse and climbed up a small staircase to the upper floor. Ducasse had paid for a suite with a view of the park.

"Don't touch anything else," she admonished Ducasse while she herself pulled on some gloves.

"Okay, but my fingerprints are all over the room."

An open travel bag made from thick black cotton lay on the unmade bed.

"Did you spend the night alone?"

"Of course, you don't really think..."

"When I warned you yesterday, you had female company."

"That was purely a business meeting," he replied with fervent indignation.

"Good, then we don't have to worry about Madame Savier's fingerprints or other signs." The way Sandrine judged the woman, she thought she would hardly be averse to taking a rich lover as a bonus to the book's selling price. She had to think about her future after all.

Sandrine pulled open the bag's zipper further. It was empty apart from one 100 euro note, abandoned at the bottom. "The burglar left something behind."

"A little tip." Hermé stepped next to her.

"The joke's at my expense." Ducasse walked past them and looked out of the window. "The thief steals my money and then makes fun of me. I hope you catch them."

"Chances are good," Sandrine replied calmly. She did not miss the sceptical look from the prosecutor, but she was convinced that once they found Savier's killer the contents of the bag would also be discovered.

"There are no obvious signs of a break-in, neither on the

door or the windows," said Hermé. "The theory that the burglar stole a master key seems plausible."

"What's your plan now?" she asked the art collector. "Will you stay here, or will you do without the sale?"

"I can take the loss, especially since you're optimistic of getting the money back. Otherwise, it only extends the business transaction with Madame Savier by a few days."

"You still want to buy it?"

"Of course. Nothing has diminished the value, quite the opposite in fact."

"For it to have been the reason for a murder should only increase the interest in the book," she agreed with him.

"You're right. Though I don't plan on selling it on."

"What else?"

"It will become a central piece in my collection." The man nodded as if he agreed with his own statement.

And only a chosen few will be allowed to see it. That would infuriate the women from the reading group. Maybe one of them wanted to avoid exactly that. She decided to speak to the ladies again.

"There's nothing else for us to do here apart from wait for forensics." Sandrine pulled off her gloves and shoved them in the pocket of her jeans.

"We will post a policeman in front of your door." The prosecutor looked at his phone. "They should be here in half an hour the latest."

"And in that time, I'm not allowed to enter my own room?"

"I'm sure that the manager can offer you a replacement. If not, the area is quite pretty and very nice for a little walk."

His drooping mouth showed only too well what he thought of a walk. Ducasse checked the watch on his wrist. It was a Chopard on a leather band and must be worth six figures.

"I'd prefer to drive to Saint-Malo. There should be an acceptable restaurant."

"I would assume so," she agreed with the man. The colleagues from forensics would finish faster if the man was not constantly peering over their shoulders. She refrained from proposing a restaurant to him. They certainly frequented different establishments.

"We will update you," Hermé promised.

"I'm expecting your call and to hear that you found my money."

"We will do our best."

"Whatever that might be." The man could not swallow the pointed remark.

Sandrine ignored him, went down the stairs and walked past reception in the direction of the parking lot.

"Madame," someone called after her, though in a voice so timid that she nearly missed it. She stopped and looked back. An older man in a waiter's uniform approached her with quick steps.

"Can I help you?"

"You're from the police. So, yes."

"Did you notice anything out of the ordinary last night?"

"Out of the ordinary? Not at all," he replied. "Someone stole my bicycle's air pump. This seems to have become a habit."

From out of the corners of her eyes she saw Sébastian Hermé's eyebrows rise slightly. This was not exactly a crime they were interested in.

"I'm sorry, if you want to you can file a report."

"This is the third time. In one year. You can't even leave your things here. Someone has to do something about that." He looked at her intently until she nodded.

"Where was it stolen?" Sandrine asked.

Hermé looked towards the exit. He wanted to get out of

here, and not waste his time with a trifle like this. Isabelle Savier was still awaiting interrogation.

"There are bike stands behind the house. The pay here isn't that great, and not everyone can afford a car. The pump was with my bike when I arrived, but now it's gone."

"Do you have a suspicion?"

"I will drive ahead while you attend to this gentleman's business," Hermé whispered.

"I will be with you shortly."

The prosecutor nodded his goodbye and marched briskly through the foyer and outside.

"I see you're only interested in the problems of the rich staying here."

She ignored the anger that had crept into his voice. If she was the one who had to serve snobs like Alain Ducasse every single day, she would probably share his sentiment.

"Maybe I saw the guy."

"When?"

"During my smoking break. I went out the back with Fabienne, the sous-chef. There I saw someone ride off on a bike. But he was nearly on the road already."

"Can you describe him?"

"From behind, with dark clothes and a big backpack which probably included my air-pump? No, I can't. How could I?"

"That's unfortunate. It would have really helped us." Most likely he saw the burglar. *I bet the backpack contained more than just the air-pump for 10 euro. Ducasse's 250,000 euro must have fit in there snugly.*

"But I recognised the bike. It was one of those bikes people buy to brag about, screaming red with studded tyres. The type with which the young guys race through the woods."

"A mountain bike?"

"Yes, I think that's what they're called." He shook his head as if in disbelief that someone might find enjoyment in driving off the beaten track.

"We will take care of it," she promised the man, who only threw her a sceptical look.

"It's the third one this year. And here in the countryside. I even bought a recognisable one, black with golden stars."

"That was clever."

"Well, you see how little it helped."

"If we find it, we will hand it over to you," she promised.

"I'm waiting for a miracle." He turned away from her and walked without another comment back to the restaurant.

Marie had taken the work off Adel Azarou and questioned the forensic technicians. She was loved and respected by everyone, and a chat between colleagues in a department was hardly noticed. Still, she came away empty-handed. The car had been properly dismantled the day after the fire in the barn. Drugs were found, registered and handed in by the kilo. She could not find any error in the documentation. The inventory lists were accurate to the gram.

Without much hope, Adel pulled into the parking lot of the towing company that had loaded up the Firebird and taken it to the police station's yard. Two cars were parked in front of the building, the others were on their way to collect illegally parked or broken-down vehicles. The office was in a small, glazed extension of an old industrial building. The secretary looked up as he stepped through the door.

"Can I help you?"

"Police," he said and showed his badge.

"You don't look like a policeman," she replied and winked at him. The woman did not seem opposed to a little flirtation.

"I'm here about a car which your company towed for the police." He handed her a sheet of paper with the date and place.

She typed on the keyboard, eyes fixed on the screen.

"To the commissariat in Saint-Malo?"

"Yes."

"A Firebird Trans Am. With night surcharge."

"That's the one I'm looking for."

"There's no entry that anything happened. Are there any complaints?"

"Not at all, but I still have to talk to the driver."

"Sure, he's just taking his break. What did he do?"

"Can you call him?"

"Not necessary. He's outside." She pointed at the court. In the shadow of a hedge sat a man holding a baguette. A thermos stood next to him on the bench.

Adel said goodbye and went over to the man.

"Do you have a minute?"

"Sure. What's going on?"

"Do you remember having picked up a Firebird Trans Am and bringing it to the commissariat?"

"Who could forget something like that? You don't see that type of car a lot. I also had to wait until the firefighters extinguished the fire. That added quite a lot of overtime."

"You loaded up the car and drove to Saint-Malo?"

"That's my job. It was tricky because the hood was very dented. The bumper fell off in the process, but that wasn't my fault."

"Was there anything special about the drive?"

"Nothing I remember. I delivered the car, a guy from the police-workshop signed for it and that was that. Sorry I can't help."

"Thank you anyway."

Adel turned and walked in the direction of his car when the man called after him.

"Or is it about the pills?"

Adel returned quickly.

"What pills are you talking about?"

"The car was full of drugs. I don't know much about them."

"Tell me."

"As I said, the hood was looking terrible. Who does something like that to a car?"

"Not so important."

"I attached the tow rope to the body and pulled it slightly, and the bumper fell off."

Adel looked at the man until he continued.

"With the bumper fell a parcel full of pills. It must have been hidden there."

"What did they look like?"

"Was heard to see in the dark, but I think they were red. Lots of round skulls. Strange."

That's it. Adel remembered all too well the red ecstasy pills pressed into the form of skulls.

"What did you do with them?"

"What would I do with that stuff? I handed it over to the policemen."

"Do you remember the names?"

"No idea, two men in everyday clothes like you. Both older than you, but I didn't look at them too closely."

"If you remember anything else, please give me a call." He handed him his business card.

"Keep it. I was busy with the car and didn't have time to take a closer look at them. I won't be able to tell you any more."

"Still, thank you very much. You have been very helpful."

"Always a pleasure to help."

. . .

Adel went back to his car and called Inès.

"I found where the drugs came from. They really are from the car which Sandrine discovered in the old shed." He told her the most important points of the driver's tale.

"One second." He heard her typing. "That's what I thought. Poutin and Dubois were working that evening and drove out to the crime scene. Maybe the man handed over the ecstasy to Poutin, and he kept it."

"To him or Dubois or any other person just standing around which he could have mistaken for a police officer. That doesn't help us."

"Dubois will be able to tell us." She did not sound very optimistic which Adel understood all too well. He felt the same.

"Do you think he will tell on his best friend? I don't think so. He's trying to escape the responsibility, and that's why he's off sick. Most likely, he will only show up next week when the press conference is over and de Chezac has publicly crucified Sandrine."

"How can we help her?"

"Talk to Matisse, maybe he has an idea. Above all though, call Sandrine. It's her head on the line and she needs to know what's going on."

"I will."

For a moment, both stayed silent until Inès hung up.

"*Merde*," cursed Adel and hit the steering wheel repeatedly. There was nothing that came to mind he could do or say that would make Dubois tell the truth. They were not the best of friends. *I hope Sandrine comes up with something.*

* * *

The house where Savier's secretary lived was on the village square, barely a stone's throw from the Farz Gwad. Sandrine tilted her head back and looked at the half-timbered house with its exposed beams and yellow mud plaster. The upper floor protruded over two benches which invited people to sit down and rest in the shade or find shelter from the rain. Pointed dormers with decorative turrets on the gables rose from the steep roof, and colourful blossoms shone behind the blue-painted mullioned windows on the first floor. It was almost too idyllic for her taste.

"You were faster with your little Citroën than me." Hermé stepped next to her and jingled his car keys.

"You like to drive fast?" she asked.

"Why do you think that?"

"The writing on the key looks like the 'A' of a Renault Alpine. It's not really a family car. I would assume it's an older model with character." She looked at him with a cheeky grin. "Most likely in a sporty colour."

"It seems to be true what they say about you. It's an Alpine A110, built 1972. And yes, in a bright rubber-duck yellow."

"I would imagine that sports car fits you." The man clearly stood out with his nonchalant elegance, at least compared to all the prosecutors she had met in the past.

"You also surprised me with your 2CV. An edition Charleston as well. I didn't expect that. You look more like someone who prefers sports cars."

"It's a beloved heirloom." Her aunt Celine had always driven her around in the red and black 2CV. Sandrine had spent many happy childhood summers at her aunt's. "She always gets me where I want to go."

"And faster than my sportscar."

"I'm standing in a no-parking zone closer to the house," she said and looked at her car.

"All good, we're here for work after all," he said to her surprise.

"You think Major Destin will play along?" she asked sceptically, but half-joking.

"We won't tell him and let the ticket disappear mysteriously." She thought she heard the man chuckle quietly, but he quickly returned to the reason for their visit.

"Do you believe the housekeeper?"

"She didn't accuse anyone or assume anything and simply stated what she noticed. She left it to me to draw conclusions. We don't have another option. We need to speak to Madame Descours. I'm curious to hear what she has to say."

Sandrine walked to the door. She could not see a bell, but a metal doorknob hung on the front. She grabbed the handle and hit it against the metal-plate, but only silence sounded from the inside.

"Maybe she isn't home."

Sandrine did not really want to come back later so she knocked again, and this time louder.

"There's no way she wouldn't hear the knocking," said Hermé.

"You can hear it over the entire square," Margritte Violinet addressed them from behind their backs. "What did poor Jocelyn do that is making you try to destroy her door?"

"I'm sorry, sometimes I'm impatient," Sandrine apologised. "We just want to talk to her. Routine things."

"She should be home, we wanted to meet." The bookseller lifted a woven basket which was hung over her arm. "I have a few things for the booth which the reading group puts up for the book market. It's very practical, directly in front of her door. Strange that she isn't answering." She took a few steps back until she left the shadow of the house and looked at the mullioned windows upstairs.

"She's sitting there," she said, shaking her head in wonder. "In her reading chair."

Sandrine stepped next to her. A chair with a high backrest stood at the window with its upper corner just visible. Someone sat in it, unmoving. She could not tell if the person was Jocelyn Descours.

"She must be napping," Margritte assumed. Determined, she went to one of the windows, lifted one of the plant-pots and pulled out a key from underneath.

"The woman clearly doesn't have trust issues," asserted Hermé.

"Ah, no worries. We do it like this here in town. No one breaks into anyone's house in the countryside." Saying it, she halted. She must have remembered the incident in the Rabelais. She stepped to the door and unlocked it quickly.

"I'm invited and you can come with me."

They followed the woman into the narrow hallway. The walls were covered with pictures of the Britannic coast, and a vase with drooping flowers stood on a tiny table.

Margritte held her finger into the vase. "They could use some fresh water."

"Jocelyn," she called out, but no one answered.

Sandrine felt an uncomfortable feeling creep up her back. Something was wrong in the house.

"Please, look around down here, I will check on the woman," she said to Hermé and began to climb the stairs. Hermé barred Margritte's way so that she could not follow. A similar feeling must have come over him.

She knocked against the simple wooden door but did not receive an answer. For a split second she thought about pulling her gun, but decided against it. Her stomach twisted not from fear for her safety, but from the foreboding feeling of what might await her as soon as she opened the door. She pressed against it with her flat palm and it swung open with a creak. She entered cautiously. Opposite her stood the chair, and someone was sitting in it with their back towards her.

"Madame Descours?" she addressed the woman. She did not receive an answer. It didn't surprise her. A rope, maybe as long as her forearms with one loop at each end, lay on the floor.

Book-filled shelves covered most of the walls. The two chairs and a small table formed a cosy looking reading corner. A lamp with a beige lampshade hung over the scene. There weren't many more pieces of furniture in the room.

The floorboards creaked ominously as she approached the woman. A red line crossed her neck, and her eyes stared lifelessly through the curtains, at the Farz Gwad on the opposite side of the square.

Hermé came up the stairs and entered the room.

"Call the people from forensics. With any luck they're still at the hotel," she told him.

"A doctor?"

"Yes, a doctor too, but he doesn't have to hurry." *Any help is too late by now.* She pulled on the rubber gloves, knelt next to the chair and put her hand on the woman's arm. *Would she still be alive if I had talked to her a bit earlier? Most likely not. She would not have admitted knowing anything about the book. A new life with loads of money is too tempting.*

Hermé joined her.

"She is dead." He stated the obvious.

"Murdered," she replied.

"Another affect action?"

She pointed at the rope. "Not this time. Something like this doesn't just lie around a living room. The loops were knotted before, and they only serve a single purpose, strangulation."

"The perpetrator holds one loop in each hand and strangles the woman."

"Just like Savier, she knew her murderer and trusted him or her. Both were killed from behind."

"A lot of strength is needed to strangle someone. It's harder than one thinks."

"That's what the loops are for. The murderer must have planned the act. They just had to be patient and not let go too early. Very cold-blooded."

"How long will this continue?"

"This is the end," said Sandrine.

"Why do you think that?"

"They must have found what they were looking for. At least it looks like it."

"And those?" He pointed at a couple of novels which lay in the corner.

"They might have fallen down when Jocelyn fought for her life. Maybe she kicked the table."

"The murderer could also have thrown them down while searching."

"We know what they were searching for. *Birds of America* is a large format work with more than 400 pages. Why would he or she go through a stack of thin novels? That doesn't make sense." She looked at the shelves. "And there too, nothing was searched through. I bet it lay here open, and the perp just took it."

"Then the murders will stop?"

"If I'm right, then yes. Unfortunately, there are two options, and I don't like either of them."

"And those are?"

"The thief either lies low and leaves as soon as it's safe for them without being noticed by everyone."

"That would bring us under a lot of pressure." Hermé's face twisted into a grimace. He clearly did not like this option.

"Or they stay here and live on as if nothing has happened,

put the 10-million-euro book on a shelf and look at it from time to time with a good glass of wine."

"And then?"

"We will never catch them," replied Sandrine. Her voice sounded a lot calmer than she felt on the inside.

His shoulders slumped forward, and he placed his hands on his knees. "A nightmare," he mumbled, more to himself than to her. Two unsolved murders, a lost art treasure and an angry Ducasse with excellent political connections could mean the end of his career. Things were not looking good for Sandrine either. She was sitting next to the corpse of a woman only a few years older than herself. A sight that put much of what was happening to her into perspective. A sacking from the police would hit her hard, but it would not kill her.

"Did you reach forensics?"

Hermé nodded. "They're on the way. It's only a few kilometres after all."

Sandrine leaned down. In between the books on the floor lay a long letter. She picked it up and opened it.

"If we had any last doubts about the identity of Savier's lover, now they are definitely destroyed." She pulled out a plane ticket. "Florida from Paris Charles de Gaulle. Same flight as his."

"Then Madame Savier was right with her hunch. The man had an affair."

"Exactly like the anonymous caller claimed."

"Jealousy is a strong motive," said Hermé.

"She's still waiting for us in the interrogation room. That will be an interesting interview."

"I'm curious too, but first I'll wait for forensics."

"We will meet in the gendarmerie." She said her goodbyes.

. . .

Margritte was waiting for her at the end of the steps. From her face, it was obvious that the woman knew what they had found upstairs. She was an astute observer.

"Like Savier?" mumbled Margritte and Sandrine nodded. She was not allowed to give any details, but soon everyone would know that Jocelyn Descours was dead. It would become the reigning topic of discussion in town.

A knock sounded from the door. Before she could answer it swung open, and Doctor Duchamps looked inside.

"If it's you calling me, I already know what I will find. It's Jocelyn, I assume?"

"You will find her upstairs. One of my colleagues is with her." She stepped aside to let him pass.

"We'll go and have something strong." Margritte grabbed her arm and pulled Sandrine out of the house. The prospect was enticing to her, and she followed the woman over to the café. She sat down on the terrace while her companion disappeared into the shop.

"Madame Perrot. Everything okay?" Alfonse stepped to her table.

"Come, sit with me." She pushed a chair away from the table, and the young man sat down.

"You look tired. The case is hard?"

"As soon as one stops caring about looking at corpses one should change profession." She forced a smile on her lips. "But I'm not that far yet."

"Happy to hear that."

"And how is it with you?"

"That depends on what will happen with the Rabelais. I liked working here. It's a good antique shop, and the books have grown close to my heart."

"Monsieur Neville will have to answer to his money-laundering in front of a court."

"Will he go to jail?"

"Only a judge can decide that, but it doesn't look good for him." She did not want to lie to the young man. It would be even harder for him if she tethered his hopes to a sinking ship.

"I will keep the business alive for as long as I can, but it will be hard without my boss."

"I'm sure that you are an excellent bookseller and an asset for the Rabelais." She gave him an encouraging smile, and he sat up straighter and nodded in agreement.

"I hope Monsieur Neville sees it the same way." Alphonse's tone was sceptical.

Margritte returned holding a tray with espresso cups, three schnapps glasses and an opened bottle of Calvados.

"Normally I use it only for cooking, but now I need a little sip." She poured the liquor and pushed the glasses towards them. "To poor Jocelyn and to the perpetrator getting caught soon." She looked at Sandrine as if she was waiting for a confirmation that the murderer would be brought to justice. Sandrine could not give that to the woman without risking a lie.

"We're doing all we can," was her evasive answer. She took one of the glasses and drank the Calvados in one gulp. The alcohol burned in her mouth, and she exhaled deeply. "Strong. One is definitely enough for me."

"Homemade by Marcel." The bookseller put her empty glass back on the table.

"I have to go now. There are still a few preparations to be done for tomorrow. There will be lots of visitors because of the book market," said Alfonse, and disappeared back inside the store.

Sandrine stayed on the terrace and enjoyed the calming warmth spreading through her stomach. She refrained from asking for another glass. Otherwise, the 2CV would wobble even more than usual on the way back.

"The man understands his work." Margritte screwed the bottle shut.

"The name sounds familiar to me. Is he one of the treasure hunters?"

"Marcel owns the store in which the members of the club get their finds newly bound if necessary."

She remembered the lanky man who had tried to vanish when she had questioned the treasure hunters. In all the stress during the last few days she had completely forgotten about him. *Maybe I should pay him a visit.*

"Why would someone do such a terrible thing?" Margritte looked at her questioningly.

"We would have found that out a lot quicker if everyone at this place, including you, was not so adamant about keeping secrets."

"What secret are you talking about?"

"I'm talking about Audubon's book which Savier wanted to present in your shop."

"I didn't know what book it was, only that it was supposed to be rare and valuable. At least that was what he claimed. I was sceptical. Fréderic was known to brag."

"Not in this case."

"Unbelievable. A true Audubon, and in my shop. It's a catastrophe that it's vanished." She shook her head, unscrewed the Calvados again and poured herself another glass. "You think the murderer was after the book?"

"At the moment, I can't imagine another motive."

"What has that to do with Jocelyn? She was working for Fréderic, but she didn't get along with the man all too well. She didn't even hide that fact."

"We will find out," Sandrine promised. She kept the truth about the woman's and Savier's relationship to herself.

"I hope so. I don't think I will get a moment of sleep tonight.

Just the thought that the murderer might be from Bécherel is unbelievable."

"Not just an inhabitant, but also someone who comes to the Farz Gwad."

"Because of that vase?"

"Who can enter your kitchen without anyone noticing?"

"Well, me, of course." She looked at Sandrine. "You don't suspect me, do you?"

"No, I don't, but it was important to the murderer that Savier's blood got into your Farz Gwad and that the treasure hunters ate it."

"Disgusting." Margritte shook herself. "Thinking about it I would like to stand up, throw away the baking tray and scrub the kitchen again." She lifted her hands in front of her. "They are sore from all the cleaning."

"So who has access to the kitchen apart from you?"

"My daughter who runs the shop, and the temps working here during summer. You have already met Bernard. Alfonse and Louis Neville stop by from time to time to get a coffee as their machine is broken. And of course, the women from the reading group."

"Florence Cassian, the lawyer and Fleur Garaine?"

"Exactly. You suspect them?"

"They had a connection to the victim," she replied. "But no, so far I'm not suspecting anyone."

"I can't imagine the two of them killing someone."

Most likely Margritte did not think anyone capable of murder, while Sandrine had learned that everyone, under the right circumstances, was.

"Did Isabelle Savier visit you from time to time?"

"Fréderic's wife? I can't remember her ever visiting. She's not interested in books. I don't think she's set a foot in a bookstore in her life."

"I thought so."

"I would like to stay here for a while and calm my nerves, but I have to prepare the room for Rosalie's presentation."

"It will happen? Despite the murders?"

"The book markets happen every month. Fréderic would be shocked if we cancelled because of him, and Jocelyn would think the same thing. No, we will commemorate the two and have a special type of church service."

"Yes, you are right. I will finish my espresso, and then be off to the gendarmerie."

After the Calvados she did not mind leaving the 2CV behind and walking the few hundred metres on foot.

The bookbinding shop Margritte had spoken about was on the way. She stopped in front of the window and looked at the display. Books bound in leather and cloth, but also carefully arranged tools used by bookbinders in the olden days were displayed. The shop exuded the owner's pride in his craft.

Madame Savier will probably be able to wait a few more minutes. Sandrine pushed open the door and entered the shop. The smell of tanned leather and glue filled the space, which was barely larger than her living room. A trimmed cover lay on a table, along with some templates and cutting tools. She immediately recognised the man standing at a bookbinding press. He held a brush with glue in his hand and looked at her in amazement.

"What can I do for you?" he asked slowly, stressing every syllable as if he wanted to win time to mentally prepare for her questions.

"We met the other day at the treasure hunter meeting. You might remember me. Capitaine Perrot."

"Of course."

"You have a very nice workshop. Bécherel must be the ideal place for your craft."

"You want to have a book rebound?"

"Unfortunately, I'm here for work."

The man put the brush on the lid of the glue pot and sat down on a chair.

"I wouldn't know how I could help the police. I'm only indirectly connected with the treasure hunter's business. Sometimes, they send me books to restore, but that's it."

"We aren't accusing you of anything. We have the business records of the Rabelais, after all. Your name doesn't show up in it."

"Then I'm not sure why you're here."

"How was your relationship with Monsieur Savier?"

"Good, as far as I can say. He came here once or twice per month with a book that needed some love. The last few weeks he came more often." He pointed at a shelf. "There are a few tomes I promised to finish before today. Unlikely that he will pay me for my work though."

Sandrine went to the shelf. None of the books had the dimensions she was looking for. They were too small and too thin. Most likely they were some of the inherited first editions he had wanted to sell through Neville. His wife would hardly miss them, and from the sale the man would be able to cover his costs.

"You knew that Fréderic Savier wanted to exhibit a very valuable and rare book at the market on Sunday?"

"Just like everyone else. That's all I can tell you about it though."

"It seems to be an Audubon. *Birds of America*."

"Oh, I didn't expect that of him."

"Why not?" she followed up.

"No one who's sane would part with a treasure like that at a flea market or an auction. The collectors would have swarmed like piranhas. Also…" He stopped. "I don't want to sound condescending."

"I wouldn't assume that."

"Frédéric collects fiction. Nothing too special, and only known names: Rousseau, Voltaire and Hugo. Things you know from school. He would have had a hard time recognising a real Audubon. He didn't follow in his grandfather's footsteps."

"How can I understand that?"

"Did you look around his library?"

"Not in depth."

"The old Auguste Savier was an admirer of nature scientists and illustrators, just like Humboldt, Darwin and Audubon." A wide smile spread over his face. "But also, of other, more exotic illustrations."

"I think I understand what you're getting at."

"Two weeks ago, he brought over an excellently preserved edition of the *Kama Sutra*. He wanted me to give it a fitting cover. That was definitely from his grandfather. Frédéric was too much of a prude. Most likely it's somewhere with Neville now and waiting to be sold. What a shame."

In this case he was wrong. It was on the bedside table of Fleur Garaine, who evidently appreciated the book and its illustrations more than her late employer. *It probably won't find its way back to the library.*

"Would you let me know if you hear anything about the book?" Sandrine handed him her business card.

"Of course, but that won't happen. If I was the one who stole it, it would already be in a safe somewhere in Paris waiting for its new owner."

"Most likely you're right."

She said goodbye. She had not found out much, though she had expected nothing else.

. . .

"Bonjour, Monsieur Neville," she greeted the man who stood in front of the gendarmerie, smoking.

"Oh, you." The corners of his mouth dropped, and his brow furrowed. He threw the half-smoked cigarette on the floor and crushed it under his boot.

"You're giving a statement?"

"You're misunderstanding everything. We didn't do anything criminal. We just traded some old books. A hobby and nothing else."

"Even if I did believe you, my hands are tied. Major Destin is in charge of the case. I'm just a temp who will leave as soon as the murderer of Fréderic Savier and Jocelyn Descours is caught."

"Jocelyn?" He looked at her in disbelief. "That can't be. I just saw her this morning with Margritte."

"I'm sorry."

"Murdered you say?"

"I fear so, yes."

"She never had any business with Fréderic or this damned book. Why would someone hurt the woman?"

"That's what we're trying to find out."

"I have nothing to do with the murders. They nearly got me, too." He brushed his hand over the back of his head, just where the burglar's blow had struck him.

"You had more luck than the other two." *Or the perpetrator wanted to keep him alive.* "What will happen with the antique shop?"

"I'm innocent," he repeated. "That will be shown during the trial. So, the Rabelais will continue as usual. In case I am the victim of a lapse in justice, Alfonse will take care of the bookshop in my absence."

"He's a real booklover."

"Maybe I will take a silent partner with me into the business," he said thoughtfully.

With the money laundering gone, most of his income had probably crumbled into dust. It was hard for her to imagine him finding someone who might be talked into investing in an old and shabby antique shop.

"I wish you the best of luck," she said, and she meant it. "In the trial and in the search for a partner."

"Thank you." He looked at her with surprise. He clearly had not expected to find sympathy with her. "I have to go now. Tomorrow is the book market and Alfonse has big plans. Most likely we will prepare until late into the night. Margritte's café will also be open until late. That's how it is in Bécherel on an evening before a market."

Sandrine found Major Destin at his desk. Sébastian Hermé sat opposite him leafing through a file.

"How's our suspect doing?"

"She's getting on my nerves with her attitude and extra requests. Apart from that, she is threatening to sue us for deprivation of liberty," said Destin.

"Is she ready for questioning?"

Hermé put the file down. "More than ready. She's twitching like an addict in rehab. Only she doesn't shout for drugs but for getting back home."

"I can understand that," said Sandrine. "There's a million-euro treasure hidden somewhere which she wants to find. She's scared that Fleur Garaine will search the library, find the book and vanish, never to be seen again. That's what she would do."

Isabelle Savier sat at a table in a plain room with barred

windows. As soon as Sandrine and the prosecutor entered the room, she jumped up.

"I demand you let me go this very instant," she asked, her voice trembling.

"We will decide that after we've had a thorough chat with you." Sandrine sat down at the table and switched on the microphone. She quickly ran through the necessary details of time and people present. She would take the lead in the questioning while Sébastian Hermé held back.

"Get to the point so this is over quickly."

"Since when did you know of the book?"

"Since Monsieur Ducasse called. He talked about the contract and demanded I hand it over to him. The day you interrupted our dinner."

"You had no interest in your husband's hobby?"

"Not at all. As long as he didn't spend more money than he brought in, he could hang out at those lousy flea markets and with those broken lives from that bookstore." She reached for the gold chain around her neck and centred the big crystal pendant in the deep neckline of her dress. "That the man really found something valuable..." She shrugged her shoulders. "Who would have thought that? Definitely not me."

"A deposit of a quarter million is a nice sum."

The woman's tongue appeared between her lips, and a greedy twinkle flashed in her eyes. She was probably thinking of the significantly larger final payment that would have enabled her to live a carefree life in luxury.

"I earned it," she said after a short pause.

"How?"

"I spent ten years with that man. That's worth something."

"You married him of your own accord, or were you forced?" Hermé interjected.

"He showed off with his property in Brittany and presented

himself as a successful businessman. I grew up in modest circumstances and fell for him. The so-called businessman turned out to be an ordinary village notary, and the estate is nothing more than an old building at the ass-end of the world eating up most of the dwindling fortune for maintenance. There was just enough left for a summer holiday in Provence. Not in a fancy hotel, but in my sister's guest room." She dropped the crystal pendant she was still holding down her cleavage and arched her back like it hurt. Sandrine smiled. Sébastian Hermé was not going to be very receptive to the charms of the woman.

"And then, when he expects a ton of cash he cheats on you with some woman, plans for a divorce and tries to hide the money from you. How ungrateful," said Hermé.

"Exactly," she hissed. She had not noticed the irony. "He'd been planning to leave me for months. Me! Who did he think he was?" Her husband's impertinence in rejecting her apparently shook the woman to the core. The Saviers' marriage could hardly be described as happy. Sandrine began to understand better why she was spending the summer in Provence and why he preferred pursuing his hobby to spending time at home. An affair and divorce seemed inevitable.

Sandrine pulled the list of transactions made through the Rabelais from the file. "Your husband was slowly selling his fortune which was the library. Only in the first quarter that was nearly 50,000 euro. Tax free." She put back the sheet. "Who knows for how long he had been planning for his future?"

"No idea. I barely ever stepped foot in that musty closet of his." Her saucy tone only showed how hurt she was. The marital fraud probably affected her much less than the financial one.

"Did you know of his affair?"

"I didn't know, but I suspected it."

"I'm certain that if my partner betrayed me, I would notice", said Hermé.

Her eyebrows twitched at the mention of his partner, and she crossed her arms in front of her cleavage. Confusion crept into her eyes. She was one of those women who ruthlessly used her charms to achieve her goals. But they would not help her in this interrogation room.

"Are you accusing me of being a bad wife? If that was a crime all the prisons would be full."

"We're not accusing you of any crime yet," Hermé said calmly.

"Then why are you keeping me here?"

"We have to get a clear picture of what happened the night of your husband's murder. You're sitting here because you have lied to us repeatedly."

Isabelle Savier pressed her lips together until they were nothing more than a thin, light line. Her jaw muscles twitched, and she breathed audibly. Sandrine leaned back. The next step had to be initiated by the woman, and it was important for determining in what direction this questioning would go.

"Okay," she pressed out. "Maybe I wasn't entirely honest with you, but I was panicking. I didn't know what to do."

"Start at the beginning."

For a couple of deep breaths there was silence. Hermé pulled the file close and seemed to want to stand up and leave.

"Fréderic had acted even stranger than usual during the last couple months. He stayed at his work until late, and his trips were longer with overnight stays. I found it hard to believe that he was having an affair. He wasn't a very passionate man. He preferred to hide behind his books. But it seemed that way."

"And then you discovered his affair?"

"I would like to claim that. However, I wasn't that observant. Only a comment from the housekeeper woke my suspicion. By now I think she wanted to warn me in her terribly discreet way."

"You still drove to Provence."

"That was clearly a mistake," she mumbled.

"Why the quick return?" Hermé asked.

"As I told you before, I received a message by an unknown person saying my husband was cheating on me. The sender claimed that his lover would be spending Wednesday night at the house. That made me jump in the car and race there."

Sandrine checked the data from the toll company. It supported the woman's statement. She could hardly have reached the property before 11:00 p.m. Right around that time her husband was killed, and it matched the testimony of Arnault Gaudry, who saw her driving away.

"You tried to save your marriage?" In contrast to Isabelle, Sandrine did not miss the irony in the prosecutor's question. He too must believe that she wanted to catch him in the act to get a better position when it came to a divorce.

"Exactly."

"You entered the estate and met your husband. Was he alone or with company as you thought he would be?" Sandrine continued.

"He was already dead when I found him in the library." Her hands covered her mouth as if she was fighting with herself to not be sick. "All that blood," she stammered, as if reliving the moment.

"It's always shocking to find a corpse, especially if it's someone close."

Isabelle Savier nodded without another word.

"What did you do afterwards?" she continued.

"I... I ran out of the house, jumped in the car, and drove off." She looked at Sandrine and linked her fingers into each other. Not even that could hide how much her hands were trembling.

"You took a room in Rennes." The prosecutor pulled the copy of a receipt from the file.

"Yes, some random hotel next to the highway."

"You checked in at 00:15 a.m. How long does one take from Bécherel to Rennes? Roughly 30 minutes?"

"Yes, that should fit. I remember arriving shortly after midnight. Everything is very hazy."

"You marched into the house and went to the library to find your husband *in flagrante*. Instead, you found him dead. Then, rather than contacting the police, you left the scene and drove to a hotel in Rennes. Is that correct?" While talking, Hermé tapped the end of a pencil on the table as if he was crossing off items on a list. He had taken on the leading part of the questioning. Sandrine moved her chair back a bit and simply observed the woman.

"Yes."

"How can you explain the cup we found in the kitchen?"

"It must be from Fréderic, or from someone who visited him that evening. Who knows who else was there."

"Madame Cassian never drinks coffee. She prefers tea."

"Maybe there wasn't any damned tea in the house," she snapped at him. Fear was written all over her face. Sandrine assumed that the woman felt cornered.

"We also found only your fingerprints. The brand of lipstick you use also matched with the one we found on the cup."

Isabelle Savier's posture collapsed. The prosecutor had closed the trap.

"I didn't touch a cup. You have to believe me. Why would I have left it in the kitchen? So that you can find my fingerprints? I'm not that stupid."

"As you said, you were panicking, and not because of the corpse you claim to have found."

"About what else then?" A last resistance of the woman who could feel the noose tightening.

"He told you he wanted a divorce. You could not deal with

his rejection and hit him in affect with the first object you could get your hands on: the bust from his table."

"That's nonsense," she mumbled.

"The evidence doesn't allow any another conclusion." Hermé closed the file as if everything had been said and she was now convicted. "If you confess you might get away with a milder punishment."

She lifted her chin and looked the man straight in the eyes. "I want to talk to my lawyer," she demanded in a last fight. She looked to the side and wrapped her arms around herself. Sandrine switched off the microphone and stood up. They would not get any more statements from Isabelle Savier today. Hermé followed her outside.

"What are we going to do with the woman?" asked Major Destin who awaited them in the hallway. He had watched the interrogation on screen.

The prosecutor threw a questioning look her way, but she held back with her thoughts.

"If we take the forensic triathlon, she ticks all the boxes: motive, means, and opportunity," Hermé said. "We have a witness who saw her at the scene at the time of the crime."

"Which she doesn't dispute," Sandrine replied.

"With the motive we have a choice: her injured pride having been cheated on by her husband, or her greed. Maybe she talked too much and mentioned the book and Ducasse's offer. She took the opportunity and saved the inheritance," Hermé continued.

"She is definitely lying. The used cup with her fingerprints did not stand in the kitchen for four weeks. First having coffee with her husband, and then beating him with the bronze bust shows a tremendous unscrupulousness. I think the woman more capable of that than panicking at the sight of a dead body and fleeing headlong." Major Destin looked at the narrow window to the interrogation room. "I am convinced she is guilty, and we should charge her."

"What do you think, Capitaine Perrot?" The prosecutor turned to Sandrine.

"I agree with Major Destin. Everything speaks against the woman. She's temperamental, and I also think she could have hit her husband with the bust in a fight. Whether she wanted to murder him or just injure him, a judge has to decide. We also have the blood stain on her trousers. The lab will take a bit longer until they find out whose blood it is."

"Do we agree to arrest her on suspicion of having killed Fréderic Savier and Jocelyn Descours?" Hermé asked.

"Yes," Destin agreed. Sandrine hesitated for a moment, but then she nodded as well. There were still a couple of inconsistencies to clear up, but all in all Isabelle Savier looked guilty.

"I'll prepare the paperwork," said Hermé.

Sandrine's phone vibrated in her trouser pocket. It was a message from Inès which she skimmed over quickly.

"I have to go to Saint-Malo, if I may that is."

"Of course," replied the prosecutor. "It's Saturday after all. You did more than enough extra hours, and nothing world-changing should happen until Monday. The murderess sits behind bars, and now we have to deal with the flood of paperwork."

"We haven't found the book yet."

"My people will turn the Savier's estate upside down," Destin promised. "If it's hidden there, we will find it."

"Then I'll be on my way."

"Enjoy the rest of your weekend," Hermé wished her on the way out.

. . .

In her car Sandrine looked at her watch. To her surprise, it was only close to 1:30 p.m. *Maybe there will be something left of my weekend after all.* She remembered the press conference which de Chezac had planned for today around 4:00 p.m. She had another 150 minutes, and then she would watch him destroy her career.

She took out her phone and called Inès. For a while she listened quietly, nodding from time to time.

"Adel is with me. What shall we do?" asked the office manager.

"You won't do anything. This is my own business." She sounded ungrateful but did not care. They had already helped her more than she could have expected. She would not let them risk their own careers. She had to take the next few steps alone.

"But..." she heard Adel in the background.

"I will tell you exactly what I want you to do. Please listen. It's 1:30 p.m. It takes me roughly one hour to drive back with the 2CV. Give me one more hour, and then we all meet at my place for a glass of wine. Either we will drink to my resignation or there will be a reason for celebration."

"Wouldn't it be better if we..."

"You don't meddle with anything," she interrupted the young woman. "4:30 p.m. at my place. Adel's job is to choose the wine. He's got better taste than me." She hung up. To keep discussing with Inès, who could not bear to just sit back and watch, would not get her any closer to a solution, and at the moment every minute counted.

She started the engine and drove off. Rocking, the duck turned into the main road and accelerated as far as its 27 hp would allow. She loved the car, but at that moment she would have preferred Hermé's Renault Alpine or her motorbike.

* * *

Sandrine stopped on a small parking site above the Plage du Saussaye, a sandy bay surrounded by dark cliffs. It was less than 200 metres to the Pointe du Grouin, but only a few tourists found their way here. The wider Plage de Port Mer with its restaurants and brasseries was more easily accessible for tourists.

A dirt path led down to the beach. The tide was nearly at its highest, leaving little more than a narrow strip uncovered. Apart from the brigadier, there was only one family with small children on the beach. They were romping in the water wrapped in wetsuits.

"Bonjour, Dubois," she greeted the man who sat on a folding chair surveying the sea.

"Capitaine Perrot?" He looked up, surprised to see her there.

"It's a very nice spot that you have chosen here."

"How did you find me?"

"Your wife told me where you are."

He nodded. "I was expecting a visit from you."

"Of course. You're an excellent policeman whom I value highly."

"I don't know if I will be able to help you," he said and looked out over the sea to a ship sailing past them.

"Technically, I'm your boss, but not on the weekend. Right now, I'm just a colleague who is worried about you."

"About me?" He sounded surprised. *He's probably right, I should be more worried about myself than him.*

"You have been on sick leave for a couple of days now. I have been assured that something like this has never happened before."

"I'm already a lot better. I will be back at work next week."

"I thought so. That's why I was looking for you."

"You want to check if I really am unfit for work?"

"No, I wanted to say my farewells."

"You want to leave us?" he asked.

"Not at all, but after finding drugs in my friend's office, I'm no longer acceptable to the police. In an hour, prosecutor de Chezac will be at a press conference to announce whether I will be charged with corruption, maybe even drug trafficking." She put a hand on his shoulder. "You're part of my team and I wanted to take this opportunity to assure you that I haven't done anything illegal."

"Poutin did..." he began, but she did not let him finish.

"He did his job and followed orders to run a raid."

Dubois fell silent. Poutin was an old friend, and they had been partners for years. Policemen learned to work and stick together on the streets.

"What's your plan?"

"It's the weekend, the weather is wonderful, and we're sitting at the beach."

Sandrine took off her shoes and socks, unbuttoned her jeans and slipped out of them. Her t-shirt fell down over her hips, but Dubois still looked away. He seemed to find it embarrassing to see his boss in her underwear. She ran into the surf until the water reached up to her thighs. Goosebumps raced over her skin and the cold pierced her flesh like tiny needles. She laughed loudly. It felt amazing and refreshing after the long car ride. It felt freeing. It did not seem so important anymore if Dubois was ready to help her. She would stay at this place no matter what happened. She had found friends here, maybe even someone for a stable relationship. *Maybe I will rival Rosalie and write some thrillers*, she thought and laughed again. A wave hit her thighs and water splashed up. She wiped over her face and tasted salt on her lips. The t-shirt was stuck wet to her stomach. She began to shiver and returned to get her things. Dubois' eyes followed every single one of her steps. The man reached into the bag next to him and pulled out a towel. He handed it to her.

"What do you really want from me? Poutin and I have been friends for decades. I'm the godfather of his eldest daughter." She could see from his eyes that the man was torn inside.

"I can piece together what happened that night. The driver of the tow truck handed Poutin a bag of drugs which he had found under the Firebird's bumper. Poutin took it and kept it. I don't know why. I don't think he's a drug dealer. He took them with him to the raid and claimed to have discovered them in the safe. I know that, but I can't prove it, and that's what matters in the end. I definitely can't prove it without your help, and certainly not within the hour." She checked her watch again and corrected herself. "The next half hour."

The brigadier opened his mouth, but she gave him a sign to stay silent.

"I met you as an honest policeman and will remember you as one. I can't ask you to betray your best friend, but you already know that you have to live with the decision you made. You know that, otherwise you would be sitting at your desk in the police station doing your job instead of sitting here and staring melancholically across the sea for hours. But ultimately, it's your choice." She picked up her clothes and held out a hand to Dubois. "It was a pleasure to work with you."

"Thank you," he said and shook her hand. Still, he avoided making eye contact with her. She left him at the beach and went to her car. From here it was only a few minutes to her house. She had sent a message to Rosalie and Léon and had asked them to keep her company. They were most likely already sitting together with Adel and Inès on the terrace.

* * *

The car rolled down the short but steep driveway and stopped in front of the garage. With both hands clamping the steering wheel, she leaned her head back and took a few long breaths until her pulse slowed down.

"*Rien ne va plus*," she whispered. Sandrine had made her move. Now all she could do was wait and see if she had judged the man correctly or if she had miscalculated. It was hard to break old friendships. *Let's see what jobs there are for ex-policewomen.*

She went over to the house. The voices of Inès, Marie and Rosalie sounded from the terrace behind the small house. A light plume of smoke rose into the cloudless sky. *Adel and Léon must be at the grill talking about the best marinade for the steaks or the fish.*

Inès stepped around the corner of the old sheep stable. As soon as the woman spotted her, she jogged over and gave her a big hug. She pressed her face into Sandrine's shoulder.

"It's okay. The world won't fall down because of this," she tried to console Inès, though she felt her heart clench.

"Are you trying to console me?" She lifted her head and grinned widely. "There's no reason to. It's time to celebrate. The press conference was postponed."

"Really?" The weight which she had collected on her shoulders over the last couple of days fell away, and she took a freeing breath. *Thank you, Dubois.* She had not put her faith in him for nothing.

"The journalists were already crowding in the commissariat, like crows around a dead sheep, when the cancellation was announced."

"Did they give a reason?"

"No. I only know that Matisse talked to de Chezac, and the prosecutor left the commissariat shortly after without saying another word to the journalists. At least that's what Arianne Briand from the local radio station is saying. She asked you to call her back, by the way."

"After everything you have risked for me, I would say you're a real friend."

"I think so too," the office manager winked at her. "And we will toast to that."

Sandrine stretched onto her tiptoes and kissed Léon's cheek.

"It looks like all accusations have dissolved into smoke." He wrapped his arm around her and pulled her towards him.

"I'm not off the hook just because a press conference was cancelled."

"Call me naïve, but what else could happen? The way I understood it, this brigadier took the drugs and left them in my safe to frame me. You're out of the whole thing."

"That's not official, though. There will most likely be another investigation."

"In which they won't find anything to blame on you. And, to my relief, not on me either. At least, that's what my lawyer is claiming. She wants to sue Poutin for faking a crime, but I put a stop to that. After all, he's your colleague."

"I will think about it. I'm sorry that I didn't trust Simone to the degree she deserved."

"It's okay. You don't know her as well as I do." He looked at her and stroked his hand over her cheek. "It meant a lot to me that you believed me."

"I knew you wouldn't lie to me."

"Thanks for your trust."

"No man should lie to a woman who has a gun and knows how to use it."

They looked at each other for a couple of seconds, then laughter bubbled up. Adel, who stood at the grill with a shining white apron, turned around, and Sandrine waved at him.

"You've made some friends since you moved here."

She looked around. Rosalie, Marie and Inès sat at a table and talked to Alain Thibaud, the vegetable farmer. He had appeared with a box of green things from his farm. She wondered where Dubois was at this very moment. *Most likely he's with Poutin, and they're talking like real friends should.* She was convinced that he would be back at his desk on Monday. Commissaire Matisse had to decide what will happen to Poutin.

"I need a moment for myself." She excused herself from Léon and entered the house.

The documents she had asked Inès to compile lay on the breakfast table in front of the kitchenette. The office manager was extremely efficient, and unlike Major Destin's people, she knew by now exactly what information Sandrine was looking for.

She took an espresso from the machine, sat down at the table and leafed through the background reports. She put aside the thick file about Fréderic and Isabelle Savier without reading it. The two interested her little. Should there be an indictment, it was the task of the responsible prosecutor to find out details about the spouses which were relevant to the investigation. Destin and Hermé assumed they had closed the case. The means, motive and opportunity fit well, and the chain of evidence was solid. The chances of putting Isabelle Savier behind bars for the murder of her husband and his lover were more than good.

"It's not your case anymore," she mumbled to herself. Something was bugging her though. It was too easy. Isabelle Savier might be ignorant and condescending, but was she stupid enough to leave a cup with her fingerprints at the crime scene? *I missed something.*

Normally, Fleur Garaine would have been her main suspect. The woman had been at the estate at the time of the crime and had a deep interest in literature. Perhaps she had believed Monsieur Savier's boasts and knew what his treasure was. *Such a sum is tempting for everyone.* Sandrine sighed and put the papers aside. The woman had an irrefutable alibi. Arnault Gaudry was a most credible witness.

The report about Margritte Violinet was quite short. Apart from a few fines for false parking, she had never brought any attention to herself. Louis Neville had not been so inconspicuous. Just like Pierre Salazar he had never managed to live from his books, and so had decided to join the circle of booksellers years ago. The Rabelais had been one of the first antique shops in Bécherel. She leafed through the copied newspaper articles. In the last one he was posing with Alfonse in front of the Rabelais, letting himself be celebrated for having given a young man his dream job.

It has to be somewhere. She pulled a sheet from the pile. *Alfonse Vatel.* Grew up in Nantes. Uncompleted training in a bookshop. Committed several small crimes. Mostly shoplifting. Lived on the streets for a number of years or stayed with friends from time to time before being placed with Louis Neville through a private welfare agency which paid most of the salary. *Would Savier invite the young man to his library after dark? Rather not. Also, what reason would there be for him to show up that late?*

He had an alibi for the night Neville was mugged. She put the short report down.

Sandrine pulled the newspaper report from the pile. A few sheets slipped to the side and sailed to the floor. She left them there and stared at the picture. *How could I have missed that?*

"What happened?"

Léon stood in the living room and looked at the floor which was covered in paper.

"All good. I will clean it up later," she said quickly and

pulled her phone from her pocket. With trembling fingers, she typed the number.

"Sébastian Hermé," the prosecutor answered after a moment.

"Sandrine Perrot here."

"I assumed you were enjoying your much-earned weekend. Gossip has it that you have a very good reason for a glass of champagne."

"It might be a bit too early, and I don't like the stuff much. I prefer a Britannic Cidre or a glass of good wine."

"What can I do for you on a Saturday evening long after closing time?"

"I need a search warrant for the apartment, garage and the Rabelais of Louis Neville."

"Neville? Why?"

"I will explain later, when there's more time."

"Isabelle Savier is in pre-trial detention, and the indictment against her is being prepared. Louis Neville is only on money laundering charges, nothing that can't wait until Monday."

"Madame Savier didn't commit the murder."

"Did I miss something?"

"Just a few details that don't make sense together."

"And I'm lacking the female instinct?" Judging by his slightly ironic tone, she could easily picture him smirking on the phone. She would miss working with him.

"Policewoman-instinct if you want to be precise."

"Are you sure that your hunch is worth torpedoing my dinner for? The soufflé is in the oven and will be ruined if it doesn't come out in time or if it gets cold."

"I think it will be worth it."

"Alright. I trust your instinct. I'll get you the search warrant."

"Can you send it to the gendarmerie in Bécherel? Destin should take a few of his men."

"I will. It's 6:00 p.m. now. Shall we meet at the antique shop in one hour?"

"It's not necessary that you come too. I don't want to completely ruin your evening. Destin and I can manage on our own."

"No chance. Either we catch a murderer..." his voice dropped to a whisper, "which is clearly worth ruining a soufflé for, or you get the opportunity to personally apologise to me for putting my relationship to the test."

"I hope an apology won't be necessary."

"Same for me," Hermé said and hung up.

"I have to leave for a bit," she told Léon.

"I can come with you."

"You would do me a favour if you could take care of my guests for one to two hours, then see them out and lock the door behind you. I will clean tomorrow." She threw the key at him which he caught nimbly.

"They will miss you and ask why you left."

Sandrine looked out the window and onto the terrace.

"Nonsense. They're well-entertained. They won't even notice that I'm gone. Also, most of them work for the police. So, for them it's nothing unusual."

"If you say so." He held up the key. "Where shall I leave this after locking? I could give it to Rosalie."

She hesitated before answering.

"It's best you keep it."

"Are you serious?" Surprise was written in his face, and he did not even try to hide it.

"Yes, for emergencies," she stressed, and took her motorbike trousers from the shelf. "I have to go now. We can talk later about it."

She dressed, grabbed her helmet and gloves and was on her way.

I really have to buy a box of wine for Rosalie, she thought while watching Inès saunter down from the house with two bottles in her hands.

"Have you... did you already call Arianne Briand? It sounded like it was important."

"Not yet, and now I'm driving to Bécherel."

"Leaving your own party?" She twisted her mouth in displeasure.

"To solve my case."

"Okay, that's a good reason. Shall I come too?"

"On the motorbike?"

"Better not. I might have had one or two glasses too many. What shall I tell Arianne? She'll call again."

Sandrine considered her question and stepped closer to Inès.

"Arianne treated me fairly. I owe her something."

Inès nodded.

"Tell her I am on the way to Bécherel to catch a murderer at the Rabelais. I will call her on Monday morning when I'm back in the office."

"Understood," replied Inès. "I'll let her know. She'll be happy to hear that."

* * *

The Renault Alpine and two police cars were parked in front of the bookshop. Major Destin, in uniform as always, and the prosecutor, in a light, sporty outfit as if he had come from sailing, stood in front of the blinding-yellow sports car and were talking. Cars seemed to be one of the few things they could talk about, apart from work.

"I assume you have proof to throw around the investigation like this," Destin greeted her before she had even stopped the BMW. She took off her helmet and handed it to the policeman.

"Could you hold it a second?"

Sandrine tilted the motorcycle onto the side stand and got off. "You have the papers?" she asked the prosecutor.

"All done. It's your show now and we're all curious."

Margritte stepped out of the door.

"The police. And so late in the evening. Did something else happen?"

"You have a garage behind the house, right?"

"Yes, but it's stuffed with bric-a-brac. And a few things from the guys upstairs." She pointed up at the windows of the top floor.

"May we have a look inside?" Sandrine asked. Technically, the garage was not included in the search warrant. She had forgotten to mention it in all the stress.

"Of course. The door is open."

Sandrine went through the small walkway which led to the back of the house. The gate opened easily and almost silently; someone had greased the hinges. The neighbours would hardly notice if the garage was opened at night.

Major Destin shone a flashlight inside.

"What do we have here?" A grin spread on her lips. Her suspicion seemed to be correct.

"Two bikes," he replied. "How does that help us?"

"One is a bright red mountain bike. Exactly like the one seen by a witness behind the fancy hotel. It was roughly the time when Ducasse was robbed."

"There are tons of those. It will be hard to prove that it was exactly that one," Hermé interjected.

"It's just a piece of the puzzle. We're going to collect the others in a second."

She turned away and towards Margritte who was waiting at the door of the Farz Gwad to see what the police wanted from her.

"Are the two upstairs?"

"Louis and Alfonse? Sure. The boy convinced him to put out another display." She pointed to a foldable pavilion made of strong canvas under which stood two tables. "I don't know how he did it. So far, Louis has always resisted it."

"Perhaps a wish from his new partner," said Sandrine, walking past her towards the stairs. The bookseller looked after her with a puzzled expression on her face. She had clearly heard nothing about a partner.

"Monsieur Neville?" she called, but no one answered. "Most likely they're on the top floor."

Hermé and Destin followed her upstairs under the roof. The heat that had built up during the day hit them. The open windows in the dormers did not provide any noticeable cooling on the windless evening.

"The police?" Louis Neville sat at the writing desk, straightened and turned towards the apparent invaders. Opposite him sat Alfonse.

"We want to have a look around and ask you some questions," she said, walking past the man and to the posterior part of the attic.

"Are you allowed to do that?" he called after her.

"We have a search warrant." Hermé pressed the sheet in his hand.

"Again? You're constantly here."

"Back then we didn't know what we were looking for," answered Sandrine without turning around.

"You won't find that damned book here. If that's what you're after you can turn the place upside down until next week," he snapped at her angrily.

"I know. It's not here." She stopped in front of an old shelf which was resting against the gable wall of the house and looked at Louis Neville. "I bet Savier never showed it to you and just boasted of his discovery."

"If you say that, it must be true." Judging from his displeased tone she had hit the mark.

"Must have been a big disappointment when you learned that he wanted to display the book in Margritte's shop and not yours, right?"

A deep growl sounded from his throat, and he did not need to answer.

"You helped him smuggle a substantial sum past the tax office over the last few years, and did he thank you? Not in the slightest. Who can blame you when you lose your temper?"

Neville crossed his arms in front of his chest and stared at her in anger.

"You don't have to say anything. We could hear you very well from the terrace downstairs," she said.

"I'll go then," mumbled Alfonse and reached for his backpack.

"No, please stay. We also have some questions for you."

"For me? I don't know how I would be able to help you."

"Who has a key for this cabinet?"

"Is that thing locked?"

"Looks like it."

"No idea. Must be full of ancient rubbish. We never use it," replied Neville.

"Can you help me, Alfonse?" Sandrine asked and pulled on rubber gloves.

The young man shook his head. Hermé and Destin were

watching closely. So far, they did not seem to understand what she was after.

"Do you like to cycle, Neville?"

"I have a bike, but it has been standing around for an eternity." He looked at his temp. "Alfonse is the cyclist of the two of us."

"Is that true?"

"I can't afford a car, and recently I have mostly walked. Bécherel isn't very big after all," Alfonse answered.

"How long have you been working here?"

"Roughly half a year."

"Do you like it?"

"Why all these questions?" Neville interrupted. Destin stepped behind him and placed a hand on his right shoulder. The antiquarian twitched and fell silent.

"It was always your dream to work as a bookseller, right?"

Alfonse nodded. His eyes drifted towards the door, but Hermé, who was a lot taller and more built than him, barred his way.

"It didn't work in Nantes. They fired you. How did that happen?"

"I was supposed to sell trash to people. I couldn't do that and so the owner threw me out."

"Bad experience," she said in an understanding tone. "And you didn't want to experience that again. The next bookstore would be your own. Or didn't you intend that?"

"I wish it was like that. I have a hard time paying rent. Where would I have found the money to start my own business? Do you think a bank would give someone like me a loan?"

"Good question," she agreed.

"You were always here, heard and saw everything. Certainly Savier's bragging too. The book would have solved your financial worries," speculated the prosecutor.

"Of course I heard what was going on. I'm poor but not dumb."

For the first time, aggression coloured his voice. So far, he had successfully hidden it. He must feel like an animal cornered in a trap. "I wasn't interested in that fucking book. Audubon was a monster. He shot hundreds of birds every day to set up their dead bodies and draw them. Hopefully, he's burning in hell for that."

"I believe you, Alfonse. You aren't stupid at all, quite the opposite in fact, and you weren't after the book."

He looked at her with suspicion flashing in his eyes. "I have an alibi for when my boss was assaulted. I was in Nantes the whole night and have witnesses for that."

"Your motive is a different one. You wanted the Rabelais for yourself, didn't you?"

"Who wouldn't like to own a treasure like this?" said Neville, but she ignored him.

"He put you up for bookkeeping. How long did it take you to figure out the dirty business happening behind the scenes?"

The young man gave Neville a disdainful look. To him, a bookshop was a sacred place, a temple of books that his boss had desecrated with his criminal activities.

"A few weeks. It struck me as odd that even though we sold a lot online, he never brought packages to the post office or had a courier pick up anything. The blatant lack of knowledge of literature by these so-called treasure hunters was evident. I'm not even sure if all of them can read."

"Alfonse," Neville hissed at him. "Don't talk like that about our customers."

"It's true. This Montfort only reads his bank statements."

Sandrine pulled the long, narrow tin box in which she kept her lock picks out of her back pocket and looked for the right one.

"Once you discovered your boss's weakness, you began to hatch a plan for how to get rid of him gracefully without suspicion falling on you."

"I don't know what you're talking about."

"You were more than willing to print out Fréderic Savier's transactions for me and subtly point out similar ones from the other treasure hunters."

"Shouldn't honest citizens do that as soon as they learn of a crime?"

"That would be desirable, but why only after several months, why not immediately?"

"I don't know. I didn't mean to hurt Monsieur Neville, he's a good boss. But then Monsieur Savier was killed."

"You knew he was going to jail. Commercial money laundering on this scale doesn't qualify for parole, but he wasn't allowed to disappear too early. First, you had to find some money to continue the Rabelais on your own."

"The antique shop is mine. A prison sentence won't change that." Neville tried to jump up, but the major pressed him back into the chair.

"Be honest, the shop doesn't make any money the way you run it. You would have ended up behind bars, and Alfonse would have continued the shop in your absence. Still, the income wouldn't have been enough to avert bankruptcy." She looked at the young man. "You would then have taken over the Rabelais."

The angry look the antiquarian gave his temp was unmistakable. She had hit the mark with her guess. But Alfonse ignored him. He just stared at Sandrine who selected one of the picks and used it on the lock.

"I'm sure we can find the key," Destin suggested.

"No problem. A bit of practice is always good." With an audible crack, the door opened.

"You seem to have had more than enough practice," Destin retorted. He apparently disliked his employee acting like a criminal.

Sandrine pulled out a backpack, opened the upper compartment and turned it around. A flood of money bundles and an air-pump, black with golden stars, rained onto the floor.

"I'm not sure who will be happier: Ducasse to get his money back or the grumpy waiter to receive his air-pump." She leaned forward and reached deeper into the shelf. "And what do we have here?"

"The book?" Destin pressed harder to keep Neville on the chair.

"No, not that, but something equally helpful." She held a crowbar in her hands. "The lab will definitely find your fingerprints and traces of paint from the chancellery's office door on it," she concluded boldly.

Alfonse's posture crumbled in on itself. His face looked pale and waxy.

"I'm sure you didn't plan on murdering Fréderic Savier. What happened? Did you get into a fight?"

"I had to talk to him. He had the Audubon and wanted to sell it to this guy who would have locked it away. He planned on keeping all the money for himself and moving away from Bécherel. I couldn't let that happen. I begged him to change his mind."

"How did he react to that?" Sandrine asked. As Fréderic Savier had not survived the evening it felt obvious what he had thought of the young man's wishes.

"He laughed." He proved her guess accurate. "He laughed at me. He said I couldn't even imagine the sum in my dreams. Afterwards, he babbled on about his new life and insulted me. He wanted to make Monsieur Neville kick me out."

"That made you angry? I can understand that very well."

He shrugged his shoulders. "All I remember is that I hit him with the bust from his table."

"But why the blood?"

He lifted his head and returned her gaze. A grin spread to the corners of his mouth. A hint of insanity crept into his eyes which made a cold shiver run up her back.

"For these dumb people books are no more than a ware, just like sausages to be put on the grill and gobbled up. Savier didn't deserve anything else. They were going to eat him, his dear companions. At least a part of him."

"The coffee machine didn't break by coincidence, right?"

"No. I needed a reason to be in Madame Violinet's kitchen without being noticed. She liked my idea of serving a Farz Gwad to the treasure hunters. To swap the blood was easy." He turned to Neville. "The way they praised the Far and stuffed themselves. Just like cannibals. I could barely stop watching. It was my time to laugh at him."

Neville swallowed and held his hand in front of his mouth. The idea of having consumed a part of Fréderic Savier was clearly still making his stomach churn.

"And Madame Descours? Why did she have to die?" Hermé asked.

"I won't say anything else. Are you sending me to prison?"

"What other option is there?" Sandrine shrugged her shoulders and walked towards him.

He bent down and grabbed his small backpack. Instead of picking it up, he pulled out a piece of garden hose roughly the length of his forearm. She tried to jump back, but she was too slow – she had not expected an attack. Alfonse yelled out and hit her. The hose hissed through the air and crashed against her knees. The force of the blow knocked her off her feet. She screamed and hit the floor.

He jumped over the desk, elbowed Destin in the stomach,

and ran past. Dodging the blow with the hose, Hermé grabbed the young man's arm and threw him against a table covered in records. Alfonse landed hard on the floor. The stack toppled and the vinyl rained down on him. Destin recovered quickly. He grabbed one of Alfonse's arms and handcuffed him to the massive oak table.

"What a boy." His breath was heavy, and he massaged the place he had been struck.

Sébastian Hermé offered a hand to Sandrine and she pulled herself up.

"A garden hose stuffed with lead balls. Easy but efficient."

"Is anything broken?" The prosecutor sounded seriously concerned.

She let herself fall on a table and patted her knees.

"Protectors for motorbike driving. Never thought that I would need them in a bookshop."

"Lucky," said Destin. "Without them your kneecaps would be broken."

Sandrine looked down at Alfonse who was scrabbling out from underneath the vinyl. *What a bastard.*

"You reacted well," she praised Hermé.

"Judo. Black belt."

"I could see that."

Two policemen appeared at the door. All the noise must have alerted them.

"One of you take this guy and throw him in a cell. The other one take the money," she commanded the men and handed the keys for the handcuffs to one of them.

"Come with us," she said to Neville who stood up, stared at the pile of money for a bit too long and finally followed them.

She massaged her hurting knee and congratulated herself on having taken the motorbike.

"I hope this is enough of an excuse for having ruined your

Saturday evening," she said to Sébastian Hermé. "I'm sure your partner went through a lot of work to cook."

"I think it will be a good excuse." He sat next to her. "I love him a lot, but his soufflés are straight from hell. Sooner or later, I'll have to tell him."

"Honesty always wins."

"Don't get me wrong, I like you, but you're not really allowed to give advice about honesty."

"I don't know when I have lied to you," she replied hesitantly. "If you question whether I thought that Isabelle Savier was a murderer, I wasn't sure. Everything was pointing at her."

"How did you get to Alfonse?"

"Through a newspaper article. Neville was posing with him in front of the bookshop. A mountain bike stood at the edge of the terrace. It was a black and white photograph, but I could have bet on it being red. Neville is big and heavy, so unlikely to be an ambitious cyclist."

"What did I miss?"

"Arnault Gaudry mentioned having nearly run over a cyclist when he left the Savier's estate around midnight. One can also be seen on the surveillance video at roughly the right time. He even drove in the direction of the chancellery. Unfortunately, we couldn't make out who exactly it was. Then he made a mistake and stole that air pump from the Château. He had a quarter of a million in his backpack and couldn't walk past a ten-euro pump. It's the little things that bring one down in the end. He had already committed small thefts in Nantes. It's hard to break old habits."

"But where's the book? He won't just tell us."

"I don't even think he has any idea where it is."

"The guy looks like he might faint at the sight of blood and has killed two people. Incredible."

"Only one person. Only Fréderic Savier."

"Why do you think that?" Hermé sounded more than just surprised. He sounded shocked. "More female intuition?"

"Simple policework."

"Tell me."

"Jocelyn Descours mentioned in the first questioning that Neville was rotten and Alfonse spooky. She was strangled from behind while sitting in her reading chair. I wouldn't turn my back on someone whom I thought weird and spooky. The murderer must have been a person she trusted. Most likely the same one who knocked Neville out. Alfonse has an alibi for that."

"And Audubon's book is with that person? I'm really curious."

"Then let's go." She offered her hand to him. "I might need some help staying on my legs."

"You know where it is?"

"I think so."

He pulled her up and she linked her arm with his. She would not be able to climb down the steep stairs without his help.

The flash of a camera pierced her eyes, and she pressed them shut for a moment.

"Capitaine Perrot, have we just witnessed the arrest of a double killer?" She heard the call of a familiar voice. She wiped her free hand over her eyes and limped a few steps forward.

"Were you hurt during the arrest?"

"Madame Binet. What a surprise to see you again." She evaded answering. *What is the woman doing here?* To her real surprise, Arianne Briand stood next to her. The journalist from the local radio with the short, colourful hair, tight trousers, and bulky Doc Martens, and the always conservatively dressed

Binet in her beige shift dress were a strange sight to behold. *What a weird couple.* She had mentioned the information about the impending arrest to Inès as a small thank you for the support of the local radio. An alliance with the *Ouest-France* surprised her.

"I'm very well. Thank you," said Sandrine. *The day before yesterday the press would have tarred and feathered me. Let's see what will be in tomorrow's Sunday editions. Hopefully something nicer.* Her bruised ego could use a few pats.

"Will you take care of this?" she asked Sébastian Hermé.

"It was pretty much your case, shouldn't you talk to the press?"

"I'm not very good at that," she whispered.

"Alright."

She limped to one of the police cars which were parked on the square and leaned against the fender. There was no trace of Alfonse. Most likely he was already behind bars.

"Sandrine." Arianne Briand came her way. "Everything okay?"

"For a few days I won't walk like an elegant swan, but limping around being grumpy isn't bad either. So, apart from that, I'm good."

"You have a good reason to strut with pride. This brigadier informed Matisse that his colleague had the drugs before they went on the raid. He obviously planted it on your friend. You're both cleared. If that's not a reason to be happy, then what is?"

"I'm happy for Léon. He was in a bind because of me. Apart from that..." She opened the car's door and slumped into the driver's seat. "A case will be opened against an officer I was responsible for, and another will receive at least a good reprimand and an entry in his previously immaculate service record. Not really a reason to be happy."

"There's more, right?"

"The brigadier would never have dared to plant drugs with Léon just to hurt me if he hadn't had backup from someone high up in the hierarchy."

"The prosecutor?"

"I don't know."

"Honestly?"

"I wish it was different."

"What will happen now?"

"For a few days I'll put my feet up. As soon as I can walk properly again, I'll be back at work and hoping for a quiet time in Saint-Malo. You wanted to talk with me about something?"

"Exactly. The woman we saw in the park."

"Fleur Garaine? I'm on my way to her."

"I knew I had met her before, but in a completely different context."

"In Nantes, I assume."

"Exactly. She was a student of Professor Connesson and wrote her dissertation on Audubon. She was part of an interview last year. Is she connected to the murders?"

"At the moment I can't tell, but if she is we would," she looked at her watch, "arrive with her at the gendarmerie in less than an hour."

"I understand," said Arianne. "Good luck. Maybe Deborah and I will hang around here for a while and watch the preparations for the book market."

"Capitaine Perrot, can we leave?" Sébastian Hermé opened the passenger door of his Renault Alpine. "I don't think you should ride your bike."

"I'm not sure if I can manoeuvre myself into this tight thing either. You would have to pull me out later, and I don't need that embarrassment in my life. I'd prefer to accompany Major Destin in the police car."

"I'll see you there," he said and got in his car.

"Where can I drive you to?" The policeman sat down next to her and started the engine.

"To the Savier's estate."

"Madame Savier is still in a cell."

"But her housekeeper isn't."

"The woman whose alibi you thought was waterproof?"

"Exactly that one."

"I'm curious."

He put the car in first gear and drove off. The engine of the Renault Alpine roared behind them, and the car followed.

In front of the stairs leading to the main entrance was parked a Renault Kangoo with its tailboards open. Sandrine got out and hobbled over. Two suitcases and some books were in the trunk of the van.

"The lady is ready to leave." Hermé stepped next to her.

Fleur Garaine appeared at the door with a big duffel bag in hand.

"You're going on a trip?" the prosecutor asked.

"Not at all. I'm driving home. As you are here, I can lock the estate and give the keys to you. You will surely hand them over to Madame Savier."

"With pleasure." Hermé sauntered towards her and reached out his arm. She came down the last few steps and let the key fall casually into his hand.

With a half-stifled groan, Sandrine sat down in the back of the van.

"Are you quitting?"

"My employer is with the Rennes Medical Examiner and

his wife is in one of your holding cells. The odds of getting paid for my trouble are extremely slim."

"You took the books we saw in your room?"

"Monsieur Savier gifted them to me. He's not into romance, and his wife doesn't read at all. Nobody will miss a few books. A meagre compensation for the wages that are still due to me."

Sandrine stroked over the hard leather binding of the *Kama Sutra*. "Marcel, the bookbinder, made it for Monsieur Savier just before he died. His last assignment, so to speak."

"Is that so?"

"An excellent work. Do the illustrations match the quality of the cover?"

"I can't judge that, the past few days have been extremely chaotic at the property, as you know. Unfortunately, I didn't get to take a look inside."

"May I?" asked Sandrine. "One hears a lot about this book, but I have never had one in my hand."

"I would prefer it if you didn't touch it. The pages are old and brittle."

"The books were part of the library, right?"

"True," she said slowly and stretched the word like gum.

"Then they are from the crime scene." She looked at Sébastian Hermé. "Do I have the right to look at objects from the crime scene?"

"Of course. You're the leading investigator."

She pulled on a pair of gloves and pulled out the book from the pile. She opened the large-format book. Fleur Garaine turned away with deliberate indifference and gasped. Behind her stood Major Destin, blocking her escape route.

"Very strange erotic drawings," Sandrine mumbled and switched pages. "Unless someone had a serious bird fetish." She turned it around and showed a page to the woman which displayed two artful prints of cormorants resting on a tree stump.

She handed it to Sébastian Hermé who had also armed himself with gloves.

"The cover isn't fixed to the block. You can slide in the original book and fasten it with loops on the inside. Very clever. I have seen it with you once before but didn't pay much attention to it. How stupid of me."

"I didn't know anything about this. You have to believe me," Fleur Garaine assured. Her head turned from side to side as if she was searching for a way out. However, there was none. Behind her stood the major, and the prosecutor was barring the way to her car. She could not escape the two trained men on foot. *At least not in her pumps.*

"We already know that Monsieur Savier was killed by Alfonse."

"Then he must also have murdered poor Jocelyn. A murderer with no conscience." She did not hesitate to blame everything on her accomplice.

"I don't think so," retorted Sandrine.

"Who else could have done something so terrible?"

"Stop playing theatre with us," she snapped at the former housekeeper. "You were too clever and took it too far. Intelligent people tend to do that."

"I don't understand what you're talking about." She looked at Hermé as if she was appealing to his manly guardian instincts, but the man was too professional to be easily manipulated.

"It would have been enough to tell Madame Savier anonymously about her husband's affair. Like a marionette controlled by you, she jumped into the car and drove here. You also used Arnault Gaudry to get the perfect alibi for the time of the murder and made him go to the window and see Isabelle Savier flee the scene."

"You really think me capable of that?"

"'Oh, there's someone at the house. Must be a burglar, I'm scared.' Even a mediocre actor, and you're better than mediocre, would have managed to make him get up and take a look."

"As you say, I have an alibi for the murder. It would have been impossible to simply sneak out, kill Fréderic and jump back into bed with my lover."

"We're not accusing you of having killed your employer. Alfonse already admitted to committing the crime. He also told us he stole from Ducasse. He didn't come up with that himself but had an accomplice: you."

"That's nonsense. The boy must be crazy."

"The cup in the sink was simply too much. Madame Savier's story is believable. On the drive from Nice to Bécherel her anger swelled. She was scared to lose her financial freedom and angry with her husband. I think it is quite far-fetched to believe that the two of them sat together in harmony, had a cup of coffee, then she tidied up, came back and struck him with the bust."

"And where do you think the cup came from?"

"You were responsible for the dishes in the house. It must have been easy to get a used cup, not wash it and put it by the sink the next day. Of course, forensics had to find it. If that wasn't enough, you also had the clothes with the blood stains in the laundry bin."

"Why would I have planned all of this? I have been working in the house for a while, but the book was only discovered a few weeks ago. How could I have known about it?"

"We know you were a student of Professor Connesson. Your focus was on Audubon's works. Fréderic Savier was a big admirer of Audubon. I assume he mentioned in his letters to the

Audubon Society that he was in possession of one of his books. We will check up on that."

"That is a very wobbly theory which you will not be able to prove."

"I think we will. Your purpose when entering the household was to search for the book. Did you find it? Unlikely that Fréderic Savier did."

"I will not say anything to that."

"It's not easy to sell a work like this if you can't prove where it came from. You needed your employer who inherited it from his grandfather. No one would question that. What happened? Did he decide to keep your share? Without you he would never have learned of the treasure hidden in his house."

"You cannot prove any of that."

"Oh, yes we can. It will take a while but step by step we will be able to prove everything." She waved her arguments away. "Which we don't even have to."

Fleur Garaine's head twitched to her. She was clearly alarmed and searching for hints on where she could have revealed herself.

"The book will convict you," said Sandrine.

"Unlikely."

"Fréderic planned on starting a new life with Jocelyn Descours. I can't tell if he gave it to her for safekeeping or if she took it from his safe. What we do know is that it must have been in her apartment at the time of her death. The fingerprints will prove it. She leafed through it after all."

"You don't really want to cover the book with that dust?" It burst from her. "You will destroy a unique piece of art. Are you even aware of that?"

"To catch a murderer, that's a price we are willing to pay."

"You c-can't do that." The woman stumbled over her own words.

"We found it in your possession. All of the rest might only be clues, but this is very hard to refute."

Fleur turned around and walked past Major Destin. She sat down on the lowest step. "I turned the house upside down to find it. It was in the attic in between all kinds of bric-a-brac. Can you imagine that?"

Sandrine nodded to show her empathy.

"You were right. I could not prove its origin and needed that idiot Frédéric. He wanted to betray me, but I could not let that happen. I had already invested too much into the whole thing."

"You knew Alfonse from his time in the bookshop in Nantes, right?"

"Yes. When he was thrown out, he stayed with me for a while, and I pulled the threads to give him the job with Neville."

"He was so thankful that he murdered for you?" Hermé asked.

"No, it was like he was manic to get the Rabelais for himself. He had already worked out the plan before I even started work for the Saviers. He was only lacking the finances to get rid of Neville and carry on the shop alone. There we found a common interest. Fréderic wanted to take our share, and that made Alfonse pretty mad. No wonder he struck him down."

"He searched the library afterwards and broke into the chancellery without any success. I assume you were the burglar in the Rabelais."

"True. He had to have hidden the book somewhere after all. There were not too many options."

"You struck Neville."

"Yes, Alfonse gave me that lead-filled garden hose for the reason that came to pass in the end." She looked up. "But I did not want to kill him. To knock him out was enough."

"I believe you," Sandrine assured her. "He was not allowed

to die yet. Otherwise, Alfonse's great plan would not have worked. How did you think of Madame Descours?"

"I knew that he was having an affair and wracked my brains to figure out who it could be. In the end I still had no idea. I nearly gave up when Jocelyn showed up talking about a book he had given her which the police was searching for. Of all the people, she came to me and asked how much she could get and who might be a good buyer. Stupid cow."

"You took it from her."

"It was mine. I found it. If not, it would have rotted in the attic."

"Was it worth the life of two people?"

"If it had worked, definitely. I would have been able to get a better price with Fréderic's help, but there are always collectors who are not too concerned about the origin as long as the price is right."

"Escort the woman to a cell," the prosecutor said to Major Destin. "And put the book in a safe."

Sandrine sat on the loading space and looked after the police car.

Hermé sat down next to her. "How do we rescue the situation now?"

"What do you mean?" she asked, confused.

"You can barely stand. Nothing seems to be broken, but you will have two huge bruises by tomorrow. I won't let you drive your motorbike."

"I will call a friend to pick me up."

"Nah. I'll drive you. That's the least I can do." He gave her a sign to wait. "Big promise: no one will see you scramble out of the car. I won't take any pictures and will shut up about it."

"Really?"

"Of course."

"Then I'll take you up on your offer. Thank you."

He pulled her up and she grabbed his arm.

"Now that your problem in Saint-Malo has cleared up, do you want to know why the prefecture asked about you?" he asked her out of the blue.

"Do I want to know?"

"Definitely."

"Then hit me."

"You were recommended for a post."

"By whom?"

"The prefect from the branch in Manche talked to the prefecture in Rennes."

"I've never met him."

"He's a friend of the prosecutor Bonnard with whom you solved the case of Le Mont-Saint-Michel."

"The world is small. Especially in this area."

"The leader of the commissariat in Cherbourg is retiring and is looking for a successor. A woman would be favoured and Commissaire Matisse thinks highly of you."

"Commissaire Perrot. Sounds good. My mother would have a heart attack," she mumbled. "Then de Chezac did me a favour after all. An offer that's hard to refuse, but I would have become unhappy in the end."

"That's the impression I get from you. You need the excitement of investigation like a fish needs water."

Sandrine laughed and limped to the car.

Book Market

A hot bubble bath, what was left of the smelly ointment Blanche Barnais had given her during the case at Le Mont-Saint-Michel, and a good night's sleep had worked wonders. She still did not feel elegant and nimble, but she could walk again without any help despite every step hurting. *In a few days, I'll be okay again.*

Margritte came towards them. "There you are. The people are already waiting," she greeted Rosalie and Sandrine.

"No problem. They can wait a bit more," Rosalie said and gave the woman a hug. "Waiting increases the anticipation."

"We had something to take care of." Sandrine excused their delay. She had kept her promise and returned the air pump to the grumpy waiter. At least one that looked very similar to the stolen one which was now stored in the evidence locker.

"Did you not want to bring some books to sign?" Margritte asked.

"They're still in the car. A friend will bring them over."

Léon had refused to let them carry even a box of the new cookbooks. Sandrine looked over her shoulder and smiled. He appeared on the opposite side. The crates were neatly stacked on a hand truck. He was extremely organised, she had to give him that, something she often lacked in her personal life. In front of the terrace was a pavilion with the two tables on which mostly old records were piled. Neville sat in a folding chair in the shade and avoided looking at her.

"You have a real treasure on display?" Rosalie asked to be sure.

"Yes. *Birds of America* by Audubon. It's nearly worth more than our entire town," she exaggerated just a little. The bookseller beamed, most likely because she was proud that such a book was being presented in the Farz Gwad. "All due to Sandrine. Without her, the book would have vanished."

"Nonsense. A lot more people had their hands in this than just me." She brushed off the praise, wondering how the book had gotten here in the first place. It was supposed to be in the safe of the gendarmerie as evidence.

"I really have to see that." Rosalie linked her arm with Margritte's and pulled her towards the bookshop.

Sandrine followed the two, past the counter crowded with cakes and sweets. The murmur of guests, the clatter of dishes, and the smell of books and freshly brewed coffee filled the room. She had to fight the temptation of settling into one of the armchairs with a delicious-looking rhubarb pudding tart and a large coffee and spending the rest of the day there. *Afterwards, when Léon has delivered the boxes*, she consoled herself.

"It's over there."

A red, velvet-covered rope separated a small room at the end of the bookstore. In its centre was a table with a sloping pedestal on which lay the open book. Though her attention was drawn to Alain Ducasse who was sitting in a chair next to it, careful to keep children's sticky fingers away from the pages.

A whiff of cedar wood wafted towards her. Sébastian Hermé walked up to her and gave her a good-natured smile.

"New deodorant?" she asked.

"It's for Sunday trips only. You should enjoy your fame today. You were the one who found the book in Madame Garaine's car while I just stood there like an idiot."

"How did you get Isabelle Savier's approval to display it?"

"The widow has a signed contract. She doesn't care much what Ducasse does with the book as long as he pays on time. I'm convinced that the family's estate will be on the market soon."

"I hope she will be happy with the money."

"People like her always search for more. That's why they're never happy."

She gave Ducasse a friendly nod, but only received a sour look in return.

"He had the choice," Hermé said quietly. "It was Savier's heart's desire to have his find exhibited here. Our collector was generous enough to grant it to the dead man."

"Wouldn't it be better if the book was in police custody? After all, it's evidence."

"That was the alternative. But he preferred to present the book to the general public for one day and then take care of its safety himself. He can probably afford a better alarm system than the police."

"I don't doubt it," she said.

"What's your plan now?" A more serious note crept into his voice.

"I won't manage to get past these rhubarb tarts."

"You know what I'm talking about."

"Not much will change. First, I will stay home for a few days and take the time I need to recover." The commissariat could definitely wait. At the moment, it was like a wasp nest someone had kicked. Soon all the excitement would calm down, and she would return to work when everything was back to normal. *I only have to keep an eye on de Chezac.*

"The post in Cherbourg is still open."

"Can you imagine me doing a desk job?"

"Not really," he agreed.

"Here you are. Where shall I put the boxes?" Léon pushed his way through a group of tourists, a box of books in his hands. The two men looked at each other appraisingly for a moment, they nodded at each other. It seemed they had passed each other's test, at least for the time being.

"They're waiting for me," Sébastian Hermé said as a goodbye. "It was a pleasure to work with you."

"Same for me."

She looked after him until he left the room.

"Seems to be a nice person, considering he's a prosecutor."

"Yes, but not nice enough to make me wish for another murder in the area."

She went over to one of the armchairs and let herself fall between the pillows. She would enjoy being pampered by Léon for the rest of the day. *I earned it.*

List of Characters

- Sandrine Perrot: Leading investigator from Saint-Malo.
- Adel Azarou: Sandrine's partner with a soft spot for fashionable outfits.
- Léon Martinau: Club owner accused of drug dealing.
- Rosalie Simonas: Successful thriller author and Sandrine's friend.
- Inès Boni: Office manager with all the connections.
- Luc Poutin: Brigadier on the wrong path.
- Renard Dubois: Brigadier in a moral dilemma.
- Major Destin: Leading investigator of the police department in Rennes.
- Sébastian Hermé: Prosecutor or juge d'instruction from Rennes.
- Margritte Violinet: Bookseller and ambitious baker with a love for old Breton recipes.
- Fréderic Savier: President of a well-known book club and passionate book collector.

- Isabelle Savier: Hates books and longs for a luxurious life in the Provence.
- Fleur Garaine: The Savier's housekeeper, and a prolific reader with a penchant for savoury stories.
- Florence Cassian: Lawyer and business partner of Fréderic Savier.
- Jocelyn Descours: Secretary in a notary's office and member of the reading group.
- Louis Neville: Owner of the antique shop Rabelais.
- Alfonse Vatel: Temp at the antique shop Rabelais.
- Alain Ducasse: Wealthy art collector keeping the truth to himself.
- Arnault Gaudry: Gardener, who is a lot less harmless than he seems.
- Antoine de Chezac: Prosecutor from Saint-Malo

Thanks

I am delighted that you joined Sandrine Perrot and Adel Azarou in their investigation in Brittany and Normandy. Feedback from my readers is very important to me. Critique, praise and ideas are always welcome, and I am happy to answer any questions. My email address is: Author@Christophe-Villain.com

Newsletter: To not miss any new publications you can sign up to the newsletter and get the free novella: Death in Paris - The prequel to the Brittany Mystery Series.

Free Novella

Subscribe to the newsletter and receive a free eBook: Death in Paris.

Sandrine Perrot's back story, her last case in Paris.

Sandrine held the warm coffee cup in her hands and looked out through the café window. The gusty wind drove dark clouds across the sky and swirled leaves along the boulevard. Pedestrians zipped up their jackets and scrambled to keep dry before the impending rain. She wasn't particularly excited about the prospect of having to take her motorbike on the road. Sandrine forgot to shop most of the time and hated to cook. Café Central was her salvation so she wouldn't turn up at work with her stomach growling.

"Would you like anything else to drink?" asked the waitress, who regularly saw Sandrine during her morning shift. She bet the young girl was a student who worked here to earn a few euros. Judging by her distinct accent, she was probably from Provence.

"Thank you but I have to get on the road pretty soon."

"Not a nice day." The young woman took a peek outside and picked up the used plate on

which the remains of scrambled eggs and baguette crumbs lay.

"That's why I hold on to my coffee cup for a while and enjoy the warmth in the café before I have to go to work." A bad feeling swept over her that she couldn't pin down to any specific event, but it nagged at her, as if the day could only get worse. The case she was investigating was stuck in her head and she couldn't shake it, which she usually could.

"No hurry," said the waitress, looking around the half-empty café. "It doesn't get crowded again until lunchtime, so until then I don't have much to do."

Sandrine's cell phone, which was lying on the table in front of her, vibrated and she glanced at the display.

"I'm afraid I have to take this call."

The waitress took the hint and took the dirty dishes into the kitchen. "Hello, Martin, what's up?"

She listened to her colleague in silence for a while.

"On the Richard Lenoir Boulevard? I'll be there in fifteen minutes."

Sandrine ended the call and cursed under her breath. Her gut feeling had proved to be right; the day lived up to its promise. She put money on the table, pulled on the waterproof motorcycle jacket and picked up the helmet that was lying on a chair.

She quickly drank the rest of the coffee. The waitress gave her a friendly wave as she left.

Her motorcycle was parked on the wide sidewalk between two trees. She wiped the wet seat with her sleeve before climbing on and pulling on her gloves. She took a deep breath and started the engine. Shortly thereafter, she merged into traffic.

Half a dozen patrol cars and an ambulance were parked by the Saint-Martin Canal. The paramedics were hunkered down in the car and puffs of smoke rose through their slightly ajar windows. They were more comfortable than their police colleagues, who had to go out to cordon off the area. The first onlookers were already gathering on one of the narrow bridges that spanned the watercourse. Sandrine drove through a gap in the metal fence separating the canal from the boulevard and parked the motorcycle on the wide pedestrian promenade. Bollards – stocky

vertical posts – were set at regular intervals, but today no boats were moored here and the lock gate was closed.

"Good morning, Sandrine," a grey-haired man with angular features greeted her. His badge identified him as Major de Police. "Kind of shitty weather to be out on a motorcycle."

"Hello, Martin. It's still a lot quicker than driving a car. Not to mention parking." She stuffed her gloves and scarf into her helmet and stuffed it into one of the panniers. "Is it our guy?"

"The Necktie Killer? Looks like it."

"Is that what they call him now?" She shook her head in disgust. "Far too friendly sounding. He's a sadistic murderer and should be considered and referred to as such."

"I didn't invent it. We owe that to the journalists who needed punchy headlines." He held up his hands defensively.

"I'm sorry. I was thinking of the victims."

"That's all right. Whenever things like that don't get to you anymore, it's time to change careers."

"In there?" she asked, looking toward the entrance to the Saint-Martin Canal, which ran underground for the next few miles. Even on sunny days, this gloomy place seemed ominous to her. "Who from our team is here?"

"Brossault, the medical examiner with the forensic guys and some cops cordoning off the area. The big boys are on their way, it was probably too early in the morning for them."

Sandrine laughed softly. The chief of homicide and the juge d'instruction, the prosecutor in charge of the investigation, would not be long in coming. They were forced to demonstrate that

the police were doing everything they could to take the perpetrator off the street since the series of murders was dominating the front pages of the newspapers. However, they hadn't even come an inch closer to him since they'd found the first victim in the summer. It was now February and two more dead women had joined the list of victims.

"Let's go then," she said, walking towards the scene of the crime.

The rain started, pattering on the dark water of the canal. Major Martin Alary pulled up the collar of his raincoat and walked faster across the slippery pavement. A uniformed cop stepped aside and waved them through the barricade.

"Was it closed?" Sandrine asked, looking at the lock where the water was damming up. The Saint-Martin Canal was just under two-and-a-half-miles long, and connected the Bassin de la Villette in the north with the Seine in the south. It had a total of five locks – enclosures with gates at each end where the water level could be raised or lowered.

"Most people only use the exposed area: a few tourist boats, but mostly paddle boats and small motorboats used for family outings in the Bassin de la Villette. Hardly more than a dozen boats a day traverse the entire length of the canal."

"The less water traffic, the more noticeable things are. Let's hope someone noticed something."

They entered the tunnel through an open metal door guarded by another police officer. Martin Alary wiped raindrops from his shoulders and adjusted his gun holster. A brick path, on which two people could comfortably walk side by side, ran along the length of the canal. The dim light of the rainy day reached only a few feet deep into the tunnel, and the antique-looking lamps that hung at regular intervals on the wall allowed one to see the way, but were useless for forensic

work. The forensics team had already set up blazingly bright spotlights so they wouldn't miss a thing.

A thin man with a pointed beard and a bald head walked towards them.

"Ah. Capitaine Perrot and Major Alary. Already here?" Marcel Carron, the forensics manager, patted Sandrine's companion on the shoulder and gave him a wink before turning to face her. He refrained from giving her a chummy pat on the back.

"How far along are you with securing the crime scene?"

"Almost done. However, there was hardly anything to secure."

"What can you tell me?"

"An employee of the city building department discovered the body during a routine examination. She was floating in the water. He informed us immediately and left the site. Very prudent."

"Is this also the scene of the crime?" the major asked.

"There's no evidence thus far," Carron replied. "We've searched the path for evidence of a struggle, but to no avail. The corpse is unclothed, but we couldn't find clothes anywhere."

"Not surprising."

"I concur."

"Any idea how the body got here?" Alary asked.

"There aren't many options left. There is no current in the canal sufficient enough to move a human body. She would have been spotted within one of the locks."

"Then she was put here," said Sandrine.

"The question is how." The forensic scientist pointed to the metal door at the entrance to the tunnel. "Entry is forbidden and the door is normally locked. However, there's no problem climbing over the door but dragging a corpse of an adult person up and over would be almost impossible without risking being discovered."

"Then there's only one option left," Sandrine said, stepping up to the railing that was too dirty to touch. "The perpetrator threw her off a boat at this point."

"An ideal location," the major agreed. "Nobody would notice since people seldom come in here."

"I'm assuming there's no security camera in the tunnel." Despite saying this, Sandrine looked around.

"Maybe the doctor can tell us more." She wasn't particularly hopeful. So far, the killer had left no usable evidence.

"Good luck."

Sandrine pulled a pair of disposable gloves and shoe covers out of her jacket pocket and put them on. Even though the forensic scientist assumed there wouldn't be anything of interest here, she played it safe.

A few feet away, she found Doctor Brossault standing next to the victim, a blue blanket spread over it.

"Bonjour," she greeted the older man in a dark suit, bow tie and handkerchief in his breast pocket. He turned to face her and used his forefinger to push his rimless glasses up the bridge of his nose. "An ideal place to dump a body, isn't it?"

"Absolutely." He nodded enthusiastically. "The murderer has a soft spot for historical places. You have to give him that."

"The canal dates back from the early 19th century, from what I remember from my history class." "1825 if you want to be exact, but who cares about that anyway?"

Sandrine suppressed a grin. The medical examiner was the type of person who always wanted to be as precise as possible and didn't withhold his knowledge.

"The canal, anyway. The structure built over the canal did not take place until much later: in 1860. At first, it was designed by Haussmann to improve traffic in the city."

"At first?" Sandrine asked. The man loved sharing his knowledge of history and enlightening those around him. It made him happy, so she let him have his fun.

"Naturally. Napoleon III was not exactly a popular head of state. Resistance to his rule simmered particularly in the revolutionary neighbourhoods such as Faubourg-Montmartre and Ménilmontant. So the plan to build over the canal came in handy. A wide swath through the city along which to send cavalry to maintain law and order."

"Interesting," said Major Alary, who Sandrine heard come up behind her. "But it didn't do him any good in the end."

"Fortunately," the doctor agreed.

Sandrine knelt down next to the body and looked inquisitively at the medical examiner. Only when he nodded did she lift the blanket under which the victim lay. A young woman's bloodless face stared at her with lifeless blue eyes. Blonde hair clung damply to pale skin. She wore a silk tie around her neck, where strangulation marks could be seen.

"She was strangled," Sandrine murmured, more to herself than to Doctor Brossault. "Just like the previous two victims," he confirmed.

"What can you tell me?"

"I'd put the woman in her mid-twenties, blonde and attractive like the other victims. She was strangled with the necktie. There are cuts on her wrists. Without wanting to commit myself, I would conclude that plastic restraints were used. The police use those things, too."

"Any other signs that she fought back?"

"I can't imagine that she didn't, but she had no chance of surviving. Not with her hands tied. Of course we are also looking for narcotics."

"Maybe the tie will get us further."

"A silk tie. Quite expensive and downright exclusive. Forensics will confirm that, although I can't imagine Monsieur Carron being an expert on the subject."

She looked up at him probingly.

"Have you ever seen the man properly dressed before?" His brow furrowed as if surprised at her lack of awareness.

"What's so special about these ties?"

"The quality of the silk is impeccable. In terms of design, I would guess mid-century. In addition, our killer is able to tie a perfect Windsor knot, something that is becoming increasingly rare these days. People either forgo a tie completely or fasten it sloppily. I would narrow the circle of perpetrators down to people with style and money."

He finished the sentence and straightened his bow tie.

Sandrine put the blanket back over the woman's face. She would see her again in the medical examiner's office. She'd seen enough for now.

To subscribe to the newsletter, please use the QR code.

Other Books

Emerald Coast Murder

Sandrine Perrot's investigation takes her from the picturesque fishing towns to the rural hinterland of Brittany's Emerald Coast.

Police Lieutenant Sandrine Perrot is on leave from her post in Paris and has settled in Cancale, the oyster capital of Brittany. She is temporarily assigned to the Saint-Malo police station for this case. The body of an unidentified woman is discovered on the Brittany coast path along the bay of Mont- Saint-Michel.

With her new assistant, Adel Azarou, she takes on the investigation, which leads them to a cold case from Paris, but also deep into the tragic history of a venerable hotelier family.

Saint-Malo Murder

Death of an influencer

The tranquillity of the picturesque old town of Saint-Malo is shattered by a gruesome murder. The dead woman is a well-known influencer and radio presenter who has made many enemies in the region with her controversial opinions and themes. The killer has not only professionally staged the body and crime scene, but also meticulously recorded the crime.

Will she find the perpetrator in the dead woman's private surroundings, or will she have to dig deep into the victim's past?

Deadly Tides at Mont-Saint-Michel

A dead woman loved by all.

Instead of spending a pleasant day with Léon on the coast and at Le Mont-Saint-Michel, Sandrine Perrot is called to a fatal accident in the Saint-Malo marina. The driver's death touches her personally, as she had just met the woman. In the course of the forensic investigation, she discovers that there is more to the alleged accident than she first suspected.

Her investigation leads her into the world of a well-known family in Le Mont-Saint-Michel, a family marked by antiquated traditions but also by conflicts between siblings.

Another person soon disappears without a trace. Was he trying to evade interrogation, or was an unwelcome witness being silenced?

Printed in Great Britain
by Amazon